praise for Tricia Stringer

'Popular author Tricia Stringer returns with another engaging tale of friendship, family drama and changing times ... [she] once again demonstrates why she is one of the best chroniclers of small town Australia.'

—*Canberra Weekly* on *Keeping up Appearances*

'... another great story of family and friends with Tricia, [who is] a master at producing authentic and real people and places that take you right to the centre of the community.'

—*Great Reads and Tea Leaves* on *Keeping up Appearances*

'"Masterful" gets used a lot in reviews, but Tricia Stringer really is. With Birds of a Feather, she firmly takes her place as one of Australia's most accomplished writers.'

—*Better Reading*

'Warm, sincere and thoughtful, *Birds of a Feather* is an engaging contemporary novel sure to delight readers, new and old.'

—*Book'd Out*

'A good, warm-hearted read with relatable and empathetic characters.'

—*Canberra Weekly* on *Birds of a Feather*

T0363648

'*Birds of a Feather* is the latest offering from Aussie favourite Tricia Stringer. Her books always strike a chord with her faithful following. On this occasion, Tricia gives us a multi-generational family drama but with the emphasis on what exactly is family? A fantastic theme to ponder in these new and uncertain times.'

—*Great Reads and Tea Leaves*

'A book you can't put down ... Stringer's skill is in weaving the experiences of different generations of women together, with sensitivity and familiarity, gently showing how context can shape women's decisions ... A moving, feel-good, warm read about strong, loving women ... the exact book we all need right now.'

—*Mamamia* on *The Family Inheritance*

'... a polished family saga ... all delivered with intelligence, wit and emotion in equal measures ... Perfection!'

—*Better Reading* on *The Family Inheritance*

'Tricia Stringer is an intuitive and tender-hearted storyteller who displays a real ability to interrogate issues that affect families and individuals. *The Family Inheritance* is another gratifying read from Tricia Stringer.'

—*Mrs B's Book Reviews*

'This book is the equivalent of a hot bath or a box of chocolates, it's comforting and an absolute pleasure to immerse yourself in ... If you enjoy well-written family sagas, look no further. *The Model Wife* is perfect.'

—*Better Reading*

'A witty, warm and wise story of how embracing the new with an open heart can transform your life.'

—*Herald Sun* on *Table for Eight*

'... a moving, feel-good read ... a warm and uplifting novel of second chances and love old and new in a story of unlikely dining companions thrown together on a glamorous cruise.'

—*Sunday Mail* on *Table for Eight*

'A wonderful story of friendships, heartbreak and second chances that may change your life.'

—*Beauty and Lace* on *Table for Eight*

'Stringer's inviting new novel is sprinkled with moments of self reflection, relationship building, friendships and love.'

—*Mrs B's Book Reviews* on *Table for Eight*

'... a really moving tale ... This truly was a delightful read that left me with that feel-good happy sigh ... be enticed by this tale of love and laughter, trauma and tears, reflection and resolution.'

—*The Royal Reviews* on *Table for Eight*

'This winner from Tricia Stringer ... is a light-hearted and easy-to-read novel with twists and turns along the way ... enjoyable and fun.'

—*The Black and White Guide* on *Table for Eight*

'Tricia has no trouble juggling a large cast and ensuring we get to know and connect with them ... captivated me start to finish; if it wasn't the wishing myself on board for a relaxing and pampered break from reality, it was connecting with the characters and hoping they managed to find what they were looking for. Definitely a book I didn't want to put down!'

'A heart-warming novel that celebrates friendships old and new, reminding us that it's never too late to try again ... If you enjoy stories that explore connections between people and pay tribute to the endurance of love and friendship, you will love Stringer's new novel. *Table For Eight* is a beautiful book ... If you're looking for a getaway but don't quite have the time or funds, look no further – this book is your next holiday. Pull up a deck chair and enjoy.'

about the author

Tricia Stringer is a bestselling and multiple award-winning author. Her books include *Back on Track*, *Birds of a Feather*, *The Family Inheritance*, *The Model Wife*, *Table for Eight*, and the rural romances *Queen of the Road*, *Right as Rain*, *Riverboat Point*, *Between the Vines*, *A Chance of Stormy Weather*, *Come Rain or Shine* and *Something in the Wine*. She has also published a historical saga; *Heart of the Country*, *Dust on the Horizon* and *Jewel in the North* are set in the unforgiving landscape of nineteenth-century Flinders Ranges. Tricia grew up on a farm in country South Australia and has spent most of her life in rural communities, as owner of a post office and bookshop, as a teacher and librarian, and now as a full-time writer. She lives in the beautiful Copper Coast region with her husband Daryl, travelling and exploring Australia's diverse communities and landscapes, and sharing her passion for the country and its people through her authentic stories and their vivid characters.

For further information and to sign up for her quarterly newsletter go to triciastringer.com or connect with Tricia on Facebook or Instagram @triciastringerauthor

Also by Tricia Stringer

Table for Eight
The Model Wife
The Family Inheritance
Birds of a Feather
Keeping up Appearances
Back on Track

Queen of the Road
Right as Rain
Riverboat Point
Between the Vines
A Chance of Stormy Weather
Come Rain or Shine
Something in the Wine

The Flinders Ranges Series
Heart of the Country
Dust on the Horizon
Jewel in the North

TRICIA STRINGER

keeping *up* appearances

First Published 2022
Second Australian Paperback Edition 2023
ISBN 9781867287278

KEEPING UP APPEARANCES
© 2022 by Tricia Stringer
Australian Copyright 2022
New Zealand Copyright 2022

Published by
HQ Fiction
An imprint of Harlequin Enterprises (Australia) Pty Limited (ABN 47 001 180 918), a subsidiary of HarperCollins Publishers Australia Pty Limited (ABN 36 009 913 517)
Level 19, 201 Elizabeth St
SYDNEY NSW 2000
AUSTRALIA

® and TM (apart from those relating to FSC®) are trademarks of Harlequin Enterprises (Australia) Pty Limited or its corporate affiliates. Trademarks indicated with ® are registered in Australia, New Zealand and in other countries.

A catalogue record for this book is available from the National Library of Australia
www.librariesaustralia.nla.gov.au

Printed and bound in Australia by McPherson's Printing Group

MIX
Paper | Supporting responsible forestry
FSC® C001695

For Jo and Annabel

Hensley Family Tree

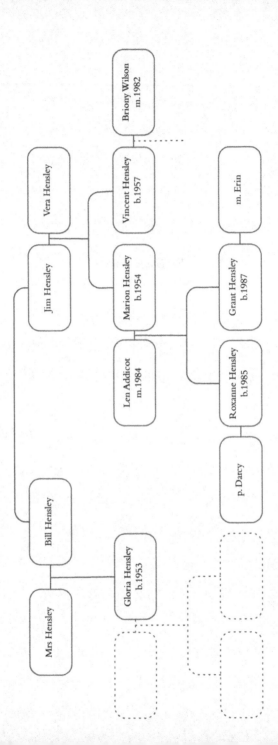

Wilson Family Tree

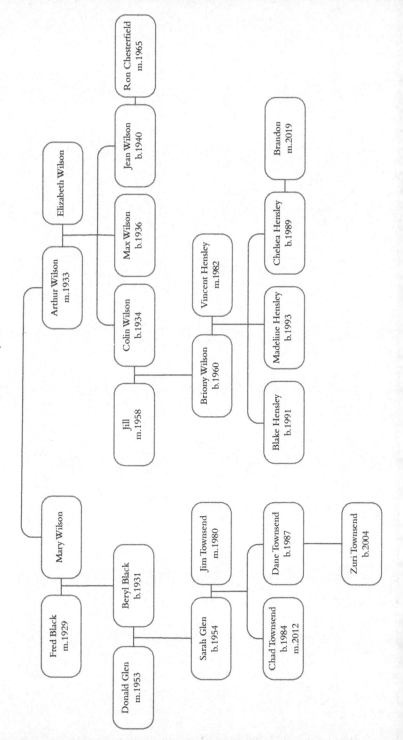

THE COUNTRY COURIER

24 November 1970

There was a spectacular turnout for the Back to Badara celebrations last weekend when more than five hundred past and present residents attended a variety of events over three days. The sunny spring weather gave an extra fillip to the festive mood that existed for the celebrations, which began at the Badara Hall. The hall, which has recently been extensively refurbished, and with the addition of a kitchen and supper room, was officially re-commemorated on Friday afternoon by mayor of the district, Donald Glen.

Mayor Glen spoke highly of the efforts of the Methodist congregation and the wider community to restore and improve the hall for the future use of all people in the district. In particular, he thanked local farmers Mr Arthur Wilson and Mr Jim Hensley for the time they had put in leading the committee, fundraising and carrying out many hours of work themselves. Both the Wilson and Hensley families have been faithful members of the congregation and tireless workers for the community for generations.

The speeches were short and sweet. Mayor Glen then cut a ribbon reopening the hall, trees were planted on the northern side by local schoolchildren, and a time capsule was buried at the rear of the hall to be opened in fifty years.

The hall became the focus of the rest of the celebrations, hosting a concert on the Friday night, a dinner dance on Saturday night and a church service followed by a strawberry fete on Sunday.

The town was decorated with flags and pennants, adding colour to the Saturday street parade which was led by the South Australian Police Band and ended at the oval where various sporting activities were held. The whole weekend was heralded a huge success.

Photo above: Mayor Glen cuts the ribbon, assisted by committee member Mrs Mary Addicot, as the large crowd throw hats and streamers in the air.

Photo left: Sweet little Briony Wilson presents a posy to Mayoress Beryl Glen before the dinner begins.

Photo right: Mayor Glen, flanked by Mr Wilson (left) and Mr Hensley (right) prepares to bury the time capsule.

one

It's not easy to disappear. Hard enough for one person let alone a mother and three children, but Paige believed she'd pulled it off. Sun streamed in through the kitchen window, warming the canary-yellow benchtops where she was slicing fruit for the kids' after-school snack. She lifted her gaze to the row of brightly coloured geraniums lining the fence beyond the window and allowed herself a smile.

They'd been in the little town of Badara in rural South Australia for six weeks and no-one had come looking for them, and there'd been no unexpected knocks on her door or weird deliveries. She had a new phone and a new number that, apart from the children's schools, only her best friend Niesha had, plus she'd given it to her parents but they rarely made contact, and Levi's other grandparents who lived in New Zealand.

It had been hard not to stand out when they'd first arrived. Badara was a town of around three hundred people if you also counted those living on nearby farms. Anyone new was

3

immediately under scrutiny. Naturally the locals had shown interest in the newcomers. Paige knew how to be polite without giving too much away and so far she'd managed to keep people at arm's length.

The house had been a surprising windfall. She'd had no idea where to hide and Google had come to her aid. Her frantic search for a rental that was both cheap and far from Melton, Victoria, had turned up this fabulous old house, with its large rooms and high ceilings. It came partly furnished, and the best part was the ridiculously cheap rent. After driving for three days, with road-side campouts, she'd been exhausted and the kids cranky and she'd been terrified that she might have dragged them all this way to a non-existent house. In the dull light of that grey after-noon it had looked a bit worse for wear and the garden was part overgrown and part dead, but the house had been true to the photos and her distant landlord's promise of being weatherproof and liveable.

"Mummy, I'm hungry."

Levi's plaintive voice and big imploring brown eyes brought her back to the present.

"Have some apple." She handed him a quarter of the fruit she'd been doing her best to cut the bad bits out of. That was the only thing that hadn't changed – the difficulty she had trying to feed her kids. She'd used her meagre savings to move them, and buy the new phone and some extra bits of furniture. It hadn't left a lot to build up her staples.

"I'm still hungry," Levi wailed.

She handed him a second piece of apple and put the remains plus another apple and a pear into a bowl.

"We'll have the rest after we get Kodie."

"Yay!" The little boy clapped his hands.

Paige strapped him into the stroller and set off to meet her daughter at the school gate. Levi was chanting his sister's name and kicking his legs in time to the beat.

"Kodie! Kodie!"

The sound of the school bell rang out in the distance. Paige picked up her pace. Luckily it wasn't very far from their place to the school.

Kodie was already waiting at the oval gate, kicking her foot against the wire of the fence. Paige bit back the command for her to stop. The shoes had been new at the start of the school year. But she could tell from the scowl on Kodie's face they'd end up in an argument. *Pick your battles*, she'd been told once by a mum with five kids. It had been good advice.

"Hey, kiddo," she said instead.

"Kodie!" Levi called.

The scowl slipped from Kodie's face and she bent into the stroller to hug her brother. She stayed half in, half out tickling him. Levi kicked and laughed. The stroller was a flimsy thing bought at a second-hand shop and the faded material was already ripped in a couple of places.

"Steady up, Kodie," Paige said.

The little girl gave her brother one last tickle under his chin and stepped back. He tugged off her hat and dropped it to the ground. She stuffed it in her bag. Paige resisted telling her fair-skinned daughter to put it back on her head. Instead, she turned the stroller in the direction of home.

"There's a newsletter," Kodie said and handed over a crumpled page. "Some of my class are showing their constructions."

Paige glanced at the newsletter, which had several smiling kids holding up buildings made from cardboard, pipe cleaners and coloured paper.

"Mine's not there."

Kodie's statement was matter of fact but Paige felt a stab of conscience. She'd asked the school not to include Kodie in any photos that may appear online. Kodie didn't know that, of course.

Paige glanced over the rest of the newsletter and her eyes stopped at a notice about a fitness group, Tuesdays at the local hall. Now that they were settled she should make the effort to mix more in the community.

"Have a good day?" Paige asked.

"Yes."

"How did your morning talk go?"

Kodie shrugged and strode ahead. Her little legs might be thin but they were strong. Her close-cropped blonde hair tufted up as if she'd been dragging her fingers through it and her backpack banged against her back with each step.

"Would you like me to hook that on the stroller?" Paige asked.

"It's not that heavy."

"I know but..." Paige was silenced by the determined jut of Kodie's jaw.

A willie wagtail hopped ahead of them singing cheerfully then fluttered up onto a fence as they passed.

"I could walk by myself, you know," Kodie said, ignoring the little bird that once she would have stopped to admire and talk to. "Jayden does."

The only thing that had bothered Paige about Badara was that there was no high school so her oldest, Jayden, had a twenty-minute bus trip to Wirini Bay Area School each day. The bus picked up and dropped off the students at the primary school gate. Even though it drove right past their door Jayden had to walk to the primary school to catch it.

She didn't like that he was so far away from her during the day, but at thirteen he was street smart and knew not to give too much away. She'd also told him the reason for their move – not the real one. She felt guilty making Levi's grandparents the scapegoats but Jayden would never have come with her otherwise. He was a good kid but he'd dug his heels in at the idea of leaving his friends behind in Victoria. She'd had to come up with something to change his mind.

Ahead of them a car came a bit too fast around the corner and slewed to their side of the road.

"You're big enough to walk by yourself, Kodie, but it's the other silly people we have to worry about." Paige nodded towards the car.

It slowed and continued along the street at a more sedate pace. The young P-plater kept his eyes straight ahead as he passed them.

"That's Jayden's friend."

Paige looked back as the car turned the next corner. "How do you know?"

"He's been at the playground when we've been there."

The poor excuse for a playground was dirt, with some swings and a small climbing frame. Badara was a pretty little town, nestled between some low hills and a dry creek bed – there were plenty of nice gardens and big trees but like some of the houses and older buildings, the park had been neglected. It was at the other end of the main road that ran past their place. She'd taken Kodie and Levi there not long after they'd moved in. Paige had found the unloved park depressing and hadn't gone back. It was Jayden who'd offered to take his brother and sister there a few times lately.

It had surprised her. Often helpful with his younger siblings in the past, since the move he'd spent a lot of time on his own in his room. She put it down to him turning into a teenager and having a room of his own at this new house – something he'd never had in the flats they'd lived in most of his life.

She should be pleased he'd made a friend but he was only thirteen. A P-plater would have several years on him and what kind of seventeen- or eighteen-year-old wanted to hang out with a much younger kid? A knot formed in her stomach and the worry that had left her for a couple of weeks returned. She'd let her guard down.

They crossed the road and Kodie hurried ahead. The place they were renting was on a corner. The house itself faced a side road, and the old shopfront attached to the house was on the main road. The owner had said they could use the big room in the old shop if they wanted to. There was a door into it from the house. Paige had liked the notion of the big space. Not that she had any idea about what to use it for other than extra space for the kids on a rainy day; they'd had not a drop of rain since they'd arrived.

They could hear the loud music thudding from the house before they even got part way along the drive.

"Jayden's home." Kodie took off at a gallop and Levi strained at his seat straps.

"Jayden," he echoed.

They both adored their big brother. She hoped he was in the mood for their attention. She rounded the house. Jayden had opened the louvre windows and the thud of the bass boomed.

She frowned. It was too early for him to be home.

"Steady up, buddy." She bent to unstrap Levi, who was straining so hard against the straps they threatened to rip from the stroller fabric.

Paige was the last inside. Jayden's door was shut and Levi was hitting it with the palm of his hand.

Kodie stuck her head out of the kitchen. "He said he'd play ball with us, Levi, but we have to leave him in peace for ten more minutes. I've set the timer on the microwave."

Levi hit the door again. "Jayden," he called. Ten minutes or ten hours, the time meant nothing to Levi.

Paige knocked then opened the door. Jayden was lying on his bed, his eyes closed and the old radio he'd commandeered turned up as high as it could go. They were hit by a wall of sound. She scooped Levi into her arms and covered his ears.

"Jayden!"

She stepped into the room and turned down the music.

"Hey!" Jayden sat up, the smile that had been on his lips dissipating.

Levi struggled to get out of her arms. "Jayden, come play ball," he called.

"I told Kodie I'd play in a while." Jayden scowled at his little brother as Levi slid to the ground.

"What are you doing home from school?"

"I got a ride with Zuri."

"Who's Zuri?"

"My mate. He goes to Wirini Area and he lives on a farm the other side of town. He drives to school some days and he offered me a ride."

Paige did a quick calculation. Jayden finished earlier than Kodie but there was still no way he could be home at this time, even with a ride.

"Did you skip a class?"

"It was only art. Dracula doesn't care if we're there or not."

"Who's Dracula?" Kodie was peering around the door, wide-eyed.

"Mr Drakus. He's got two long pointy teeth." Jayden bared his teeth at her and gnashed them together.

"I care." Paige folded her arms. Back in Melton, Jayden had fallen in with a group of boys who were ambivalent about school attendance. It was another of the reasons she'd wanted to move.

"Don't make a fuss, Mum. It was one lesson and one ride." Jayden spoke with the authority of an adult. "Zuri told me footy practice starts soon. He said I should come and try out. The under-fifteens are short on players."

Paige's jaw dropped. Jayden had never shown the slightest interest in sport before. "I thought this Zuri was old enough to drive. How could he be in the under-fifteens?"

"He's almost eighteen. He's playing A grade. He's been telling me about the footy."

"Do you even know any of the rules?"

"I watch the footy on TV and I've played a bit at school."

Paige studied her oldest son as her youngest climbed onto his lap. Jayden had always been lean and short for his age. He was showing no sign of the growth spurt she'd heard could come with boys reaching their teens. It was hard to imagine him surviving on a football field with older and bigger opponents. "I don't know—"

"You said we were here to make a new start, Mum. It's a way to meet people."

Kodie sidled into the room and leaned against Jayden's bed. All three of them were looking up at her.

"I'll think about it."

"Sweet." Jayden jumped up as if she'd said yes and hoisted his little brother to his shoulders. "Get the ball, Kodes. Let's go out the back."

The backyard was an overgrown mess that Paige had partly tamed with a push mower and a small saw she'd found in the garden shed. On one side, just beyond the back of the house, was a cement slab where a building had once stood. The kids used it to play basketball and handball and any of the other ball games they made up that could include Levi.

Paige watched them through the window. How had the conversation gone from skipping school to playing for the local footy team? She shook her head, grateful the kids were at least happy and outside for a while. It was two days before her Centrelink money was due and the groceries she'd bought a week ago were almost gone.

There was no takeaway food here, no nearby shop of any kind apart from the place she collected her mail. It had a faded sign saying mini-mart but sold nothing except a few second-hand books and magazines. She had enough bread and milk to get them through the next day. Then first thing Wednesday morning she'd have to drive to Wirini Bay to do a quick grocery shop, fill the car with fuel, drop some lunch at school for Jayden and then get back to Badara in time to make some lunch to drop off for Kodie. Right now she'd have to be very creative with whatever was in the cupboard to make something to feed her kids tonight.

She wandered into the kitchen. Her heart sank when she saw the fruit she'd cut up was all gone and the empty bread bag was on the bench. Jayden must have made himself a snack when he got home. That meant only half a loaf of bread in the freezer and there wasn't much cereal left. She sagged to a chair. Sometimes she didn't want to be a mother. The weight of the responsibility was overwhelming. The newsletter she still gripped in one hand caught her eye. She read the ad for the fitness group again. It was Tuesday tomorrow, perhaps she'd go. It was time she got out of the house and did something for herself.

two

Briony Hensley glanced out her kitchen window. Inside her house was cool but outside the temperature was rising and charged with the electricity that came with hot windy weather. It was the first of March, officially the first day of autumn but summer hadn't finished with them yet. She hated days like this and doubly so if she had to go out in it like she did today.

The timer sounded on the oven at the same time as the back door banged and footsteps thudded along the passage. The steps were light and quick.

"Have you still got your boots on, Madeline?" Briony closed her eyes and drew in a breath at the thought of her new Persian hall runner.

"Mum?"

She opened her eyes. Madeline was in front of her, a puzzled expression on her face.

"Are you going to fitness class?"

Briony glanced down at the pink and grey lycra she'd ordered online. "It's Tuesday."

"I didn't think you liked fit—"

"Why do you still have your boots on?"

"Dad's hurt himself."

Briony's heart skipped a beat, the rule about removing boots forgotten. "Where? How?"

"He says he's okay but the tractor tyre fell against the bench. His hand was the meat in the sandwich. I don't like the look of it."

Briony sighed. "Where is he?"

"I've left him sitting out on the verandah seat. He's all greasy and there's some blood." Maddie looked down at her boots then back at Briony. "Can you take a look? I have to meet the horse truck. Miss M is arriving today."

"I thought you were collecting her."

"There was another horse coming this way so she hitched a ride. They'll be here any minute."

"You go. I'll see to Dad."

Madeline spun away, then glanced back. "He reckoned he'd be right, wanted to keep working but I insisted you look at it."

Briony smiled at her youngest. She could do anything with horses but she was as soft as butter when it came to humans. "I'll patch him up. Is the tractor finished?"

"No. I've told him to wait till I get Miss M settled."

"You've told him?"

Maddie grimaced and tugged at her ponytail protruding through the back of her cap.

"You know what he's like, Mum."

"I do."

With a flick of her ponytail Madeline was gone, the sound of her boots echoing back along the passage. Briony followed her, detouring via the laundry to grab an old towel, the first-aid kit and a bucket of warm water.

By the time she reached the back door, Vince was pacing the verandah, his hand wrapped in one of his handkerchiefs and clutched to his chest.

"What've you done?" Briony waved him towards a seat.

"Jammed my hand. I swore a lot and there was blood. Maddie panicked…" He looked her up and down. "Is it your fitness class day? I was hoping you'd help me finish the tractor."

"You know I have to go."

Vince frowned and shook his head. "Just because Marion organises something, you don't have to—"

"I enjoy fitness."

It wasn't exactly a lie but some days, like today, she'd gladly skip the class but then she'd have to explain why to Marion and that was fraught with difficulty. Briony busied herself cleaning up Vince's hand. Once she'd rinsed off the grease and blood she could see he'd lost some skin, two of his fingers had deep lacerations and there was general bruising. A small black fly hovered.

"Can you move all your fingers?"

"Of course." He lifted them, dispersing the fly, and fresh blood trickled across his hand.

"You might need stitches. I suppose suggesting you see a doctor is out of the question?"

"I'll be fine."

"You could put some ice on it."

He met her glance. "Don't fuss, Briony."

She eased herself up from her crouched position beside him. "Do you want me to bandage it?"

"It'll only get in the way."

"Just try to keep it clean."

Briony studied him as he inspected his injuries. His thick hair was plastered to his head where his hat had been. It was in need of a cut. There was a couple of days' stubble on his chin and a smudge of grease across his cheek. His shirt was an old one with several rips she'd patched and his jeans were covered in grease. He looked tired and way older than his sixty-five years.

"If you do go to the doctor you'll change first, won't you." People would think they were on the bones of their bums if he went to Wirini Bay looking like that.

"I don't need a doctor." He brushed his lips over her cheek. "Any chance of a coffee before you go? There's something we need to talk abou—"

"Oh hell, my frittata's still in the oven." Briony bolted for the door. "Leave the first-aid stuff – I'll pack it up later."

She reached the kitchen and caught the first whiff of the overdone frittata.

"Damn! Damn! Damn!" She removed the bubbling brown dish from the oven, dumped it on the wooden bread board and lifted the edge with a knife. She groaned at the sight of the blackened base.

"Now what!" She glanced at the clock. No time to make another. They had lunch together after fitness class and everyone brought something. She tugged open the fridge. For a brief second her hand hovered over the container of sandwiches she'd already made for Vincent and Madeline's lunch, then she spied the remains of the roast chicken. She had the makings of a salad. That was all she had time for.

Once the salad was safely sealed in a bowl, Briony scraped the burned frittata into the chook bucket and gave the bench a final wipe down. She looked towards the window as a sudden gust of wind shook the standard roses along the fence. If only she'd deadheaded them yesterday. Now her neatly clipped lawn would be covered in white petals.

She headed to the bedroom, past Madeline's room and the mound of sheets still waiting to be washed after her daughter's weekend visitors.

"Damn!" She'd totally forgotten about them. Briony could happily stay home from class today. There was a stack of paperwork to do as well, Madeline would want help with the horses when she got back and Vincent had said something about shifting sheep to Warrow's paddock later in the day. She really was too busy to go to fitness. To top it off it'd be awful in the old church hall with its ill-fitting windows and two ancient ceiling fans that barely stirred the air.

She sighed. It was easier to go than face Marion's displeasure.

In the bedroom she straightened the cushions on the neatly made bed, then sagged onto the soft doona and wondered what would happen if one day she stayed in bed and slept. As if that was ever an option but some days…She smoothed the quilt, picked up her bag and made her way through the house with one last glum thought for her ruined frittata.

Outside, the first-aid kit sat open beside the seat Vince had occupied. She stopped to close it, and remembered he'd started to tell her something before she'd dashed off to save her frittata. She sighed. She'd deal with it when she got home, whatever it was.

Briony tipped the bucket of dirty water onto the garden and strode off. If she put her foot down, she might just make it on time for the class.

A sudden gust of wind whirled across the yard flinging dust in her eyes.

"Yuck!" She swept her tongue over her lips and swallowed to erase the grit. "That's all I need. A hot dirty day."

Inside a house fifteen kilometres away, Marion Addicot's hand paused over the toaster as another whirlwind swirled across the yard.

She glanced up at the yellowed ceiling then leaned forward to peer outside in time to see the dirt and rubbish rattle against the window and hear it rain debris over the rusting tin roof, then the wind deviated slightly to trouble the branches of a large gum before it whirled off across the house yard and on to the next paddock. The wind was from the east and her mother always said an east wind blew no good. A shiver prickled her spine in spite of the warm morning.

"Just a dust devil." Her husband, Len, put his phone down on the table. His gaze had followed hers to the window. "Bureau's forecasting a warm one today. March is more summer than autumn these days. We'll be lucky to see any rain before May. Might have to dry seed again."

Marion put two slices of toast on the plate in front of him and gritted her teeth. He'd said the same thing every morning at breakfast for over a week.

"Thanks, duck," he said as she turned away. She shrugged off her irritation and resumed work on the sandwiches she was making for his lunch.

"Any chance of another cup of tea?" Len asked.

"Should be some in the pot," she said over her shoulder as she put his sandwiches in his lunch box.

"So there is."

Marion always made enough for at least two cups and she only drank coffee.

"I'll put these sandwiches in the fridge," she said. "There're sausage rolls as well. Give them a quick zap in the microwave."

"Where are you off to?"

"Into town for fitness class."

"Is it Tuesday already?" He shook his head, his thick white eyebrows accentuating his hangdog look. "I guess I'll manage on my own."

Marion gritted her teeth again. He made that half joking complaint any time she left him alone these days. Len had always been competent when it came to managing on his own but since she'd retired he'd become almost clingy, asking for her help to do farm jobs he'd previously managed alone; sitting in the kitchen as she prepped each evening meal but not offering to help, although he always washed up; dropping in to the house for morning and afternoon tea.

Marion had only recently retired from teaching. After working full-time since their own children had been in high school, she still wasn't used to being permanently at home. She clung determinedly to the events and routines that took her away from the property: a weekend or two at their beach shack at Port Kent, church once a month, shopping and a visit to her mother in the home at Wirini Bay once a week, Wednesday afternoon mahjong and her Tuesday morning fitness class. If she didn't have those things, she'd go mad.

Today they'd slept in. It had been a hot night and they'd both been restless. Even so they usually woke at six every morning without an alarm. This morning it had been well after seven when they'd stirred and now she was going to be late if she didn't get a move on. It was her job to unlock the hall and she liked to be there early to make sure everything was shipshape for the class. Luckily there were enough sausage rolls for Len to have a couple with his sandwiches and for her to take for the pooled lunch after they exercised. Everyone enjoyed her sausage rolls.

She startled as Len brushed his lips across her cheek, his stubbly chin rough on her skin.

"I'll feed the chooks," he said.

"I can do it." She felt a stab of guilt. Len was a good man, a hard worker, a loving father and husband, but right now she could cheerfully trade him in for…what she didn't know. There was this prickly feeling inside her. Some days it was rampant – like today. It churned in her stomach and spread to every corner of her being, creeping under her skin, an itch she couldn't scratch.

"You get ready for your big day out." He chuckled as he collected the scrap bucket from the bench. "Will you be home to get dinner?"

"Of course I…" Her exasperation faltered as he patted her hand away from the bucket.

"Have fun with the ladies, love. Don't gasbag too much."

He winked, pushed his battered hat onto his head and went out.

Marion leaned over the faded laminex bench and gripped it tightly beneath her fingers. She took long, slow breaths. Only when she heard the back door shut did she release her grip and step away.

three

Marion tried for another surreptitious glance at her watch midway through an ab crunch. The hall was hot and stuffy, and, compounded by the noise coming from the instructor's sound system and the pain in Marion's midriff, the fitness session was dragging on.

"Come on, ladies – you can do it." Courtney's strident tones echoed around the hall, chasing the thudding sound of the electronic chaos that she called music. She was moving her toned torso up and down to the beat with ease. "Don't forget to breathe. Muscles need oxygen."

Marion managed one more upward jerk and collapsed back on her mat. Thankfully Courtney had had enough as well.

"Good job, ladies. Roll over onto those tummies now."

There was a collective subtle sigh of relief as several other women released their screaming ab muscles and relaxed onto their stomachs. Marion thought longingly of the lunch and long glass of lemonade that would follow.

Around her, six women of various ages and shapes rolled and stretched their way through the final few minutes of their weekly fitness class. Outside the easterly wind stirred dust and wailed around the poorly fitting windows of the old hall. Underneath their feet, the wooden floor dipped and sagged. They were using the front half of the hall. Marion tried not to think about the back corner that only last week had been cordoned off due to white-ant damage in the bearers supporting that section of the floor.

The hall was managed by the church that stood next door and there was no money to pay to have it fixed. Marion knew all about it. She was a member of the small congregation and the hall had been discussed at length. There was a lack of finances, of course, but even if money was available only half the members wanted it fixed. The others said the ongoing decline was inevitable and it would be throwing good money after bad.

"Last five," Courtney bellowed. "Four, three, two, and one. That's it, ladies – good job."

Marion cringed at the patronising tone of her voice. Courtney patted at her neck with a towel but her face looked as neatly made up as when she'd arrived. Even on the hottest day Marion hadn't seen Courtney's make-up run.

"Thank god. Those last few minutes nearly killed me," a voice hissed beside her.

Marion turned to Gloria, whose plump red cheeks dripped with perspiration that ran in rivulets from her forehead.

"Doing us good though, Gloria."

On her other side, Marion's sister-in-law Briony patted at her face. "I hope so. I found it hard work too." Briony gave Gloria an encouraging smile. "And it is rather hot in here." She looked up and Marion followed her gaze to the ceiling where two fans were doing little to move the air.

"It's not that hot a day." Marion spread her towel over her yoga mat and lowered herself to it. "We're not fit enough yet, that's all."

"That easterly wind's miserable." Jean's smile was sweet, as was her complexion. "You girls are doing a great job." Jean had recently celebrated her eighty-second birthday and had lived in Badara since the day she'd been born. *Girls* was an affectionate label for any woman younger than her.

"You're amazing, Jean," Briony said. "You're so fit."

"I walk every day, eat and sleep well." Once again Jean smiled sweetly. "And enjoy my evening glass of wine."

Courtney clapped her hands. "Come on, ladies. Time for cool-down stretches."

Marion glanced across to the edge of the group and their newest member, as Briony settled on the mat beside her. "It's good to have a new face."

"Yes."

"Do you know who she is? She's only managed half the exercises with the little one in tow." Marion stretched one leg in the air and tried valiantly to get her toes to point in the right direction.

"Other leg now, ladies," Courtney called. "Point those toes towards your face for a nice deep stretch of those calves and hamstrings."

"She's moved into the old bakery house." Briony lifted her foot and reached out to grip it.

"Not another single mother."

"I don't really know much about her." Briony glanced furtively past Marion, who twisted to follow her gaze.

The young woman who'd introduced herself as Paige was on the outer edge of the group, and was managing to get her foot almost to her face. Her little boy was beside her munching his way through a container of biscuits.

Marion's leg stayed defiantly at a ninety-degree angle from her body and that was closer than it had been several weeks prior when they'd first started. She wondered how long Paige would stay. A string of young women with assorted children had rented the old bakery house over the last few years but they didn't last. The children would be enrolled at school for a term, maybe two, and then they'd be gone. Badara was an isolated town, with few services, and they soon realised the extra cost of fuel and lack of supermarket, medical and other facilities subverted the cheap rent.

"I want to go home," the little boy grumbled.

Marion glanced in Paige's direction again. Pity she wasn't married with a partner who was employed locally. The town was dwindling when it came to useful contributors and there was little to attract newcomers, apart from cheap housing.

After retiring at the end of last year, Marion had been keen to get a few things happening in their little town. Just after Christmas she'd surveyed the locals for a list of options. Lots of things had been suggested: a community garden but the school already had one, a swimming group even though they were at least thirty kilometres from the nearest ocean, learning to play croquet with not a flat surface or a blade of grass available. Several had suggested an exercise group and Marion had picked that as the easiest to arrange and a good starting point.

She'd organised for them to access the hall for a small fee, and for their instructor, Courtney, to make the twenty-minute trip from Wirini Bay to run the class for a slightly larger fee. Trouble was Courtney had said they'd need at least eight in the class to make it viable for her and they never knew how many would turn up each week. They'd averaged seven until today when there were only six and two of them were attending for the first time; Paige and another woman, Claire, who was married to the new primary school principal.

Marion had only met her once before when there'd been a welcome barbecue. As a local and a recently retired member of staff at nearby Wirini Bay Area School, Marion had been invited. She'd gone along to do the charitable thing. Since she'd retired she'd kept away from schools, hadn't done any relief teaching like some of her friends. She'd slung her hook and kept right out of it. She wasn't going to be one of those people who kept sticking their nose in after they'd retired.

"Slowly rising to your feet now," Courtney crooned. "Take your time, ladies. I don't want anyone falling over."

Marion and the five other women staggered up with varying degrees of mobility. Paige's son clung to her leg but she still managed to rise steadily upright.

"Deep breath in." Courtney dipped her hands below her knees, swept them in a high arc above her head and flung her arms out as they came down. "Throw away your cares."

Marion always felt a little ridiculous at this point. She glanced to her right where Jean was joining in with gusto, a peaceful smile on her lips.

"Good job, ladies." Courtney flicked off the music and tugged the headpiece from her neatly plaited hair.

The momentary silence was such a relief.

"Thanks, Courtney." Marion mopped her neck. "That was a good workout."

"Pity there were only six of you." Courtney pouted.

"Two of them are new so that's good." Marion glanced around at the other women, swigging from drink bottles or rolling up mats.

"Well, let's hope they keep coming," Courtney said. "Although we'll need a creche if there are children. They're too distracting." She glanced in Paige's direction then turned to pack up her things.

Marion grimaced. Paige had been looking their way but ducked down quickly and started to gather up the assortment of toys her son had spread around.

Marion moved across. "Hello, again."

Paige straightened. She had that darting look of someone who didn't want to chat but Marion never let that put her off.

"Do you think you'll keep coming? We could do with the numbers. And we have a pooled lunch afterwards." Marion waved a hand towards the back of the hall. "There's always enough for extras if you'd like to stay."

Paige had one hand on the stroller now piled up with all her things and her son clutched with the other. "Thanks but I need to get Levi home."

"Perhaps we could help you find a child minder for next time," Marion said.

Paige looked uncertainly over Marion's shoulder.

Courtney had moved across to join them and flashed one of her rare smiles at Paige. "I hope you're going to be a regular. Nice to have someone younger. Are you able to get childcare? You'd get more out of the class without the distraction of your little boy."

Paige's mouth opened but Courtney changed her focus to Marion.

"I did tell you we'd need eight each week to make it viable."

"A few people are away." Marion had managed to get ten women from the district to come along to their first class five weeks ago. Since then some hadn't returned and, like today, a few new ones had come along but she couldn't seem to get a regular quorum of eight as Courtney had requested.

"Keeping fit is a commitment." Courtney's eyebrows arched.

Marion was aware of Paige edging away.

"Let's hope the numbers pick up," Courtney said.

"I'm sure they'll be back next week." Between now and next Tuesday Marion would have to make a personal visit to each woman who'd said she'd commit. It'd be disappointing if her first attempt to get some action happening in Badara fell over before it was barely started. She and Jean had a small mahjong group going and there was the CWA of course, but there was little else in the tiny town to keep minds and bodies active.

"I must get going. I have another class at Wirini Bay this afternoon." Courtney fixed her with an expectant look.

"Oh yes, your money." Marion took an envelope from her bag and handed over the five dollars she'd collected from each attendee before they'd begun. They'd actually paid seven dollars each but two of that went to the hall fund.

"Thanks." Courtney stashed the envelope in her bag. "It's good to have a cross-section of the community here but you will need a regular eight in attendance."

Paige was moving steadily towards the door now with Claire not far behind her. Bad luck neither were staying for lunch. Marion would like to have pinned them down for next week. Perhaps she could visit them, take a batch of her sausage rolls, make sure they were committed.

Another gust of wind hit the front of the hall and fine powder floated in the air, a mix of dust and plaster.

"I'm really not sure how structurally sound this place is." Courtney sniffed. "Are you sure there's nowhere else we can meet? Did you try the school?"

"They make use of all their spaces on Tuesdays and that was the only day you could fit us in. Anyway, the hall will be fine. The walls are solid."

"Just everything else that's not." Courtney slipped a piece of chewing gum into her mouth.

"There're a few small issues." Marion turned her back on the cordoned-off area. She was determined to keep the hall operating. Badara needed it. "We're looking into getting some grants."

Courtney gave an eyeroll suited to a teenager. Then again, Marion thought, she was only in her early twenties, so she was barely more than a teenager.

"I'll see you next week. Make sure you have the numbers."

Marion stiffened, but before she could reply Courtney drew her tall, toned figure up to full height, took a grip of her trolley handle and set off after Paige and Claire with her sound system trundling behind her across the uneven floorboards.

There was a whoosh of wind as Paige opened the wooden door at the front of the hall. The force wrenched it from her grasp and the door hit the wall. A heavier shower of plaster fell from above and clattered onto the wooden floor.

Paige yelped and jumped back, dragging her son and stroller with her. Above the door there was a cracking sound. Courtney shrieked. A large clump of plaster came away and hit the floor, disgorging a narrow cylinder that was propelled across the wooden surface and stopped against the toe of Courtney's sneaker.

"I told you this place wasn't safe," Courtney yelped as she hurried out the door. Paige and Claire glanced back at Marion then up at the wall above before dashing out after her.

The door swung back and another trickle of plaster showered the floor.

"They're a jumpy lot." Gloria secured the door. "It's only a bit of plaster. Not as if the roof's going to fall in."

"The old hall's got good bones," Jean said. "No damage that a bit of repair work can't fix."

Marion was grateful for their confidence.

Briony looked sceptical. "Do you think Courtney will come back?"

"I'll get Len to fix the plaster then I'll ring her," Marion said.

"She seemed a bit grumpy today," Briony said.

"We promised her at least eight each week or it barely covers her petrol money." Marion put her hands to her hips. "It wouldn't hurt her to smile a bit more though."

Briony looked momentarily startled. "Her workouts are good but I have to admit her taste in music is not my thing," she said quickly.

"I don't care what she plays as long as she comes back next week."

Marion patted at another trickle of perspiration rolling down her neck, while beside her Briony looked as if she'd been sitting in a cool room all morning instead of spending an hour doing ab crunches, lunges and squats. She'd even managed to reapply her lipstick.

"Is that a new outfit?" Marion asked.

"I'd hardly call gym gear an outfit but yes, this is new. It's very comfortable."

"You look fantastic. I wouldn't dare wear something that tight." Gloria chortled and patted her ample backside. "If I squeezed it all in I'd be worried it would erupt somewhere else."

Marion looked down at her own grey trackpants and baggy black t-shirt. It was an exercise class, not a fashion parade, but Briony always dressed to impress.

"It was a fun class, wasn't it?" Jean joined them. "I told Claire about lunch, she said maybe next time, and I also mentioned our mahjong."

Marion nodded. Jean could always be relied on to help spread the word. "At least there're four of us for lunch."

"I can't stay. We've got shearers," Gloria said. "And I won't be here next week either."

"Why not?" Marion snapped.

Gloria scowled. "Specialist appointment in Adelaide. We'll be away a couple of days. Not that it's any of your business, Marion." She waved in Briony and Jean's direction and left.

Marion frowned after her. She'd known Gloria all her life. They were cousins and a similar age but had little in common except a family tree and living in the same district.

"I can't stay for lunch today either, I'm afraid." Jean picked up the gym bag at her feet. "I've promised to help my friend in Wirini Bay clear out and sort some of her house. She's downsizing."

"Oh." The air rushed from Marion's mouth like a popped balloon.

"But I'll be back next week. Such a good workout I wouldn't miss it." Jean's face crinkled in a broad smile and she leaned closer. "It's only that jolly noise young Courtney calls music I don't like. No wonder the walls vibrate."

As if to emphasise her words another little clump of plaster fell to the floor.

Briony moved towards the scatter of debris and looked up.

"They widened the door and put a new frame and lintel over it back when they did the renovations," Jean said. "It probably just needs patching."

"November 1970. That was a while ago." Briony leaned closer to the plaque on the wall and read out loud. "*The addition, including a kitchen and supper room, was erected for the use of the people of the district and in recognition of the work of many Methodist congregations. Opened by the mayor of our district, Mr Donald Glen.*" She glanced around. "I'd even forgotten that the three denominations came together. I only ever think of it as Uniting Church these days."

"You know, I've not given a thought to the date," Jean said, peering at the plaque. "We were supposed to have another celebration fifty years on from that."

"That would have been two years ago – 2020." Marion wrinkled her nose. "We had enough on our plate that year and barely had enough members for church, let alone a committee to organise something that demanding."

"Thank goodness our numbers have improved," Jean said.

Jean was always optimistic. The new principal and his wife had attended each month since arriving at the start of the year. Marion supposed two more people in the congregation was a small increment.

"Your dad and mine were the driving force behind the renovations," Jean said.

"Were they?" In 1970 Marion would have been sixteen and at boarding school. A time of her life she rarely thought about. She had a vague recollection of coming home for the opening and not being happy to have her exeat weekend taken up with town stuff but that was about all. "It was a long time ago."

"What do you suppose this is?" Briony had retrieved the cylinder that Courtney had kicked aside.

They gathered around to look at it. "It's a piece of poly pipe clamped at both ends." Jean looked up at the hollow space above the door. "If it was buried up there it could be what's caused the plaster to crumble."

"Do you think there might be something inside?" Briony said brightly. "Maybe a roll of bank notes?"

Marion frowned. "You wouldn't fit too many notes in there."

"Oh!" Jean clapped her hands. "I love surprises. Let's open it."

Marion took the dusty tube from Briony and inspected its sealed ends. "How?"

Jean dug in her gym bag and took out a multi-purpose tool, brandishing it in the air. "Keith gave it to me for my sixtieth. Best present ever. I never go anywhere without it."

Marion handed over the tube. In a flash Jean had one end open. She tipped it and a small plastic bag slid out with something rolled inside.

"Not money, unless it's a cheque," Marion harrumphed.

Jean carefully opened the bag and the paper slipped out. "It looks like a piece of newspaper." The small roll was held in place by a rubber band, which disintegrated as Jean tried to slide it off. With care she unfurled the black-and-white page. "It's a clipping."

Marion and Briony moved in and peered over her shoulders.

"It's the page from the local paper about the hall reopening and the Back to Badara celebrations," Jean said. "How marvellous. I bet my dad put this up above the lintel. I remember they had to use the side door for the celebration weekend because this part wasn't finished in time." She pointed to one of the photos. "That's our fathers with the mayor."

Marion lowered her head closer to the clipping. "How can you tell?"

"Their names are underneath," Briony said.

Marion shot her a sideways look but Briony's gaze was firmly on the page.

"I remember that weekend so well," Jean said. "The police band came and played at every function." She sighed. "Keith and I danced the night away."

"And that's me." Briony waggled a finger at the yellowed photo of a little girl with a frilly dress and a ribbon in her hair holding out a posy to a woman wrapped in a fur. "I'd totally forgotten about that. I had to present flowers to the mayoress and I was terrified."

"What wonderful times they were. I'll take this home and make a copy for you both." Jean carefully rolled the page and slid it back into the plastic bag. "It'll be easier to handle."

Marion marvelled at Jean's memory. Her own recollections of that weekend were very sketchy. She looked back at the crumbling plaster above the door and wondered if Len could fix it before next week.

"We should do it this year," Jean said.

"Celebrate the hall?" Briony frowned.

"The hall's just an excuse. It might help give everyone something to focus on as a town. It's so quiet around here these days. And this is the only shared space the community has."

"There's the sporting club." Briony still didn't sound interested.

"It's smaller and out of town," Jean said. "The CWA uses this hall, and the school uses it for concerts and things."

"So do the mums-and-bubs group," Marion said. "And there's been the odd birthday or anniversary gathering here."

"The old-time dance group are keen to use it again once the bearers are replaced." Jean tapped her foot. "It's got such a good floor."

Marion cast a quick look at the patch in the corner that had been lifted. "A celebration event might be a way to raise some money for repairs and upkeep."

"It'd be a lot of work," Briony said.

"Many hands would make light of it, I'm sure." Jean nodded sagely.

Another strong gust of wind hit the front of the hall and more plaster trickled down.

"We'd better get something done about that," Marion said. "I'll get Len to come and take a look."

"Good idea. My Keith's beyond getting up ladders these days but I'm sure he'd help if Len needs someone to hold the ladder."

Jean fluttered her hand in a wave. "I must be off. See you at mahjong, Marion." She set off out the door with the agility of a much younger woman.

"And then there were two," Marion said.

"Such a shame."

"You don't want my company?"

"I didn't mean—"

"Don't look so mortified. I'm teasing. I know what you mean. We're family. It's nice to meet up with others."

"I guess we can share what we've got."

"Yes." Marion did her best to smile. Her sister-in-law wasn't the stimulating company she'd hoped for that morning when she'd set off from home. "It won't take long to warm my sausage rolls."

"Why don't we take lunch back to my place?" Briony said.

"I suppose Vince and Maddie will be there, at least."

"Not sure. I left them sandwiches and cake to get for themselves."

"Oh."

"I can make us a decent coffee instead of boiling the kettle here. And Madeline's new dressage horse has arrived. We can check out the divine Miss M."

"A fancy name." Marion dragged her lips up into a smile. Madeline had always had horses since she'd talked her father into buying her a pony for her seventh birthday. Marion had no idea how many shows, gymkhanas and events Vince and Briony had attended since and she'd been to quite a few herself, hauled along to watch Madeline on whichever horse she had at the time.

Marion suddenly felt defeated. She was hot and tired and not in the mood for pretending to be interested in yet another horse. She'd tried so hard to get this fitness group going and it was more often than not her and Briony and one or two others who stayed for lunch. "Thanks for the offer, Briony, but I think I'll go home.

Lots to do." That was a lie. Marion had no idea what she'd do to fill the rest of the day.

"All right," Briony said quickly. "I'll see you next week then."

Marion shut the door on her departing sister-in-law and swept up the plaster. Instead of the lack of things to occupy herself with she turned her thoughts to Jean's suggestion of a celebration. That it could also be a fundraiser had merit. Marion would talk to a few others about that to see if she could drum up some interest. That would give her something to do when she went home. She'd make a list of potential women who'd get involved and what kinds of activities they could organise. She hoped Jean would be part of it. She was one of the oldest residents of the town and her recall was sharp as a tack.

Something niggled at the edge of Marion's memory. Something to do with the Back to Badara weekend and the hall...she wriggled her shoulders to dispel it. Jean had been right when she'd said Marion's parents had been stalwarts of the church back in the sixties and seventies. They'd rarely missed church back then, when services were held weekly. And they'd been involved in every aspect of the community, from sporting clubs to the school. Her dad had died many years ago but her mum was in residential care in Wirini Bay. Vera's short-term memory wasn't good but she often recalled things from her younger days. Marion would chat to her about the hall on her next visit. It was always good to have something other than the weather and the garden to talk about.

She shut the door firmly as she left and was dismayed to hear the clatter of another trickle of plaster hitting the floor behind her.

four

Briony gripped the steering wheel hard all the way home. She knew if Marion ran with this hall celebration idea it would be bigger than Ben Hur and Briony would have to be on the committee. There was no saying no to Marion when she got her teeth into something. It was all right for her, being retired. Briony couldn't picture a future where that was even possible and she had plenty on her plate without Marion adding to it.

She turned down the driveway that ran beside the house then stopped. A large trailer loaded to the top with household items was parked at her back gate. She frowned and opened her door.

"Mum!"

Briony startled as a pair of arms wrapped around her and squeezed tight.

"Chelsea?"

"Thank goodness you're here." Chelsea looked over her shoulder. "Dad and Maddie aren't home. I was beginning to think you'd all gone away."

Briony looked from her eldest daughter to the trailer behind her.

"What's going on?"

"Didn't Dad tell you I was coming?"

"Not a word."

Chelsea's face crumpled. "Oh no, I thought he would have told you some of it. I can't go through it all again." She put her hands to her face.

"What can't you go through?" A million scenarios flew through her head: Chelsea had an incurable disease, or maybe Brandon; something had happened with the property. She'd thought Brandon's parents had overextended when they'd bought it for the kids.

"It's all too much." Chelsea sobbed into her hands.

"Go inside, Chels. Turn on the coffee machine. I'll make you a cup and you can tell me about it."

Chelsea didn't need further encouragement. She twisted away and almost ran inside.

Briony retrieved her gym bag and the small esky she'd taken to keep the lunch cool. Her heart sank as she passed the trailer. Stacked inside the stock crate were boxes labelled *bedding, kitchen appliances* and *winter clothes*. An assortment of other bags and boxes were packed around a clothes dryer, a small table and two chairs, and the thing that bothered her the most, the antique dresser Chelsea had taken with her when she'd left home to marry Brandon. Briony moved on to the car. It too was jammed full of bags and boxes. She pursed her lips and hurried inside. It looked like her daughter was moving and Briony had the worrying thought that it was to her old home.

"What have you done to Blake's old room?" Chelsea was standing inside the back door looking into the sunny room that ran across one half of the back of the house.

"I told you I was turning it into a family room slash library."

"You just said you were rearranging."

They looked into the room, which had been stripped of furniture and window dressings. The old carpet had been removed and drop sheets covered the cement floor. Briony had only recently washed and scrubbed the walls ready for the paint that was sitting in the corner waiting for when she had time to begin.

"I didn't realise you were doing a total makeover." Chelsea sniffed. "I thought you were getting rid of the bed and adding a few chairs and shelves. Where will Blake stay when he comes home?" She turned a forlorn look on her mother.

Briony gave a brief wistful thought to the son who'd left Australia three years ago to work in London. She hadn't seen him in the flesh, hadn't had a decent conversation with him – video calls were all very well but not the same – or hugged him close in all that time. She straightened her shoulders. "When he comes home there will be a place for him to stay."

"I hope you haven't changed my room." Chelsea started up the passage.

"Boots off, please," Briony said, noting her daughter's tears had evaporated as quickly as her concern for her brother.

"Mum," Chelsea groaned, but reached down to slide off her elastic-sided boots.

"I'm trying to protect my new hall runner. Hopefully this one will last longer than the previous one. And your room is ready, as it always is for when you and Brandon come for visits."

Boots off, Chelsea went on up the hall.

Briony glanced after her then went into the kitchen. She'd toyed with the idea of making Chelsea's room at the front of the house the library but…Her thoughts trailed off. An assortment of cups and plates were stacked on the sink, and the cake tin was closed but still on the bench, with the empty container that had held the sandwiches she'd made for Vincent and Madeline beside it. She put the cake away and stacked the dirty dishes in the dishwasher then retrieved the salad from the esky.

Next she made a beeline for the coffee machine. Besides her Thermomix it was her most prized kitchen accessory. She took in the mess of ground coffee and the cup of slops. Madeline had made coffee and not cleaned up. Briony began to sweep coffee grounds from around the perimeter as Chelsea came into the kitchen. The fact that she'd gone off to see her bedroom gave Briony hope that she wasn't sick.

"Now tell me what's up?" Briony asked.

"I...I've left Brandon." Chelsea sagged to a chair.

Briony took a step towards her daughter and faltered. She needed a drink and it was too early for wine. "I'll make us a coffee and you can tell me what's happened."

"Brandon's...he's..." Staccato sobs and hiccups swallowed Chelsea's words.

Briony reached out and took her daughter's trembling hand. "He's what?"

"He's taking ice."

Briony's stomach sunk to her feet and a hard lump formed in her throat. She tried to imagine the happy-go-lucky Brandon taking that path. He wasn't much of a drinker and he didn't smoke. At least as far as she knew.

"Are you sure?"

"Of course I'm sure." Chelsea's tear-filled eyes flashed. "Do you think I'd leave him if it wasn't true?"

Briony tried to think of what she knew about ice. Very little and it was all bad. "When you say he's taking ice—"

"He's an addict, Mum. It started out small. We...he...his mate gave him some. It was recreational, like having a few beers, but now he can't stop. I've tried everything...he won't..." Chelsea took a deep breath and between bouts of sobbing she told Briony about her life as Brandon had declined into heavy addiction, her fears and misery and the final straw when she'd finally realised he wasn't going to stop. She talked on and on until eventually her words dried up but not her tears.

Briony hugged her then, rocking her like she had when she was a child and been hurt. Only this was a hurt Briony knew wouldn't be fixed by rocking. Her own thoughts were in turmoil as she tried to understand something that had come as a complete bolt from the blue. They caught up as a family a couple of times a year, spoke on the phone regularly – how could she not have known something as big as this was happening?

By the time her sobs finally stopped, Chelsea was exhausted and Briony suggested she try to get some sleep. After settling her daughter on her bed, she returned to the kitchen and eased the door shut. She took a breath and held it like she used to do when the children were babies and down for their naps. For a moment the house was silent. She hoped Madeline and Vincent wouldn't return for a while and Chelsea would get some rest. Briony blew out the breath, drank some water then made herself another coffee. She still couldn't reconcile her image of Brandon with that of an ice addict.

And during her outpouring Chelsea had said she'd told her dad what was going on the previous evening. Briony was surprised Vincent hadn't told her about Chelsea's call, then remembered she'd been at a Women's and Children's Hospital Auxiliary meeting and he'd been asleep by the time she'd got home. This morning they'd had no time. She assumed that's what he'd been going to tell her when she'd dashed off to save the frittata in the oven.

Chelsea said her dad had offered to come and get her. She'd put him off, thinking she'd give Brandon one more chance. He'd gone to his mate's place but as much as she'd wished it, he hadn't come home. Her chat with her dad, along with Brandon's absence, had given her the courage to leave. She'd hooked up the stock trailer, loaded it up with as much of her stuff as she could and left.

Briony sipped her coffee as a raft of emotions crowded in on her; anger at Brandon, sorrow for her daughter, fear for how they'd deal with this. And how would it work having Chelsea at home again? She and Madeline were like chalk and cheese. They were the oldest and the youngest. Chelsea liked frilly clothes, pop music and new things while Madeline liked denim and horses, nothing else mattered. If they were together for more than a day or two the sparks flew. Their brother Blake had always been a mediating influence but he was too far away to help this time.

Briony sat up at the sound of a vehicle. A dog barked. It would be Vincent back from shifting sheep. She slumped down in her chair, unable to drag herself out of the funk she was in, and listened as his steps came closer along the path, then his boots thudded to the ground, first one then the other, the slight squeak of the screen door, water running in the bathroom and then he arrived in the kitchen.

He looked around. "Where's Chelsea?"

"Sleeping, I hope."

"Hell, that's a ten-hour trip without any stops. Why didn't she let me go and get her? Share the driving."

Briony stared at him, only recalling as he said it what a huge drive it would have been for Chelsea on her own. "She said after your chat, Brandon rang her high as a kite saying he was staying at a mate's place and she decided then and there to pack and come home." Briony felt something twist inside her. What a terrible mother she was. She had no idea how to cope with Chelsea's problems. She put a hand to her head.

"Have you got another headache?" Vince switched on the kettle. He'd refused to learn how to use the coffee machine.

"Another?"

"You had one a few days ago and then a couple of nights before that. It's not like you."

Briony frowned as he turned away to get out cups, then she remembered. A warm flush of guilt spread across her face. She'd snapped at him about something, had immediately realised how petty it had sounded then instead of apologising had blamed a headache. And the night before that Vincent had been amorous and wanted sex and she hadn't been able to muster any interest. She cringed to think she'd used the headache excuse then too. Mind you, there was a throbbing behind her temple at the moment. With all that was going on it was no wonder.

"What's going to happen, Vincent?"

"About what?"

"Chelsea."

"She's been through a lot, love. Let's give her a bit of space before we ask her to make decisions."

"Space!" Briony clapped a hand to her head. "Where's she going to put all her stuff?"

"We'll find a spot."

"Have you seen the trailer! And her car's crammed full. There's too much for her bedroom."

"We'll squeeze it in somewhere. Maybe I can find space in a shed for some of it."

"The sheds aren't vermin proof."

"Don't worry about it." He patted her shoulder. "Finding somewhere for her stuff is the least of Chelsea's worries. She's just left her husband, Briony. I'd like to give that idiot Brandon a thrashing."

The kettle flicked off and he turned away to make the tea. Briony fancied another coffee from the machine but three in a row would be a bit much.

Marion carried her fitness gear inside and Len called to her from the kitchen. "Want a cuppa, duck?"

She stuck her head in the door. He was waving a cup in the air and dressed in his favourite baggy trackpants and a t-shirt.

"Yes, thanks. Have you showered already?"

"Knocked off for the day."

She glanced at the mail bag lying on the end of the kitchen table. "I stopped to pick it up but you beat me to it."

"I was in the paddock next door when I remembered we hadn't collected it yesterday."

They had a roadside mail delivery three times a week. Mostly it was accounts, catalogues or one of the magazines Marion subscribed to but at least it was something else to look at. It wasn't often the bag was empty but, on the days when it was, she felt the hollow knock of disappointment.

"I'll get out of these gym clothes and be back."

Instead of coming straight home after fitness she'd called on Cliff Tiller. He was in his late eighties and lived alone in a little run-down house over the back fence from the hall. He had no family and Marion liked to check in on him. She'd first started calling on him when she'd still been teaching and had discovered he liked to read. Then she'd only called in once a month to swap his books from the library in Wirini Bay, but since she'd retired she popped in more often. He wasn't very mobile and he loved her sausage rolls. He'd invited her to stay and eat with him. She had but not before she'd cleaned his benches and cleared a space at the table for them. She'd been pleased to have a reason not to rush home.

When she returned to the kitchen, Len had put the cups on the table and cut two slices of cake. The mail bag had been emptied and the contents stacked neatly at the end of the table. As Marion had predicted it was a mix of catalogues and some windowed letters, probably bills, but on top was a postcard. She slipped on her reading glasses. It was a cartoon image of a set of enormous breasts with a glass of champagne overflowing from the cleavage and *Having a bubbling good time on the Gold Coast* printed across the top.

She sat and picked it up immediately.

"I don't know where Darcy finds these postcards." Len chuckled.

Darcy was their daughter Roxanne's partner and he had a wicked sense of humour. Roxanne travelled up and down the east coast a lot with her work and Darcy sometimes went too. He spent some of his time sourcing quirky gifts and cards.

"I think he scours every shop to find the worst card he can." Marion smiled. "He says he wishes we were there and that the card reminded him of me. Cheeky man." She flipped back to the front. "Not sure if it's the big boobs or the glass of bubbles?"

"Both, I'd say." Len winked.

Marion stuck the card to the fridge next to the one Darcy had sent a month before, which had a koala silhouette on a yellow sign that warned of drop bears for the next fifty kilometres. She kept them there on display for a while, a happy reminder of the bond they shared, even if so distant. She had a drawer full of postcards from various destinations around the world as well as Australia.

The wave of melancholy she'd shaken from the morning swept her again. She missed her kids, especially now she was retired.

Roxanne and Darcy lived in Sydney and her son, Grant, and his wife, Erin, lived in Perth. They all joked about Len and Marion being piggy in the middle. They were almost exactly halfway between the two cities as the crow flies. Such a long journey to visit either of them. She picked up her cup and blew on the weak milky coffee before she took a sip. And the thing she longed for, a grandchild, was nowhere on the horizon.

"Are you okay, duck?"

She looked up. Len was studying her across the table.

"Of course."

"You seemed a bit glum this morning and now..." He cocked his head to one side. "You've got that sad faraway look in your eye."

"Do I?" Marion pulled herself up straighter and tugged her lips into what she hoped was a smile. "Haven't seen the kids for ages. Missing them, I guess." It was more than that but how could she explain it to Len if she couldn't explain it to herself?

"How was your fitness class?"

"Good." She was pleased to change the subject. "Numbers were low. I'll have to get around and see a few people about coming more regularly or I'm worried Courtney won't continue. Oh, and I need you to come and look at the lintel above the hall door too. It might need some patching. It appears to be crumbling where they widened it during the renovations."

"That was a long time ago."

"Over fifty years. Jean's keen to have another big celebration like the Back to Badara they held when the hall was reopened."

Their landline rang. Marion was closest and got up to answer. She didn't rush. These days landline calls were usually someone trying to sell her something, a recorded voice saying they were from the tax office and she was going to jail if she didn't pay up, or someone wanting to conduct a survey. She put the phone to her ear and waited.

"Aunty Marion?" the male voice echoed.

She pressed the receiver tightly to her ear. "Blake?" Her nephew, Vince and Briony's son, lived in London and rarely called. They usually only spoke on birthdays and at Christmas. "Is everything okay?" She turned to look at Len, who raised his eyebrows.

"Yes, I'm fine. I'm...I'm actually in Sydney."

"Oh, that's wonderful, Blake. Are you coming home? I saw your mum today – she didn't say."

"She doesn't know yet. I...I'm coming next week and I...well, I thought I'd surprise the folks."

"Oh." Marion screwed up her face. She wasn't sure how well Briony would cope with a surprise, albeit a welcome one. She was such a flighty being and Blake hadn't been home in three years.

"I wanted to check in with you, to make sure they weren't going anywhere. I only spoke to them last week and they didn't say but I know they're often away with Mads and the horses."

"They're home at the moment and as far as I know they're not going anywhere for a while. When are you planning on coming?"

"I haven't booked yet. But I was thinking early next week."

"How long are you staying?" Marion wished it was one of her own children coming home.

"I'm not sure – maybe a couple of weeks or it could be longer."

"Your family will be so excited to see you."

"Actually, I've got a favour to ask. Last time I spoke to mum she was talking about turning my room into a library or something. I'm sure she'll want me to stay there but I wondered if I might stay in the shack at Port Kent then I can spend a bit of time with you and Uncle Len as well."

Marion was surprised but then she shouldn't be. She'd always felt closer to Blake than to her nieces and he'd had a special rapport with Len.

"You're most welcome to stay here but, yes, the shack's not being used."

"Thanks, Aunty Marion. I'll ring you when I've got the date sorted. See you soon. Say hello to Uncle Len."

Marion looked at the receiver as if Blake's face might be imprinted on it then replaced it on the base.

"I caught bits of that." Len beamed at her. "Sounds like Blake's coming home."

"Yes."

"Won't that be great. Did he say when he was leaving London?"

"He's already in Sydney."

"What? And he hasn't told anyone?"

Marion resumed her seat and took a bite of the cake she wasn't going to have. "He wants to surprise them."

Len's bushy white eyebrows shot up.

"Don't you say anything, Len Addicot. He wants to surprise them so it's not our place to tell."

"My lips are sealed." Len made a show of turning an imaginary key and throwing it away.

"Hmmm," she said.

"I can keep a secret."

Marion took another sip of coffee, which was almost cold now. It wasn't that Len was a gossip but he was guileless and sometimes things had a habit of popping out of his mouth when they shouldn't. At least with her nephew back home there would hopefully be some family get-togethers to look forward to.

five

Paige took a sip of coffee and swept her bleary gaze over Levi and Kodie, both tucking into their breakfast. It was seven thirty on Monday morning and she'd already been up for an hour. Just for the moment it was quiet, the two of them positively angelic, eating pancakes.

Last night she'd stayed up late watching a movie and then Levi had come into her bed in the early hours and taken over most of the space, giving her little sleep. He'd woken early and played noisily with his cars, waking Kodie who was immediately cranky. Paige had bought herself some peace by making them pancakes.

She glanced at the clock, took another fortifying slurp of coffee and stepped out into the sunroom to call Jayden. As expected he grumbled and burrowed under the covers. He was harder and harder to get out of bed these days. Keeping a wary eye on the clock, she gave him a few minutes then called him again.

A yelling match ensued. Paige took a breath. There was little she could bargain with him over – he needed his laptop for schoolwork but he loved his old battered radio. She threatened to take it away for a week if he missed the bus. He dragged himself out of his room, his straight dark hair sticking up every which way, and plonked himself at the table to pull on his socks. He ignored his siblings' cheery good mornings but was glad of their help when he couldn't find his shoes. There was a mad flurry as they turned the house upside down. By the time Kodie found them outside the back door, Paige just had time to shove Jayden's lunch box and a pancake at him before he made a dash for the bus. She rested her head against the wall and took a moment for herself.

Jayden had been at her all weekend to play footy. He'd done lots of research and had presented it to her over their late breakfast on Saturday. She'd put him off, wondering how she'd afford the subs, the boots and the fuel to get him to games, some of which, she'd discovered, would be as much as a one-hundred-and-fifty-kilometre round trip.

They'd been discussing it again loudly after dinner Saturday night when there'd been a knock on the back door. Levi was just out of the bath and had run naked to answer it. Paige was amazed to see Marion standing there, a small box in her hands. She'd apologised for visiting so late and acknowledged the children with a contorted twist of her lips that Paige realised was a smile. Levi had immediately wrapped himself around Paige's legs and Kodie had retreated to the kitchen.

Marion had brought them sausage rolls she'd made herself and pressed Paige about coming back to fitness.

"Don't worry about Courtney and her creche ideas," she'd said and leaned down closer to Levi. "You can come with your mum, that's fine."

Levi had poked his tongue out at Marion. Paige had put a hand over his mouth, thanked Marion for the sausage rolls and said she'd think about the class. It wasn't only having to take Levi with her that was the problem. She hadn't known it would cost her seven dollars each time.

They'd eaten the delicious savouries for lunch on Sunday. It had been a special treat and Paige had even managed to save a few for their lunch today. She went back into the kitchen and zipped up Kodie's lunch box.

"Nearly time to go, Kodie. Have you got your reading book?"

Kodie and Levi were playing some kind of game with the cars and didn't respond.

"Kodie, come on."

"Don't go," Levi cried as his sister climbed to her feet.

"We're going too, for a walk," Paige said.

Kodie couldn't find her reading book and once more a search ensued. They finally found it under a pile of dirty clothes they'd sifted through earlier looking for Jayden's shoes. Kodie protested yet again at having to be walked to school and Levi had grizzled all the way back, partly because it was a windy day again and partly because he was often out of sorts on Mondays after having his siblings to entertain him all weekend.

Paige threw the washing into the machine and started on the kitchen with Levi clinging to her leg wanting her to read him a story. She gave up on the dishes and sat on the floor. With her back to the cupboard, she dragged the little boy onto her lap and read several books before her bum went numb. Levi immediately began to grizzle. She glanced at her phone. It wasn't even nine thirty. The dishes she'd started still languished in the sink. The games they'd played on the weekend were stacked, some not put away, on one half of the table along with the papers and textas Kodie had been using. A basket of shoes was upended and cupboards hung open where Levi had helped in the search for first Jayden's sneakers and then Kodie's book.

She bribed him with a biscuit while she finished tidying up. When they'd first moved in it had taken her a while to unpack the things they'd brought with them in the hired trailer. The house had been partly furnished, thank goodness, and she'd spent the weeks since scouring any op shop or second-hand place within driving distance. She was happy with the furnishings now but after all that activity it left her with little to do to fill her days.

Levi finished his biscuit and wanted another. She tried to get him back to playing with his cars but he wouldn't be distracted and outside the wind was whirling around the yard stirring up dust. There were beds to be made and rooms to tidy to keep herself busy. She could put on the TV but she tried so hard not to let Levi spend too long in front of it each day.

She cajoled him to help her make the beds, making a game of it as best she could. Her bed was the last. She pulled up her doona from the pile it had made on the floor.

"Here's a bunny," Levi cried and plucked one of her fluffy slippers from the floor. They'd been a gift from her friend Niesha the previous Easter – a pair of fluffy pink bunny slippers with a chocolate egg in each. She retrieved the matching slipper from far underneath the bed and Levi slipped his bare feet into them. He slid around the floor chanting, "Pink bunnies, pink bunnies!"

Paige thought longingly of Niesha, who'd been her closest friend back in Melton. They'd been neighbours, helping each other with childcare, having the odd girls' night out with a couple of other neighbours they were friends with, even a movie together sometimes. Niesha had been there for her when the worst had happened.

Paige took a sudden breath. It was weird how a random reminder of Ari's loss still caught her out of the blue after more than three years. She closed her eyes and took a calming deeper breath.

Two years after the accident that had killed her partner and Levi's father, Paige had been slowly getting her life back together when Niesha's husband had lost his job and they'd had to move away from Melton to the other side of Melbourne for his new one. It had been a huge blow and the people who had moved in to their house had been awful; noisy and coming and going at all hours of the day and night. Jayden had started chumming up with one of the boys who lived there. The boy had been rude, disrespectful and had no curfews. Another of the reasons for Paige to move her own family away.

"Can I paint, Mummy?" Levi had ditched the slippers and was waving a paint brush he'd found under the bed. His big brown eyes and dark curls were so like Ari's.

Paige took another steadying breath. "How did that get there?" Levi loved to paint but she wasn't a fan. She kept a small collection of kids' paint pots and she'd set him up outside with them a few times when the other two had first gone back to school.

"Painting, painting!" Levi marched around her waving the brush in the air.

"It's too windy outside," she said as she stepped out into the passage, Levi's feet pounding the floor behind her.

Just inside the front door was another door leading to the adjoining shopfront. "Let's go in here." She turned the big old key in the lock and opened the door, letting Levi run in first.

"Lellow!" he yelled and ran around in big circles, his bare feet making thudding echoes on the wooden floor in the all-but-empty room.

Judging by the old signs and bits left behind on the shelves, the shop had been used for different businesses over the years. Now it was a huge empty space with newspaper-covered glass doors and windows facing the road. There were shelves on one wall behind a solid wooden counter that had been badly defaced. The wooden floorboards had been coated in varnish but had lost their sheen, and the paint on the walls was a dull dirty brown except for the wall opposite the counter, which had been painted a vibrant yellow. Levi couldn't do too much harm in here.

She put a large cardboard box and pots of washable kids' paint on a plastic sheet with the extra protection of layers of newspaper then slipped one of Kodie's old t-shirts over Levi's clothes. It almost touched the floor and he danced around, eager to begin.

He was happily painting to music by The Wiggles playing from the old CD player, another lucky find, when her phone vibrated in her pocket. She dug it out and frowned. It wasn't a number she recognised. She moved out into the passage and accepted the call.

"Hello, Ms Radcliffe?"

"Yes," she replied warily, not recognising the male voice.

"It's Tim Clark, Jayden's homegroup teacher. We met at the start of the term."

"Yes." Paige's heart thumped harder.

"Jayden's fine, by the way. I'm just ringing to chat about his work."

"Okay."

Tim told her Jayden was behind where he should be with some subjects and he wanted to touch base with her to discuss a few strategies. By the time Paige ended the call she wasn't sure whether to be reassured or worried. Tim Clark sounded confident and on the ball, but Jayden would need to make some improvements. His teacher had suggested tutoring but she wasn't sure how she was going to manage that. First she'd have to convince Jayden, then she'd need to find someone and then there'd be the cost. While she was still pondering that, her phone buzzed again.

This time she smiled when she looked at the screen. It was Niesha. She peeped at Levi who was still happily painting and sat on the floor to answer the call. It was so good to hear her best friend's voice. Between them they shared the highs and lows of the last few weeks. It was a relief to have someone else to share her concerns over Jayden with, and Niesha had her in stitches over the state of the house after her day spa outing, when she'd left her husband in charge of the kids.

"The place was a shambles when I got home but having the day to myself was worth it." Niesha sighed. "How are you doing? It must be tough out bush on your own."

"We're settling in okay. The house is like a castle compared to what we had."

"And no unwanted visitors."

"So far so good."

"Mummy, Mummy, look at my painting," Levi called.

Paige dragged herself upright and crossed to the shop door.

"Levi!" Her hand flew to her mouth.

The little boy's grin was wide with delight. He stood beside the yellow wall that now had stripes of colour down it. There were splodges of paint all over him, even his hair and face had splatters, and he'd left paint footprints on the wooden floor.

"I painted a rainbow," he said brightly.

"Oh, no!" she wailed. "Sorry, Niesh, gotta go."

"What's happened?"

"Levi's painting has gone beyond the box I gave him."

She tossed her phone aside and advanced on her son, who was waving his paint laden brush in the air. Drops of colour splattered left and right.

"No, Levi."

"I like painting."

She lurched forward to catch his arm. "Keep the brush still."

His bottom lip wobbled.

"It's okay." She reached out her other hand. "Pass me the brush. I think we've done enough painting for today."

He hesitated and a giant drop of paint ran down the handle and dripped to the floor.

She whipped it from his hand, gripped him beneath his arms and hoisted him up and onto a patch of clean newspapers.

He began to wail.

"Mummy's going to wipe you down then I'm going to run you a big bath. We need to get the paint off."

Levi's wail stopped abruptly. "With bubbles?"

"Sure."

By mid-afternoon when they headed off to meet Kodie, Paige felt as if she'd done a month's housework in a few hours. Besides the mess in the old shop, somehow little splodges of paint had ended up on her bedroom floor, the passage wall and around the bathroom. Everywhere she took Levi, the paint travelled with him, transferring to surfaces she hadn't realised he'd come into contact with. She'd scrubbed and soaked and cleaned until the skin on her hands was red and stinging.

"Kodie!" Levi cried as they approached the school gate.

Paige looked up and her frown deepened. Kodie was trailing across the oval, her bag over one shoulder with the principal walking beside her.

"Hello, Paige. I was going to ring you but then I realised the time and thought I'd catch you here."

Paige glanced from his smiling face to Kodie's frown. "Is something wrong, Mr Howell?" Kodie had been in trouble a few times at her last school but none since they'd been at Badara. She hoped she wasn't behind with her work like Jayden.

"Please call me Richard. And everything's fine. I've been talking to Kodie's teacher and she says Kodie's settling in well."

Kodie leaned in to the stroller to hug Levi, then the three of them stared back at the man on the other side of the school fence.

His glance moved between them then came back to rest on Paige. "It's Levi I've come to chat about. Kodie tells me he's three?"

Paige nodded.

"He might be eligible for our kindergarten's early start program."

"Oh?" Paige had thought she'd have to wait until the following year before Levi could start pre-school. "He's not four till August."

"We have some flexibility due to our relative isolation. I'm sorry, I should have got onto it earlier for you but I didn't realise you had another child until the other day. The session runs on Tuesday mornings. If you come in first thing tomorrow and do the paperwork Levi could start then and see how he goes."

"Oh," Paige said again. Any further words deserted her as a strange liberating sensation surged up through her chest. If Levi went to pre-school she could have a morning to herself, and unlike her friend Niesha there'd be no price to pay when she got home.

"I know he has older siblings but there aren't many social opportunities for pre-schoolers here. I'm sure you're a fantastic mum but he might enjoy some different stimulation."

Paige opened her mouth but nothing came out.

"And you might enjoy some time for yourself." Richard smiled.

"I...are you sure?" Paige stammered. "It's six months till his birthday."

"I'm sure he'll meet the criteria and if you leave him for a while tomorrow you can go to the exercise class."

"Oh." Paige couldn't believe so little coherence was coming from her mouth but her brain was a whir of thoughts. What could she do with several hours to herself each week?

"That's if you want to, of course. Claire said some of the ladies were a bit intense but she's going to give the class another go." His face lit up in an encouraging smile. "There's not much else to do in Badara on a Tuesday morning."

She grinned back. "You're right there."

"I want to get out." Levi kicked his legs.

"We're going now." Paige tipped the stroller and jiggled him back in the seat. "What time should I come tomorrow?"

"When you bring Kodie to school will be fine. Call in at the office and we'll sort out the paperwork."

"Thanks."

"See you all tomorrow." He waved and walked back across the oval.

Paige pushed the stroller steadily, oblivious to Levi's calls to get out. She loved her kids dearly but to have half a day a week to herself was a luxury she'd never had since…well, since Levi was born. Ari had been such a hands-on dad with Jayden and Kodie even though biologically they weren't his. And he'd been so looking forward to being a new dad with Levi, something he'd never experienced. She took a breath, carefully closing the door on any thoughts that might stray back to that time and Ari's death, and walked on, a spring in her step for the first time in a long while.

six

Marion watched the car park beyond the hall door while making a pretence of inspecting the lintel above. It was one of those lovely days autumn could bring: sunshine, a soft breeze and a few fluffy clouds to dot the azure-blue sky. They'd left the door propped open to let the air into the old hall.

Len had managed to plaster up the cracks but it was the lack of class attendees that had Marion keeping watch. So far only Jean, Claire and Paige had turned up. The three of them were chatting, mostly Jean with the odd murmur from Claire. Paige didn't say much but she appeared more relaxed without her little boy in tow. Evidently he'd been accepted into some early start pre-school program and she seemed rather happy about it. Mothers these days wanted children then were all too keen to palm them off. Paige hadn't brought anything for lunch so Marion assumed she wasn't planning to stay.

On the other side of the hall Courtney was setting up her sound system. Marion was keeping a surreptitious eye on her as well and noticed the instructor also casting glances towards the door, her face set with a sour look.

Since last Tuesday, Marion had managed to call on every woman in the district who'd originally professed interest in a fitness class. Twenty-two in total, and a couple of them entailed a forty-kilometre round trip. Not all were at home but she'd left them notes then followed up with a phone call, and the rest she'd reminded personally of their promise to come along. There'd been so many excuses. Gloria wouldn't be here either, of course, but surely Briony would come.

Marion checked her watch again. A car roared into a space out the front, Briony's four-wheel drive. That made five.

"Time to get started, ladies." Courtney's voice echoed loudly through her headset then her music started.

Marion waited for Briony and took the lunch container from her hands as she hurried through the door. "You get your mat out, I'll put this in the kitchen for you."

By the time she'd returned, the others were all marching on the spot and Marion joined in. The exercises were more strenuous than any they'd done before. They were twenty minutes in and Marion had decided she could do no more when Courtney paused for them to have a drink. "Good job, ladies," she intoned and took a sip from her bottle.

Just as they were ready to start again a burly man in a hi-vis shirt stuck his head in the door.

"Can I help you?" Marion asked.

"My boss asked me to look at the flooring job that needs doing."

"Oh," Marion said. "Who's your boss?"

"My nephew," Jean said.

"Are you Mrs Chesterfield?" the young bloke asked.

"I am." Jean turned to Marion. "You remember I've got a nephew who's a builder, my youngest brother's son?"

Marion didn't. Jean was from a big family and she was the only girl. There were a lot of Wilsons in the district and the youngest brother had moved away.

"He's obviously freed up some time to come and do this work for us," Jean said.

The bloke nodded. "I was coming this way on another job. I said I'd take some photos and some measurements so he can order what he needs."

"But there's no money," Marion said.

The bloke looked perplexed.

"My nephew's doing his dear aunt a favour." Jean winked and led the young man to the corner of the hall where the bearers needed replacing.

"How long will he be?" Courtney asked.

"I don't know," Marion said.

"Well, I'm not having my ladies exercising while there's a worker in the hall."

Paige snorted then ducked her head as Courtney eyeballed her.

Marion frowned and looked over as the bloke lowered himself through the space where the floorboards had been removed and disappeared from sight. She was pleased that there was progress with the repairs but did it have to be right when they were holding their class?

Jean was bending over the hole talking.

"Perhaps just let him get on, Jean," Marion called.

Jean stayed where she was, her head bent as if she was listening then she gave a sharp nod and came back to the group.

"He's going to be several minutes and I was finding out when they'd be doing the work," she said crisply. "The only days they have free are next Monday and Tuesday and the young man seems to think they'll need all that time if we want them to put the floor back together properly."

"So we'll have to miss next Tuesday." Courtney's eyebrows rose up to meet her fringe as she glared at Marion.

"I didn't know this was going to happen," Marion said.

"It was too good an opportunity to pass up," Jean said.

"Perhaps we could use the supper room." Even as Marion suggested it she knew it wasn't possible. The supper room had a number of tables and chairs and had become a storage area for other bits of furniture; a rarely used Sunday school cupboard, the mums-and-bubs equipment, tubs of costumes from the last school play and the old piano. It would take half a day to clear out and then they'd have to put it all back.

"We'd already canned that idea when the problem with the floor first happened," Briony said.

"I really don't think this is working, Marion." Courtney's hands were on her hips now. "You don't have the numbers we agreed on, you don't have a suitable venue and I'm not sure that your hearts are truly with the whole keeping fit concept."

"Of course they are," Marion snapped.

"Following a workout session with sausage rolls and cream cakes is not in the spirit of keeping fit, really, is it?"

Marion scowled back at the condescending look on the young upstart's face. "Socialising is important for morale."

"And we do have salad," Briony squeaked.

"I only bring cream cakes when there're a few left over." Jean's tone was affronted. "It's not every week."

Courtney shook her head. "I'm sorry, ladies, but I'm calling today off."

"Well, we won't be paying you then," Marion said.

"Suit yourself but I'm certainly not coming back until you've got the numbers and a decent venue." Courtney turned on her heel and unplugged her music. There was a heartbeat's silence and then the sound of a whistled tune coming from the hole in the floor.

Marion took in the faces of the other four attendees. Briony looked surprised, Jean's brow was furrowed, Claire had a startled look and Paige's brown eyes were dull with disappointment. They stood around awkwardly – the only sound besides Courtney packing up was the cheery whistle from below the floor. Without a backward glance the young instructor strode off with her speaker in tow.

Marion was the first to move. "I'm sorry about that." She dug out the envelope with the money she'd collected and began handing it back.

"She's an outspoken young lady, isn't she." Jean was looking towards the door.

"I guess it wasn't quite what she bargained for," Briony said.

"Young ones today," Marion muttered. "No stamina."

Paige was next in the line to receive her money back. She met Marion's look with a steely gaze.

"I guess that's the end of classes till the work's done and we've got more people," Briony said.

"Such a shame," Jean said.

Footsteps echoed back across the floor as the young man returned. "Got what I need, thanks," he said.

"Tell my nephew to ring me when he's got a start time," Jean said. "I'll meet him here with a key."

"Will do." The man strode away, the sound of his whistled tune following him out the door.

Marion felt the last vestiges of her fitness group drifting off after him. "We need a space to continue our workouts. Thinking caps on, ladies."

"We'd need an instructor," Briony said.

"First things first." Marion put her fingers to her lips and tapped. "Where else could we meet?"

There was silence for a moment. "I could ask Richard if there's somewhere at school," Claire said.

"Already tried that," Marion said. "Unless we change our day."

"What about the old bakery?" Jean said.

All eyes turned to Paige. She flicked her gaze between them.

"The place you live in was originally a bakery," Marion said.

"Oh, I thought it had been a second-hand store."

"It was, but that was after the general store cafe," Briony said.

"Which came after the bakery," Marion said with a firm nod.

"It had a lovely wooden floor," Jean said wistfully.

"It still does," Paige said.

"That's so wonderful of you to offer." Jean clasped her hands to her chest.

"I—"

"Yes, thank you." Marion wasn't sure that Paige had offered nor if her place was suitable but they were desperate. "Could you put together a few exercises, Claire?"

Claire's mouth fell open and she took a step back. "Me?"

"Didn't you say you used to go to a fitness class in Adelaide?"

"That was quite a while ago and—"

"That doesn't matter." Marion was determined to hang on to their group if only by a fingernail. "As long as you can remember a few exercises, I'm sure we could all muddle along."

"Oh." Claire looked startled again.

"That's all right, dear." Jean patted her back. "Perhaps between us we could come up with a routine. Why don't we all plan a few exercises each? It won't matter if some are the same."

"And you want to use my place?" Paige finally got a word in.

"Yes, dear." Jean nodded and smiled encouragingly.

"What about music?" Marion said.

"There's plenty on Spotify," Briony said.

Paige coloured. "I don't have wi-fi and my phone data is limited."

"I have Spotify," Briony said. "We can use mine."

"Right, that's settled," Marion said. "Next week we meet at the old bakery."

"Thank you, Paige." Jean smiled her sweet smile. "Why don't we have an early lunch to celebrate?"

"Now?" Marion glanced at her watch. It was barely eleven o'clock.

"I didn't plan to stay," Paige said. "I have to pick up Levi."

"Nor me today." Claire had found her voice.

"What about next week?" Jean said. "Since Paige is having us her way perhaps we could bring enough to share."

"We always do," Marion said.

"Yes, but in this instance Paige is supplying the venue so she doesn't have to supply food."

Paige opened her mouth to speak but Briony jumped in.

"I'm happy with that," she said. "You'll stay and eat with us next week, won't you, Claire?"

Claire glanced from Briony to Paige, whose look was beseeching.

"Yes, I'll bring something."

Marion felt the tension in her body ebb away. Their little exercise club would continue.

"I've been wondering," Jean said. "About holding a 'fifty years on' celebration to raise funds for the hall. We're a mixed representative of the district. Why don't we throw some ideas around over lunch next week? It would be good to have input from different age groups, those who've been in the district forever and those who've not been here so long." She beamed in the direction of Paige and Claire.

"What a good idea, Jean." Marion nodded, wishing she'd thought of it herself although she really didn't know what input Claire would have, she hardly said boo to a goose, and Paige would possibly not be here long enough to see it through. Still Jean's suggestion had merit.

Paige walked at a brisk pace along the edge of the road. The footpath in this section was only dirt and the road was better for walking. Not that she was taking much notice of where she walked. Holding next week's fitness club at her place filled her head. How had she let them talk her into that? She'd be a bit early to get Levi but she had to escape before those wily women had her roped in to do something else. She'd have to make sure she had her supplies topped up; milk, tea and coffee. They liked to have lunch and even though they said they'd bring it she couldn't not prepare something.

Perspiration cooled on her skin and she shivered as she walked into the shade thrown by the giant grain silos on the other side of the road. They'd been a hive of activity when Paige and her children had first moved to Badara back in January. Levi especially had been entertained by watching the trucks coming and going. Today the yard appeared empty and there was no sound or sign of anyone.

From further along the road, the sounds of children laughing and playing drifted on the slight breeze. Once more Paige shivered. She undid the windcheater she'd tied around her waist and slipped it on. It seemed silly on such a beautiful day but since she'd cooled off after exercising she hadn't warmed up again. Instead of continuing on to the school where the pre-school was tucked in one corner, she turned down the side road and walked the couple of blocks to the main highway. Not that you could call it a highway. The bitumen which ran between Wirini Bay and Badara ended a few k's the other side of town and became a dirt road.

The only business still open in Badara, the postal agency, was on the corner and that's where she was headed. That it was a 'business' was debatable and if it was open it would be a surprise but Paige went anyway. Mail came to Badara three days a week: Mondays, Wednesdays and Fridays. Paige didn't bother calling in to check very often because she rarely got mail. On a couple of occasions there'd been something too big for the box and she'd had to go inside, which she didn't like doing. Mr Carter who ran the place wasn't a pleasant fellow. His hostile manner put her off, as if she wasn't entitled to ask for her own mail, and his personal hygiene wasn't good.

The first time she'd gone in all three kids had been with her and he'd growled at them to keep their sticky fingers off the merchandise. Not that she would have let her kids touch anything in that shop. There was a dusty stand of greeting cards that looked as if they'd been there forever, and several second-hand magazines, books and DVDs, and that, along with a few post office items, was the extent of his merchandise.

Anticipation battled with unease when she opened her box to discover a slip signalling something to be collected. There were no cars parked outside the worn-out building but Paige hoped someone else might already be inside collecting their mail. She tentatively tried the door and to her surprise it opened. Mr Carter advertised he was open weekdays between eleven and twelve but a couple of times before she'd been there and the place had been locked up.

The shop was dark as usual and the fusty shut-up smell mingled with that of stale cooking and strong body odour. She tried not to breathe deeply as she approached the counter. There was no-one there but she could hear television noise coming from the room beyond.

"Hello?" she called.

The sound of cars screeching ricocheted out from the back.

Paige cleared her throat. "Hello!"

There was a grunt and then movement. She steeled herself as Mr Carter waddled slowly through the door, squinting at her from behind grubby glasses.

"Yeah," he said.

"I've come to collect a parcel." She placed the note on the counter.

"Right." He grunted, picked it up and leaned across to look behind her. "No-one with you today?"

"My children are at school." Paige was forced to take a breath through her mouth. "I'm on my way to pick the little one up, actually, so I'm in a bit of a hurry."

"Yeah, righto." He shuffled to a set of pigeonholes against the side wall and leaned down.

Paige glanced around the dingy shopfront. She'd love to throw open the doors and windows and get in here with a broom and mop and bucket. The poor man couldn't be comfortable living in this mess, surely.

"Your lucky day." He picked a package from the bench and shuffled back to the counter. "A parcel."

Paige eyed it suspiciously.

"You taking it or what?"

"Yes." She reached for the postbag. "Thank you. Have a good day." She spun away and out the door as he harumphed behind her and gave a wheezy cough.

Outside Paige took a big breath of fresh air and read the sender's details. She'd thought maybe it was from Niesha but the parcel was from her mother. It wasn't anyone's birthday so it was a bit unusual. Although she'd been known to send random gifts before, this was the first communication since they'd moved to Badara. There'd been no texts or calls between them, except a short response to the message Paige had sent with their new address and phone number, and now there was a parcel. Paige turned the bag over. It was soft and pliable – maybe clothes. She tucked it under her arm and set off to collect Levi.

He was tired after his busy morning so they hadn't got far when he started to complain. Paige piggybacked him home and made him some lunch. Once he was settled with his food and ABC Kids on the TV she picked up the parcel and slit it open. Three t-shirts and an envelope slid out onto the table. She picked up the shirts. An expensive brand name was emblazoned across the front of each one. Black with white writing for Jayden, way too big but he'd grow into it. Pink for Kodie with sparkle in the writing – she hated pink and sparkles. The smallest t-shirt was grey with darker grey writing. It was a rare and random gift, probably ordered online with little thought, and Paige felt not the slightest bit of gratitude. Her mother either wanted something, which once again was unusual, or she felt guilty about something, also unusual.

Paige picked up the envelope. An obviously hurried note was scribbled across the front. *Hello Paige, I agreed to send on this letter so am enclosing something for the children.* Paige frowned. What was her mum up to? *Love Mum and Dad. PS Don't shoot the messenger but we think you should give the contents serious thought.*

So she obviously knew what was in it. Paige ripped open the envelope, curiosity overriding her annoyance that a rare communication from her mother had an ulterior motive. Inside was a letter. Paige unfolded it. Her gaze swept straight to the sender's name at the bottom and her anger returned. Lucinda and James. Jayden's other grandparents had used her mother to make contact again. At least her mother hadn't given them her address – yet anyway.

She glanced briefly at the words: they wanted to send money, how much they cared – she nearly choked when she read that – he could attend his father's old school. She stopped. That was new. She re-read that sentence then crumpled the page to a tight ball in her hand.

"No bloody way!"

She snatched up her phone and typed a text to her mother thanking her for the t-shirts and asking her not to forward any more letters. Her finger hovered over the send button. She went back to the text, put on caps lock and typed a reminder not to give anyone her address or phone number. Then she jabbed send.

"Mummy, I'm hungry." Levi's plaintive voice drifted from the lounge. Probably a break between shows.

"Turn the TV off and come and see what Mimi has sent."

At least her kids had got a new t-shirt each out of her mother's con.

After Paige and Claire had left the hall, the remaining three women sat at the servery in the kitchen and enjoyed their shared lunch. The tea had just been poured when Jean remembered her photocopies.

"I had the devil of a job," she said as she ferreted around in her gym bag. "First our scanner wasn't working then the printer was out of ink. I had to make a special trip to Wirini Bay yesterday but here they are." She handed the pages to Briony and Marion. "The clipping was bigger than A4 so I had to do it over two pages. The photos have copied quite well."

Marion slipped on her reading glasses and scanned the article about the Back to Badara celebrations held on a November weekend in 1970.

"That's my mother-in-law, Mary, holding up the ribbon for the mayor to cut," she said.

"Doesn't she look glamorous?" Briony said. "With that hat and those pearls she could be the queen."

Marion snorted. "She thought she was."

"Mary was a fabulous sewer and milliner," Jean said. "She could make a silk purse from a sow's ear. She would have made that outfit."

"I remember Mum made my dress," Briony said. "It was a big deal at the time."

"She was a grand sewer as well," Jean said. "We all made so many of our own clothes back then."

Talk of clothing jogged Marion's memory. "Oh! My best friend, Gail, and I wore jeans most of that weekend. Neither her parents nor mine were happy about that." The uneasy feeling stirred in her stomach again.

"All I'm any good at is mending ripped jeans and shirts," Briony said. "I wish Mum had passed on her sewing skills to me."

"She died before she had the chance." Jean reached across and patted Briony's hand.

Both women looked momentarily lost. Briony's mum, Jill, had died not long after Vince and Briony were married. There were so many family connections in the district Marion had forgotten Jill and Jean had been sisters-in-law.

"I've spoken to a few people about the fundraiser," Marion said. "There's a lot of interest. Perhaps we could re-create some of these moments for it."

"There was a time capsule," Jean said. "That's the photo of the mayor with our fathers."

Now that she was wearing her glasses Marion could see her dad clearly in the photo beside the mayor, who was holding a shovel in his hands. She peered closer. In the background was her mum, and partly obscured was a girl with cropped hair wearing pants. Marion shook her head at her teenage image. The pants were her new denim jeans and she'd had her hair cut short. Her mother had hated it. Marion had been so sure of herself back then, so cocky so...A gasp escaped her lips as the unease turned to a surge of dread. "The time capsule!" she blurted.

"We could dig it up and bury another one," Jean said. "People always love that kind of thing."

"No!"

Both Briony and Jean were startled.

"Not for a fundraiser anyway," Marion said quickly.

"It'd be the perfect thing." Briony frowned at her.

"People could pay to put something in the next one." Jean clapped her hands. "Another way to raise money."

"No." Marion shook her head quickly. "It's not quite right for an event like this. We need something grand to get people putting their hands in their pockets. Time capsules have been done to death." She knew she was blathering but she had to put a stop to the time capsule reveal.

Like a bolt from the blue, seeing her teenage self in the photo had brought it all back. She didn't like to admit it but she and Gail had been a pair of bitches back then. Fifty years into the future had seemed beyond them. Even a few years, Marion thought sadly.

They'd had no idea in 1970 that three years later Gail would succumb to leukaemia. Marion wondered how different life would be now if her best friend was still alive. How would Gail have responded to the predicament they'd created? There was no use wondering. Marion had to go it alone, but one thing was for sure: revealing what they'd put into the capsule would cause so much hurt to the small community she now thought so fondly of. She couldn't let it happen.

She glanced up from the pages she gripped tightly in her hand. Both women were frowning at her. Marion hoped her face didn't give away her fear.

"Let's think of as many ideas as we can and pool them all next week when we discuss it with the others after fitness. I'm sure there'll be lots of far more interesting and money-making suggestions."

She took a gulp of tea. So many futures depended on that time capsule staying buried.

seven

Briony glanced around her kitchen table. It was set for six – not usual to have visitors for dinner on a Tuesday night, especially given it was Marion and Len who'd invited themselves. She'd tried to put them off but Marion had been insistent. It was very strange. Their family dinners were usually on weekends and not that often any more now that Vincent and Marion's mum, Vera, no longer joined them.

The spicy aroma of the chicken curry she had simmering in the slow cooker filled the kitchen and the sounds of the TV drifted from the room next door. Madeline and Chelsea were both in there watching a quiz show – Madeline seemed to be a calming influence on her sister for once – and Vincent was in the shower. Everything was ready. Marion was bringing pavlova for dessert so there was little else for Briony to do but wait.

Sitting at this hour of the night was rare. After the crazy day she'd had, if she relaxed any more she could easily go to sleep sitting up. They'd had a busy start, shifting sheep early but, thankfully, after Courtney's walk-out, Briony had been home earlier than she'd expected from her class. Marion had been suddenly eager to get away after her proclamation they all were to come up with fundraiser ideas. She'd been quite distracted and then to ring an hour later and ask if she and Len could come for dinner was very strange. Dinners with Marion and Len were for birthdays, Christmas and the odd planned get-together in between, not out of the blue on a Tuesday night. Briony had told her Chelsea was home. Not why, of course. She'd made it sound like a visit.

Luckily Briony had already planned the curry and there was plenty. She'd set it going, wrangled in washing and run out some drums to Vincent in the paddock. Both girls had momentarily disappeared and when they did come back from a trip to Wirini Bay she'd pressed Chelsea to finish sorting her things. Some of the boxes had still lined the passage and with visitors expected Briony wanted a tidy house. Vincent had left the furniture on the trailer for now and stored the whole thing in the old barn, which had a cement floor and a ceiling. Madeline had made herself scarce again as Briony had cajoled a sullen Chelsea into stacking and sorting the rest of her gear into her room. And now the last thing Briony felt like doing was entertaining.

Vince shot past the door heading up the passage wrapped only in a towel. "Heard a car pull up," he called.

Briony adjusted one of the place settings. Marion always put her on edge. Briony felt her sister-in-law had long ago weighed her up and found her wanting. It really was very strange to invite herself for dinner. There must be something she wanted to tell them as a family, but why hadn't she asked them to come to her place? With Chelsea home they were a group of four now but cooking never fazed Marion. She'd whip up a meal for visitors out of nothing. Not Briony – she liked plenty of notice when it came to preparing food. Perhaps Marion or Len were ill and it was easier to come here, or maybe they were selling up the property. They'd talked about it a few years back but nothing had come of it.

"Hello!" Marion's voice boomed up the passage.

Briony gave one last glance around her kitchen, took a deep breath and stepped out to meet them.

Her squeal brought an instant response from the rest of the family who pushed in close behind her.

"Blake!" She wrapped her arms around her son's frame. He was thin yet muscly beneath her grip. Over his shoulder Marion and Len hovered in the doorway, both beaming widely.

"Where...how?" Briony spluttered.

Vince stepped up, his shirt not fully buttoned, gripped Blake's shoulder then pulled him into a hug. Both Madeline and Chelsea were there too, shrieking their delight. It took some time for the ensuing hullabaloo to settle. It was Marion who ushered them into the kitchen.

Briony sat Blake at the head of the table, lowered her shaking body to the chair beside him then leaped up again. "We need another place set."

"I'll do it," Chelsea said.

Len popped a bottle of champagne he must have brought with him and glasses were handed around.

Vince got a beer from the fridge and one for Len. "One for you, son." He waved the can at Blake.

"I'm happy with bubbles for now," Blake said and raised his glass in the air. "It's great to be home."

"Oh, don't you sound posh," Madeline said.

"Do I?" Blake shrugged.

"You've acquired an English accent," Marion said. "It's more obvious in the flesh."

"We only spoke a week ago." Briony tried to recall the conversation. He'd given nothing away to indicate he was leaving London although now that she thought about it their call had been brief. "How long will you be here for?"

"I'm back in Australia for good."

"Really? But why didn't you tell us you were coming?" Briony clutched his arm, worried she was imagining him and he'd disappear like a mirage if she let him go.

"I wanted to surprise you."

"Well, you've done that," Madeline said.

"When Blake said he was arriving today I thought I'd get you to have us for dinner here," Marion said. "That way we knew you'd all be home."

"He told you he was coming?" Briony looked from Marion to Blake.

"Only so I knew you'd be home," he said. "I told you, I wanted to surprise you."

"I still wish I'd known." Briony gave Blake's arm a squeeze. He really was there.

"So you could kill the fatted calf?" Chelsea smiled but there was a hint of sarcasm in her voice. Things had been tricky since she'd come home. She'd been getting constant calls and messages from Brandon and his parents, pleading with her to go back to him. Briony knew she was hurting but she had been morose and difficult to live with. Just that morning she'd almost bitten off Briony's head when she'd suggested they go to fitness together.

"No." Briony swallowed her annoyance. "So that I'd have time to adjust to the shock. It seems all my children are surprising me lately."

"Not me." Madeline smiled, a smug look on her pretty face.

"Give it time," Vince muttered and Madeline's smile slipped.

"Is the food ready yet?" Chelsea asked. "I'm starving."

Briony leaped to her feet. "I haven't put the rice on."

"I'll help," Marion said.

"I hope there'll be enough curry." Briony tried to remember how much chicken she'd added.

"I made a tuna mornay as well, just in case." Marion nodded at the casserole beside the pavlova. "I'll pop it in your oven to keep it warm while we do the rice."

Behind them the conversation picked up again. Vincent and the girls were firing questions at Blake. Briony kept an ear on their chatter not wanting to miss anything. She got as far as opening the rice container and spilling some of the contents before Marion took over.

"You go back and sit down. I'll get the rice going." Marion shooed her away.

Briony sat back beside Blake just as he asked Chelsea how Brandon was.

Chelsea immediately burst into tears. Vince, seated on his daughter's other side, put an arm around her shoulders. Madeline's face was crestfallen and Len fidgeted with the serviette in front of him.

Blake reached across to take Chelsea's hand, a shocked look on his face. "What's happened?"

"Chelsea's come home for a while," Briony said quickly.

"I...can't...go back." Chelsea's words came out in stutters between her sobs.

"It's a bit of a story," Vince said. "Bottom line is Brandon's got into drugs."

"Oh no, really?" Blake said. "Bad?"

Chelsea nodded. "He's addicted to ice." A giant sobbed jarred the words from her mouth.

"I'm so sorry, Chels."

Briony glanced at Marion and Len. Marion was poker faced as usual but Len looked uncomfortable. They would have to be here tonight and hear all this before Briony had a chance to smooth out the story.

Vince passed Chelsea his hanky. "This is clean."

She took it, blew her nose noisily then pushed away from the table. "Sorry to spoil your homecoming."

"You haven't." Blake smiled.

Briony wished Chelsea had managed to hold it together. Just until Marion and Len had left, at least. Their children had both gone to university, found suitable partners and were living perfect lives. Briony would have preferred to keep Chelsea's news quiet until they were sure what was to be done. She and Vincent needed to speak with Brandon's parents. It wasn't that she didn't believe her daughter but Chelsea was prone to exaggeration. Briony hated the thought of any addiction – many lives had been ruined by them – but was it as bad as Chelsea said? Maybe this was only a hiccup. Marriages had downs as well as ups but Chelsea hadn't been married long enough to learn that.

"I'll go and wash my face." Chelsea sniffed and wobbled to her feet. "Back in a minute."

Marion had moved back to the table and looked from Vince to Briony. "You didn't say Chelsea was home for more than a holiday."

Briony felt the judgement in her look and her tone.

"I gather this is recent," Blake said.

"She's been grappling with it for ages, poor kid." Vince shook his head. "Finally last week she got up the courage to tell us and leave him."

"Sounds like there's a full house here," Blake said.

Vince clapped a hand on his shoulder. "We'll squeeze you in, son."

"I hear Mum's turning my room into a library."

"I've only just started," Briony said. "It's a bit of a mess."

"The girls can bunk in together."

"No way, Dad," Madeline whined, echoed a second later by Chelsea, who'd come back into the room.

"Great to see you too." Blake pulled a face at his sisters then grinned. "Don't worry. I'll stay at the shack at Port Kent."

"But that's so far away," Briony said.

"Not that far."

"Surely we can organise something here." Briony looked imploringly at her husband. "It wouldn't take much to clear out Blake's old room."

"Tonight?" Vince yelped. "You've got stuff everywhere."

"We can't have people thinking we've turned out our son after all this time he's been away."

"Mum." Blake shook his head and smiled. "It's just somewhere to sleep and I'll see you during the day."

"If you're sure," Briony murmured and looked across at Marion, who'd moved back to check the rice. Somehow her sister-in-law had taken over, as she often did.

"I hope you haven't gone soft working in an office in London," Vince said. "I could do with some help. There's a bit of stock work to do over the next few days."

"Do you still ride?" Madeline leaned in. "We can go for a farm tour on the horses."

"I need some help shifting furniture." Chelsea gave her brother her sweetest smile.

"There's a paint brush and tin of paint at the shack." Len added his piece. "A few window frames need some attention there."

"Give the man a break," Marion said, her authoritative voice cutting over the top. "How was your trip home, Blake? When did you leave London?"

Briony sat back while the chatter went on all around her. She studied her son, drinking in every feature. Blake had always kept his hair short but now the sides were very closely clipped and it was thicker at the top in a soft wave that swept back from his forehead. His long, thin sideburns were neatly trimmed, his face clean-shaven and his clothing fitted his trim and muscly body.

She could see only glimpses of the boy who'd left home to do his senior schooling at boarding school, then gone on to university and his first job with an international company in Sydney as a health and wellbeing adviser before heading overseas. He'd still seemed so young at Chelsea's wedding and Briony's heart had almost broken when a week later they'd waved him off overseas. The job and then circumstances had meant almost three years had passed since she'd last seen him in person. He was truly a man now and yet almost a stranger.

She was disappointed he wasn't staying here with them but had to admit to being relieved at the same time. They needed the chance to get to know each other all over again. Yet how would she do that if he was off with the others all day and spending his nights at Port Kent? What would people think if he wasn't staying full-time with them? And word would soon be out that Chelsea had left Brandon. She couldn't bear the thought of her perfectly constructed family becoming the subject of gossip.

"Dinner's ready to dish."

Marion's call cut through the turmoil of thoughts whirling around Briony's head. She put on her best smile, crossed the room, and was relegated to the position of helper in her own kitchen.

eight

The next morning Marion and Blake arrived at the shack in Port Kent, both cars loaded with supplies. They hadn't told Briony but the shack hadn't been quite ready to occupy and Blake had stayed the previous night at Len and Marion's. The day before his arrival Marion had gone to the shack to drop some basic groceries and make the bed and had discovered mice had been in. It had taken longer than she'd expected to clean and she'd carted all the sheets and bedding home to wash.

Together they put everything back to rights. Marion had been surprised by how useful Blake was. Living away had obviously been good training for him. Briony had done everything for her children, still did if the previous night's lack of help from the two girls was anything to go by. In contrast Blake had cleared the table and offered help on several occasions and today was pulling his weight with setting up the shack.

Marion gave the kitchen bench one last wipe and went outside. Blake was standing under the front verandah, gazing out to sea, the last bag he'd gone out to collect lying at his feet.

"I didn't realise how much I've missed this."

Marion followed his gaze over the ocean gently lapping the white sand of the bay stretched out in front of them. Such a contrast to the dirt roads, endless paddocks and straggling tree lines of the farm. "It's a long time since you've been back to Port Kent." Once he'd moved to Sydney he hadn't come home often.

"It's not just Port Kent but the white beaches and blue water and the weather. It's so much warmer here than London." He lifted his arms wide. "So good to feel the warmth."

Marion eyed off his skin, which was as white as English snow. "Better not get too much sun or you'll be burned before you know it."

He dropped his arms back to his sides. "Uncle Len said you might move here when he retires."

"Did he?" Marion was surprised. Len rarely talked of retiring. She'd mentioned moving to the beach a few times but he'd put her off and it hadn't come up in a long while. Now that she was retired she couldn't picture the two of them in this tiny place with nothing to do but look at each other and the view, no matter how engaging that view was. "You two stayed up late last night." It had been almost eleven when they'd returned from her brother's. She'd been more than ready to fall into bed but Len had got out his port and offered Blake a nightcap. Marion had been surprised when he'd accepted. She'd left them to it.

"It was good to catch up. I feel as if I was only a boy the last time we had a decent chat. I didn't realise we had so much in common."

"I thought you'd have been too tired." She studied him closely. There were shadows under his eyes and the morning stubble across his chin gave him a grey complexion. She wondered again what had brought him home without telling anyone he was coming and what he and Len had talked about so late into the night.

"Still running on adrenaline, I guess, but it's caught up with me now." He glanced at his phone. "Mum will be expecting me for lunch."

"I have to be off too," Marion said. "I have a bit to do."

"Of course, thanks for your help. I really didn't mean for this to put you out."

"It hasn't."

He smiled and the weariness disappeared from his face.

Marion rested a hand on his arm. "It really is good to have you home. And you're welcome to stay here. At least until you work out your next move." He'd been definite he was staying in Australia when Briony had asked him last night but vague about what he was going to do and where he was going to live. Marion didn't think it her place to press him.

"Thanks, Aunty Marion." He took her empty cup. "It's been good to see you and Uncle Len again. I love that he still calls you 'duck' after all these years."

"A ridiculous name," Marion snorted. When they'd first been married she'd wanted to keep ducks. They'd ended up being the bane of her life and Len had thought it hilarious and called her the duck queen, which had ended up simply being duck. "Don't you get any ideas about calling me that." Marion glared at Blake then tried for a softer look "But we can probably dispense with the Aunty and Uncle. It's sounds odd coming from adults. I've suggested your sisters drop it off too but they won't."

"Mum wouldn't like it." He grinned. "I'll stop in and say hello again one night soon."

"Call first just in case," she said and set off for her car, spinning her wheels in the gravel as she backed away.

Thoughts of Blake were immediately replaced by what was on her agenda next. She had some tidying up to do at home and a meal to prepare. Today was her mahjong afternoon at Jean's place and she liked to get everything ready before she went in case she was late home. The other two women who played would also be useful sounding-boards for ideas for the hall celebrations. The thought of organising something for the town that involved the whole community had put a zing in her step. The only downer was the blasted time capsule but she had plenty of time to derail that.

She'd just made it inside the house when her landline rang. She eyed it suspiciously then picked up.

"Is that you, Marion?" a voice croaked.

"Jean? Yes, it's me."

"I'm sorry, dear, but I have to cancel our game today. I've woken up with a sore tooth and I need to visit the dentist."

"Oh, that's no good." Marion's enthusiasm for the day ahead rushed from her like air from a balloon.

"They can fit me in after lunch."

"Can I bring you something? Some of my special chicken soup?"

"Oh, no, dear, but thank you. I've got plenty to eat and Keith manages under supervision."

"You take care then," Marion said. "Hopefully you'll be okay for fitness club next week."

"Oh yes, I'll be fine by then. I'd hate to miss that. So good of Paige to have us her way. What a valuable addition to the town she's proving already."

Marion said goodbye and put the cordless phone back in its cradle. She thought Jean's optimism a bit early where Paige was concerned. Marion still didn't think she'd last long in town but while there was somewhere for their fitness group to continue she was grateful.

She tucked a chair back under the table and wondered what she was going to do with the rest of her day now that mahjong was cancelled. She'd seen her mother only last weekend but Vera Hensley was quietly in la la land and time meant nothing to her. Perhaps a trip to Wirini Bay would brighten Marion's day and Vera's. And she could show her mother the newspaper clipping. You never knew what memories would be triggered. Through the window she saw Len walking across the yard towards the house. If he knew she was going to be home he'd want her to help him with something. She had to make it clear she still had plans for the afternoon even though mahjong was cancelled.

By the time he arrived in the kitchen she had the kettle on and lunch started.

"Saw you come back," he said. "Thought I'd come in for a cuppa."

"We can have one with an early lunch. My mahjong's been cancelled." Marion turned away from the hope that filled his face and poured his tea. "I'm going to the Bay. I need a few things from the shop and I'll visit Mum."

"Oh." There was disappointment in his voice. "That'll be nice for Vera. Say hello for me."

Marion suddenly felt mean. "Are you busy? Why don't you come too?"

"Having trouble with the harvester."

"Still?" The old machine had been temperamental over harvest but it had made it through. Len had pulled it apart to work on it and clean it as soon as harvest had finished. That was months ago.

He sighed. "I've been putting it off. Needed a part and by the time that came I was busy with other things. I have to get it done now though so I can pack it away. There've been a few mice about and I want to make sure it's put away properly."

"I told you about the mice at the shack."

He nodded.

"I hope we don't end up with a plague again. It's impossible to keep them out of the shack, and this place for that matter."

Marion finished the cold meat and salad she was preparing while Len sipped his tea.

"Busy dinner at your brother's last night," Len said as she put their lunch on the table.

"Yes. Fancy Chelsea being there. And Brandon's into drugs. Did you know about that?" Marion eyed her husband. He and Vince had the odd men's weekend at Port Kent when they played golf or went fishing. Sometimes the two of them discussed things they kept to themselves.

Len shook his head.

"Sounds like she's left him for good."

He blew a breath over his lips, making a low whistle like a bomb dropping. "It'll cause a ruckus."

"It already has. Chelsea's obviously distressed and Briony's acting like a startled rabbit."

"I meant with Brandon's family. His dad bought that property when they married. What's it been, three years?"

"Almost three. Evidently it's leather."

Len cocked his head to one side.

"The anniversary. Their third anniversary is coming up and the gift is leather."

Len still looked at her blankly. "Perhaps it was mentioned when you men were outside looking at Vince's new tractor. Chelsea was upset about the matching leather jackets they'd organised to give each other." Marion pictured Chelsea's pout as she'd told them about the jackets. "Evidently they'd arranged to have them made and it was too late to cancel the order."

"That'd be the least of their worries."

"I thought the same thing," Marion said. "A bit of clothing is small against the loss of a relationship." She loved her brother's kids, of course, but they'd been indulged as children.

"I was thinking about the property."

This time it was Marion who tipped her head to the side.

"Brandon's family bought the farm next to theirs for Brandon and Chelsea."

"Oh, I see what you mean."

"Sorting out farms when a marriage breaks up is a nightmare. Remember the Townsends nearly lost everything when their daughter-in-law walked out two years ago."

"Walked!" Marion scoffed. "She ran and who could blame her? That Townsend lad was a liar and a cheat. A gorgeous wife, three lovely kids and he was making those secret trips to Bali. He deserved to lose his farm."

"I agree. I have no sorrow for him, but his parents and his brother didn't deserve to have their livelihood threatened, nor their reputation."

"They didn't have the affair."

"You know how this community loves a scandal. It was all any-one talked about for months." He picked up his fork and moved some tomato around his plate. "It's often the innocent who are left to face the shame."

Marion glanced at her husband but his head was bent over his plate and all she saw was his thinning grey hair. "Len?"

He looked up and she almost gasped at the sorrow she saw etched in the lines of his face. "Is everything all right?"

There was a moment's pause, a moment in which Marion's life danced before her eyes, the pain, the sacrifices, then he smiled and reached for her hand, gave it a squeeze.

"Of course it is, duck. Just feeling my age today."

She let out the breath she'd been holding. Made her voice light. "You're going to be seventy next birthday. Perhaps it's time we went back to the accountant and crunched the numbers again."

"Perhaps." The single word rose and faded and with it any suggestion that Len Addicot would retire.

Marion was both saddened and pleased by that thought.

Sun streamed through the big windows overlooking the sea as Marion entered the aged care residence where her mother had lived the last few years. The entrance and shared living area always felt welcoming and comfortable, which eased Marion's guilt at encouraging her mother to move in when the first signs of dementia had begun to show.

Marion had still been teaching and neither she nor Vince could care for Vera at home, but that hadn't stopped him from trying to convince Marion she should. They'd argued about it on and off for ages. He'd wanted her to give up teaching and have Vera live with Marion and Len. Apart from the fact that she loved teaching, their farm income wasn't as lucrative as Vince's and her wage often bought basics. And their house was small with one bathroom, not at all suited to someone needing care.

Marion had suggested he give up farming and look after their mother. And when she'd told him she was serious he'd backed off. Finally, he'd agreed an aged care home was the best option but he'd wanted their mother to move into a home in one of the bigger centres much further away.

Once again Marion had fought to get their mother a place at Wirini Bay. Vera had settled well into her room with a sea view and the staff were wonderful. In the early days Marion had brought her either to her place or Vince and Briony's each weekend and taken her on shopping trips, but gradually Vera had become more and more agitated if she left the home. These days she only went as far as walks in the garden. Marion had called on her mother nearly every day while she was still teaching but now that she'd retired and didn't travel to Wirini Bay each weekday, her visits were less often and she felt bad about that. Daughter guilt was like mother guilt, never far away.

Marion walked down the long passage towards her mother's room. It was a wide space with intermittent alcoves housing shared seating spaces and she recognised her mother's voice as she neared the last group of chairs. She was seated on a couch with her back to Marion and Mrs Cant, who'd been Marion's tennis coach back in the day, was seated opposite.

"Hello, Mum." Marion gave her mother a minute to work out who she was before she bent and kissed her on the cheek.

"Oh, Marion." Vera patted the empty space beside her. "I haven't seen you for ages."

Marion didn't correct her. There was no point. "Hello, Mrs Cant."

"Who are you? How do you know my name?" Mrs Cant waved a leathery hand at Marion.

"You remember my daughter, Marion," Vera said. "She lives on a farm out near Badara where you and I both used to live."

"Did we?" Mrs Cant frowned. "And this is your daughter?" She leaned in towards Vera. "She's not as attractive as you, is she? Must take after her father."

Marion ignored the comment and handed her mum the small bunch of flowers she'd thrown together, a few daisies and lavender from her sparse garden with some gum leaves.

"How pretty." Vera put the bunch to her nose. "Are they from your lovely garden?"

"Yes." Marion knew her mother wasn't with it when she called Marion's basic house yard a garden. Vera had maintained a magnificent garden both at the farm, which Briony had taken over, and then at the house in Wirini Bay. Once more Marion lamented the dementia that had robbed her mother of her independence and of the ability to have a meaningful conversation. They'd become especially close after Marion's dad had died and she missed being able to talk with her mum about everything from farm life to children to getting older.

"Where do you live?" Mrs Cant asked.

"Badara," Marion said and then was surprised as a figure sat up from a nearby lounge chair.

"I want my hair washed," the frail old woman wailed.

"They'll wash it tomorrow, Ruby," Vera said in a kind but raised voice.

Ruby blinked but her eyes didn't appear to focus, then she settled back on the chair again.

"Mum, do you remember the Back to Badara celebrations?" Marion reached into her bag for the newspaper clipping.

"No." Vera shook her head. "I don't think so."

Marion placed the photocopy of the clipping on her mother's lap and lifted the glasses that hung around her neck. "There's a photo of you and Dad."

Vera adjusted the glasses on the end of her nose and peered at the page.

"What's that?" Mrs Cant waggled her fingers once more.

"It's a page about the Back to Badara celebrations from 1970," Marion said. "You would have been there, Mrs Cant."

"Where?"

"Badara."

Ruby suddenly lurched forward. "I want my hair washed," she wailed again.

"Tomorrow, Ruby," Vera said and the old lady slowly settled back.

Marion pointed to the photo featuring her parents. "You and Dad did a lot for the church and the community back then."

Vera was silent a moment, leaning closer to the page. "Yes. Renovating that hall was a huge job but at least it will get more use now that it's got a proper kitchen." She spoke as if the project was only recently finished.

"It's had lots of use," Marion said. "Thanks to the efforts of you and Dad and other locals."

"You were so cranky that weekend." Vera chuckled.

"You remember it?"

"Of course I remember. You were home from boarding school but you wanted to go with that girlfriend of yours to the Bay."

"Gail." Marion recalled the two of them had thought themselves above their small hometown celebrations. They'd hoped to spend the weekend in Wirini Bay, going to the pictures, hanging out at the deli and down at the beach. What a pair of upstarts they'd been. Marion felt a pang of regret for the angst she'd caused her parents in her younger years.

"She's a troubled girl, that one," Vera said.

"Who? Gail?"

Vera nodded. She was looking down but Marion got the feeling her mother's thoughts were somewhere else beyond the page.

"Poor thing," Vera said.

"Sad she died so young."

"Did she?" Vera looked worried. "I must have missed hearing about that."

Marion remembered the huge funeral. Everyone from the district had been there, including Vera.

"She was never happy with her lot, that one. Being a mechanic's daughter wasn't good enough for her." Vera leaned closer. "You were a good friend to her but she wasn't a good influence on you. It's not kind to say but if she's passed you're probably better off without her."

"Do you remember there being a time capsule, Mum?"

Vera frowned and tipped her head to one side then her face brightened. "Oh yes. Your father spent hours chasing people up for their contributions. Don't you worry, he made sure your page went in the jar with all the other high school kids' notes. He didn't want you to miss out just because you'd gone off to boarding school. He was so proud of you."

Marion sighed. She'd hoped that perhaps the page she'd put together with Gail may have somehow been left out but she should have known her father wouldn't have let that happen.

Vera patted Marion's leg. "She was jealous of you, you know."

"Who?"

"Gail."

"I don't think so, Mum. We were good friends." Marion had never heard her mother mention Gail in that way, ever.

"She was a fair-weather friend," Vera said.

"What's your name?" Mrs Cant waved at Marion, wanting to be part of the conversation again.

"Marion," she said, and bent to retrieve the page that had slipped from her mother's lap.

"Oh, look at these flowers." Vera plucked the rough bunch from the seat beside her. "Did you bring these from your garden in Badara?"

Marion nodded.

"Where?" Mrs Cant barked.

"Badara," Marion and her mum said in unison.

"I want my hair washed." Ruby lurched forward and her knee rug slipped to the ground.

Vera stood. "They'll wash it tomorrow, Ruby," she said and picked up the blanket, which she tucked lovingly around the frail old woman then patted her gently until she relaxed into her chair again.

"I'd better get going, Mum." Marion could see the conversation was only going to deteriorate further. "Is there anything you need before I go?"

"Oh no, dear." Vera came back and sat on the couch. "We're well looked after here, aren't we?" She reached out and patted Mrs Cant's hand.

"Of course we are."

Marion kissed her mother's cheek and walked away. Behind her she heard Mrs Cant ask Vera who the gangly, awkward-looking woman was who'd sat and talked to her. Marion much preferred visiting her mother when she was alone in her room.

nine

Paige hummed as she washed the lunch dishes. She'd had a very successful morning in Wirini Bay. She'd found bargains at the op shop and had made her grocery money stretch further than she ever had before due to a few good specials at the supermarket. One of which had been the large chicken now simmering on the stove and filling the kitchen with delicious smells. It had been marked down, and she'd be able to make soup and a casserole and have some cold meat for sandwiches out of it.

Levi was happily playing with a set of Octonauts figures he'd found at the op shop and Paige knew Kodie would love the Power Rangers figurine he'd also discovered there. Jayden was harder to buy treats for these days. She'd decided to quietly offer him the five dollars she would have spent. He was saving his money for a PlayStation. It would take him forever but he was keen and she was happy to encourage his saving habit. She also thought money might be an incentive for him to apply himself to his schoolwork. She'd had a chat to him about his teacher's call but Jayden had become defensive and she'd let it slide for the moment.

A fly buzzed past her and hovered around the simmering saucepan. "How did you get in?" She reached for the fly spray she'd had to keep handy since living in this house. The fly momentarily went quiet. Paige stepped closer, peering around the saucepan and stovetop.

She was startled by a tentative knock at her back door. Why was it people in Badara always came to the back door? The yard was a shambles, there was a huge crack in the sunroom window beside the door and paint flaked from the walls, whereas she'd cleaned and tidied the front verandah, put out a mat and added a cheery plant in a pot.

She put down the can and immediately the fly buzzed around the saucepan again. She frowned and stepped tentatively into the sunroom. Beyond the frosted glass in the top half of the door she could make out a shape. She still didn't know that many people in town. Perhaps it would be Marion with more sausage rolls. The food would be welcome but Paige still wasn't sure how to take the brusque leader of their little exercise group.

She opened the door and was surprised to see a tall guy with his back to her surveying the yard. He turned and his lips tugged up in a lopsided smile. A deep scar snaked up his left cheek, stopping just beside his eye.

"Hi," he said.

"Hello."

He flapped a fly from his face. "Saw your car in the drive so thought I'd call in."

She assessed the green cap pulled low over his forehead. *John Deere* was printed across the crown in large cursive writing and he clutched a folder in one hand. Who or what was John Deere? She glanced warily out into the yard. This was the country. Did they get door knocking scammers out here?

"I'm looking for Paige?" he said.

She frowned. "Who are you?"

"Sorry." He shoved out a hand. "I'm Dane Townsend."

She accepted his brief shake, still wary. Perhaps this guy was another of Jayden's teachers on a house call.

He shuffled his feet. "Sorry," he said again. "I'm looking for the mother of a boy my..."

At that moment Levi came to the door and wrapped his arm around Paige's leg, looking up at the tall stranger. She put a protective hand on his head.

Dane smiled at Levi and lifted his hand for a high five. "G'day, mate."

Levi stepped forward, slapped his hand then gripped Paige's leg again.

"Does Jayden live here?" Dane glanced back at her. "Or perhaps someone else has a boy called Jayden? My son seems to have palled up with him."

"Your son?"

"Zuri."

"Oh." Paige shook her head. This guy was Zuri's dad. "So it was your son who gave Jayden a ride home from school without my permission?"

"Did he?"

"You should tell him that's not okay."

"I will. Sorry." He took a step back. "So...you're Jayden's mum?"

"Yes." She drew herself up but her eye level was only to the height of his shoulders.

"I thought maybe you were his sister."

Was he trying to flatter her or just being honest? People sometimes mistook Jayden and Paige for brother and sister. "Ditto with you and Zuri." Not that she'd had a good look at Zuri but she knew roughly how old he was and this Dane guy didn't look much older than her.

His face broke into a wide grin. "Touché, I guess. I'm sorry if Zuri overstepped the mark. He's a good driver but I'll talk to him about offering rides without checking in first." A blowfly buzzed past them and inside.

"Darn." Paige tugged the door shut. "Blasted things."

"Sorry."

"You keep apologising but you can't be responsible for everything."

"Shouldn't keep someone's door open when they're cooking."

"The flies get in even when the door's shut."

"Maybe down the chimney. This old place probably needs fresh flywire over the opening and a screen door."

"Probably." Paige folded her arms. "My landlord's in Adelaide. The cheap rent means I have to do any repairs myself. I don't plan to be doing much except maintain."

"Sor—"

She raised her eyebrows, stopping him mid-word. "What was it you wanted to see me about?"

"Zuri said Jayden was keen to play footy."

She'd thought Jayden would give up on the footy but only that morning he'd mentioned it again. There was no way they could afford it.

Dane opened the flap of the folder. "I brought the forms for you to fill out."

"Oh, I thought you were here to sell me something."

"Sell you something?" He frowned.

She waved her hand at him. "The hat and the folder."

Dane lifted his hat and looked at the front of it as if he'd never seen it before. The thick brown hair that had been trapped beneath it fell forward over his face. "John Deere's farm machinery. Every second person around here has one of these." He shoved it back on his head.

Levi tugged on her leg. "I'm hungry, Mummy."

"Sorry to keep you." Dane fiddled with the folder then thrust some pages at her. "Fill these out and Jayden can bring them with him to practice. I'm the team manager. My number's there if you have any questions." He backed away. "I'd better get going."

"But…" Paige looked up from the papers he'd pushed into her hands but saw only Dane's back as he loped away around the side of the house.

Two more blowflies buzzed around the door. Paige batted them away and hurried Levi inside, not sure how she was going to let Jayden down yet again.

Briony had been fussing around the house. That was the only way she could describe her erratic visits to various rooms where jobs were half done then abandoned as she moved on to the next. She'd been expecting Blake since mid-morning, and had been disappointed when he hadn't arrived for morning tea with the rest of the family, listening at every open and close of the back door, hoping to hear his voice. She was busting to spend time with Blake, some one-on-one quality time to discover more about the man he'd become.

She'd always thought herself closer to her girls – they'd done lots together when they were younger. Briony had been the one to drive them to ballet lessons, to sport, pony club, take them away on shopping trips. Vincent had taken Blake wherever he needed to go but Blake had shown no real interest in farm work, football and fishing, all things that occupied Vincent's time. It had been a source of unspoken friction between the two and so it was almost a relief when Blake had accepted a place at uni and made it clear he didn't want to farm.

His Bachelor of Health Science had led to his first job in Sydney with a global company and then the job in London. They'd been proud of his achievements, but had taken a while to accept their only son wasn't planning to carry on the family tradition of the male offspring taking over the farm.

It didn't surprise her that Len and Marion's son, Grant, had chosen a different path – their farm barely earned them a living. Blake on the other hand would have taken over a property of quality and substance. Vincent hadn't dwelt on it for long but a small part of Briony still wished their son had been a farmer. It was a tradition.

The back door banged. She stuck her head out of the laundry as Chelsea came past. Her eyes were red and puffy.

"What's happened?" Briony asked.

"I was out helping Dad with the sheep and I got another call from Brandon. He wants me back and he sounds so remorseful, Mum."

"Are you sure this isn't just a blip?" Briony said.

Chelsea frowned. "What do you mean?"

"I suppose everyone deserves a second chance."

"But it's more than a second chance. This would be the fourth or fifth."

"Really?" Briony gasped.

"I've left him before, Mum." Chelsea's lip wobbled. "I've stayed with a friend or at a motel and then I've gone back and things are okay for a while, but this time…"

"But you didn't tell us." A lump formed in Briony's chest.

"I didn't know how. And anyway, I believed him when he said he was going to stop."

"Surely you knew about the drugs before you married him."

"It was recreational back then. I tried some pills too but—"

"You used drugs!" The lump inside Briony exploded, sending burning tendrils up through her body. She stared at her daughter as if seeing a stranger.

"A couple of times but I didn't like it. I didn't realise Brandon had kept it up until it became a problem."

"I've got a drug-taking daughter?" Briony put her hand to the wall to steady herself.

"I tried some twice, Mum, years ago."

"Does Dad know?" Vince and Chelsea had been particularly close since her return home.

Chelsea shook her head.

"Best he doesn't, nor anyone for that matter." The sound of an approaching vehicle distracted her. "That might be Blake."

"Mum?"

Briony turned back. Chelsea looked small and vulnerable, a mouse instead of the strong young woman she usually was. Being married to Brandon had certainly changed her.

"Go and wash your face and put on a smile. Blake's here for the rest of the day. We've got lots of catching up to do. We'll talk about Brandon later." Briony checked her lipstick in the mirror. She didn't want anything spoiling Blake's return. She pulled her face into a smile too, tucked away a stray strand of hair and straightened her skirt then hurried out to meet him.

"Hello," she called. She took in his fitted pale blue t-shirt and low-slung jeans. Last night he'd looked smart in chinos and a check shirt. Blake had always liked trendy clothes and even though today's look was simple he could have stepped out of a magazine.

He waved and reached back into the car, bringing out a take-away coffee cup.

"Where on earth did you get that? I've got a machine here, you know." She gave him a squeezy hug. He smelled good too, some kind of aromatic herbal scent.

"I know but Port Kent has a cafe with a coffee machine so I couldn't resist one for the drive." He waved the empty cup. "It was good."

"I thought you'd be here earlier."

"Had a bit of sorting to do and then I couldn't leave the view and remembering all those summers we spent at the shack."

"They were good times." Briony wrapped an arm around his waist as they moved towards the gate. "I hope you still like chicken and mushroom risotto. I've made it for lunch."

"Anything you make is good, Mum."

"You're a keeper." She grinned, enjoying his flattery. He was always one to compliment her cooking; she'd missed that.

"I passed Maddie on the way in. We had a quick chat. She's off to see someone about a horse show or something."

"Yes. They're hoping to revive the horse events at the Wirini Bay annual show."

"She loves her horses."

"More than anything." Briony was thankful at least one of her daughters had her head on properly.

He stopped to slip off his loafers.

"You don't have to," she said.

"Old habits."

Briony ushered him inside, stopping beside the door to his old room. "I've decided to tidy up in here and bring a bed back in, just while you're home. Then you don't have to drive back and forth and we can—"

"Don't do that." He cut her off abruptly.

Briony turned in surprise.

"I don't know how long I'm staying, Mum." Blake's voice was gentle again, placating almost. "I've just got myself settled at Port Kent. How about instead of dismantling the work you've put in, I help you finish it instead?"

"Painting?"

"Yes, and last night Dad said something about shelving."

"I ordered it but it's all flat packs and he hates putting that stuff together. He's stored it in the back of one of his sheds for now."

"Putting flat-pack furniture together is something I've become good at."

Briony gave him a hug and they both stared at the bare room.

"I kept all the things from your drawers."

"Couldn't have been anything exciting."

"They're in a box. Mostly it's trinkets, an old school uniform, some scarves and badges, a few games. I didn't have the heart to throw them out. You'll have to look through them while you're here."

The sound of music drifted from further up the passage.

"Is Chelsea inside?" Blake asked.

"She's just come in. She's been working sheep with your dad."

"How's she coping with this Brandon thing?"

"Not well."

"I'll go up and say hello."

He walked up the passage, knocked gently on Chelsea's door and went in. Deflated, Briony went to the kitchen to check on the risotto. She'd wanted some time with Blake by herself and was disappointed he'd gone to see Chelsea instead. It would be good for Chelsea to have his calming influence. Briony hoped her daughter would keep the news of Brandon's addiction and their separation within the family. Imagine if it became widely known? Chelsea's admission she'd tried drugs had shocked Briony but maybe it wouldn't come as a shock to Blake.

Briony clapped her hand to her mouth. Perhaps he took drugs himself. Her son had lived away for so long she had no idea what he might have done in that time. Their video sessions and phone calls had always been about his travels, his work, his friends, but really he could have been a mass murderer and Briony would have been none the wiser. Madeline was the only one of her three children who Briony felt she truly knew. What kind of terrible mother did that make her?

She took some comfort from the fact Blake must be planning to stay in the area for a while if his offer to help do up his old room was anything to go by. That would give them one-on-one time. Her thoughts drifted to her plans for the library. She hadn't imagined it would be needed as a spare room but it might be sensible to put in a good quality sofa bed. Then there'd always be an extra bed in the house. With the table set, the salad made and the baked risotto out of the oven she took out her phone to start looking. By the time Chelsea and Blake got to the kitchen and Vince came in to join them, Briony had already bookmarked a couple of possible sofas.

ten

Tuesday morning Paige had been awake before Levi. It was fitness club day and they were coming to her house. She'd tried to put it out of her head all week but now that the day was here she was restless.

To add to her unease Jayden had gone off in a huff to catch the bus. He hadn't given up on the idea of playing football and he'd been cross with her for telling Zuri's dad about the car ride.

"Now he thinks I'm a crybaby," Jayden had yelled at her. "He probably won't come near me any more."

Somehow they'd gone from that to an argument about his schoolwork. It did Paige's head in the way conversations with Jayden ended up on a completely different topic to the one they'd started on. After he'd left and she'd calmed down, she'd dropped Kodie and Levi at their respective classes on the dot of start time and dashed home again to make sure everything was ready.

She hadn't thought the women would see the rest of the house then sometime in the night, as she'd tossed and turned, it had hit her that they were bringing lunch and would probably need to use the kitchen, which was also the only place with a table and chairs, and maybe the bathroom. She'd risen early and rushed around tidying the house, even the rooms they wouldn't see. In the kitchen she'd put away toys and anything out on benches and washed every surface.

She sipped her coffee as she gave the room a final glance. So much for keeping to herself. She'd invited a group of almost strangers into her home, or maybe been pressured into was a better way to describe it. Home had always been her safe place, up until last year. Being a single mother with three children she often felt judged. If she was running late she wasn't organised; if she didn't have enough money she should be grateful for what she was given; if her children didn't have full lunch boxes she didn't care for them. There were many ways people expressed their disapproval. And the biggest one was the way they looked when they discovered each of her children had a different father.

Paige picked up her phone, opened her photo gallery and scrolled to the folder labelled Ari. At times like this when she was feeling anxious, she would find solace in the photos of their life together. She used to end up crying as she scrolled through but gradually that had changed and now they made her smile. Especially the one of him with his mouth open wide and his long tongue poking out trying to make a scary face. His dark brown eyes were as round as twenty-cent coins and shone with laughter. She'd been giggling so hard it had taken her a few goes to get a clear photo. She flicked on to the last photo she had of him. It had been taken the day Levi was born. Ari had his tiny son in his big strong arms, gazing down with such a tender look of love she caught her breath every time she looked at it.

The sound of a car stopping and then a door shutting echoed along the passage. Paige put the phone away. She'd left the wooden front door open hoping the women would all come that way rather than round the back. She rinsed her cup then felt a flutter of nerves as she heard a knock at her back door. She stepped out into the passage. Beyond the screen at the front of the house she could see a car parked and someone leaning into the open boot.

She frowned and turned towards the back where the knock had come from. Through the frosted glass of the sunroom door she could see a shadowy figure. She opened the door, startled to see Dane with a toolbox in his hand.

"Hi," he said. "Hope this isn't a bad time but I mentioned to Mum about your fly problem and she remembered we had an old screen door in the shed. I also found a spare roll of flywire I could fit over your chimneys for you."

"I—"

"Hello?" a voice called from the front.

Paige swivelled from back to front and then back again. "I've got visitors coming."

"Sorry," Dane said. "I would have called first but I didn't have your number."

"I—"

"Hello?" The front screen door rattled.

"Come in," Paige called.

"Sorry to be early," Briony's apologetic voice carried along the passage.

"No worries," Paige replied. "Head into the shop."

"I shouldn't get in your way putting the door on," Dane said. "And I can come back another time and do the chimneys if it's easier."

Paige spun back to him. She was swivelling so much it was making her dizzy.

"I thought I should get here before the others," Briony called from behind her. "Make sure my music would work."

Paige nodded at Dane. "Sure, okay, thanks." Then she hurried along the passage, confused again by his actions. Was he interfering or being kind?

"Oh, I'd forgotten what a great space this is." Briony was standing in the middle of the shop slowly turning around. "It'll be much better for our little group than that huge hall."

Paige was relieved it wasn't Marion here first but Briony was nearly as intimidating. As usual she was wearing a trendy fitness outfit – today's was black and lime green – with hair neatly done and make-up applied as if she were going out for dinner rather than to exercise class.

"I've brought my bluetooth speaker." Briony lifted the bag she was carrying. "And some lunch."

"Would you like me to put the food in the kitchen?"

"Great." Briony removed her towel and speaker and handed over the bag. "It's only curried egg sandwiches and there's a dozen eggs as well. We've got an oversupply at the moment. I thought perhaps with three children you'd probably go through a few."

"The eggs are for me?" Paige glanced from the bag to Briony, who was already setting up her speaker on the old shop counter.

"Yes, if you want them," she said.

"Thank you."

The sound of hammering carried from beyond the back door as Paige took the food to the kitchen. She was returning along the passage when another face appeared through the screen. It was Claire and behind her a car was pulling up. Briony's music filled the empty shop space as Paige opened the door for Claire and waited for Jean to make her way in.

"This is great," Claire said as she stepped into the shop.

"I haven't been here since the Blacks ran it as a second-hand shop," Jean said. "That was years ago." She smiled at Paige. "I grew up in this house."

"Did you?" Both Paige and Claire spoke at once.

"My father was the baker here and this was our home." Jean was still in the passage, looking around. "I haven't been into the house itself since my brother, Max, sold the bakery and moved to Wirini Bay. Goodness, that was in the late seventies." Jean smiled expectantly at Paige.

"Hello." Marion arrived at the door carrying a cardboard box, a delicious savoury smell floating in with her. "Sorry I'm late. I thought I'd make an extra batch of sausage rolls so I could leave some for the children." She pushed the box at Paige. "I'll just go back for my mat and towel."

"I brought you some apples too," Jean said and popped a paper bag on top of the box. "Our tree was loaded this year. I've made an apple cake for our lunch. Shall I pop it in your kitchen, dear?"

"I've got a savoury slice," Claire said. "And I made a batch of biscuits to leave with you. Children always love biscuits, don't they." She smiled.

Paige felt a niggle in the pit of her stomach that tingled and grew to form a lump in her throat. An extra dozen eggs, a bag of apples, sausage rolls and biscuits. They must think her a charity case.

"Let's put everything in the kitchen." She turned swiftly on her heel and led the way.

Behind her she heard Jean exclaim, "This used to be my room."

Paige looked back. Jean was waving a hand at Levi's door as she passed. Paige was thankful she'd shut the doors to all the bedrooms. She didn't want these women snooping.

"The kitchen's quite different," Jean said as she and Claire put their food on the bench. "The lovely old wood oven's gone and the yellow laminex is very bright and cheerful, isn't it?"

Paige looked at the more modern oven that had been built into the space below the chimney. If Dane was to be believed, the chimney was the source of some of the flies that plagued her. Just at that moment he called out. They all looked to the back door.

"Hello, Aunty Jean." He smiled and the scar disappeared into the creases of his face.

"Hello, dear, what are you doing here?"

Paige frowned. Briony had also called Jean 'aunty'. She looked from Dane to Jean wondering if 'aunty' was a term of respect or meant Jean was actually an aunt to them both.

"Paige was having trouble with flies. Mum thought this old door might help." Dane propped the screen across the open frame.

"That was thoughtful of her," Jean said.

Right on cue a blowfly flew in.

"Sorry." Dane winced at Paige. "I have to leave the door open while I do this part."

The fly buzzed around the box of sausage rolls. Paige shoved the box in the oven.

"I have trouble keeping them out of the old schoolhouse too," Claire said.

"Maybe some new flywire for the chimneys as well?" Jean smiled at Dane.

"Yep. I was planning to…" Dane gave Paige a questioning look.

She sighed. "Go ahead. We'll all be up in the old shop anyway."

"It's our fitness class this morning," Jean said. "Paige has kindly allowed us to use her place because of the floor being fixed at the hall."

"I saw there was someone working there as I drove past."

Of course he would have. Paige folded her arms across her chest. It seemed everyone knew everything that happened in Badara and what they didn't they made up.

Jean was busily telling him all about the work on the hall floor.

"I think we should get started," Paige said. Claire nodded her support and the three of them went back to the shop where Marion and Briony were fiddling with the music.

"Good, you're back,' Marion said. "I was about to send out a search party. How did everyone go planning something for today? I've managed a set of warm-up movements."

"I've thought of a few aerobic exercises," Claire said.

"I think I can remember the strength and balance focus that Courtney did," Jean said. "But some of us might need a chair for that."

"I'll get some." Paige strode back to the kitchen. The various gifts and lunch contributions that didn't need the fridge lined the bench. She decided she'd leave the cheese toasties she'd made for the kids to eat after school. They didn't meet the standard of the rest of the offerings.

Through her kitchen window she could see a ladder against the wall and overhead footsteps crunched across the tin roof. She hadn't realised Dane would need to get up there. She turned her back on the bench and the evidence of her social and personal failings and went back to the shop.

"We're hoping you might recall some of the ab exercises," Marion said. "Briony has offered to lead our cool-down."

"Sure," Paige said, relieved. They were the ones she remembered from Courtney's session.

Somehow, between them all, they managed to do a raft of exercises. There was the odd moan when a new song blared from Briony's speaker, a few groans at some of the exercises, several bouts of giggling when one or the other of them found themselves in a tricky position and a collective intake of breath as Jean almost missed the edge of her chair when she sat for the ab exercises, but they got through it and everyone was smiling, even Paige. Claire was the one who kept them all on track. She seemed to have a better recollection overall of the exercises than the rest of them put together.

"I think we've earned our lunch," Jean said.

Paige glanced at her watch. "I'll have to go and collect Levi soon."

"It's not a full day of care then?" Marion said.

"No."

Marion raised her eyebrows then glanced around the shop. "This has gone well today. The old shop is the perfect place for our exercise club. Except for that ghastly yellow wall. Why do people feel the need to do that?"

Another thing, along with Levi's early finish, she obviously wasn't happy about.

"It gives the place a lift," Jean said. "I always thought the shop was a bit dreary with the beige walls when the Blacks ran it."

Marion turned away from her scrutiny of the wall. "It must seem funny coming back here after all this time, Jean."

"I admit to being a little curious."

Jean looked at Paige and then it felt as if they were all staring at her.

"The bedrooms are pretty basic," she mumbled, then, intimidated by their collective gaze, she shrugged. "Have a look if you want."

Marion immediately strode forward and opened the door to the room across the passage. Paige hung back as they all looked inside.

"You're not using it as a bedroom?" Briony said.

Paige had taped together a pile of their smaller moving boxes to make bookshelves. Between her and the children they had a few books and there were always plenty at op shops. She'd put a couch in there one day but for now it had a mat and some cushions and a piece of brightly coloured sheer fabric draped across the window. She cringed as the other women cast their judicious gazes around the sparsely furnished room.

"This room and the one behind it were my brothers' bedrooms," Jean said. "The three older boys in here and my three younger brothers in the other."

"It's perfect for a reading-come-family room," Claire said.

"And this was Mother and Father's room." Jean hesitated beside the closed door further along the passage.

Paige nodded and Jean opened the door.

"Oh, I'm so glad you've made this one your room, dear," Jean said. "It was always such a cosy room and, in the winter, Mother kept the fire going."

Once more the other women looked in. Paige had to admit she loved the high, patterned ceiling and corner fireplace with its intricate wood surrounds and inlaid mirror. It was the only other room besides the lounge that had a fireplace. She was glad the bed was made. She hadn't been able to afford wardrobes but in her room there was a clothes rack so her things were hanging at least.

The women continued on, opening the doors on Kodie's and Levi's rooms then peering at the bathroom.

"I'm pleased to see they've modernised that and added a toilet," Jean said. "We had a long-drop toilet down the back when we lived here."

Paige wasn't sure what that was but she didn't like the sound of it. Was there some hole in the backyard they hadn't discovered? "There's a second toilet in the laundry," she blurted.

"Very useful," Briony said. "We've only recently added an en suite off our bedroom. I wish we'd had a second bathroom when I had all three teenagers at home."

Paige was bemused. Briony made it sound as if Paige herself had managed the update to the old house.

They moved on into the lounge. "There used to be a wall here." Jean held her arms wide. "It separated the lounge from the passage but it's a much better use of space having it opened up like this."

Once more everyone stopped to look.

"What a gorgeous rug." Claire ran her hand over the crocheted rug Paige had thrown over the second-hand couch.

"My gran made it for me."

"It's very on trend," Briony said. "You have a great eye for decorating."

Paige looked at her in surprise. She'd thrown the rug over the old couch to hide the stains. It was hard to believe anything she had would live up to Briony's standards.

"And it looks like Dane has finished putting on your screen door." Jean nodded towards the sunroom where the inside door was open and a screen now stood between them and the outside.

"What was Dane doing here?" Marion's tone was sharp.

"Being helpful as he often is," Jean said and smiled at Paige. "He's very involved in the local community."

"Pity he didn't bring Sarah with him," Marion said. "I've done my best to get her to come to fitness."

"I visit her as often as I can," Briony said. "She doesn't come into town much. She's still finding it hard to face people."

"So silly," Marion huffed. "It's not as if she did anything wrong."

Paige assumed Sarah was Dane's wife and was wondering what that was about when Briony cut in.

"Your children are all quite different in looks, aren't they?" She was standing in front of the photo of Paige and her kids with

Father Christmas. He'd been set up with a photographer in a shopping mall the previous year. Levi and Kodie had been busting to sit on his knee and Paige had had to work hard to convince Jayden to be in the photo with them. It had turned out well. A happy photo and a good likeness of them all, just the four of them. It was the only one she had out on display.

The other women crowded around, peering at her family with the same scrutiny they'd given her house. Paige felt as if yet another layer of her life was being peeled back and laid bare.

"We should start lunch if Paige needs to get her little boy soon," Claire said with an encouraging smile. She hadn't leaned in for a close look like the other three had.

The women followed Paige into the kitchen and began setting out their contributions. Paige removed Marion's box of sausage rolls from the oven and found a plate for her to put some on. Soon all five of them were around the table sampling the assorted food. It felt strange to have these women in her kitchen chatting about everything from the weather to friends and family, people Paige knew nothing about. Nor Claire, Paige guessed from her silence.

Paige dashed off in the middle of it to get Levi. She took the car even though it was only a short walk. She didn't want to leave the women in her house for long. When she came back they'd made themselves teas and coffees and the discussion had moved on to the progression of the hall floor, except for Claire who'd had to leave. Paige was sorry. Maybe because she was new to the town and a bit younger than the others but Claire was the only one of the four she felt comfortable with.

Levi clung to Paige's leg like a periwinkle to a rock to begin with but soon worked out these strange women in his house had food and he was easily bribed. Paige settled him at the kindy table in the lounge with some lunch and ABC Kids on the TV.

"There's so much TV for children these days, isn't there," Marion said as Paige sat back at the table.

"Three on your own is hard work," Briony said.

"Their father isn't with you?" Jean asked.

"Aunty Jean," Briony admonished.

"Well, we don't know that he's not one of those flying out and in workers and we simply haven't met him yet."

"He's not." They all turned at the sharpness in Paige's voice. "In fact, none of them are." The woman from child support services back when it was just Jayden and Kodie had asked her the same question. She'd prodded and poked into Paige's private life trying to find out if she was getting a secret supply of money from one of their fathers. *As if!* Paige had sneered.

"None?" Briony shook her head.

"My three children have three different fathers and none of them were FIFO workers, to my knowledge. They're not with us in any shape or form. I'm raising my three alone. Does that answer your question?" Paige stared at each woman in turn. They all looked surprised.

"I didn't mean—" Jean began.

"There's no need to get hostile," Marion said.

"No?" Paige jumped up and paced the kitchen. "You've been looking down your noses at me ever since I joined your exercise group. Single mum, a child in tow, and two more kids. I know what you're thinking."

"Really?" Marion said derisively. "And what is that?"

"That I don't belong here. And now you've come today, bringing food for the charity case." Paige stopped and flung out an arm. "Inspecting my house to see if I'm up to scratch."

"You invited us," Marion snapped.

"I didn't get a choice. And then Dane turns up at exactly the time you all arrive saying his mother suggested he fix the flywire.

You expect me to believe that's not a set-up. I don't even know his mother. I didn't ask for your charity. I manage very well. I don't expect to be given handouts and to be...to be judged."

"Oh, my dear girl." Jean reached out a hand and placed it on Paige's arm. "Is that what you think we've been doing? I'm so sorry."

The compassion in Jean's voice and the worried look on her face made Paige falter.

"We were being stickybeaks, that's all," Briony said gently. "But none of us came with the intention of passing judgement." She cast a quick look in Marion's direction.

"Of course we didn't," Marion huffed.

"This was Aunty Jean's home," Briony said. "We were being curious, that's all. Your home is lovely. Your kids are lovely."

The rest of Paige's speech was sucked from her mouth by Briony's smile. She sagged back to her chair and put her head in her hands.

"I think we've all had a big misunderstanding." Jean spoke so gently Paige bit her lip to hold back her tears. "I hadn't been in my old home for so long it truly was just a case of wanting to see it again. I'm sorry that made you feel uncomfortable. It was thoughtless of me."

"And the food's not because we think you're a charity case," Marion said. Her manner was still gruff.

"People just do that here." Briony's words settled like a soothing blanket. "When we go to each other's places we take something for the hostess."

"Especially when people are new to the district," Jean said.

"And as you were having us at your place we didn't think it fair you had to provide lunch as well," Marion continued.

Paige was too afraid to lift her head. Was that truly what this had all been about? Generosity? Shame for her behaviour washed through her and formed a knot of dread.

"We should get going then," Marion said. "Leave you to it."

Paige, stiff with embarrassment, was aware of Marion and Briony rising from the table but Jean's gentle hand still patted her arm.

"Is it all right if we tidy up first, dear?" Jean said. "It's something else we're used to doing. Not leaving a mess for the hostess."

Paige swallowed her groan and, not daring to speak, she simply nodded.

"Hopefully the hall floor will be finished by next week," Marion said over the clinking of cups and plates.

"Oh no, it won't be," Jean said.

The sounds of washing up stopped. Paige risked a sideways glance at Jean as she stood to pick up a tea towel.

"I'd forgotten to tell you all. My nephew says it's a bigger job than they thought. He needs more wood and he won't be back till late next week."

"We'll just have to skip a week," Briony said.

Paige swallowed the huge lump of regret in her throat. "You can..." Her voice was little more than a squeak. She cleared her throat. "You can come back here...if you still want to."

There was a heartbeat's silence.

"That would be lovely, dear. Wouldn't it, girls?" Jean said.

Paige risked lifting her eyes. Marion's face was set in her usual wonky grimace but Briony and Jean were smiling at her.

Paige cleared her throat again. "And thanks for the things you brought."

"Our pleasure," Jean said. "Now this time I truly am being a stickybeak but had you noticed Dane has left you a note?" Jean lifted a piece of paper from the bench. "There's a get-together for the footy and netball club. He's written on the flier."

Jean handed it to her. A note was scribbled across the top. *Hope the screens help with your fly problem. If Jayden's still keen on footy you should all come to the Family Day. Let me know if you need more info or a ride. My number's on this flier.* Paige scanned the flier and once more her heart sank. Jayden would want to go and then she'd have more pressure for him to play.

"The social events are usually good fun," Briony said. "We used to go when our girls played netball but Madeline hasn't played for a few years."

"It's a good way to meet people," Marion said.

"And they'll all be lots younger than us." Jean waved a hand to include Marion and Briony. "You'll meet people your own age."

"My son Jayden's keen to play football," Paige said.

"And from the look on your face, you're not." Marion's eyebrows raised.

"I...I wouldn't mind him playing." Paige swallowed the dry lump that had formed in her throat, not sure how much she was prepared to confide but she'd been on her own without anyone to discuss things with for so long now. "It's the cost."

No-one spoke. Paige's cheeks warmed. Why had she admitted that? She folded the flier and tucked it away with the pile of notes and school newsletters.

"Hell, yes." Marion was the first to break the silence. "It was a long time ago but I remember when my son, Grant, played. A pair of footy boots alone set me back a small fortune."

"Children grow so quickly," Jean said.

"I think the club runs a second-hand pool." Briony tapped a finger to her cheek. "Uniforms, boots, anything kids grow out of that are still in good condition. Dane would know who organises it these days."

"And I'm sure they'd have a payment scheme for subs and things," Marion said. "There would be quite a few families in similar positions. Don't the Smarts have four kids involved in the club?"

Briony frowned. "Five now, I think. Keeping them in shoes and uniforms must be a nightmare."

"You should chat to Dane." Marion looked Paige straight in the eye. "We're not all middle-class over-sixties here. And he's been through some difficult times."

"And a very nice young man to boot," Jean added. "Even if I am a little biased."

Paige not only felt overwhelmed but also embarrassed by their attempts to help.

"I have to get going," Briony said. "Blake and I are going to finish painting the library this afternoon. Some mother-and-son bonding time. I've hardly had him to myself since he's been home."

"What a shame we didn't get around to discussing the fund-raiser events," Jean said.

"I've made a rough agenda and a list of people I've contacted already. I brought it with me." Marion waved a hand towards her bag. "Perhaps next week we should make sure we leave time to discuss it."

"Yes, good idea." Jean looked to Paige. "If you don't mind us turning your kitchen table into a meeting space, dear?"

Paige shook her head vigorously. She wasn't keen to have them back but she'd do anything to make up for her embarrassing behaviour.

"Keith and I have been pondering ideas to turn the time capsule into a fundraiser," Jean said. "We're thinking we should retrieve it beforehand. Put it on display for all to view and then charge five dollars a family to have something included for the next capsule."

A flash of despair crossed Marion's face then she quickly gathered her things. "I have to go," she said.

"Me too," Briony said. "And that's a great idea, Aunty Jean. We'll give it a proper look over next week."

"See you next week, Paige," Marion said sharply, concern etched in her face.

They all left together. Paige shut the front door; the noise it made was a hollow clunk. She wandered slowly back along the passage, buoyed by the happy sound of Levi singing along to a tune on the TV. Today had been a strange one that had begun with trepidation. Now, as she thought about the eggs and apples, the sausage rolls and biscuits all brought out of generosity, and that she could leave her back door open for the breeze and fresh air, she felt a little more like she belonged rather than being an outsider. Instead of being intimidated by the older women in the fitness group, she realised they were simply being neighbourly. Although Briony was rather pretentious, and Marion still scared her a little. Her tone was often sharp and what that pained look when she left had been about Paige didn't know. She'd dashed off in a hurry with the air of someone with her mind on something else entirely. All that aside, today had definitely been a big step forward for Paige and the best thing of all was the glimmer of hope that maybe Jayden could join the local footy team.

Marion turned onto the main road and watched in her rear-view mirror as Briony and then Jean also turned onto the main road. Both drove in opposite directions. Marion knew Jean wouldn't be deflected from the time capsule. She could create a new one to be buried but there was no way Marion would allow the report she and Gail had written over fifty years ago to be exposed for all to see.

She drove on in the direction she would normally head for home and when the other cars were out of sight she turned left, drove the three blocks to the other side of town and along the road to the hall. A builder's ute was parked out the front and the door was propped open. She turned into the space between the church and the hall and drove as far along the block as she could so her car wouldn't be in plain sight from the road.

She got out and made her way between the two buildings. To her left, behind the church, was a small toilet block. It had been upgraded to a more modern two-toilet besser brick building about twenty years ago. The path between the church and the hall led to it but little had been done with the bush garden behind the hall since it had been planted after the renovation reopening. One of the previous ministers and his family had shown some interest but they were long gone.

Marion stared in dismay at the overgrown garden, wondering where exactly the time capsule had been buried. She pushed her way past bushes, stepped over exposed roots and around little stone borders. Someone had attempted to edge the paths at some stage. She'd hoped to find a plaque or a rock marking the time capsule burial site.

She closed her eyes, imagining the space as it had been fifty-two years ago. One of the farmers, it could have been her father, had cleared the back of the block in readiness for the garden. She tried to picture the day they buried the capsule in the bare yard. She was in the background of the photo. She opened her eyes. The fence that bordered the neighbouring house's yard had been behind her in the newspaper photo. The fence that was now crowded with bushes. That meant the capsule had to be a few metres in from it, about the middle of the bush garden, where there had once been a birdbath. Sadly it had fallen or been knocked over and broken and never repaired or replaced but it would have been the perfect thing to sit atop a time capsule burial site.

Marion worked her way to a more open area, now thick with weeds and overgrown plants. She could start looking here once the builders in the hall had left but she'd need some tools, a rake and a shovel. With a heady sense of relief she retraced her steps back to her car and drove home.

eleven

Sun shone through the bare windows of what had been Blake's bedroom and music played softly from the speaker. Even though painting wasn't her thing, Briony felt content as she applied the paint edger to the wall. Blake was working along from her, rolling the paint on after she'd done the cutting in.

It was his playlist they were painting to, an eclectic mix of the songs she remembered him playing in his teenage years: Beyonce, Mariah Carey, Madonna, Pink and, to both his sisters' disgust, Robbie Williams. Sometimes the three children had put on concerts. Blake would choreograph the whole thing, organising the girls. They'd all be wearing outfits to match whichever of the latest songs took their fancy. Chelsea loved to dress up so was easily coerced, but Madeline had sometimes rebelled. Briony and Vincent would share a quiet laugh at their youngest daughter's pouting face, her little arms folded tightly across her chest. Briony had been determined her kids would have a happy childhood, so different from the closed doors and long silences she'd experienced, and she was pleased she'd achieved that even if it hadn't always been easy.

So many times she'd had to make a stand that her children, especially the girls, railed against. Chelsea had had a steady boyfriend before Brandon. She'd only been seventeen but had decided she wanted to have sex with him. Briony had put the kybosh on that and had read the riot act to her daughter about the stupidity of having sex at her age and with someone who was unlikely to be husband material. Chelsea had had the good sense to blush when Briony had reminded her of that talk when she'd first become engaged to Brandon. Although as it turned out, saving herself for him hadn't necessarily worked out for the best.

And Briony had been the mother from hell, according to Madeline when alcohol hadn't been allowed at her eighteenth birthday party. Several of those planning to attend were still under eighteen and Briony hadn't been prepared to chaperone underage drinkers.

They were some of the run-ins she'd had with her children. Vincent had tried to talk her round a few times – not about sex, he was happy to leave that side of parenting to her, but Madeline had pleaded with him over the alcohol. She'd thought she'd be the lamest kid in school. Vincent had been swayed but quickly accepted Briony's stance when she'd said she wouldn't stay home for the party and he could manage it all by himself.

Blake had rarely rocked the boat. The worst had probably been the time he'd told her he was planning to go to a karaoke bar he'd heard about. He was at boarding school and at eighteen of legal drinking age, but he'd been a late developer and she didn't think him mature enough for city bars. He loved to sing so she'd encouraged him to join the school choir instead.

She studied his profile now as he rolled on the paint. His head was nodding to the beat of Kylie Minogue singing 'Can't Get You Out Of My Head' and he was lip-syncing to the vocals. He hadn't ever joined the choir. Briony wondered if he frequented karaoke bars now.

He turned and his cheeks coloured. "What?"

"It's just good to have you home."

"It's good to be here. And I'm glad you're giving my old room this makeover. It'll make a great library. Although I haven't noticed anyone in this family sitting still long enough to read." He smiled at her. It was a bright cheeky smile that warmed her even more.

"We do read." She defended the rest of her family although she had no idea about Chelsea's reading habits these days. "I'm also going to put a desk and a small TV in here. Madeline likes to watch different shows to what your dad and I do." Briony tried not to think about her brief head in the door of the lounge the previous weekend. Madeline and her girlfriends had been drinking cocktails and watching the Gay and Lesbian Mardi Gras. Heaven knows why? "We can use this space when she has friends over. Give them the lounge to themselves."

"Looks like you're not getting rid of Maddie or Chels any time soon," he said.

"Chelsea's turning up was a surprise."

His smile dropped away. "She can't go back to Brandon, Mum. He's no good for her."

"I…"

"I know you want what's best for her and from what she's told me that's not being with Brandon."

"He seemed so right for her. They had the fairy-tale wedding, a property they worked together, the perfect life…they still could." Briony shook her head. "He's such a nice young bloke. Or at least we always thought he was. I don't understand why they can't sort it out. Why can't Brandon see what he's throwing away?"

"People make wrong choices, Mum, they change. Sadly sometimes for the worse. It would do Chelsea no good to go back at this stage."

"I still can't believe how grown up you are. You sound like you're speaking from experience." Her hand stilled part way along one edge of the doorframe. "You haven't taken drugs, have you?" She glanced at him then turned away, not wanting to see his face when he answered.

"Not my scene," he said. "Although there were plenty of opportunities."

"What about girlfriends?" Now that he'd answered the drug question she felt brave enough to press on. It was something Briony had often wondered but never felt she could ask over the phone or video call. She stopped scraping with the edger altogether and studied him. "You've introduced us to plenty of your friends via video from London but you've never mentioned a girl-friend. Even when you lived in Sydney there were lots of friends but no girlfriend. Was there never anyone special for you?"

Blake opened his mouth, closed it again and an odd look passed across his face. Briony couldn't quite pick it – nervous perhaps? He was wearing an old loose shirt of Vince's over his clothes. A lock of his hair had fallen forward across his forehead and there was a smudge of paint on his cheek. For a minute he looked like the boy who'd left the farm to go to boarding school, young, vulnerable.

"There has been," he said. "But it didn't work out."

His tone was wistful. There was something more, she was sure. She sat the edger carefully on a piece of newspaper.

"Did something bad happen? Is that why you came home?" A string of panic-inducing scenarios ran through her head – the girl had dumped him and his heart was irretrievably broken; she was pregnant and was forcing him into marriage; he wanted the baby and she didn't or...Briony pressed a hand to her lips, he'd caught some terrible disease.

"It was part of the reason." Blake put his roller down on the paint tray. "My work never got back to normal after 2020, and our relationship became toxic; you really get to know someone well when you live in the same small apartment for months and months on end. And then, just when I thought I'd pack up and come home I met another Aussie. We hit it off from the start. We have so much in common, Mum, it's crazy. It's as if we were destined to be together." His face lit up with happiness. "Gab had been making plans to return to Sydney and I had nothing to stay in England for, so we travelled back together."

"And it's serious between you?"

"Gab's the one, Mum." His deep brown eyes shone.

Briony hugged him, careful to avoid getting paint from his shirt on her own coverall. "Will she come here? I'd love to meet her. We all would. Or perhaps I could convince your dad to take a trip to Sydney. It's ages since we had a holi—"

"Mum!" Blake stepped back a little, his smile gone, replaced by that anxious look again.

"What is it?" Briony gripped her hands together. Perhaps the girl had a different cultural background. Briony told herself that would be all right. Or maybe she was pregnant or maybe she had children by a different father. Like poor Paige. Three different fathers for three different children, she was one mixed-up young woman.

"Mum, Gab's not...Gab's not a she...Gab's a bloke."

"What do you mean Gab's a bloke? You're being silly. You're teasing me."

Blake locked his steady gaze on her and slowly shook his head.

She took a step back, one hand to her chest.

"I'm gay, Mum."

"No." Briony shook her head vigorously.

"I am. I've known since I was a teenager but—"

"That's a lie." Briony thought back to those years. She'd have known. He'd been a social animal at high school with a string of female friends. He did go to an all-boys boarding school for his final years, but when it came to events like formals he'd taken some delightful young women and he'd been asked to partner others on several occasions to their formals. She clapped a hand to her cheek. "Was it boarding school? Did something happen?"

"No, Mum." He had a wry smile on his face. "If anything, it made me realise what I was feeling but I kept it to myself then. It wasn't until I started uni that I let myself experience—"

"No, no, no." Briony shook her head, fear swelling up inside her and beating in her chest. "I can't...you never..."

He shrugged. "I went to Sydney and on to England. I could live my life without telling you."

"Why now then?"

"Because I'm back in Australia to stay. I'd like to come home more often." His voice was almost pleading and his smooth features creased into worry lines. "It's who I am and I don't want to hide it from my family. I've met the love of my life. Gabriel is thirty-five, his family live in Sydney. He has two sisters, like me, but they're both younger. His parents are doctors, divorced but not nastily. They're really happy for us. They're great people – you'd get on well with them, I'm sure, and—"

"Stop," Briony hissed. "You've kept it to yourself all these years and now you suddenly..." she flung her arms in the air, "come out or whatever it is they call it and you expect us to accept this news with open arms!"

"I presumed—" His cheeks were pink again and his look distressed.

"Have you told your dad or your sisters about this?"

"That I'm gay?"

"Stop saying that word!" Briony said.

Blake faltered, as if she'd slapped him. "This is the twenty twenties, Mum. Australians voted for gay marriage."

Briony stepped away from him. "Not in Badara we didn't."

"How do you know? Has the whole town discussed it?" Sarcasm dripped from his words.

"Now you're being ridiculous."

"I wasn't sure of the best way to tell you. I knew it would be a shock but I had hoped you'd be a little happy for me. Gab's going to come, that's why I thought it best for us to stay at Port Kent. We'd give you some space. Aunty Marion—"

"You've told Marion!" She pressed her hands to her cheeks. "Oh my saints, Blake, how could you?"

"I haven't told Marion I'm gay, I just asked if she'd mind if I had a friend to stay."

"No." Briony backed towards the door. "No, Blake. You mustn't tell anyone else."

"Why the hell not." He took a step forward, knocking the roller, and paint slopped from the tray onto the drop sheet beneath it.

"There's no need for that language. It's bad enough Marion and Len know about Chelsea's marriage problems. We'll keep it between us until I work out what to do."

"What do you mean 'work out what to do'?"

"I need a coffee." Briony hurried out the door, then stopped and put her head back in. Blake was staring at her, the worry gone, his angry glare gone, replaced with a look of...a look of disappointment. Briony tasted the bitterness of regret. "Would you like one?"

He held her gaze a moment then slowly shook his head. "No thanks. I'll finish this off and head back to Port Kent."

"What about dinner?"

"I'm capable of cooking my own dinner, Mum."

She turned away, unable to bear the sorrow etched on his face. In the kitchen she ignored the coffee machine and lowered herself to a chair instead. The contentment she'd felt only a short time earlier had evaporated. A shiver wriggled down her spine. She hunched over the table. First Chelsea's news and now Blake's. Her beautiful family was falling apart. What on earth was she going to do?

The late afternoon had turned a little grey as Marion drove around the town block that the church and hall took up almost half of. There was not a soul about when, for the second time that day, she turned in between the church and the hall and parked her car. She opened her boot and withdrew the shovel, rake and pick she'd brought from home. It was a strange afternoon – not a breath of wind and the air felt heavy and warm. So unusual for them to have muggy heat. No doubt something was brewing. She closed the boot, threw a surreptitious look over her shoulder and hurried off to the bush behind the hall.

Once in the centre of the garden she was out of sight from the road. The trees that had been planted fifty-two years ago stood tall now between the road and the car park on the other side of the hall. Marion began with the rake. She dragged it across the dried weeds. Some of them pulled away and others remained firmly embedded in the ground but she cleared enough of a patch to start digging. The first jab with her shovel made a ringing sound that vibrated up through her arms and jarred her teeth. No rain had fallen in Badara for at least a month and then it had only been a fleeting summer storm. The ground was rock hard.

She tossed aside the shovel and took up the pick. By the time she'd swung it several times, perspiration rolled off her forehead and down her neck and her muscles felt like she'd done a week's worth of Courtney's arm strengthening exercises. Biceps and triceps and everything in between screamed at her to stop. Marion looked in despair at the small space she'd cleared and the shallow hole she'd made. The blasted time capsule could be anywhere. How would she ever find it?

"Hello, dear."

Marion lurched around at the sound of Jean's voice.

"I wondered who on earth was scratching around out here."

"What are you doing here?" Marion couldn't disguise the surprise in her voice.

"I thought I'd see how far my nephew had got with the floor." Jean peered around Marion at the place where she'd been digging. "What are you doing here?"

"I...it's...it's for the Badara celebration—"

"I know what you're up to." Jean smiled and winked conspiratorially.

"I...you do?"

"I've been thinking myself what an eyesore this bush garden has become. No-one has looked after it since the previous minister left and it's grown into a mess. It's grand of you to try to tidy it up but it's way too big a job for one person. We need a working bee."

"You're right. I just thought I'd come and see what it was like first. What might need doing."

"Better to get your Len in with his tractor and bulldoze the lot. We need someone to come up with a plan. We could make it a shared garden."

"We don't really need a community garden in Badara. Everyone has a house yard and the school has the vegetables covered."

"I meant a more manageable garden, so that when we have events at the hall people could sit out here if they wanted, children could play. It's such a mess now and a haven for snakes."

Marion glanced around warily. She hadn't given a thought to snakes while she'd been scratching around in the dry grass.

"If it was laid out better with a watering system," Jean went on, "it could be easily maintained."

"Watering systems, paving and plants don't come cheap."

"It could be a memorial garden." Jean's smile grew wider as she glanced around. "We could ask people to sponsor parts of it in memory of past residents."

"I was doing a bit of a tidy-up. To see what the ground's like, what would need to be done. We can't do anything major without consulting..." Marion glanced around the bedraggled garden, "the others."

"No-one's bothered that it's gone to rack and ruin, but you're right. I've been thinking about the Back to Badara idea. Most of our plans for the celebration would centre around the hall, which would also involve the church so I think we need to let the congregation know."

"Don't you think a garden like you're talking would be a lot of work, Jean?" Marion madly scrambled to deflect the older woman. "None of the congregation are that young any more."

"But that's the beauty of it. We'd have more of the district involved and get the younger ones to do the heavy work for the festival."

"Are we calling it a festival now?"

"The festivities have to have a name. I thought the Back to Badara Festival had a nice ring to it. The service is here next

Sunday. Some of them might like to be on our committee for the celebrations."

Marion could see Jean was set on her idea. The only way forward was to go along with her.

"I guess we could put the idea of a celebration to the congregation. If people are keen our group can discuss it further after fitness next Tuesday as planned."

"You're such a good organiser, Marion. I hope you'll volunteer to chair the events. We need someone at the helm with a sensible head on their shoulders."

"That's a thoughtful suggestion but we should ask for expressions of interest if we're going to do it properly." Besides, there was no way Marion could concentrate on planning events until she got rid of the blasted time capsule. Her phone vibrated in her pocket. She glanced at the screen. It was a message from Blake. "I have to get going, Jean." Marion scooped up her tools and turned away.

"Don't forget this one, dear." Jean pointed to the shovel.

In Marion's rush she'd overlooked it leaning against a bush. It was Len's good one. "Thanks."

"See you at mahjong tomorrow." Jean smiled and gave a little wave as Marion spun away and strode back to her car.

"Blast and dammit!" Marion muttered as she put the tools back in the boot. It would be Jean who'd come along and found her poking around. Not that it mattered. Marion had already worked out there was no way she'd be able to dig very deep in the rock-hard ground unless she soaked it first. She looked to the sky. The grey clouds were sadly not rain clouds. Somehow she'd have to soak the soil herself. And who knew if she even had the right spot. She slammed the boot shut. It was all so frustrating.

Back in her car she looked at the message. Blake was asking if they were home. She replied that Len was there and she was on her way. They hadn't seen Blake since his arrival last week. It would be good to have his company, and maybe he'd like to stay for dinner. Someone different at their table would be a welcome distraction.

twelve

"Where's Blake?" Madeline stood inside the kitchen door, looking from the table set for four people to Briony.

"He's gone back to Port Kent," Briony said.

"Already? He didn't let me know." Madeline got out her phone. "He was going to come for a ride when he finished the painting."

"And he was going to help me bring in some of my things from the shed." Chelsea had come in behind her sister.

"He was tired from painting," Briony said. "He'll be back tomorrow."

"I'm out all day tomorrow following up horse show stuff and I'll probably stop in Wirini Bay for dinner afterwards," Madeline said.

"Are you ever home?" Chelsea snapped. "I don't know how Dad managed before I was here to help."

"I'm around most of the time," Madeline muttered and fiddled with her phone.

Briony glared from one to the other. "And so am I." The dull headache that had developed with Blake's departure strengthened. "I am your father's extra help when he needs it, although I do

agree this horse show is taking up a lot of your time, Madeline."
Briony switched her gaze to Chelsea, who was helping herself to
a bottle of wine from the fridge. "And what are you bringing in
from the shed? Your bedroom already has furniture."

"Blake helped me shift some things while you were at fitness.
We've made room to bring in my chest of drawers and my comfy
chair and a few other things."

"You're settling in then?"

"Yes. Unless you want me to move into one of the sheds?"

Briony flinched away from Chelsea's glare.

"Blake's having dinner at Aunty Marion's." Madeline looked
up from her phone. "He says he thinks we all need a bit of space."

Briony turned to the sink so the girls wouldn't see the hurt on
her face. She filled a glass with water and took a sip.

"Don't tell me you told him to go back to Sydney," Chelsea
said.

"Of course I didn't," Briony snapped.

"Why would she do that?" Madeline asked.

"Classic Mum sticking her head in the sand. Out of sight
out of mind," Chelsea snapped. "She thinks I should go back to
Brandon."

"I do not!"

"What's all this shouting about?" Vince stuck his head in the
door. "Who thinks you should go back to Brandon? Has Marion
been here?"

"Aunty Marion hasn't said anything – it's Mum who thinks I
should go back to him."

Vince looked at Briony as if he'd just been told she'd thrown
Chelsea off a cliff.

"I didn't say that!" Briony blustered. "And Blake left of his own
accord. The painting is finished. He'll be back tomorrow."

"Don't think so." Madeline waved the phone she still clutched. "He said he's going to visit Nan and some old school friends in Wirini Bay tomorrow and maybe have a meal there."

Chelsea stared at Briony, the glass of wine she'd poured half-way to her lips. "He told you, didn't he?"

Once more Briony turned away and reached for the glass of water.

"Told her what?" Vince had that exasperated tone he got when Briony and the two girls were chatting back and forth about topics that flew over his head.

"Mum?" Chelsea said. "Tell me you didn't reject him."

"What's going on?"

"Why would she...oh..."

Vince and Maddie spoke at once. Vince had a puzzled look but Maddie glanced at Chelsea and raised her eyebrows.

The blood in Briony's veins felt icy in spite of the warm evening. The girls knew about Blake. Briony hadn't wanted him to tell the others yet, not till she had it sorted in her head, but she should have known he'd tell his sisters. He'd probably outed himself, or whatever it was called, to them years ago.

Briony hadn't known Chelsea and Brandon took drugs or that their marriage was on the rocks, she didn't know Blake was homosexual. She obviously didn't know her children at all. She looked at Madeline, wondering what secrets she was keeping. The last time she'd brought a guy home to meet them had been – Briony put a hand to her head – when? Years ago. Maybe she was a lesbian. The pain in Briony's temple was excruciating now.

"Everyone sit down," Vince said. "Chelsea, pour your mum some wine, and, Madeline, I'll have a beer please."

He guided Briony to a chair and immediately some of her tension eased. Vincent would know what to do. He always did – only sometimes they didn't always agree on the path he'd suggest, but he was level headed. Her knees buckled and she hit the chair with a thud. Perhaps he knew too. Was she the only one who hadn't known?

"Now," Vince said once they were all seated, "can someone tell me what's going on?"

"I'm not sure if Blake has told you, Dad, but he obviously told Mum today and she's overreacted."

"Told Mum what?"

"He's gay."

Briony watched Vince's face — there was no surprise, his features remained inscrutable. What did that mean? Did he know too?

"Is that what all this fuss is about?" Madeline asked. "Oh no, Mum!" She pushed back from her chair and leaped to her feet. "You didn't reject him, did you? He's your son."

"This has obviously come as a big surprise to your mum," Vince said.

"But not to you?" Briony was surrounded by family but she'd never felt so alone. Even Vincent had deserted her. "You knew and you didn't tell me?"

Vince scratched his chin. "I didn't know for sure. Blake hasn't actually told me." He shrugged. "It's a feeling I've had."

Briony bit back the retort that she'd had that feeling too but she'd locked it away, not allowing it air to breathe. Life was tough enough without her precious son having to fight extra battles.

Chelsea jumped up beside her sister. "Bloody hell, Mum, you didn't kick him out, did you?"

"Of course I didn't kick him out," Briony snapped.

Vince reached a hand across the table and took hers in his warm grasp. "What did you say, love?"

She lifted her gaze from the glass of wine she'd been staring into but hadn't touched. "It was a shock."

"I can understand that," he said. "It's probably not the life you'd thought for him."

"Get a grip, Mum." Chelsea waved her hands about. "Lesbians, gays, queers, whatever goes, it's all a normal part of life these days."

"It's not as if Blake's flying to Mars or turned into a zombie," Madeline said. "He's gay, that's all."

"And we're fine with that, aren't we, Briony?" Vince rubbed his hand over hers, peering at her closely.

"Don't give me that baleful look!" She ripped her hand out from under his. "Are you saying it's okay for Blake to be... homosexual?"

"You don't have to whisper, Mum," Chelsea said. "There's no-one here but us."

Vince ignored his daughter, looking directly into Briony's eyes. She shivered at the sorrow reflected back at her.

"You need a bit more time to digest it," he said. "Blake's our son and we love him no matter what."

"Don't you dare say I don't love my son."

"I'm not. I—"

"Of course I love him but I...I can't..." Briony shook her head. "He can't be gay."

Madeline and Chelsea stood behind Vince. All three of them stared at her, radiating a collective body of disapproval.

"Why do you have to whisper the word?"

Briony recoiled at the simmering anger in Chelsea's voice. Chelsea didn't understand, neither did Madeline. Briony had made sure they'd never feel the horror and pain of being different and she'd thought if she ignored the tiny little suspicions she'd once held about Blake that it would keep him safe. During his time away from Australia she'd shelved her fears completely. She looked at Vincent, took in his disapproval, another barb. He knew how she felt and yet he'd sided with the girls against her.

Tears pooled in her eyes as the pain in her head throbbed relentlessly. She stood. "There's a pie in the oven. You'll have to cook your own vegetables. I'm going to have an early night." She turned away from her astonished family and made her way to the bedroom. She needed pain relief tablets and to put her head on the pillow before it rolled from her shoulders.

"Thanks for the meal, Marion," Blake said. "I should go and let you two get to bed."

"I know we're getting old but we don't need to go to bed at eight o'clock." Len chuckled. "How about a glass of port?"

"I'd love one."

Marion knew port wasn't Blake's drink of choice. He drank it in deference to Len and she could see he was eager to stay on. "I'll have one too, thanks, Len. Why don't we sit on the back verandah? It's such a mild night."

They moved out and seated themselves in the new wicker outdoor setting.

"This is nice." Blake ran his hands up and down the armrests.

"The staff at school gave them to me," Marion said. "My farewell gift. If we ever move to the shack permanently I'll take them there."

"You will move there, won't you?"

"Still to be decided," Len said. "I'd like to one day maybe."

Marion glanced at her husband's serious face then at Blake, who was flicking his gaze between them. "Your dad has kindly said it's ours already as far as he's concerned but Len feels that's too generous."

"I thought it was supposed to be yours when Nan...well, once she's gone," Blake said.

"It will be but while she's alive and the shack is still in her name it's there for both families to use whenever they want." Marion smiled at Blake. "And it's great that you are at the moment."

"You said something about bringing a friend to join you," Len said.

"I was going to but I'm not sure now." Blake shifted in his chair and took a sip of his port. "It might not be the right thing to do."

Before Marion could ask what he meant by that his phone lit up and vibrated on the table. Blake glanced at it but instead of ignoring it as he'd done several times during the evening he picked it up. "Sorry, it's Dad. I didn't see him today, I—"

"Of course." Len waved a hand. "Go inside if you'd like some privacy."

Marion glanced over at Len as soon as Blake's voice faded beyond the door. "He seems bothered by something tonight, don't you think?"

"Does he?"

"He didn't eat much of his meal."

"No-one can resist your lemon chicken. Perhaps he's unwell."

"Len." She frowned at him. "He was so excited when he first came back. Today it's as if he's a different bloke. And why's he here, when I'm sure Briony was expecting him to have dinner their way tonight?"

"It's not really our business, duck."

"What did you two talk about that first night when he stayed here?"

"Nothing and everything. He had some things to get off his chest." Len stared into his port a moment. When he glanced up he took a breath, started to speak then swallowed his words with a sip of the deep red liquid. "We solved the problems of the universe over too many ports, which resulted in a sore head for me the next day, as I remember."

The back door opened, and Blake joined them again.

"Everything okay?" Marion asked.

"Just Dad touching base." In the yellow glow of the verandah light he looked weary. "I really should go."

"Are you all right, mate?" Len asked.

Blake hovered beside his chair while a range of emotions played across his face, fighting with each other until sorrow took over. He put his hands to his head and raked his fingers back through his hair.

"Nothing's going as I thought," he said. "I'm thirty-one and Mum still makes me feel like a child. As if I don't know my own mind." He thumped his fist into his open palm.

Marion opened her mouth to offer comfort but Len was quicker, out of his chair in a flash with one arm across Blake's shoulders, guiding him back to his seat. "Sit down," he said. "I'll get you another port."

"Or would you prefer coffee?" Marion asked.

"Just water, thanks."

Marion brought them all water. They sat in silence, the only sound the occasional cricket or the flap of a moth against the light.

Blake drained his glass and sat it back on the table. He took a breath. "I've already upset one branch of the family tonight – I might as well continue."

Len glanced at Marion, his look beseeching, and then she realised Blake was focused on her too.

"I want to tell you something."

Marion had a horrible sinking feeling in her stomach but before she could put a reason to it, Blake spoke.

"I'm gay."

The breath she'd been holding rushed from her. She'd expected Blake to announce some kind of terrible affliction. She could feel Len's gaze but she didn't look back at him as realisation dawned. Blake had been speaking to her which meant Len already knew. Once more it was only the crickets and the moths that broke the silence. Marion understood how important to both men her next words would be.

She reached out and gripped Blake's hand. "You know that makes absolutely no difference to you being the person we love," she said. "And you know we're always here for you, no matter what."

Blake managed a wobbly smile. "Thanks, Marion...both of you for your support."

"I gather it didn't go so well with your parents," Len said.

"Dad wasn't there, that's why he rang. He was..." Blake shrugged. "Okay with it but...Mum...she's lost the plot. Dad wants me to stay away for a while...from my own family!" Blake stood and stared out into the gathering darkness, his disappointment palpable. "I was worried it wouldn't go well, that's why I've put it off for so long." He turned back and Marion's heart broke at the sorrow on his face. "I thought it would be a shock then they'd be okay with it."

Marion could only imagine Briony's reaction. Having a gay son would not fit her idea of how her family should be. "What about the girls?" She wondered how much like their mother they'd be.

"They've known for a while and they're both life-as-usual with it. That's who's been sending the texts all night. Messages of support. It's just Mum and Dad...well, Mum really. I think Dad will be fine."

"He will," Len said with great authority.

Marion hoped he was right. She was glad Len was being optimistic but he couldn't truly know how Vince would react. She worried her brother would stand by his wife, and Briony had obviously taken the news hard.

"Time will help," Len said.

"But don't feel you have to be alone," Marion said. "You know you're always welcome here."

"They'll come round, mate." Len put a hand on Blake's shoulder. "They love you."

Marion blinked back tears, not sure if it was Len's loving gesture or his words that overwhelmed her.

"You're both so understanding. I wish my parents could be like you," Blake said.

Len opened his mouth but Marion spoke first this time.

"You're not our son," she said. "Perhaps that small distance makes unexpected news easier."

"You've had a long time to come to terms with your sexuality," Len said. "Your dad's right, they need some time, that's all."

His gaze met Marion's over Blake's head. She was glad Blake had confided in him first but she wondered what else they might have discussed. She turned back to Blake. "We love you too. But your parents love you more. They'll come round."

Once more Blake's face contorted as he grappled with his emotions.

"Was the friend, the one you mentioned might come..." Marion's words trailed away.

"Gab." Blake brightened immediately. "He's the one."

"We'd like to meet him," Len said.

"Perhaps give your family a bit more time," Marion cautioned.

"You two are great." He reached an arm out to pull them towards him in a squeezy hug.

Once more Marion met Len's gentle gaze. Life was full of twists and turns. She reached for the port glass, which still held a mouthful.

"If you want to keep busy I've got some tree trimming I wouldn't mind a hand with," Len said. "And some fencing."

Marion sat up in her chair as Len's suggestion led to a lightning-bolt idea of her own.

"There's some garden work at the church hall I could do with some help with," she said. A little fizz of hope rose above all the emotion of Blake's confession. He could be the one person she could get to help her dig around in the garden at the hall without having to explain too much. She could get him started while she kept Jean busy playing mahjong the next afternoon.

thirteen

"Are we going to this?"

Paige came back into the kitchen from hanging out a load of washing and Jayden was waving the Family Day flier at her. She'd put it aside the day before and then forgotten about it.

"Maybe."

"Going to what?" Kodie asked, a smear of Vegemite around her lips.

"It's a family get-together for the footy and netball clubs." The excitement in Jayden's voice was a nice change from his recent moodiness. "That's great, Mum."

"Can I play netball?" Kodie asked.

"I don't care if I have second-hand boots." Jayden hauled himself up onto the bench. "I promise I'll do lots to help with the little ones when I'm not playing footy and—"

"Hold it." Paige put one hand up. "I haven't said anyone's actually playing anything yet. We'll go to the get-together and find out more."

"I thought Zuri's dad told you all you needed to know."

Jayden had noticed the screen door when he'd come home the previous afternoon and she'd explained Dane had installed it for them.

"We didn't really discuss it. It was the ladies from my fitness group who mentioned the clothing pool and a possible payment scheme for subs but I gather there's also a lot of travel." Her car was old but reliable. If they had to do hundreds of extra kilometres getting him to football games there'd be fuel costs and the service that was due later in the year would come around much quicker.

"You always tell us to think positive, Mum." Jayden jumped down from the bench and folded his arms across his chest. "It doesn't sound like you are."

Levi swung around in his chair and knocked his milk over. It splattered across the table.

"Levi!" Jayden brushed at his shorts.

"Sorree," Levi sang.

Paige passed a damp cloth to Jayden and used another to mop up the mess. The lump of guilt for what her children missed out on sat firmly in her chest.

"It was an accident," she said, then noticed the time. "You'd better get going, Jay, or you'll miss the bus."

Without a word, he went to clean his teeth and gather his things, allowing her to brush a kiss across his cheek as he headed for the door.

"Have a good day," she called after him.

It wasn't until later in the day that she came across the flier again, lying on the bench among the breakfast dishes. She'd taken Kodie to school and Levi was playing with toys in the sunroom, so she'd started clearing up the kitchen. A closer read revealed the Family Day actually started in the late afternoon. Levi and even Kodie were generally getting titchy by that time on a Friday but a trip to the beach might be fun.

She flapped the note against her fingers then got out her phone and punched in Dane's number. It rang for so long she was about to disconnect when he answered.

"Hi, it's Paige. I wanted to say thank you for the screen door and the flywire in the chimneys."

"No problem. I hope it helps."

"No flies inside today." She gave an awkward cough and there was silence. "Hello?"

"Yeah, sorry. Was there something else?"

"Oh no...yes." Paige stumbled over her words. "Jayden still wants to play football but...I'm a little concerned because he's never played before."

"He's keen so he'll catch on quick enough. We take all comers. I like to think it's because we're a welcoming club but it's also because we're short of numbers..." His voice trailed off and there was silence again.

"Briony said there might be a second-hand pool for boots and things," Paige said.

"Yeah, although I'm not sure what's in it. Are you coming to the Family Day? I think they're planning on doing a bit of a swap and share there."

Paige chewed her lip. She didn't have anything to swap or share.

"And what about subs?" she asked. "I spent a bit to move us here and I'm still on a pretty tight budget."

"Trust me, I know what that's like. Teenage boys are busy. I was one once but I swear I didn't grow overnight like Zuri has a few times. One minute his clothes fit and the next they don't. Come to think of it, he's recently cleaned out his cupboard. There might be a few things he could pass on to Jayden."

"Oh...no...you don't have to..." Discomfort wormed through her. Now Dane, like the fitness club women, was offering things. "I gather there's a fair bit of travel involved for games," she said.

"Not every week but a few of the games are a bit of a hike. Jayden could always go with Zuri and me though."

"You don't have to do that, I just wondered..."

"I often give one or two of the younger blokes a ride. Some of the other parents are juggling other commitments so I try to help out."

She closed her eyes. He obviously devoted a lot of time to the footy club. She wondered what his wife was like.

"It'd be great if you came to the Family Day at Port Kent," he went on. "Weather's looking good for the beach and you'll meet lots of people, find out all there is to know. I'm happy to give you a ride if you'd like."

"Oh, no, that's okay. I need a car seat for Levi." And if they did go Paige wanted to be able to leave when she chose.

"Tell you what, why don't Zuri and I swing past on our way there? You can follow us and we can introduce you. I know it can be a bit daunting when you rock up somewhere new."

"Let me think on it some more." She still wasn't sure she was ready to commit, and it didn't sound as if his wife was going. She hoped it wasn't going to be an all-guys show but then if it was netball as well..."Can I message you in a day or so?"

"Sure. Let me know by Thursday and we can make a plan." There was a noise in the background, then a female voice and a dog barked. "Sorry, I have to go. Talk later in the week."

And that was it. Paige was left holding a silent phone with a bundle of butterflies flapping in her stomach. She was good at keeping people at arm's length but first the fitness group and now Dane were infiltrating her space.

The butterflies whirled as the phone in her hand started to ring. She glanced at the number – it wasn't Dane's. Perhaps one of the schools? She answered.

"Paige, please don't hang up."

The soft flutter of butterflies changed to an explosion of flapping birds inside her chest. Huge birds that battered her ribs.

"All we want is to see Jayden sometimes." The woman's voice was soft but Paige knew there was nothing soft about Lucinda.

"Paige, please," the voice begged. "It must be so hard on your own. We can help."

Paige's finger went for the disconnect button.

"You know we have the money. We could help—"

Paige pressed *end* and held the phone away from her as if it had the power to allow the caller into her home. She jumped as it rang again. The same number. With trembling fingers she blocked it. Not that it mattered. Now that they had her number they could call from any phone and she'd never know who it was until she answered. They'd tried that before – it was one of the reasons she'd changed her number. She pressed her back to the wall and slowly slid down it. The thrashing wings inside her exploded up and out of her throat in a howl, and the phone slipped from her fingers to the floor.

Two little arms came around her neck and two big brown eyes full of worry peered at her. "Mummy, what's the matter?"

She pulled Levi to her, imagining he was Jayden, who she was trying so hard to protect but thought himself too old to be hugged by her. "I'm all right, Levi. I had a fright."

He planted a sloppy kiss on her cheek. "Don't be scared, Mummy. I'll look after you." His little face was so like Ari's, so full of love and concern she had to fight hard to hold back the tears.

The phone started ringing again. A different number. She took a risk, turned it off and drew in a long deep breath. Her composure returned as she realised they might have her new number but that didn't mean they knew where she was.

"I'm hungry, Mummy," Levi whispered in her ear.

"You're always hungry." She forced a laugh and rose to her feet, tugging him up with her. "Let's have morning tea. Can you get the milk out for me?"

Levi rushed to the fridge. He loved to help. She gave him another hug as he returned, intent on the large container he carried carefully with two hands. She mustn't let the call frighten her. They were all safely hidden away here in Badara. Her bloody mother had probably given Lucinda the phone number but Paige had to hold on to the hope she hadn't also given away their new address.

Marion pulled up outside the Townsends' back gate. In the distance, towards the sheds, she could hear a dog barking and the bleating of sheep. She hoped that meant the men were busy and Sarah might be alone in the house.

She retrieved her container of sausage rolls from the back seat and let herself in the gate. She'd been thinking about Sarah since Len had mentioned the Townsends the other week. Added to that Briony had said Sarah couldn't face people and then Dane had been at Paige's place. Sarah and Briony were cousins, of course, Wilson descendants like Jean, but the Townsends lived a long way out to the west of Badara and Sarah and Marion didn't see a lot of each other except for the odd community or sporting event over the years.

Marion had rung Sarah when the fitness club had first been planned, thinking of her as a potential attendee, nothing more.

It hadn't occurred to Marion that Sarah might still be feeling reluctant to face people after the terrible time they'd had with their oldest son, Chad, and his Bali exploits, but it made sense. Sarah had always been someone who kept her personal feelings close. It must have been devastating to find out about her son's duplicitous life, to have her family broken apart and exposed to scrutiny and to nearly lose their property in the fall-out that followed. Marion should have called in before.

She could see the back door was open beyond the screen. She drew herself up and knocked. "Sarah? Are you inside?" She listened, but no sounds came from the house.

"Hello, Marion."

She turned and swallowed her surprise. Sarah was walking towards her, a couple of bulging shopping bags in her hands. It wasn't her arrival, but her appearance that shocked Marion. In the past Sarah's hair had always been well-groomed. Now it was long and limp, and the grey she'd previously hidden with colour was streaked through the brown. Sarah was tall but her shoulders were thin and rounded and her face gaunt. Marion scrambled to think how long it had been since she'd last seen the other woman face to face. Perhaps six months, maybe nine.

"I just popped in to say hello." Marion put on her cheeriest voice. "I've been cooking so I brought you some sausage rolls. Dane and Zuri might like them if you don't want them."

Sarah came along the path and stopped beside her. "That's very kind. We all love your sausage rolls. Haven't had them in a long time."

They stood looking at each other.

"Would you like to come in?" Sarah said, just as Marion thought she'd have to invite herself.

"Thanks, I'd love to if you have time."

Sarah led the way into her kitchen. "I've been over at Dane's place, clearing out some things he asked me to get."

Dane lived only a short distance from the main house in the original old farmhouse, which was much smaller than the Townsends' more modern home.

Sarah put down the two bags she'd been carrying and flicked on the kettle. "The men are doing sheep work so I've already delivered their morning tea but I haven't had mine yet." She glanced back at Marion. "Please sit. Tea or coffee?"

"Coffee, thanks." Marion sat at Sarah's table. The kitchen wasn't as fancy as Briony's, which had updated cupboards and every sparkly appliance, but it was more modern and spacious than Marion's. Except for a sewing machine on the end of the table with some jeans folded and perched on top there was not a thing out of place. The Townsends' farm was much bigger than Len and Marion's and on better land. Marion had always thought of them as being well off, but Chad's divorce must have nearly broken them financially.

"I'm sorry I haven't called before this, Sarah. It was very remiss of me."

"We're a distance apart." Sarah dragged a piece of hair from her face and tucked it behind her ear. "We don't usually call on each other."

"I know but…"

"I hear you've finished up teaching. I didn't realise when you rang me about the exercise group. How's retirement suiting you?" Sarah put out a plate of home-baked biscuits along with a milk jug and sugar container. "It must be different after teaching for so long."

Apart from relief work at the post office, Sarah had never worked off the farm to Marion's knowledge.

"I'm getting used to it," she said. "Trying to keep myself busy or Len thinks I'm his personal help." Marion forced a laugh.

"I got out of having to do much farm work until…well, now that it's just Jim and Dane…I do more again…" Sarah's voice faltered then she gave a weak smile. "Mostly I run errands, although Zuri is on his Ps and he usually volunteers. Other than shopping and the odd trip to Adelaide, I don't leave the place much."

Sarah used to be a hard worker in the community. The finality of her statement shocked Marion. "What do you do to keep busy?"

"When there's nothing left to do in the house and the men don't need me, I garden. I enjoy growing vegetables and we have several fruit trees so there's often something to do there. Sometimes Dane lets me do a bit of housework for him and I'm allowed to bake extras for him and Zuri, but they like their independence so I try not to interfere."

Marion glanced at the sewing machine. Sarah used to win awards at local shows for her needlework. "What about your beautiful embroidery? I enjoy knitting in the evenings now that it's cooler but I was never good with a needle and thread."

Sarah ran a hand over the smooth tablecloth in front of her. "I haven't done any for ages. I don't read much any more either."

"Jean and I have a mahjong group on Wednesday afternoons."

"She's told me about that, and the fitness class."

"You could come with me to mahjong today."

"That's a complicated game, isn't it?"

"I'm sure you'd get the idea quickly."

"I can't seem to concentrate very well these days."

"I do wish you'd join our little fitness group."

"Oh…no…thank you, but…maybe one day."

"At the moment there aren't many of us," Marion persisted. "You know Jean and Briony, of course, and Gloria comes sometimes and other than that there's only the two new girls. Claire, the principal's wife – she's very shy but lovely – and a young mum who's living in the old bakery, Paige."

"Dane did a bit of repair work for her. I think it's such a shame the owner doesn't maintain the place. It's a lovely old house but it doesn't surprise me that people don't stay when he won't do the simplest of repairs. Absent landlords make it difficult for tenants."

"Dane was there yesterday when I was. Paige invited us to use the old shopfront for our fitness session because of the work being done at the hall."

"Those clothes are for Paige's son." Sarah waved a hand towards the bulging shopping bags she'd been carrying. "Things Zuri has grown out of. He recently gave his room a makeover and put anything he didn't want in boxes in the spare room. Evidently he was supposed to sort it and take it to the op shop but he hasn't done it yet." Sarah smiled. "He's such a good kid…young man now, he's almost eighteen."

"You must miss your other grandchildren." Chad's family had lived on their second property, not far from Sarah.

A shadow crossed Sarah's face then the smile returned. "That's why I go to Adelaide every so often, to visit them. Thankfully my daughter-in-law and I have a good relationship. She makes keeping in touch easy, although I must admit the video calls feel a bit stilted and awkward. I always run out of things to talk about with the children but it's better than nothing and yes, I do miss them."

There'd been a rumour that Chad was working interstate as a truck driver but Marion didn't like to ask. "Are you sure you won't come to the fitness class, Sarah? We meet every Tuesday morning at ten and have a shared lunch afterwards. It's been good to do something different. You could just come for lunch if you don't want to do the exercises. Your Aunty Jean's pretty hard to keep up with, I must admit."

They both smiled at that.

"I'll see. Thanks for the offer and for the sausage rolls and the chat. It was good of you to come out." Sarah pushed back from the table and Marion understood her time was up.

On the drive home she was troubled by thoughts of Sarah, who'd become a ghost of the woman she used to be. Marion decided she would have to find some way to encourage her back into the community. It was something to ponder. For the moment she had to get home for lunch with Blake and Len.

They'd been working on fences all morning but Blake had promised to come with her to Badara in the afternoon. She'd been purposely vague about the project because she didn't want Len to know what she was doing. She'd just told them there was a bit of tidy-up gardening to do at the hall. She planned to set Blake to work soaking the ground on the pretext of preparing it for weeding and replanting, and the best bit was that Jean would be home all afternoon while they played mahjong so she wouldn't be out poking her nose in. Marion thought she'd go back and do some digging on her own later in the evening when Jean would be eating dinner. Once the time capsule was got rid of she could concentrate on plans for the Badara celebrations.

fourteen

Paige jumped at the bang of the screen door. The fruit knife slipped in her hand. There was a thud and then Jayden appeared in the doorway. She was so pleased to see him she squeezed him in an extra tight hug. He stepped back and gave her that look he'd developed recently, as if he was questioning her sanity.

"Good day?" she asked.

"Yeah."

Paige turned off her phone now that she had all her kids home safely. There'd been another call an hour ago from an unknown number. She'd let it ring and no message had been left. It could have been a spam call or it could have been them. It was doing her head in.

"Jayden!" Levi came running and wrapped his arms around his brother's legs.

"Hey, little bro."

Kodie followed. "Can we play that game we played yesterday out the back?"

"Give your brother time to get in the door," Paige said.

"Oh yeah, the door," he said. "What are those bags at the back door?"

"What bags?" Paige had gone out the front way when she'd picked up Kodie.

She followed Jayden to discover two shopping bags leaning against the outside back wall. After the phone calls, Paige eyed them suspiciously.

Jayden picked up one bag and peered inside. "Looks like clothes." He passed it to her and leaned down to get the other.

Paige lifted a t-shirt from the bag as Jayden let out a yelp of delight.

"Footy boots! Two pairs."

"Who...how?"

"There's a note tucked in one boot." Jayden passed it to her.

She'd thought perhaps Dane but the page had a flower at the top, lines like old-fashioned writing paper and a short note written in a neat flowing style.

"*Dear Paige and Jayden.*" Paige read the note.

"What about me?" Kodie complained.

"They don't know you," Paige said and continued reading. "*Dane asked me to drop off these clothes and footy gear that Zuri has grown out of. Hope some of it's useful (two pairs of footy boots, different sizes). Dane took a guess at Jayden's size but feet are tricky. Kind regards, Sarah Townsend.*" Paige assumed Dane's wife had left the things at her back door.

"This pair's my size." Jayden was already sitting on the floor trying on the boots.

Paige picked up the bag that had t-shirts on the top. There were several brand names and they were in pristine condition. Sarah Townsend obviously had a bigger budget than Paige, but she also looked after her son's clothing.

Paige lifted out a charcoal t-shirt. She caught a glimpse of a car and a gold logo before Jayden snatched it from her hands.

"*Rocket League*! Sweet!" He pulled the t-shirt on over his school shirt. It was way too big but he was grinning from ear to ear.

Paige smiled to hide her sorrow at yet another failure on her part. Jayden loved the video game but they had no way for him to play it. He'd played when he'd visited friends back in Melton but he hadn't mentioned it much since they'd moved house.

Kodie took the plastic bag that still held some clothes. "Is there anything for me?"

"Zuri doesn't have sisters," Jayden said.

"You've got that lovely t-shirt Mimi sent," Paige said.

"I don't like pink." Kodie folded her arms across her chest.

Paige wanted to say she shouldn't look a gift horse in the mouth but she glimpsed herself in her daughter's stern look and remained silent.

Jayden picked up the bags. "I'll put these away and get changed then we can go out and play handball."

"Okay." Kodie's face brightened.

"I made cake today," Paige said.

"I helped." Levi jumped up and down.

"Let's have some now," Paige said.

Levi ran to the kitchen and Kodie actually smiled.

"Be there in a minute," Jayden called.

Paige took the cooling cake from under a tea towel to excited squeals from the two younger ones. At least there were some things she could get right.

Briony did her daily chores in a daze. Blake's disclosure of the previous afternoon throbbed and niggled like a festering sore inside her. The other members of her household tiptoed around her — that was only Vincent really, it was more like stomped in the case of Chelsea and Madeline, along with sideways glares, pursed lips and head shakes. Briony ignored them all, lost in her grief that her son was not the man she'd thought and he wouldn't have the future she'd imagined for him. Vincent had tried to reassure her and remind her that they loved their son and he loved them, no matter what, but why was she the only one who could see how hard life would be for Blake?

It was late afternoon again and she was on her own for the moment prepping dinner. Vincent had tried to talk to her last night but she'd exhausted herself from crying and had gone to bed early. He'd tried again after lunch when they'd had a brief moment alone but nothing he said could make her see that things would ever be right again. Blake professed to be homosexual and Chelsea had declared at breakfast she wasn't going back to Brandon.

Briony took two painkillers and a large drink of water. She'd been fighting another headache all day. She finished peeling the potatoes for the shepherd's pie and put the left-over lamb roast into her blender to chop.

"How are you, Mum?" Madeline asked in the sudden silence after the motor stopped.

Briony's heart thumped as she whirled around. "I didn't hear you come in."

"I didn't mean to scare you." Madeline got herself a glass of water. "How are you feeling now?"

Briony stiffened. Madeline's question was a change from the disdain she'd been radiating. "I'm fine."

"Oh...that's good." Madeline smiled, delightedly. "I'm glad, Mum. It's awful when we're all fighting."

"We're not fight—"

"We've finished in the house paddock." Madeline cut her off. "Dad and Chelsea should be in soon." She flopped onto a chair and pulled out her phone.

Her hair was loose and fell in soft waves framing her pretty face. She looked so young, so innocent, oblivious to how cruel the world could be. Briony had made sure of that. Madeline didn't understand this was not some petty disagreement, this was about keeping Briony's family safe.

She swiped up the knife. Madeline was also oblivious to the demands of running a household. Briony turned back to the potatoes and took out her frustration on them as she wondered why neither of her daughters ever offered to help prepare a meal. And if Vincent didn't remind them they didn't help with dishes either. Blake always offered to help. Oh, was that a sign of homosexuality she'd missed?

The potatoes were boiling and the meat simmering in its gravy base when she heard voices from the direction of the back door and soon after Vince came in. He gave her a brief hug.

"How are you?"

"I'm fine," she said again, feeling anything but fine and wishing they'd stop asking her. "Dinner will be ready in about half an hour."

"What are we having?" This time it was Chelsea.

"Shepherd's pie."

There was a brief silence. It was a meal both she and Vincent enjoyed. Neither of the girls were fans but for once Briony didn't care. They certainly hadn't provided any help. No-one commented.

"Have you been in touch with Blake? Let him know he should come home again?" Madeline had finally put down her phone.

Briony stared at her. "What do you mean?"

"I thought now that you'd calmed down you'd want him to come back."

"I didn't ask him to leave."

"You didn't make him feel welcome," Chelsea snapped. "You rejected your own son."

"I did not!"

"Oh for f—"

"Chelsea!" Vince's sharp retort startled them all. "We need to clear the air. Let's all sit down."

"I've got the dinner to finish," Briony said.

He strode to the stove and turned everything off.

"What are you doing," she snapped. "The potatoes—"

"Can wait," he said. "Sit down, everyone."

He glared at Briony and then Chelsea until they both sat, then he did too. He gripped his hands together, staring down at them as if they might speak for him. Briony rarely saw him so openly agitated.

"Chelsea and Madeline, you've obviously got a better handle on this than your mum and I?"

"You think?" Chelsea raised an eyebrow. "Blake thought perhaps you oldies would have difficulty with it but I reassured him you'd be cool." She shook her head. "How wrong I was."

"Blake is a member of our family and it's important we present a united front for him and the community," Vince said.

"We agree on that at least," Briony said. "We can't let people find out."

"That's not what I meant, love." Vince reached for her hand. "Blake's life is one that we don't completely understand yet but he hasn't killed anyone or set fire to anything or committed a robbery. He needs to know we love him and that we support him. That's the united front we need to present to everyone else, no matter our personal feelings."

Briony snatched her hand away. "You can't be serious. People aren't homosexual in Badara."

"Actually the new people running the servo in Wirini Bay are a couple," Madeline said.

Briony gaped at her. "I thought they were sisters."

"Mum!" Chelsea groaned.

"And Melanie Brown came out a few years ago."

"That whole family was strange," Briony said quickly. "They moved away after that."

"Gee, I wonder why?" Chelsea rolled her eyes.

"You can't be different in Badara." Briony felt a tremble in her knees that vibrated up her body. Why couldn't she make them understand how horrible life would be?

"Love, we're all different." Vince spoke soothingly. "You'd be surprised by some of the differences if you knew about them."

"That's my point." Briony's fingers were trembling now. "People keep things to themselves. They don't go around shouting they're homosexual or getting divorced from the rooftops."

"Blake's not exactly shouting it from the rooftops. He's told us – his family," Madeline said. "The world has changed and maybe Badara needs to grow with it."

Briony glared at her youngest daughter. Of all her children, she thought she and Madeline were on a similar page. "What would you know about it?"

"I may as well join the rejected." Madeline stood and glanced from Briony to Vince. She drew a deep breath. "I've been waiting for the right time to tell you, but lately I don't know there ever will be so I'm just going to say it. I've met someone and I was hoping to bring him home to meet you."

Briony managed a weak smile. "Of course, but surely that's good news, isn't—"

"It's Cameron Baxter."

"But he's..."

"Forty-two, has a Filipino mum and is divorced with two kids." Madeline folded her arms across her chest. "On the other side of the balance sheet, he's not gay and not taking drugs so I'm hoping that might count as some positives."

"How long have you been seeing him?" Chelsea asked.

"Twelve months."

"What?" Briony couldn't believe Madeline had kept such a secret for so long.

"He's a good bloke," Vince said.

"Did you know about this?" Briony gasped.

"I'd heard a few rumours at Ag Bureau." Vince winked at Madeline. "Loves his horses. I assume he's on the show committee you've joined."

Madeline went a little pink and nodded.

"No-one has standards any more." Briony couldn't sit still. She rose and paced the length of the kitchen.

"What's that supposed to mean?" Chelsea snapped.

"Look at you, for example," Briony said. "You've been married for five minutes and you give up at the first sign of trouble and leave your husband, and now Madeline is trotting around with a similarly separated man."

"Divorced," Madeline said.

"Only recently," Briony snapped.

"I wasn't the reason his marriage broke down."

"I suppose you'll tell me his wife took drugs so it was okay for him to leave her and those poor children."

"She walked out on him, and Cam hasn't left the children." Madeline flung out her arms. "He has them as often as he can. He's trying for full custody, in fact."

"That makes it better," Briony scoffed.

"Stop, Briony, please," Vince said.

Chelsea shoved her chair back. "How can you take Brandon's side over mine?"

"I'm not." Briony glared from one daughter to the other. "But marriage is for life. Separation and divorce aren't something you do lightly."

"Love." Vince looked at her imploringly. "It's not the same."

Briony gasped as if he'd stabbed her in the chest with a knife.

"Not the same as what?" Madeline asked.

"Nothing." Briony sat back and drew a deep breath. "If we stick together, we will get through this."

"Through what!" Chelsea yelled.

"This tragedy!" The girls recoiled from her but it was Vincent's dismay that hurt the most. She looked imploringly from one daughter to the other. "Can't you see how hard life will be for you if…" The lump in her throat swallowed her words.

"I can't believe you'd want me to go back to Brandon." Chelsea's eyes brimmed with tears.

"I don't!" Briony groaned.

"What do you want then?"

"I…I just want everyone to be…normal!" Briony clenched her fists so tightly her fingernails dug into her palms.

"We are!" Chelsea wailed and dashed from the room.

Madeline looked from one parent to the other and winced. "I think I'll go make sure she's okay."

For a short moment after her departure there was silence and Briony's pounding head was thankful.

"I know you're finding this hard, love, but you're being too tough on them. They don't understand. I agree the end of a marriage is tragic but I don't want Chelsea stuck in a toxic relationship. And as for Maddie, well, that's a surprise but we've known Cameron and his parents for years. They're nice people.

He's a good bloke. You know why that marriage broke up. Once his wife took that job in Adelaide the writing was on the wall."

His pleading gaze rested on Briony and she looked down at her still-trembling hands.

"Times have changed, love."

She couldn't stand his gentle acceptance of their family falling apart. "And on top of all that," she snapped, "I suppose you think it's okay for our son to tell everyone he's homosexual as well?"

"I wasn't truly surprised. Remember all that Kylie Minogue?" He nudged her but Briony was in no mood for his silly jokes and his smile dropped away. "We have to accept Blake for who he is, Briony. I certainly don't think he should have to hide it. I agree with Madeline. The world's a different place from the one we grew up in and if Badara hasn't kept up, it needs to. No good will come from trying to keep it hidden."

The tablets Briony had swallowed weren't even taking the edge off the pain that throbbed in her head. How on earth would she face people if all this got out?

After mahjong Marion had returned to the bush garden to find Blake still there. He'd managed to soak quite an area and he'd pulled out weeds and dead bushes and made a pile of green waste. In the end his questions had forced her to confess she was looking for the capsule, although not exactly why.

With a bemused look he'd offered to help dig. Now as the sun was lowering in the sky they'd only managed to dig a hole a couple of metres across and about thirty centimetres deep. All they'd found were some rocks, a couple of old bottles and a rusty tin can. Nothing that resembled a time capsule.

They stopped to survey what they'd done. Marion's right palm smarted with a blister and Blake was looking dishevelled.

"It could be buried quite deep," he said.

"Or not in this exact spot." Marion cast her gaze around the sprawling bush garden. She sighed. "We should go home. I owe you another dinner."

Blake wiped the back of his hand across his forehead leaving a smear of dirt.

"Maybe there's someone who knows exactly where the time capsule is," he said.

"Is that what you're looking for?"

They both spun. Jean was standing a few metres away, arms folded across her chest.

"Good heavens, is that you, Blake Hensley?" Jean wrapped him in a hug.

"Hello, Aunty Jean."

"Look at you, all grown up now. Your mum said you were home. Don't you look marvellous." Jean patted his shoulder then turned to Marion. "Poor Cliff over the fence could hear someone out here all afternoon, he said. He couldn't see over the fence and he's not feeling the best today so he asked me to investigate." Jean stepped closer and inspected their work then she looked at Marion. "I thought it was funny you scratching around here the other day. You've never been a gardener before. What exactly are you up to, Marion?"

Marion wasn't usually lost for words but they deserted her under Jean's impaling gaze.

Blake cleared his throat, perhaps sensing the tension. "Aunty Marion thought she should dig the capsule up to make sure it's in good condition," he said. "Looks like it may have disintegrated altogether if this is where it was buried. There's no sign of it."

"You're where it was supposed to be buried," Jean said.

"Supposed to be?" Marion frowned.

"The capsule isn't in the garden."

"Oh?" Blake scratched his head.

"Where is it then?" Marion asked.

"Safe. My father worried if we buried it out here this very thing might happen. Only he thought some of the local youth might dig it up after the ceremonies were over." Jean's eyebrow quirked up. "I guess back in the seventies that would have included you, Marion."

Marion swallowed a fresh wave of guilt. "Where is it now?" she asked again.

"He found a better place for it. You don't need to worry, it's quite safe. No-one would have touched it." Jean pulled her cardigan closer. "Gosh, it gets chilly once the sun gets low. I'd better pop in and tell Cliff nothing's amiss over here. You must call in and see Keith while you're home, Blake. Come for morning tea and we can have a good catch-up. See you Tuesday at fitness club, Marion."

Marion stared into the hole they'd scratched in the dirt. A wave of defeat swept over her. "I'm sorry you did all that hard work for nothing." She picked up her shovel. "We should get going."

Blake cleared his throat again. "Are you going to tell me the real reason I've slaved over a shovel in the heat all afternoon and got blisters on my hands?"

She glanced at him. "It's complicated."

"It always is in Badara."

"I'm honestly trying to avert some heartache. Not for me, for others. Other than that I'd prefer not to say any more."

"Fair enough." Blake began to collect more of their tools.

"I really am very grateful for your help."

"Like Nan always used to say there's nothing like hard work to take your mind off your troubles."

"You haven't heard from your family today?"

"Not from Dad or Mum. Chels and Maddie are fine of course. They keep messaging me with updates." He shoved a spade into the pile of dirt they'd made. "I knew Mum would have trouble accepting that I'm gay, it's why I delayed telling them, but I'd hoped Dad…"

"They might need a bit longer but they'll come round."

"Will they though?" He pinned her with a sorrowful gaze. "Why couldn't they be more like you and Len?"

"I'm sorry, Blake. I still think with time…"

"I might as well go back to Sydney."

Marion's heart broke for him, and for Vince and Briony. "Don't rush off yet. Give them a chance."

Blake shrugged. "We'll see."

They carried their gear to Marion's boot. Blake closed it with an extra hard shove then brushed his hands even though the dirt on them was ingrained rather than loose.

"I really do owe you a special dinner tonight," Marion said. "I've prepped a pudding and I think there's even a decent bottle of red in the cupboard."

"Thanks, Marion." He managed a small smile.

"Things will get better." She gave his shoulder a quick pat. "Oh, and please don't mention the time capsule to Len."

Blake gave her a quizzical look.

"I know I'm being secretive," she said. "But you'll have to trust me. There's a good reason."

Blake's grin was genuine this time. "One of your puddings and some red wine should buy my silence."

fifteen

Paige followed Dane's car past the jetty and along a dirt track to a car park above a long stretch of sandy beach bathed in late afternoon light. She glanced at the tripmeter. They'd come thirty-two kilometres since they'd left home. She hadn't been to Port Kent before and she hoped she'd be able to find her way back again on her own. She'd asked the kids to pay attention and watch for landmarks. The long stretch of dirt road between Badara and the highway had offered few but it had kept them busy pointing out unusual mail boxes and different trees.

Once they arrived Paige finally met Zuri, who she realised was a younger clone of his father once she got a good look at him. Minus the scar, of course, and his hair was cut much shorter. Today Dane's was firmly trapped under a cap with *Toyota* printed across the front.

"I'm sorry about driving Jay home the other day without checking with you first," Zuri said.

Paige could see Jayden from the corner of her eye looking as if he'd like to find a hole to hide in.

"It was a surprise, that's all, and I don't like Jayden skipping classes."

Zuri frowned as if that was news to him.

"Your dad says you're a safe driver."

"I've had to drive him home from the club a few times."

"Hey!" Dane chided. "What's the point of having a P-plater in the family if I can't enjoy some perks?"

"Huh!" Zuri poked his dad in the chest and looked to Jayden. "Maybe you could come out our way one day and I could teach you to drive."

Jayden brightened immediately and Paige didn't have the heart to can that idea, even though she wanted to.

"Let's get our gear down to the beach," Dane said.

Jayden and Zuri helped ferry eskies and chairs then went off to kick a footy with a group of teenagers. Dane introduced her to so many people Paige was sure she wouldn't remember any of their names, but they were all friendly and Kodie and Levi were soon playing on the water's edge with several other kids.

She kept an eye on them from a small distance, settled comfortably in a folding chair Dane had brought.

"How long have you been in Badara, Paige?" The question came from one of the other mums who was also watching the little group by the water.

"We came about two weeks before school started," Paige said, trying to remember the woman's name. It had started with a 'J'. Jan or Jen?

"Sorry we haven't called in to welcome you." The other woman beside her was nursing a small baby with a young toddler at her feet.

"Jac told me there was someone in the old shop again," the other said, nodding at her friend.

Paige tried to commit the name Jac to memory.

"Life's been a bit crazy since this bub came along. Everyone said the third made a difference and they were right." Jac adjusted her hold on the baby. "Did you say your little one goes to kindy? My oldest goes but I haven't seen you there."

"Levi's only there on Tuesdays." Penny, the pre-school teacher, joined the group.

Paige smiled. At least that was one name she remembered.

"Good to see you here, Paige," Penny said. "I'm glad Jac and Jo are looking after you. The sporting club's very social. Our sons will be playing in the same team so if you ever need help with transport let me know."

"Thanks." Paige was still trying to commit the names Jac and Jo to memory. They both had their long blonde hair up in a pony-tail and they were even dressed similarly in soft white blouses and denim shorts. Paige couldn't remember the last time she'd worn anything white.

Dane passed by with a six-pack of beer. "Would you like one, Paige?" he offered.

"No, thank you. I'm fine with lemonade."

Paige enjoyed beer but there was rarely any money for alcohol in her budget so she couldn't offer some in return. She'd brought the bottle of soft drink as a treat to share with her kids but they were all busy.

"You ladies all okay for drinks?" Dane asked.

"We're good, thanks."

The other three women raised their glasses. Dane headed off towards a group at the barbecue and Penny fell into step beside him, talking about a working bee.

"With three under four I've been pregnant or breastfeeding forever." The woman with the baby shook her head towards a group of fellas chatting, each with a can in their hands. "Not that I'd have a drink if I waited for my husband to get it."

That one was Jac, Paige had it now. She was the one with the baby and two little kids.

"Dane's a gentleman." Jo winked. "He's such a catch, isn't he, Jac? I know he had a long recovery time from his accident and then Zuri turned up but he doesn't often have a date."

"Not many available women around here."

They both smiled at Paige.

"I thought he was married."

"Not Dane."

"Oh." Paige frowned. "It's just that I...Dane sent some things for Jayden with a note from Sarah."

"That's Dane's mum."

"Gosh, did she call in at your place?"

The two women studied Paige. Her cheeks warmed, she wasn't sure if from their interested gaze or for her misunderstanding.

"I didn't see her. She left the things at my door."

"She's hardly been out anywhere since the scandal over Chad – that's Dane's brother," Jac said. "Have you heard about that?"

Paige shook her head and sank lower into her chair as the other two proceeded to fill her in on Dane's brother's double life – a woman in Bali and a family on the farm at Badara. The marriage had broken up and financially crippled the Townsends and Sarah had been so distressed by all that had happened she rarely left home.

"It must be about two years since it all blew up but Sarah's taken it badly from all accounts," Jo said. "Not able to face people, I guess."

Paige was wondering how she could extricate herself from the gossip circle when Levi came running up needing the toilet. By the time they got back, races were being organised for the kids. Then she found the uniform swap operating from the boot of someone's car. She was able to kit Jayden out except for socks, but then discovered they were part of his membership package. She found the treasurer and had a discussion about payments, and by the time the barbecue was ready she felt she could finally agree to Jayden joining the football club, even if she was still a bit concerned about his lack of height and bulk compared to some of the other boys.

Later, when an exhausted Levi had fallen asleep in her arms and she was sitting on her own, she overheard a couple of people discussing team photos and Facebook in the same sentence. That swept away her happily chilled mood. She had closed her Facebook account before she'd left Melton. She'd requested no photos of her children to go online or in media when she'd enrolled them at their new schools and no-one had questioned it, but how could she refuse Jayden inclusion in a team photo?

"Here you are," Dane said. "Looks like Levi's batteries have run down."

"Yes." Paige eased forward in her chair. "We should leave before it gets dark."

"Would you like me to take him?" Dane offered.

"Thanks, but I can manage." Page struggled to her feet and adjusted Levi's floppy body so that his head was on her shoulder.

Dane picked up the tote bag at her feet as she tried to reach it. "Let me take that. You head to the car and I'll round up the other two."

She had Levi strapped in by the time Dane followed a complaining Kodie to the car. Jayden managed to cajole his little sister into her seat.

"Thanks for your help," Paige said as Dane dropped their wet towels and sandy shoes into the boot with the bag.

"I hope you enjoyed yourselves." Dane glanced back to the group spread out along the beach. "We're a pretty good club to belong to."

"I get that feeling for sure," she said but all she could think about was Jayden's photo on social media.

"And how are you feeling about Jayden playing footy?"

Paige opened her mouth to reply but Dane went on. "The club's a bit like a big family. People keep an eye out for everyone's kids."

Paige was swept along by a wave of overwhelming longing for that broader sense of family her kids had never had. Perhaps not never but…she sucked in a breath and changed the subject.

"I don't think I said thanks for the clothes you sent."

"Was there anything useful? I asked Mum to tell you to chuck whatever didn't fit or wasn't needed."

"Most of it's perfect." Paige smiled. "I didn't see your mum. The clothes were by the door when I got back from school the other day."

His face was lit by the golden light of the lowering sun, highlighting the jagged scar that ran down his cheek and exposing the flash of sorrow that crossed his face.

"It was good of her to take the time," Paige said quickly. "And for suggesting you put up the screen door. Please pass on my thanks."

"I will."

They both hesitated, shuffling their feet.

"I'd better get this lot home," Paige said.

"Watch the road," Dane said. "It's the time of night for kangaroos."

"Okay." That wasn't something Paige had ever thought to worry about before. "Jayden can be lookout."

"Yeah." Dane glanced back towards the beach. A group were setting up a small fire below the high-tide mark. "I think we might be here for quite a bit longer."

Paige felt a small pang of envy. She wondered what it would be like to stay, sit by the fire talking and drinking until late, not having the sole care of three kids to think of.

"Goodnight then." She walked around the car to the driver's seat.

"Would you and the kids like to come out our way for lunch on Sunday?" Dane asked. "It'd be a simple barbie like tonight. Nothing fancy but the kids might enjoy a run around and Jayden can have that driving lesson."

"Yes, Mum, can we?" Jayden called from inside, followed by similar pleading from Kodie.

"Sure," she said, not feeling too bad at being pressured into accepting. "I'll bring some salads."

"Okay." Dane's grin once again tucked the scar out of sight. "I'll get Zuri to call in about twelve. You can follow him back to our place. There are a few twists and turns and it's easier than giving directions. People sometimes get lost."

"Thanks. See you then."

They hadn't got far along the road towards home, only a few kilometres down the highway, before Kodie fell asleep too.

Paige flicked a quick look at Jayden in the passenger seat beside her. They didn't often get time alone together where he couldn't escape her. "Did you enjoy this afternoon?"

"It was great."

"And you really want to play football?"

"Yes, Mum," he groaned. "I've told you so many times."

Paige was looking ahead for a signpost. "We must be getting close to the turn-off." Then she saw it and slowed the car to turn onto the dirt road to Badara. "At least that's one more place I can find my way to and back again," she said lightly.

"Why won't you let me play footy, Mum?"

"I didn't say I wouldn't let you play."

"What's up then?"

"I told you I don't want people knowing where we are, and if you play footy they'll take team photos and sounds like they put them on Facebook and—"

"Have Levi's grandparents been giving you a hard time again?"

"No." Paige felt bad that she'd told Jayden that Ari's parents were putting pressure on her to have access to Levi. It wasn't exactly true – it was Jayden's own grandparents who were giving her grief – but it'd been the only thing she could think of at the time to cover the real truth for their move away from Melton.

"Why do you keep turning your phone off then?" he asked.

"I've had a couple of those nuisance calls. Anyway, it doesn't have to be on all the time."

"Mum?"

She risked a quick glance at him. The sun was getting low in the sky and every bush on the side of the road looked like a kangaroo. "Everything's fine. You don't have to worry." She did enough of that for all of them but that was as it should be; she was the parent.

"It's got nothing to do with my dad?"

This time she kept her gaze firmly on the road and gripped the wheel tighter. "Jayden, you know your dad's dead," she said softly, partly because she didn't want it to sound harsh to him and partly in case the two little ones in the back weren't fully asleep.

"Of course I know, but his family aren't dead."

"Do you want to see them?"

"No...but..."

She risked a glance his way. He was staring ahead, his young face solemn. "You've met your father's parents. They upset you, remember?"

"Yeah, I know. I didn't go for them but they really wanted me to spend time with them and I kind of get that."

He was sounding so mature. Part of her wanted to explain but part of her wanted to protect him.

Ahead of them a shadow broke away from the bushes and hopped across the road. Paige braked and the car fishtailed in the gravel.

"Mum!"

A second kangaroo followed the first. The nose of the car turned to one side then the other, and slewed to a stop in the middle of the road. Paige's heart was thudding in her chest. She reached across and grabbed Jayden's shoulder. "Are you all right?"

"Yes."

She looked back at Levi and Kodie – both slept on oblivious. Paige eased her trembling hands from the steering wheel.

"Are you okay, Mum?" Jayden's eyes were wide with fright.

"Yes, mate, I'm fine." She rubbed her hands together. "That was close."

"That first one was huge."

"Sure was. Wouldn't have wanted him to have dented our car."

"Wait till I tell Kodie tomorrow what she missed."

"She'll be miffed."

"Yeah." Jayden laughed.

Paige gripped the wheel again, eased her foot from the brake and slowly moved forward. It wasn't the distraction she'd wanted but for now she'd take what she could.

"Come back and sit down, Marion," Len said.

Marion lowered her binoculars. "They can't see me from there." She waved towards the distant strip of beach where someone had lit a fire. "I'd forgotten it's the football and netball club family get-together."

Blake came out of the shack balancing three cocktails complete with fruit and jaunty umbrellas. He offered one each to Marion and Len and kept the third for himself.

"Who's driving home?" Len said, eyeing the colourful drink in his hand.

"You could stay the night," Blake said.

"Only one drink for me," Marion said. "I'll drive."

"Better sip it then." Blake pulled a face. "I may have been heavy-handed with the tequila."

"It's got plenty of fruit in it." Marion took a sip and then a quick breath. "Mm!" She put the glass down beside her. "I think I'll take that slowly." Once more she waved in the direction of the beach where stick figures stood around a bright fire. "You should have popped down there, Blake. You'd know quite a few from your primary years."

"No-one I've kept in touch with," he said. "I did see a couple of high school friends in Wirini Bay though, when I went in to do some shopping." He tapped the glass. "I stayed and had dinner with them last night at the pub."

"Oh, that's good," Marion said. "Did you call in and see your nan at the nursing home?"

"Not this time," Blake said. "But I will."

"How are you feeling about tonight?" Len asked.

"A bit fatalistic, I'm afraid. I've gone from hurt to rejected to angry and now I'm not sure I care." The sorrow in his eyes wasn't hidden no matter how hard he tried for a brave face.

"It's been tough, mate, but don't give up on your parents yet," Len said.

"I know you both mean well but I can't see how dragging Mum and Dad here will help."

"We're not dragging them, are we, Len?" Marion glanced at her husband, hoping he hadn't coerced his in-laws.

"When I rang your dad to suggest Friday drinks he sounded happy and also relieved," Len said. "He probably wasn't sure what to do next. I simply said this is an opportunity to relax and enjoy each other's company without any pressure."

"What about Mum?"

"I didn't speak to her but Vince said they'd both be here."

At that moment they heard a vehicle pulling in and lights illuminated the carport beside them.

Blake jumped up. "I'll make two more drinks."

"You're sure this is a good idea?" Marion murmured as soon as the door shut behind him.

"It's worth a try." Len contemplated his drink. "I have every confidence Vince will come round and I have to hope Briony's love for her son will win out in the end."

"She can be very determined."

"It's what's made her."

"Or ruined her. How can she reject her son?"

"She's had a very different life to you and I."

Marion sniffed. "She doesn't realise how lucky she is that he still wants her love, no matter how much he pretends he doesn't."

They both went quiet at the sound of footsteps. As Vince and Briony rounded the corner, the screen door flew open and Blake stepped out carrying two more drinks.

"Hello," he said, an extra burst of cheer in his voice. "I've made us all a cocktail."

"Oh." Vince held up a sixpack. "I brought beer."

Briony offered a container. "Your dad didn't say if it was for dinner as well so I've brought some finger food." No smile broke the austere set of her face.

"Great," Blake said, still in an over-exuberant voice. "Here, let's swap."

They fumbled around as awkward as strangers, then Blake went back inside. Vince and Briony were left holding a glass each as if it was about to explode in their hands.

"They're good," Len said, lifting his in the air. "One won't hurt you but you won't need a second." Silence followed. Briony looked at Vince then down at the drink.

Blake came back with a couple of plates of food. Len leaped up to drag over the little outdoor table for him to put them on.

"Have a seat," Blake said, waving to the empty chairs. Vince sat easily but Briony perched on the edge of hers like a bird about to take flight.

"Here's to Friday," Marion said, picking up her glass again.

"Cheers!" The three men chorused boisterously but Briony didn't speak, her face remaining deadpan.

Briony held the slivers of watermelon and lime to one side and took the tiniest sip of the bright pink drink Blake had given her. She winced as the alcohol hit the back of her tongue and rolled down her throat. Cocktails had never been her thing. Not something they'd ever drunk much as a family. Perhaps the girls did. She had to admit she had no faith in any of her beliefs about her family now. Or perhaps cocktails were a manifestation of this new life of Blake's she didn't understand.

She glanced at him as the conversation between the other four went on around her. Could she have picked just by looking at him that he was homosexual? Did homosexual men look different to other men? She certainly didn't see any connection between her brief glimpse of the Mardi Gras on television the other night and Blake. She glanced at Len and Vince, their weathered, gnarled fingers both struggling to hold the cocktail glasses and take delicate sips. Hardly fair to compare him to two older men.

Briony studied Blake again and for the first time she saw the glint of a tiny earring in his earlobe. Why hadn't she noticed that before? Her gaze swept lower, taking in his muscled arms curving from beneath a snugly fitted patterned shirt, which was tucked into light blue chinos and ended with his tan loafers encasing sockless feet. It wasn't the way many men around the district dressed but Blake was a city boy now and he'd lived in London. He'd always been a snappy dresser but that didn't mean someone was homosexual. But the earring...

"Briony?"

She glanced up. They were all looking at her.

"Are you with us, love?" Vince patted her leg.

"Of course," she said stiffly.

"I wondered if you'd got the message from Jean that we can use the hall again on Tuesday for our fitness group."

"Oh, no. I haven't looked at my phone for a while." Briony had shut herself away from the outside world ever since Blake's confession had sent her into a spin.

"Evidently her nephew came back today and got the floor finished."

"I'm not sure I'll be there anyway."

"Why not?"

Briony averted her eyes from Marion's piercing gaze. "It's tricky without an instructor."

"Why don't you have an instructor?" Blake asked.

"She quit," Marion said. "Last week we all took turns to organise a part each. I thought it went quite well."

Briony pursed her lips. She'd stood up to Marion once tonight – she wasn't going to again.

"I could do it," Blake said.

"Run our fitness class?" Marion leaned in.

"I did my training during lockdown in London. It was so hard not getting to the gym. My partner and I…"

Briony closed her eyes. She did not want to hear about what he and his partner did together in all those months of confinement. How could she not have known he was living with a man? Well, in truth she had known. Brian had been there for several video calls but they'd shown no signs of being anything but mates.

"We both missed our gym sessions so I set up a circuit at home," Blake said. "Then I started researching to expand my repertoire and then I did an online course. I completed the face-to-face part and got my certification once things opened up. My old job was cut right back so I worked part-time as a fitness instructor up till I left."

"I remember you talking about that on one of our video calls," Vince said.

"Do you?" Briony had no recollection.

"Would you take our class?" Marion asked. "We don't pay much but we'd really appreciate it."

"It's an old ladies' class except for Paige," Briony said. "Not the kind of group you'd be used to." There was no way she wanted the women of the district to see Blake prancing around in gym gear. They'd know straight away he was homosexual.

"Running the sixty-plus class was my favourite," Blake said. "One of my group was a marathon runner and a couple of others were ballroom dancers. They were fitter than me."

"Maybe you and I should join, Len," Vince said.

"Ladies only." Marion waved a hand at Blake. "With the exception of our new instructor."

"That's sexist," Len said.

"All right," Marion said with a smug look. "Ten o'clock Tuesday morning. Wear comfortable loose clothing and track shoes. See you there."

"Oh," Vince said. "I think I've got the stock agent visiting then."

"I'm sure I have." Len laughed.

"Maybe Blake could run a men's fitness group in the evening," Marion said.

Briony looked from one to the other of them. Had they all gone completely mad?

"I'm not sure I can make it Tuesday," she said.

"See how you go." Marion reached for her drink and lifted it in the air. "I'm so pleased we'll have a proper instructor."

"You're going to stay a bit longer then," Briony said.

They all looked at Blake.

He smiled. "I'd like to."

Briony quietly let go of the breath she'd been holding.

sixteen

A little after midday on Sunday, Paige and the two younger ones followed Zuri, with Jayden as his passenger, out to Dane's farm. Dane had been right when he'd said it was tricky to get to. They'd made several turns at crossroads and T-junctions before they finally rolled over a grid and along a tree-lined driveway, passed a neat modern farmhouse and came to a stop beside a smaller plasterboard cottage.

Dane waved to them from the house gate, a brown kelpie dancing at his feet.

"Hope the kids aren't timid with dogs," he said apologetically as the dog licked each newcomer in turn.

Both Kodie and Levi giggled in delight.

"It doesn't seem so," she said.

A sheep bleated beyond another fence.

"Come and meet our pet sheep," Zuri said.

The kids followed him and Dane helped Paige get her things from the car.

"There's a lot of food here," Dane said, peering into a basket as he led the way around the house.

Paige had packed a dip, crackers and vegetable sticks, a fruit platter and two salads. "There are four of us and you're supplying the meat."

"It's only snags and chops," he said.

She gave him her best determined look.

He shrugged. "Fair enough."

They set the food out on a table under the back verandah. The table was covered in a blue-checked tablecloth and there were several containers already on it.

"This looks nice," Paige said. She felt a bit on edge with him now that she knew he didn't have a partner. She hoped he didn't think she was in the market for a relationship. She was done with them.

"Mum sent over some cake," he said. "She loves to bake and there's not much call for it around here these days. The tablecloth was in the basket so I assumed she wanted me to put it on the table." He grinned. "Mum said for you to take home anything left over."

"Is she coming for the barbecue?"

"I asked her. Dad's out till late visiting a relative in hospital so she might come over later."

"I'd like to say thanks for dropping the clothes off."

"I did tell her."

The four kids returned with the excited dog still bounding between them.

"I'm hungry," Levi said.

Paige shook her head and uncovered the dip and fruit. "Have you met my small human eating machine? I swear he eats more than Jayden."

"Jayden will probably change once he starts football. A whole box of cereal can disappear when Zuri gets home from school."

"Exaggerating again, Dane," Zuri said and poked his dad in the arm. "Do you want Jayden and I to cook the meat?"

"Jayden hasn't ever used a barbecue." Paige glanced at her son who was beaming eagerly beside Zuri.

"I've cooked sausages in the frying pan," Jayden said.

"A barbie's easier than that," Dane said. "Go for it, fellas. I'm happy to hand over the tongs."

Paige watched her children settle in as if they'd visited here many times before. Zuri was instructing Jayden at the barbecue, Levi was climbing on an old swing set and Kodie was playing with the dog.

"Everyone's happy," Dane said. "Take a load off." He waved her to a chair in the shade. "Do you like beer?"

"Yes, but—"

"That's good. I didn't think to get anything else." He took two cans from an esky. "I've got lots left over from the beach barbecue."

"I didn't bring any."

"You made all that salad. It's something Zuri and I aren't so good on." He held a beer towards her.

She looked from his warm smile to the can. "Okay, thanks."

He sat beside her and passed her a stubby holder. "So this is why we have kids," he said. "Eventually they can do the work for us."

Paige raised her eyebrows. "Maybe you're at that stage but I'm a long way off."

They both watched the two little ones playing in the sunshine. Kodie had found a tennis ball that the dog retrieved every time she threw it and Levi had actually managed to make the old wooden swing move back and forth by himself. No-one needed Paige. The autumn sun had just enough strength to be warm rather than overheat. She relaxed further into the chair.

"You can tell me to mind my own business," Dane said softly. "But how old were you when you had Jayden?"

Normally Paige would have clammed up or changed the subject but there was nothing critical about his tone and, besides, he could hardly pass judgement, he had Zuri.

"Just seventeen," she said. "What about you?"

"Twenty-two."

"Not quite so young then." Paige was surprised. She'd thought Dane and Zuri closer in age.

"Zuri was almost five when I found out about him though so, technically, I was seventeen when I became a dad."

"Oh." Paige was confused but not prepared to ask.

"I'm surprised the local gossip mill hasn't filled you in."

She took a sip of her beer, hoping it would cool her cheeks. She'd heard plenty of other stuff about the Townsends but not about Zuri.

"His mum and I were teenage sweethearts but I was in a car accident when I was seventeen. I got pretty banged up." He put a hand to his cheek. "My face was ripped open, I had internal injuries, a broken arm and a smashed up leg. I wasn't a pretty sight and she didn't cope. I don't blame her. I wasn't in a good head space either. She visited me once when I got transferred back to the hospital at Wirini Bay. Her family lived in the town but not long after they moved interstate. We didn't keep in touch."

"I can relate to that." Paige glanced towards the barbecue where Zuri and Jayden were chatting and focused on their task. "I thought Jayden's dad was the love of my life but when I got pregnant things changed very quickly. His parents and mine wanted me to have an abortion." Paige screwed up her nose. She'd rarely told anyone that, hating to say it out loud. "Of course now I can see where they were coming from – we were so young. But…I ended up with Jayden."

"Making that choice must have been tough."

"I had to fight hard to keep him." She looked towards her son who was laughing at something Zuri had said. "And maybe that need to keep my baby was about finding the love that I felt was lacking with my parents."

"How did you manage?"

"My gran was more helpful. She made sure I understood all the options – termination, adoption, keeping the baby – and she at least let me believe it was my choice rather than making a right or wrong decision. She got me to find out more about them all, and said she'd support me. I'm sure it was her influence that turned my parents around. They finally accepted my decision to keep Jayden and let me live at home so I could finish my QCE."

"You grew up in Queensland?"

Paige nodded.

"That's where Zuri's mum moved to after she…after we confirmed he was mine."

"So you suddenly had a four-year-old?"

"Yep. She turned up on my doorstep with Zuri. It was the first I knew she'd even been pregnant, let alone had a child. It was a huge learning curve but, like you, I don't regret one moment of it."

"She hasn't ever come back for him?"

Dane shook his head. "She keeps in touch but she's married with more kids. I think having Zuri complicated that new start she wanted. He seems okay with it. What about Jayden? Does he have contact with his dad?"

"Never." Paige swallowed as the boys looked over. She'd almost shouted. "He knows what there is to know about his dad, but they've never met and never will now. Rufus was killed last year in a freak work accident."

"How did you manage when Jayden was little? I missed all that with Zuri."

"My parents gave me some support for a while and then we all lost patience with each other. Living in the same house, even though they have a mansion on the Gold Coast, nearly drove us mad. My mother's a clean freak so a toddler was her worst nightmare and Jayden wasn't allowed to call her Nan or Gran. She insisted he use her name, Miriam, which he couldn't say, of course. It came out as Mimi so that kind of stuck. They had so many rules. I moved out when Jayden was three. And me having two more kids by different fathers has not just blotted my copybook, it's almost destroyed it. We keep in touch but we're not close."

"They don't want to see their grandkids?"

Paige shrugged. "They acknowledge them. My older brother and sister have both married and had kids now and live not far away. They're the golden children." Since she'd left her parents' house she'd only been back a couple of times. Paige had been determined to make a go of life on her own and she was proud of the fact that she'd never, well, almost never, asked them for anything.

"And your siblings?"

"Like Mum and Dad we don't communicate all that often. There's a big age gap and they're clones of our parents, with similar thoughts on lifestyle choices and single parenthood."

"Hey, Dane," Zuri called. "Meat's nearly ready. Have you got a tray?"

"Right there beside you, mate." Dane shook his head and chuckled. "I sometimes think I should get his eyes tested."

"It's nice that he calls you Dane," Paige said. "You could be brothers."

"I don't mind he calls me Dane but I definitely fill the role of dad. Brother's a dirty word in my house and I'm guessing you'd have heard why by now."

Heat spread over Paige's cheeks again but Dane was already on his feet. "Let's see how your cooking skills have gone, fellas," he said as he threw an arm around each boy's shoulders.

Paige wandered over to where Kodie and Levi were swinging back and forth on the tandem swing. Each of her children had such different fathers, and each seemed to be managing without them, but how could she be sure of that? Jayden and Kodie were both strong independent kids and she was so proud of them; Levi too, of course, but sometimes when she looked at him she could see his dad, Ari, looking back at her and that broke her heart all over again.

"Mum."

She turned at Jayden's call.

"The meat's cooked." The smile on his face was wide.

After what they'd all been through, her family were settling in Badara, and life had found some kind of normalcy. She put her hand in her pocket and patted her phone. She only switched it on for a while each day now and today it was staying off.

An hour later Paige was alone inside at Dane's kitchen sink washing the barbecue dishes. He'd suggested he take the kids with him to feed the sheep. With Levi safely strapped in beside Dane and her two older kids in the back, she'd offered to stay behind and wash the dishes. It was quiet, something Paige rarely experienced, so she was startled at the sound of someone coming in the back door.

"Oh, hello." The woman stopped mid-stride. Her greying hair was pulled back in a ponytail and worry lines etched her face. "I heard the tractor and the ute and thought you'd all gone off."

"I said I'd stay and clean up." Paige wiped her hands on a tea towel and smiled. "I'm Paige Radcliffe."

"I guessed that's who you were. I'm Dane's mum, Sarah." She took another step into the room. "I thought I'd clean up while you were all off in the paddock but you've beaten me to it."

"I was about to make a cup of tea," Paige said. "I wanted to try one of your cakes. I haven't had a chance yet. The kids enjoyed them though, thank you."

"I'm glad." Sarah's lips turned up in a brief smile. "I love to bake but no-one seems to want to eat too much cake or dessert these days. Except Zuri, of course, but Dane tries not to have too much sweet stuff around."

"Me too. If there's cake that always disappears first."

There was a pause. Paige felt awkward knowing more about the Townsends' personal life than she should, thanks to Jac and Jo at Friday evening's barbecue. It sounded as if Sarah in particular had been hit hardest by the actions of her eldest son and the fallout from it.

Sarah took a step back. "Well...you've got it all under control...I'll leave you to it."

"Would you stay and join me?"

The other woman hesitated, her head moving as if to shake no.

"The kettle was easy but I don't know where the cups and the tea are. I don't like to rummage in someone else's kitchen."

Sarah wavered a second longer then crossed the room, opening cupboards and setting things out. "Hopefully there's milk in the fridge," she said. "But you never know with these two men. Luckily I live just across the yard."

"I drink it black. I learned to after years of kids emptying the last of the milk carton."

"Three must keep you busy."

Paige was pleased to see Sarah put tea bags into two cups.

"They sure do. Milk evaporates and bread...I never seem to have enough. Jayden can eat half a loaf on his own and my little one too."

"And it's even more difficult without a general store in Badara any more," Sarah said. "At least you used to be able to get the basics there if you needed. Poor Mick Carter can barely organise the mail these days but when his wife was alive they kept bread and milk and a few other groceries. I used to do the odd day for them when they went away but he has let the place go and won't ask for help." She passed a mug of tea to Paige. "Shall we take it outside? It's a beautiful day."

Paige followed her out to a couple of wooden garden chairs tucked in a corner of the yard and bathed in autumn sunshine.

"So what do you do to keep busy in Badara?" Sarah asked with the hint of a smile on her lips.

"The kids and the house take up most of my time. I read a bit and we go to Wirini Bay to shop, of course. And there's a fitness group. Except for me it's all old—" Paige winced.

Sarah laughed. "A few people have asked me to come along to that. And you're right. They're all old like me."

Paige put a hand to her warm cheek. "I didn't mean..."

Once more Sarah laughed. Her eyes sparkled and the weariness that had been etched on her face dropped away. "Tell me who else goes and what do you actually do at this fitness group?"

They were sitting there chatting like old friends when Dane and the kids returned an hour later. Jayden had been allowed to drive the ute and Levi and Kodie were babbling with excitement about sheep and lambs and having a ride in the tractor. Paige gave Dane a nervous glance when Levi had said that.

"He was perfectly safe," Dane said.

It was Sarah's smile that reassured Paige rather than Dane's words.

seventeen

It was Tuesday and Briony drove into Badara, a sick feeling rolling around in her stomach. Fitness was on again in the hall and Blake was going to lead it. Like a troubled child avoiding school she'd tried to stay home but for once Vincent had been adamant she go. Of course when she'd thought about it she'd realised how bad it would look if Blake's own mother wasn't there.

Now here she was, hovering on the doorstep, regretting the second cup of coffee she'd had before she left and clutching her gym mat to her chest as if it had some kind of super power to protect her from what was about to happen.

"Hi, Briony," Gloria called as she entered.

Briony managed a wobbly up-turn of her lips in response. Jean and Claire were there as well and in Courtney's old spot Blake was fiddling with a bluetooth speaker. Briony blew out a breath. She'd been worried about what he'd be wearing but he looked perfectly sensible in loose running shorts and a pale blue polo top. Cheerful music began to play. It wasn't as loud as Courtney's so that was another positive.

Marion strode towards her. "Isn't it wonderful that the floor's fixed and the cordons are gone."

"And Len's done a great job of mending the wall," Jean said.

They all gazed up at the patch over the door. It looked solid enough. Part of Briony wished it would fall down again and put the kybosh on the class.

"Now, Blake has said he doesn't want to be paid but has generously suggested his portion of the takings could be donated to the hall maintenance fund," Marion announced as the participants each passed over their share.

"Thanks for coming, everyone," Blake said. "You'll need a chair each."

Once more there was a surge of activity as each woman carried a chair to the middle of the hall. Blake turned up the music. Soon everyone but Briony was toe-tapping to 'Girls Just Want To Have Fun'.

"Isn't it great of Blake to fill in?" Gloria said. "Get the group going again."

Briony gave a half a nod.

"We didn't stop," Marion said.

"While the floor was being fixed." Gloria waved to where the cordon had been.

"We had the class at the old bakery last week."

"Oh."

"But it is good to be back in the hall with a proper instructor." Marion's enthusiasm only lessened Briony's.

"Are we ready to start, girls?" Blake lowered the music volume. "Sorry, I don't have a mic. I'll have to keep the music down a bit so you can hear me."

Marion glanced around. "Paige isn't here yet."

"Yes I am, and I've brought a new member." Paige stepped through the door followed by Sarah Townsend.

There were welcomes, introductions for Claire and more chairs put out, momentarily distracting Briony until Blake clapped his hands.

"Ready to start?"

Had he flicked his wrist? Briony hadn't noticed him doing that before. Was that part of his gay persona?

"I'm not sure how you've warmed up in the past." Blake wriggled his shoulders. "But I like to begin with a kind of tai chi combo. First, set your feet apart and settle your weight on them, bend your knees and take a deep breath in. Draw the arms up in a circle over your head then swing down to the side and stretch out your arms and fingers."

Gloria chortled but they all gave it a try. Blake turned up the music a little and led them through the graceful movements. Briony studied him closely, watching for any sign that might give him away to the others.

"Stretch those arms out, girls," Blake called. "Push the air away with your hands then extend those long, elegant fingers."

The accompanying song was 'Like A Prayer' by Madonna. After a slow start the beat quickened and Blake upped his pace in time with it, perhaps thrusting his hips a little too far. Briony glanced around hoping none of the others noticed but they all seemed to be focused on replicating his movements. She thought about the brief glimpses she'd had of the Mardi Gras as she watched her son lead them, singing along with Madonna. By the time the music faded everyone was in step with him but Briony, who felt she had two left feet today. She almost collapsed as Blake tossed his head, flicking his thick wave of hair to one side.

The session shifted on to more aerobic activities. Briony sometimes had to twist herself in knots to keep her eye on Blake as they went through knee repeaters, side steps, skaters, mountain climbers, ab crunches. Whichever exercise Blake stepped them through the women followed but Briony was often out of step. Finally they reached the end and she relaxed a little as Blake led them through a cool-down session accompanied by tranquil instrumental music.

"Deep breath in, girls," he called and they drew themselves in and up.

"And that's it," Blake said as they lowered their arms in a collective sweep.

Spontaneously they all clapped. Briony glanced around once more. No-one seemed to be staring.

"That was great," Gloria said.

"Marvellous, dear." Jean patted Blake's shoulder. "How long will you be staying? I hope you can run our group again."

He glanced at Briony. "I'm not sure but at least one more week."

"You might be too busy," she said quickly.

"I'm sure I'll find time for a fitness class."

The others began to pack up. Blake made a beeline for Briony. The smile he'd had for the other women faded.

"A quick word, please," he said as he guided her outside.

Away from the door he stopped and dropped her arm. She blanched at the anger on his face.

"What was that about, Mum?" he hissed.

"I just thought your dad and Uncle Len might need you to—"

"I mean you watching me so hard you lost your step. And during the floor exercises you were twisted in such a knot you overbalanced."

"I...I thought perhaps you might..."

"Embarrass you?"

"No! Of course not." She fanned her face with her hand, suddenly feeling hot again.

"What then?" He folded his arms across his chest.

"I just wanted to see if you..." Briony flapped her hand harder. "Men aren't usually fitness instructors around here."

"You don't have *any* fitness instructors around here, men or women."

"I know. I thought you might..." She shrugged.

He stared at her and she cringed as the horror of realisation dawned on his face.

"You thought I might somehow act gay? Or perhaps you thought I'd announce it."

He spat the words at her and, caught out, Briony was speechless.

Inside the hall Marion was still humming 'Like A Prayer', feeling as if her prayers had most certainly been answered. Her fitness club had a regular core of people and was growing. It was a huge step for Sarah to attend. Marion would have to chat to Paige later about how she'd managed that but for now she was simply happy it was all coming together.

Blake had done a fabulous job. His cheery encouragement had made the exercises seem easy and the music was all songs they knew – the Beatles, Beach Boys, Abba. Marion had felt as graceful as a ballerina even though she knew awkward giraffe was probably more what she looked like and she hadn't glanced at her watch once.

"I hope everyone can stay for lunch." She waited for the usual excuses, but only Claire couldn't stay. Marion looked around, realising that Briony and Blake were missing. She stuck her head out the door. They were standing a little way off and didn't appear to be speaking. She hoped that Briony was as impressed as the rest of them by Blake's great session.

"We're a cast of thousands for lunch," she called. "Hope you two are staying."

"I can't, I'm afraid." Blake strode past her and into the hall. The simmering anger on his face made her heart sink.

"Is everything all right?" Marion asked, even though she could tell by the look of shame on Briony's face that it wasn't. "What's happened?"

"Not here, not now," Briony muttered and went back inside.

"See you," Blake called to the others, who thanked him again and clapped at his reassurance he would return next Tuesday.

"There's enough lunch at home if you'd like some," Briony said. Only Marion noticed the look of disappointment Blake gave his mother and her distress at his reaction.

"See you later, Marion." He waved and was gone. Marion wanted to ask Briony what she'd said because as sure as the sky was blue she'd somehow upset Blake again but they were interrupted by a call from Gloria.

"Kettle's on!"

Briony packed up her things and trailed the group into the supper room where they reconvened around the big table that dominated the centre.

Jean clapped her hands in delight at the array of food on the table. Everyone had brought something different. She handed Sarah a plate. "It's lovely to see you here."

"Marion and Briony have both asked me to join and then Paige convinced me I needed some exercise." She smiled at the younger woman.

"I hope you don't have to dash off too soon, Paige," Marion said, thinking if she left Sarah might too.

"Levi is having lunch at kindy today so I can stay a bit longer."

They all settled in, including Briony who was trying her best to cover her misery as Jean brought the discussion around to what she was calling the Back to Badara Festival. "Those of you who were at church on Sunday will know the congregation are all in favour of holding a Back to Badara Festival, and anyone else I've spoken to for that matter. I think we should form a committee and start the planning."

"The name's a mouthful for a start," Gloria said.

"What would you like to call it, dear?" Jean asked in her sugar-and-spice voice.

"What about the Badara Bash? It has a good ring to it."

"Sounds like a shed fight," Briony said. "What about the Badara Gala?"

"Too posh," Gloria said.

"I like the sound of Jubilee," Sarah offered.

"It's not exactly fifty years though," Jean said.

"Let's leave it at Jean's suggestion of Festival for the moment." Marion picked up her pen and wrote that at the top of the page. If they took this long over every suggestion, they'd be here all day. "Now what's the proposal for the weekend and what would be the best time of year?"

They spent the next half an hour making suggestions and either agreeing or not until they had a short list to work with.

"So a date in early November seems to be the best," Marion said, tapping the end of her pen on her notepad. "We'd have a welcome barbecue at the oval on the Friday night. Gloria, you've offered to convene that?"

Gloria nodded.

"Saturday morning we'd have walking tours of the town," Marion continued. "A great idea! Jean and people who live in some of the older or more significant dwellings will be asked if they'd do home tours. And we accept Paige's suggestion of a small entry fee." There were nods and murmurs of agreement.

"Then in the afternoon a family games day at the oval with food, drink and local craft stalls, and we'll ask the CWA ladies if they would be prepared to convene the stalls."

"As a member I'm sure they will," Jean said.

Marion nodded and looked back at her list. "And Sarah suggested we ask the football and netball clubs to organise the games afternoon."

"I'll talk to Dane about it when I get home," Sarah said. "I'm sure they'll want to be involved."

Marion nodded. "Then on Saturday the black-tie dinner dance here in the hall which Briony has offered to convene."

"And don't forget a church service Sunday morning." Jean smiled as Marion added it to her list.

"There's lots to organise but I'm sure we can do it in the time," Marion said.

"Getting the word out to past residents will be the hardest." Briony's face had lost its pinched look as she gathered up plates.

"Yes, we should probably advertise a 'save the date' in the *Country Courier*." Jean nodded. "With more information to follow."

"We could make a Facebook group," Paige said. "It's free and easy, and once people know about it we can share info there."

"Great idea." Marion jotted it down. "Can we put you in charge of that, Paige?"

Paige shrugged. "Sure."

"Well done, everyone." Marion beamed. "We've covered a lot of ground. Let's follow up all our contacts during the week and

reconvene after fitness next Tuesday. I assume this is a good time
for everyone?"

They all agreed.

"Oh," Jean said, just as the plates of cakes were handed around.
"I do have one piece of bad news."

They all paused to look at her.

"It's the time capsule."

Marion's pen dropped to the floor with a clatter. She ducked
down to retrieve it. Jean hadn't mentioned the blasted capsule during the meeting and Marion had hoped she'd forgotten about it.

"My dear father was worried at the time that if it was left out in
the bush garden someone might try to dig it up." Her gaze swept
over Marion. "He organised what he thought would be a much
safer place and that was under this very room."

"How?" Marion blurted.

"There's access in the corner." Jean waved to one end of the
room.

The boxes of costumes that had been stacked there had been
moved and the outline of a trapdoor was clearly visible.

"How long has that been there?" Marion asked.

"Since the supper room was built," Jean said. "Originally it
was to give access to pipes but I don't recall it ever being needed.
Over the years it's blended in with the rest of the flooring so you
wouldn't even know it was there."

Marion gripped her pen tightly. Bloody Jean and her secrets.
The time capsule had been almost under Marion's nose all along.

"While my nephew was working on the hall floor I asked if
he'd open the trapdoor and retrieve the time capsule for me. And
that's where the bad news comes in." Jean got up and collected a
shopping bag from the side of the hall.

Marion's gaze was glued to the bag. The lunch she'd recently enjoyed churned to a sickening mush.

Jean put the bag on the table and sat down. "My father thought PVC pipe the best container to keep everything safe, but the end mustn't have been fixed properly. The contents are ruined."

Marion gasped so loudly everyone looked at her. "That's a shame," she said quickly.

"It is," Jean said. "It looks as if mice have nested in it and moisture has got in. Anything that was paper, like letters and photos, have been destroyed, fabric has been shredded, cardboard turned to sludge. Nothing was recognisable. I had to throw it all out."

Marion's spirits lifted with each revelation.

"There's one small silver lining." Jean reached into the bag and pulled out an old preserving jar. "The high school teacher put all the teenagers' letters in here."

Marion's rising spirits plummeted to the bottom of her stomach, lost with her once more churning lunch.

"Unfortunately the seal has perished so some moisture has got in here too." Jean carefully lifted the lid. "I don't think it's going to be worth a big reveal at the Back to Badara Festival so I thought I may as well share it with you girls. Especially you, Marion, as you showed so much interest."

Marion barely heard Jean's words over the pounding in her ears. Her gaze remained firmly on the jar.

"I think I put something in there," Gloria said. "You would have too, wouldn't you, Marion? And you, Sarah?"

Sarah shook her head quickly. "I was sick. I had German measles and I'd been sent from school to stay with my grandmother so I didn't come home that weekend."

Sarah's cheeks were pink and Marion's stomach churned harder. That Sarah hadn't been there was true, but it hadn't been German measles that had kept her away.

"My parents were very involved," Sarah continued. "Dad was district mayor at the time. I remember feeling very disappointed I wasn't there."

"Oh, that's right." Gloria put on a posh voice. "You and Marion were away at boarding school then."

Sarah looked down at her hands.

Jean carefully removed the papers from the jar. "Oh dear," she said. "From the outside I thought some of them might be okay but looks like moisture must have seeped in here too. The envelopes are stuck together." She began to carefully tease them apart. "If yours is okay, Gloria, and yours, Marion, perhaps you'd read them to us. They might give us a laugh."

Marion's brain was a jumble of thoughts. If her contribution was still intact maybe she could knock a glass of water on it or make a dash for the door on the pretext of needing the toilet and accidentally drop it in. Or perhaps she could make some excuse about wanting to keep it private.

"Ohh," Jean said. "The names are gone and the envelopes feel solid."

Marion's seesawing emotions rose again.

"But the middle ones might be okay." Marion's heart plummeted as Jean carefully lifted an envelope free of the others. "This one says Meredith Fromm." Jean frowned. "Gosh, they left the district many years ago. We must try to track her down." Jean put the envelope aside and peeled off another. She smiled and handed it across the table. "Gloria Hensley."

"Oh, mine survived," Gloria squeaked.

"Are you two related?" Paige asked.

"Marion and I are cousins. I'm Chapman now." Gloria fiddled with the seal of the envelope.

"Open it carefully," Jean warned.

The flap peeled back and Gloria extracted a rippled page. "Not many words are readable."

"That's a shame." Marion's tone lacked the right amount of sorrow judging by the strange looks she got from the others. "I'm sure we didn't write anything worth reading though, do you, Gloria?"

Gloria was peering at the page. "*Badara news*," she read then looked up. "That's right, we had to make up a news story about current happenings and then make a prediction about what we thought might be happening in fifty years." She frowned at the page. "I can't make out what I wrote. Something about a fire."

"It might have been that one behind Petersons' garage," Jean said. "You remember the Petersons, Marion? You and Gail were the best of friends. Such a shame she died so young."

"I vaguely remember the fire," Gloria said. "It got into the tyres and they were worried about the fuel nearby. It was probably the only newsworthy thing to happen in Badara that week. Or even the month." She tsked. "There's more but all the words are blurred or soaked away altogether."

"Try yours, Marion."

Marion looked from Jean to the envelope she was holding as if it was a snake about to bite her.

"Your name is quite clear so the inside might be okay."

Marion continued to stare.

"Marion?" Sarah nudged her.

"Oh, for goodness sake, I'll open it." Gloria took the envelope from Jean and carefully prised open the flap.

"No!" Marion's hand shot across the table.

Everyone around it froze except for Gloria, who clutched the envelope to her chest and gave a gleeful giggle.

"Ooh! Did you write some secrets in here, dear cousin?" she cooed. "Something delicious, I hope." And before Marion could stop her she'd removed the envelope's contents. "Yours is much clearer than mine was. Let's see." Gloria began to read. "*Badara Untold News from 1970. Reporters Marion Hensley and Gail Peterson report on the happenings in Badara this year and ask where will these people be in 2020?*"

She looked up. "Did you and Gail write this together? It's bound to be juicy. She was such a—"

"We shouldn't speak ill of the dead," Jean said.

"Hmph." Gloria shrugged.

Marion made another attempt to reach across the table but Gloria was too quick for her. She continued to read. "*Marion and Gail are both headed for university to become a teacher and a doctor respectively. But will have toured the world and probably never return to Badara not even by 2020.*"

"Ooh! La di da!" Gloria said.

"We were kids," Marion said. "No need to read any further."

"But I do like to see you squirm," Gloria teased. "Now what's next? *Billy Brown shows innovative skills. He siphons petrol from Petersons' garage each week. Will he own his own service station in 2020?*"

Jean chuckled. "Everyone knew he did it. I didn't realise it was that often though."

"It probably wasn't," Marion said, remembering how Gail had had a special dislike for Billy, who had two left feet and thick glasses back then.

Gloria continued. "*Carol Devon is always waiting at the back door of the bakery expecting handouts. Will she be earning her own living in 2020 or still be bludging?*"

"Oh dear." Jean's smile faded.

"I don't remember the Devons," Sarah said.

"Me either," Gloria said.

"That poor family were destitute." Jean shook her head wearily. "Her husband drank all their money. My brother ran the bakery by then. He always made sure they had bread for the week."

Once more Marion remembered Gail's anger as they wrote the news report. She'd made it sound as if the Devons were spongers. "Please don't read any more," she pleaded.

"But there's so much here," Gloria said. "You get a mention, Sarah."

Marion didn't dare look along the table.

Gloria continued to read. "*Sarah Glen, daughter of the district mayor, jumped the gun and had an illegitimate baby.*"

The gasps ricocheted around the table as Marion fought to stop the contents of her stomach from rising up her throat.

"*In 2020 he/she will be fifty.*" Gloria read on. "*Will he/she know their true parentage?*"

That had been Marion's one piece of gossip. How excited she'd been to know something Gail didn't. Marion had told her how she'd seen a very pregnant Sarah in Adelaide the previous month and Gail had filled in the gaps.

"Sarah?" Paige's worried cry made Marion look up.

Sarah was on her feet, pale and swaying. Paige put an arm around her shoulders.

"I…I'm going home," Sarah mumbled.

"Perhaps you shouldn't drive," Briony said.

"I'll go with her." Paige cast an incredulous look at Marion before she guided Sarah from the room.

Those who remained stared at Marion. Her heart was pounding so hard she feared it would burst. She cast another pleading look at Gloria.

Gloria glanced at the page. Her eyes widened. "I probably shouldn't—"

"Who's next?" Briony said.

Gloria lifted her gaze. "You."

"Please don't..." Marion's voice trailed away.

"You may as well," Briony snapped. "I'd like to know what scandal my sister-in-law has made up for me."

"*Colin Wilson sells a lot of insurance at one particular house in Wirini Bay.*" Gloria's voice was little more than a whisper. "*Will he have moved there permanently by 2020?*"

Marion heard Briony's sharp intake of breath, felt the glare of her eyes, but didn't move.

"How could you?"

The bile in Marion's throat rose again as she forced herself to look up into Briony's broken-hearted gaze.

Briony didn't wait for an answer. She walked out, her feet echoing across the wooden floor of the hall, and then silence.

Jean sighed. "It was the town's worst-kept secret." She shook her head at Marion. "Jill did everything she could to keep up appearances. I think it was what killed her in the end."

"Ah, yes, I knew I'd be on the list somewhere." Gloria's voice dripped with sarcasm. "*Gloria Hensley goes behind the railway shed with any boy she fancies.* What?" Gloria glanced at Marion then back at the page. "*The latest being Rodney Tripp. Will she be...*" Gloria's jaw dropped. "*Will she be running the town brothel in 2020?*"

Gloria's mouth opened and closed like a goldfish but no sound came out. Marion flinched at the pure hatred she saw in her face.

"You always were a bitch, Marion. You and your snobby friend Gail both thought your own shit didn't stink." Gloria flung the page onto the table and stormed out of the room.

Marion's head flopped forward into her arms. The only sound was the pounding in her ears.

A gentle hand rested on her shoulder. "I'm sorry. I was so excited to find a small part of the time capsule contents hadn't been destroyed...if I'd known...I never imagined."

Marion groaned.

"You and Gail certainly went to town on this town," Jean said.

Marion groaned again and lifted her head, resting it against the palm of her hand. "I'd forgotten half of what we put in there."

Jean picked up the page. "It certainly was rather hurtful for Gloria, for all of them." She glanced down. "Oh, there's one more."

Marion couldn't remember who else they'd written about but she had no more energy to stop it as Jean read.

"Mary Addicot thinks her son Leonard is meant for Marion Hensley. That will NEVER happen. Everyone knows Leonard is a homo. Will he have been found out by 2020?"

Jean made a small huffing sound. "Well, once again it's hurtful but poor Mary's no longer with us. You were wrong about Leonard and you did end up marrying him so it was the reverse of what you wrote."

Marion gripped her face in her hands and pressed her fingers into her eyes. She remembered how she and Gail had giggled over the report, egging each other on. And today, as each piece had been read out she had recalled it, but she had no recollection of the section about Gloria and the last one about her and Len. He hadn't even been on her radar when she was sixteen. She'd known him, of course, like you did most people who lived in the district, but she hadn't liked or disliked him. He'd simply not existed in her circle of friends.

"Now I understand why you were looking so hard for the time capsule," Jean said. "I suppose at sixteen you couldn't imagine the distant future and the fallout of such a missive being revealed. I think I'll get rid of them all. Tell people nothing survived if they ask. Are you happy for me to do that?"

"Yes." Marion sighed, still gripping her face. She remembered she'd got cold feet at the last minute when she'd imagined her parents reading the news report. It had triggered her conscience perhaps. She'd told Gail they should rewrite it, temper it down but, Marion recalled, her dad had arrived to pick her up and he'd been in a hurry. Gail had said she would make some changes but she obviously hadn't bothered. What did any of that matter now anyway? The report had done its damage. She'd have to face up to people she'd known all her life and somehow apologise. Blast Gail for dying young. She'd got off scot-free.

Jean began poking the envelopes back into the jar.

"Wait." Marion sat up. Her head swam as her eyes adjusted to the light. "Can I see it?"

Jean raised her eyebrows. "If you want." She passed it over.

Marion looked at the page of untidy cursive writing. The blue ink had faded and some words were partly erased by moisture but she recognised her scrawl. Gail hadn't rewritten it at all, but the last two paragraphs were in neat print – Gail's writing. Marion had always wished she could write so neatly. Gail must have added the final pieces about Gloria, Marion and Len. Why would she have done that? Marion felt a small portion of the hurt the others must be feeling that Gail, her best friend, had made something up about her.

eighteen

Paige glanced nervously at Sarah sitting rigidly in the front passenger seat beside her. The colour that had drained from her face back in the hall still hadn't returned and she hadn't said a word since agreeing to let Paige drive her home.

They'd had to go via the kindy to collect Levi. He'd chattered about his morning, and then when he found out they were going to the farm he was full of excitement, talking about the dog and the big swing. Paige responded to his questions about the pet sheep and where Dane was but Sarah remained silent. Finally Levi's voice became a mumble and just before they reached the farm he fell asleep. Paige was thankful she'd been to the Townsends for the barbecue on the weekend. She wasn't sure Sarah would have been much help with directions.

The car shuddered as they drove over the grid and Sarah looked around as if she suddenly realised where she was.

"Thanks, Paige," she said. "You can let me out by the garage."

"Will somebody be home?" Paige didn't like the idea of leaving her alone.

"The men won't be far away. It was good of you to drive me." Sarah had the door open with one leg out when she turned back. "It's probably too late but please don't say anything to Dane or Zuri about…about what was said back there."

"I wouldn't." Paige shook her head but she couldn't imagine how such a secret had remained hidden in a place like Badara where everyone knew everyone else's business.

"I can't imagine what you think of me."

Paige reached across and gripped Sarah's arm. "I was pregnant at sixteen. It was the toughest time, an emotional roller-coaster. If what was read out was true, the only thing I'm thinking right now is how much harder it must have been for you in your day than for me."

Tears brimmed in Sarah's eyes. "You're so kind," she sniffed. "I must go."

"What will you do about your car?"

"Zuri can drop me off on his way to school tomorrow. I just need some time to…" She dug a tissue from her pocket and blew her nose. "I'll be all right." She stood and closed the door gently, peering in the back window to look at Levi who was still asleep, then she gave a small wave and walked off.

Paige swung her car around and headed up the drive. She'd just gone over the grid when a ute turned in and pulled up beside her. She lowered her window, wondering how she was going to explain her presence to Dane who was smiling at her across the space between the vehicles.

"Hello? What brings you out here?"

Paige's mind scrambled and then she remembered the empty cake containers she'd put in the back of Sarah's car when they'd met at her place before fitness.

"I was returning your mum's containers." Her cheeks warmed but it wasn't a total lie.

"Oh." He adjusted his hat on his head. "Wasn't Mum going to meet you at the hall?"

"Yes, she did. I forgot to give her the containers."

"I'm sure she wouldn't have wanted you to drive all this way. Did you stop for a coffee?"

"Oh no, only to drop off…I've got to get back. Levi will wake up soon and I've got things to do."

"Righto. Good to see you. Maybe you could come out another day? Bring all the kids again."

"That'd be great. Bye." Paige put up the window and drove out onto the road. She didn't like to lie but it wasn't her place to share Sarah's secret, and if she'd told Dane the real reason for her driving to the farm, he'd have wanted to know more. Marion's news report was going to cause the Townsends a whole lot more grief and they'd already been through so much.

Briony stepped out of the shower and pressed the towel to her face. She'd driven straight home from the hall. Thankfully the house had been empty. No sooner had she stepped inside than the emotion she'd bottled up all the way home had exploded like a cork from a bottle. The concerns she'd had for Blake taking the fitness class had paled into insignificance when Marion's report had been read out. Briony had sobbed uncontrollably until her chest had ached and her tears had run dry. Knowing someone could come home at any moment, she'd stood in the shower hoping the warm water and the steam would help return her blotchy face to normal. She dragged on some fresh clothes and bundled up her gym gear to take to the laundry. She wouldn't be returning to that class, nor anywhere Marion was likely to be.

She stepped out of the bathroom and almost ran into her husband.

"There you are," he said. "I need an extra person—" He peered at her. "What's wrong?"

Briony stepped around him and went into the laundry. "Nothing, except if I never see your sister again it will be too soon."

"That doesn't sound like nothing. What's Marion done this time? I know she's a bit bossy but you just have to stand up to her and she's fine."

"She's a miserable cow!"

Vince's eyebrows shot up to his hairline. "Hell, love, you are upset. Tell me what's happened."

"She wrote awful stuff in a news report." The tears Briony thought had dried up bubbled over again. "It was read out today after fitness."

"Wasn't Blake with you? I haven't seen him this aft—"

"He didn't stay for lunch," she wailed and flung herself into Vincent's arms. She didn't want to mention the class and Blake's anger at her.

Vince hugged her a moment then guided her to the kitchen where he sat her down. He flicked on the kettle, put a box of tissues on the table then took the seat next to her.

"Get your breath then tell me again," he said. "I don't understand. What report?"

"It was in the bloody time capsule." Briony blew her nose. "You probably wrote one too."

He screwed up his nose. "Not that I recall – when was this?"

"In 1970."

"What? You're upset by a report that was written back in 1970?"

"She told everyone about my dad and his affair, Vincent."

"Why would she do that? Especially now – it was so long ago."

"She wrote it and then it was hidden under the supper room."

"Since 1970?"

"Yes." Briony clenched her fists and banged them on her lap. "Jean uncovered it but mice had got in and there was water damage."

"To the report? How the hell could you read it then?"

"It was in a glass jar."

Lines creased Vince's brow. "I'm sorry, Briony, you just said it had pest and water damage and now you're saying there's a jar."

"Yes!" Briony groaned. "The jar was all right except it was one of those old preserving jars with the rubber seals. The seal had perished so some moisture got in and only a few of the letters were readable."

"And one of them was Marion's saying your dad had an affair?" Vince shook his head. "I still don't get why she would even write that. She was only..." He shrugged. "What? Fifteen or sixteen in 1970."

"I don't know but it was read out after lunch and now *everyone* knows." Briony dabbed at her cheeks as more tears spilled over.

He leaned in and hugged her. "To be fair, love, most people know."

She shoved him away. "They don't. My mother worked so hard to present us as a united family. Dad made a mistake, she forgave him and we went on. A few people knew but Mum made sure there was nothing more for them to gossip about."

"Who else was there when Marion read out the report?"

"Marion didn't read it." Briony thumped her legs again. "Now I know why she didn't want Gloria to."

"Gloria read out Marion's report?"

"Gloria's was damaged and Marion was being funny about not reading hers so Gloria did."

"I can understand why Marion would have been funny about it. She would have been concerned for you."

"If she was concerned for me she never would have written it in the first place."

"So who else was there while Gloria was reading a news report from 1970 that Marion didn't want read out?"

"Jean, Sarah—" Briony clapped a hand to her mouth. "Sarah had left but that was the other awful thing in the report. It said she'd had an illegitimate baby."

"What?"

"It was terrible, Vincent. Sarah went as white as a sheet. She left but Paige went with her. I hope she drove her home because Sarah didn't look capable."

"Is it true?"

"How would I know? Your sister's the one with all the gossip."

Vince shook his head. "Forget the tea – I think I'll have a beer."

"A wine for me, please."

She took a gulp as soon as he handed it to her.

"Sounds like this exercise group was a bit explosive," Vince said. "Blake told me the class went well."

Briony sat upright. "Thank goodness he'd left. I don't want the kids to hear about their grandpa. He and Mum are both gone and I don't want to tarnish their memory."

"It seems to me that keeping things quiet only causes angst later."

"What are you referring to?"

"Everything and nothing." Vince shrugged.

Briony glared at him but he met her look with one of quiet resignation.

"Buried secrets, love…they have a way of working their way to the top."

Briony took a bigger swig from her glass.

Marion battled against the weight that was forcing her down. It pressed in on her nose and mouth and she struggled to drag in a breath. From somewhere in the distance she heard her name. Someone was calling her. She pushed back against the weight and a sudden burst of light brought her back to reality.

"What on earth are you doing in bed? Are you sick?"

She blinked at Len, trying to focus her eyes and clear her head as she pushed the blanket off her shoulders and wriggled her fingers to bring some life back to her numb arm.

"Duck?" Len bent down beside her, his worried gaze searching her face. "What is it?"

"I was tired after…after fitness. I thought I'd lie down." She closed her eyes as she realised the horror she'd created had been real and not a dream. She'd driven straight home after the debacle at the hall. Jean had insisted she could manage the clean-up on her own. Marion had been relieved to find her house empty. She'd toed off her sneakers, crawled onto her bed and pulled the heavy blanket over her head, hiding herself from the world. She must have fallen asleep.

"What time is it?" she croaked.

"Five o'clock." Len's cool hand cupped her forehead. "You're a ball of perspiration. Are you sick?"

"No. I must have got too hot, that's all." Marion pushed back the covers and sat up. "I'd better start dinner."

"You're still in your gym clothes." He eyed her again. "Are you sure you're okay?"

Marion couldn't bear the kindness in his look. She dropped her head to her hands. "I'll never be okay again."

"Heavens, did Blake work you that hard?"

"It wasn't Blake," she mumbled through her fingers. "I've done something terrible, Len. Hurt so many people."

Len prised her fingers away. "I'm sure it can't be that bad."

"It's worse."

"Tell me."

Marion took a breath and the whole sorry tale of the fitness club lunch poured out. She didn't stop until it was all said, every horrible detail. Except the last paragraph of the news report. It was destroyed now – Jean had seen to that with a match from the kitchen – so there was no chance Len would ever have to hear Gail's final words.

"What am I going to do, Len?" she groaned when she finally finished. "Today for the first time I thought the fitness club was really working well and then it all fell apart. I've hurt friends and family. They'll never speak to me again."

"It seems a bit tough to punish you for something you wrote when you were sixteen."

"You should have seen their faces." Marion closed her eyes, revisiting Sarah's devastated look, Briony's hurt and Gloria's anger. And then dear Jean, who'd been so kind about it all, and Paige. Marion's eyes flew open.

"Even the young newcomer, Paige, thinks I'm the devil incarnate."

"I'm sure she doesn't."

"What am I going to do, Len?"

"You'll work it out. You always do."

The gentle understanding in his look was her undoing. Marion rarely cried but big fat tears seeped from her eyes and rolled down her cheeks.

"Oh, duck, come here." He pulled her to him and wrapped his arms around her.

Marion clung to him like a drowning woman and her sobs intensified. She cried for the hurt she'd caused but also for herself and Len. He hadn't held her this close in so long.

nineteen

It was Thursday afternoon when Paige heard a knock at her back door. She and Levi hadn't long finished their lunch. He jumped up from the game he'd been playing at her feet and ran to the door. Paige followed.

"Dane!" Levi cried out in delight as he pulled on the handle.

"Hey, little mate." Dane high-fived Levi's outstretched hand. "Can I come in?"

"Of course," Paige said, happy for some adult conversation.

Dane held out a biscuit tin. "Mum's been baking again."

"That's kind of her."

"Yay! Biscuits!" Levi jumped up and down, tugging on Dane's arm.

"Stop, Levi," Paige said. "Let Dane get in the door and then if you ask nicely maybe you can have a biscuit." She accepted the tin from Dane and led the way into the kitchen. "Would you like a coffee?"

"Thanks."

While the kettle boiled, Paige put the TV on for Levi and settled him in front of it with a couple of Sarah's biscuits and a drink.

"It's my only babysitting service," she said guiltily.

"Hey." Dane held up his hands. His face was split in a huge grin and today his wild hair was trapped beneath a woollen beanie. "No judgement here. Zuri's had far more than the allowable screen time over the years. You do what you have to to survive. I was lucky to have Mum nearby."

"How is your mum?" Paige asked. She'd been concerned for Sarah ever since she'd dropped her home but she didn't have her number, and even if she did she wouldn't have felt brave enough to call.

"She's the reason I've come, really."

Paige set the mugs on the table with the open biscuit tin between them.

Dane wrapped his fingers around his mug and stared into it. The lead-in music for *Dinosaur Train* drifted from the lounge with Levi's mumbled accompaniment.

"We…Dad and Mum and me." Dane looked up. "We wanted to thank you for supporting Mum the other day. And driving her home."

"She had a shock. I didn't think she should drive."

"It was kind of you." He glanced into his cup and back at her. "Evidently I have a half-sister."

"That must have been a surprise."

"For my brother and me, yes."

"Is your brother home?"

Dane shook his head. "Mum insisted we skype with Chad so she could tell us both at the same time."

"What about your dad?"

"He's known a long time. Mum said she couldn't marry him without telling him she'd had a baby before. They decided they'd tell us one day…but one day never came."

"Life was different for an unmarried teenager in your mum's day."

"I get that. I'm not judging. It's just that after all we went through when Zuri suddenly arrived in our lives…then my dickhead brother leading a double life. Mum knows how I feel about keeping secrets." Dane shook his head slowly back and forth. "Nothing in my family is ever how it seems."

Paige wanted to reach out and lay a hand on his but he was across the table, beyond her reach, and if she moved to him it would feel awkward.

"Are you going to meet your sister?" she asked instead.

Dane shrugged. "I'm still digesting it but even if I wanted to I'm not sure how. Mum hasn't ever tried to get in touch and there's been nothing from the other direction either. She could be dead, for all we know."

"Your poor mum. I feel bad. It was me who convinced her to go to the fitness class and stay on for lunch. I think she was enjoying the company and she got involved with the planning for the Back to Badara weekend."

"What exactly happened at the lunch? Dad and I were so happy that Mum was finally doing something in the community again, then Mrs Addicot wrecked it by telling stories. I don't understand why someone would dig up the past after all this time. Mum was a bit vague about that part but I've never thought Marion Addicot was a bitch or a gossip."

"I have to admit I find her a bit scary but you're right, she hasn't seemed like the kind of person to spread tales about others." Paige screwed up her face. "I'm not sure it was entirely her fault."

"Mum said there was a news report."

"Yes." Paige filled him in as they drank their coffee.

"So it was written back in 1970?" Dane said.

"Yes. They were teenagers. I got the impression Marion wasn't keen to have her report read out though. It was Gloria who insisted."

"Gloria Chapman? I don't think there's much love lost between her and Marion. They're cousins. Gloria was a Hensley like Marion was. Vince Hensley and Marion Addicot are brother and sister. Their dad and Gloria's dad were brothers."

"I knew they were cousins." Paige's head was spinning trying to follow his explanation. "Half this district seems to be related."

Dane laughed. "They probably are. If not by blood, by marriage."

"Well, Gloria was very determined to read out Marion's news report," Paige said.

"If I was going to say anyone tended towards gossip it'd be more likely Gloria than Marion."

"Whichever is the case, it's done now. Do you think your mum will come back to fitness class?"

"I've no idea. Dad says they've done a lot of talking over the last few days. Mum almost seems brighter since she told Chad and me about our sister."

"How did your brother take it?" Paige had to admit to being mildly curious about a guy she'd heard so much about but hadn't met.

"I don't know. He didn't say a lot at the time. He's hardly in a position to throw stones." Dane stood up and put his empty cup on the sink. "We don't talk much. We were never close and since his…" He shook his head. "The Townsends have provided plenty of fodder for local gossip."

There was a short silence between them and Paige was keen to change the subject.

"Please let your mum know I'm happy to meet up again before the class if she wants to go to fitness next week."

"Hell." Dane clapped a hand to his head. "I almost forget to tell you about the breadmaker. Mum asked me to see if you'd like one. Evidently you were discussing bread when you came out for the barbecue lunch."

Paige frowned, thinking back. "Oh, yes. We did. I think it was more about how much my kids go through and she said how hard it is when there's no local shop."

"My sister-in-law left a lot of stuff behind she didn't want. There's a breadmaker among the gear still at their house and Mum wondered if you'd like it."

"I've never used one before."

"It's pretty easy. Zuri and I have Mum's 'cause she never uses it any more."

"I'll think about it, thanks."

Paige saw Dane out and pondered the breadmaker offer. It was yet another act of generosity from Sarah – but it wasn't only her. Paige was slowly learning to accept it seemed to be the way life was in this community.

She jumped as her phone began to ring. There had been no unwanted calls for over a week. She moved towards it as it vibrated across the bench. It wasn't a number she recognised so she let it ring out, then continued to stare at her phone. If it was a teacher or someone she knew they'd leave a message.

A text message pinged into her inbox. She snatched up the phone and read: *You missed a call but the caller didn't leave a message.* Paige tapped the phone gently against her palm. She'd witnessed firsthand the destruction keeping secrets from loved ones could cause but her situation was different to Sarah's. Jayden was

a teenager, and a young one. There was no way she would allow
him to be hurt and if that meant keeping secrets then she'd do it.

Briony snipped another dead rose from the bush and dropped it
in the bucket at her feet. Deadheading roses was therapeutic. She
imagined each stem was Marion's neck and she snapped the secateurs together with gusto. No matter how hard she'd tried to put
Marion's report out of her mind it came wriggling back. Particularly when she was on her own and had time to think.

Snap! The last shrivelled bloom dropped to the bucket. Briony
looked back along the row of standard roses – not a withered head
or faded bloom to be seen. Each bush stood straight and tall, fresh
buds forming among the lush green canopy. If only her family
were so easily corralled and organised.

Her children had all been avoiding her. If they were home,
they appeared for meals which were eaten with stilted conversations, mostly with little input from Briony. She'd become a pariah
in her own family. Even Vincent had given up trying to persuade
her to his way of thinking.

A sudden image of Blake popped into her head, the excitement
on his face when he was telling her about Gab. He'd had that
same joyful look so many times over the years – in primary school
when he'd won a prize at the local show for his chickens, when
he'd got great year twelve results and been accepted into his chosen uni course, when he'd won the job in Sydney, always so open
with his emotions. She'd tried her hardest to do what was best for
him, for the girls…She pressed a hand to her chest to steady the
niggling twinge of doubt; could it be she'd got it wrong?

She stiffened at the sound of an approaching vehicle and drew herself up. This was no time for self-doubt.

The drone of the motor was accompanied by the chatter of happy voices. To her amazement, her three adult children were riding in the back of the ute, laughing and carrying on like teenagers. The ute stopped at the back gate and Vince lowered the window as the others jumped out.

"There's a big tree down in the creek paddock," he said. "We're going to cut it up and bring it back to the woodshed."

"We're taking a thermos and some food." Chelsea was first through the gate.

"Do you want to come, Mum?" Madeline was two steps behind her sister.

Briony shook her head. "There are fresh biscuits cooling on the bench. Take some of those if you want. And plenty of apples." She met her husband's resigned look.

"I'm going to hook up the trailer," he said.

Blake stepped back from the ute as it pulled away, his smile tentative.

"Why don't you come with us, Mum?"

"I've plenty to do here," she said stiffly.

Blake walked through the house gate but instead of following his sisters inside he came to a stop beside her.

"What happened after I left the hall the other day?"

"We had lunch." Briony turned back to the rose bush, desperately seeking another dead bloom to snip but there were none.

"Dad said someone upset you."

"He shouldn't have," Briony snapped. "It's all fine."

"So you'll be at class next week?"

A shiver wriggled down Briony's spine despite the warmth of the afternoon sun. "I'm not sure about that."

"Is it because I took the class?" His smile changed to a look of irritation.

"No," she said quickly. "Nothing to do with you. Your Aunty Marion's the one with the big mouth."

"What did she say?"

"It doesn't matter." Briony folded her arms. "Nothing you need to worry about."

"I'm an adult, Mum. You don't have to keep protecting me."

She glanced at him. He was half-turned away from her, staring across the yard. His usually smooth wave of hair was an untidy jumble, no doubt from riding in the back of the ute, and in spite of his protest there was a vulnerability about him that made her want to wrap him in her arms.

"Blake?"

He turned back. "Yeah."

"You are sure, aren't you?"

"About?"

"You know..." She waggled a hand at him.

Realisation dawned on his face. "Are you asking me if I'm sure I'm gay?"

She winced at the word and nodded.

"Of course I'm sure."

"It's just that sometimes people try things, like your sister and... drugs." Once more she waggled a hand in the air.

"Mum, I've always been gay and I'll admit it wasn't easy at first and I'm sorry I didn't talk to you and Dad about it then but..." He shrugged.

"If only you had."

He slowly shook his head. "To be honest, I'm glad I didn't. I don't think your disapproval would have helped me back when I was still trying to understand it myself."

Briony pressed her fingers to her lips to stop the gasp that erupted, the pain of his words too strong to bear.

The rattle and rumble of the ute returning with the stock trailer on behind filled the silence between them. Madeline and Chelsea burst out the back door arguing about who was riding in the front of the ute.

"Ready, Blake?" Chelsea called.

"Coming." He turned back to Briony. "Are you sure you won't come with us, Mum?"

She shook her head. "I'll make sure dinner's ready for when you get back."

He opened his mouth to speak again then closed it, gave a small shake of his head and went to join the others.

"We'll be a few hours," Vince called.

Briony nodded and waved as the ute drove off with her precious family aboard.

Her children were lucky. They'd never suffered any big hurts in their growing years. She'd made sure of that. They had no idea of what it was like to be marginalised. People could be so hurtful if you were different. She wanted to protect them from that forever if she could.

Briony moved along the standard roses to the lavender bushes either side of the gate. She kept them nicely shaped but a few stalks protruded at angles. She lifted her secateurs and began to snip.

twenty

The following Tuesday morning Paige walked up to the front of the hall as Blake pulled into the car park.

"Are we the only ones coming, do you think?" he asked.

"I don't know." Paige looked along the otherwise deserted street. "I guess you heard there was a bit of a blow-up last week. Sarah won't be here today but I don't know about anyone else."

"Mum wouldn't say much except she wasn't sure if she was coming. Did Marion say something to upset someone?"

Paige winced. She didn't want to add to the anguish that had already been created. "Not exactly."

The hall door creaked open. "Hello, you two," Jean said. "I came through the back way. Are we it?" She looked around. "Oh, good, here comes Gloria."

"And Mum," Blake said as another car rolled into the car park. "And my sister."

A younger woman exited the passenger side of Briony's car.

"Hi, little bro." She winked. "Thought I'd help lower the average age of your class."

"Enough of your sass, Chels. We've got a good cross-section of ages, thank you," Blake said. "Have you met Paige?"

Paige said hello and followed them inside. Blake had similar hair and brown eyes to Briony but Chelsea was fair and blue eyed. Perhaps she took after her dad. And he was Marion's brother, Paige reminded herself. It took some keeping up with all the family connections in this town. She'd been trying to explain some of them to Niesha during their chat the previous evening but had failed, only confusing her friend completely.

Paige rolled out her mat and wriggled her shoulders to dispel the strange feeling of tension in the hall. She noticed Briony jump at the slight clunk of a chair placed on the floor, conversations were spoken in hushed whispers and Briony and Gloria kept glancing towards the door as if they were watching for something or someone. Like Paige, it seemed no-one had brought lunch.

By the time Blake had his music set up and chairs out, they were all lined up to begin: Paige, Jean, Gloria, Briony, and the new addition of Chelsea. No Claire today. Paige was sorry Sarah hadn't come either but Marion's absence was a relief. Her presence would have made it more awkward than it already was.

Not even Blake's mild cajoling and calm music could get everyone to focus. There were far more missteps, wobbles and groans than usual. They were barely into the warm-up when Jean clapped her hands and asked Blake to stop.

She stepped up beside him and turned to face the group. "I think I need to speak to everyone before we go any further."

Unease tingled in the pit of Paige's stomach. Surely there wasn't going to be more trouble.

"Last week Marion was caught up in an unfortunate business that affected some people in this group. I spoke to her this morning and she feels she is unable to come to class because of the hurt she's caused."

Paige noticed a questioning look pass between Blake and Chelsea but everyone remained silent.

"I sent text messages to you all to that effect," Jean said. "Except you, Paige, as I don't have your number. We are a small community and I'm sure none of us wants anyone to suffer unnecessarily. I've apologised to Marion for my part in what happened."

Briony gasped and Gloria muttered under her breath.

For a second, Paige felt the full force of Jean's resolute look before her gaze continued on over the rest of the women.

"Marion wrote something as a child—"

"Hardly a child," Gloria muttered.

"When you get to my age, teenagers are children," Jean said. "And she didn't write it alone. It was a silly news report she forgot all about and then, when it came to light and she remembered her part in it, she was full of regret—"

"Didn't want her true colours revealed to everyone," Gloria said.

"She was full of regret, as we would expect of someone of Marion's calibre," Jean continued. "She's an integral part of this community and I think we should give her a chance to move on from this."

"We didn't write those awful things," Gloria snapped.

"But we did uncover them," Jean said, her gaze directed at Gloria. "And read them out against Marion's wishes."

Gloria muttered something Paige couldn't catch.

"I wouldn't have come today if I hadn't got your text letting me know Marion wouldn't be here," Briony said.

Chelsea was openly making faces at her brother now. Paige could read her lips as she mouthed *what's this about?*

"Marion was the driving force behind this girls' club." Jean gave Blake one of her sweet smiles. "I hope you don't mind me calling it that?"

Blake shook his head, a bemused look on his face. "Not at all."

"It's not the same without Marion. And there's the Back to Badara Festival to consider. Marion has done a lot of the legwork already and is overseeing everything. If you won't work with her then someone else will have to step up and it won't be me. I'm too old." Once more Jean's gaze swept the group, pausing at each person then moving on to the next.

There was a general shuffling of feet and clearing of throats. Paige wished she hadn't come herself, she felt so uncomfortable. Even though Marion wasn't physically present, her presence was with them.

"I wanted us to think on that so we can all do our bit to help mend the relationships when the time's right." Jean turned to Blake again. "Now I'm looking forward to ironing out my kinks to some of your lovely music, dear. Shall we start again?"

Blake switched on the music and led them through his tai chi warm-up. Paige concentrated on him, trying not to think beyond the exercises.

"Zip the core, girls," Blake said with a grin in Jean's direction. "And tuck that tail."

Jean chortled like a schoolgirl while beside Paige, Chelsea gave an eyeroll and muttered, "Please!"

Chelsea said very little on the drive home. Briony had been on edge all the way, expecting a barrage of questions about what had happened with Marion but instead Chelsea's only conversation had been about what a good job Blake had done, even though he played oldies' music and Aunty Jean was flirting outrageously with him.

Briony had been relieved to escape to the shower but when she returned freshly dressed to the kitchen to prepare lunch, both Chelsea and Blake were waiting for her. Immediately she tensed under their scrutiny.

"We want you to tell us what Aunty Jean was prattling on about," Chelsea said.

"Now?" Briony strode past them and switched on the coffee machine.

"I promised Blake I'd wait till he got here."

Briony pursed her lips. That's why Chelsea had said little on the way home. She'd been biding her time.

"You can't say it's nothing, Mum," Blake said. "Obviously Marion said something that has upset you badly if you don't want to see her."

"What's going on with Aunty Marion?" Madeline joined her siblings at the table.

"Where did you come from?" Briony hadn't heard her come in, which meant her boots were off at least.

"I was finishing off with the horses when I heard the cars." She sat at the table. "Thought it was about lunchtime."

"Bloody hell, Maddie," Chelsea snapped. "Do you ever make your own food?"

"Of course I do, but Mum's usually here and she does it. Anyway, I don't see you or Blake getting your own food."

"I made the sandwiches for lunch today, actually," Chelsea snapped. "And Blake always helps with the cleaning up."

Briony kept her back to them as they bickered, gripping the bench so that she didn't pick up the nearest thing and throw it at them.

"Settle, you two – this isn't the time," Blake said sternly.

Briony took a breath and risked a look behind her.

He patted the seat beside him. "Come and sit down, Mum. Maddie can make the coffees in a minute."

Madeline opened her mouth to protest but Blake gave her a playful push and she sat back and folded her arms.

Briony looked at each of her three children, the older two studying her with expectant looks while Madeline pouted. There was no escaping them this time but what could Briony say to smooth this over? Her brain scrambled as she took a seat beside Blake.

"I hate that you've had a falling out with Aunty Marion," he said. "What's it about?"

"I'm amazed she hasn't told you." Briony had been wondering how much Marion had divulged. "You two are as thick as thieves."

"I haven't seen Marion this week," he said. "I've helped Len with the fencing a couple of mornings but he's always sent me off before lunch and said Marion either wasn't home or she was busy. I thought it was a bit odd because she usually plies me with food when I'm there."

"That is odd," Madeline said. "Aunty Marion always insists on food."

Once more three pairs of eyes were focused on Briony.

"It's all to do with the blasted time capsule," she snapped. "Marion wrote a news report to go in it back in 1970 and it was full of awful things, some about my family and some about others. It got read out at our lunch after fitness last week."

Chelsea shook her head. "All this fuss over something Aunty Marion wrote half a century ago?"

"Why would she read it out now?" Madeline said.

"What was in it that upset you so much?" Blake asked.

Briony glanced down at her hands gripped in her lap. After Jean's lecture today and now the kids making it sound so simple how could she make them understand her hurt?

"It was about your grandparents." She drew herself up. "It put them in a bad light."

"Gosh, Mum, they've both been gone for a long time now," Blake said.

"I know but—"

"Is it about Grandad's fling?" Chelsea asked.

"What fling?" Blake and Madeline spoke in unison.

"There was no fling!" Briony snapped and eyeballed her eldest.

"I heard about that years ago," Chelsea said, ignoring Briony. "Supposedly, way back in the day, Grandad had a 'liaison'," she made air quotes with her fingers, "with a woman in Wirini Bay."

"Who told you that?" Briony felt her small grip on protecting her parents' good name slipping away.

"I don't know." Chelsea shrugged. "It was when I started at Wirini Area and kids were hurling insults one day. Someone tried to make a big deal of it but it was years ago; who cares?"

"Go, Grandad," Madeline said.

"Madeline!" Briony snapped. "Infidelity is not something to be taken lightly."

"So it was true?" Chelsea said. "I never believed it at the time. Just thought it was some Wirini Bay kids trying to sling mud."

"We understand that might have been a hurtful time for you, Mum." Blake gave Chelsea a stern look. "But true or not, it was a long time ago."

"It didn't happen," Briony said. "My mother, your dear gran, worked hard to dispel that terrible rumour. It's not fair to bring it up again."

"Really? Is that the big secret?" Madeline's voice was incredulous. "Who cares what people think? Especially after all this time." She pushed to her feet and strode across the kitchen. "I need coffee."

"Me too," Chelsea said.

"Yes, please," Blake added.

Briony sat back and once more stared at her children. "You can be blasé about things but I care about what people think."

"Mum," Chelsea groaned. "You're always so worried about what others think – but what about your own family?"

"Everything I do is for you." Briony found the strength to get to her feet.

"Is it?" Chelsea jumped up too. "From where I'm standing it's as if you don't care about me and that my marriage is over because the guy I fell in love with can't choose me over drugs. You care more about covering it up so other people don't find out."

Briony almost wilted under her daughter's blazing glare.

"And you can't be happy for Blake, who has fallen in love with a guy who sounds wonderful, and for Maddie, who's also found the man of her dreams. Instead of standing by us you're more worried about what people think. Well, how about worrying about what we think for a change?" Chelsea flung out an arm. "It'd be nice if the Badara community supported us but they're not the ones that count. It's your love and support we need, Mum."

"Chels, that's enough," Blake said. "Calm down."

The room fell silent. Briony managed to stay upright even though her knees trembled, while around her the three people she loved more than anything in the world remained as rigid as if they'd turned to pillars of salt, Madeline with one hand on the coffee machine, Blake still seated and Chelsea glaring at her from across the table.

From outside came the sound of a vehicle approaching.

"That'll be your dad coming for lunch. Are you staying, Blake? Chelsea's made plenty of sandwiches. Can someone set the table, please? I need to pop up to the bedroom for a minute."

She turned away from their surprised looks and walked as quickly from the kitchen as her wobbly legs would take her.

twenty-one

Marion looked at the clock for the umpteenth time that day. Fitness class would be finished by now and they'd probably be settling in for lunch. The nausea she felt every time she recalled her news report had been encased in sorrow as she woke that morning and realised it was Tuesday and she wouldn't be joining the exercise group.

Jean had rung after breakfast to see how she was and suggested she needed to come and see everyone but Marion had firmly said no. For once in her life she was burying her head in the sand. She had neither the courage nor the strength to face the women she'd hurt. She knew she'd have to apologise but even after a week she hadn't got the strength to face it yet. She'd hardly left the farm in all that time. Len kept checking on her and trying to get her to help with jobs he could manage perfectly well on his own. She'd run out of things to keep herself occupied and the prickly feeling inside her was driving her crazy.

She paced the floor again then stopped and snatched up her keys. She'd go to Wirini Bay for a change of scene and visit her mum. Even though the conversation would be stuck in a loop about weather and food and flowers, it would be somehow reassuring.

She was pleased to find Vera sitting in her room alone when she arrived.

"Hello, Marion," Vera smiled brightly. "Haven't seen you in ages."

Marion and Len had made the trip in to see Vera the previous Saturday. The bunch of daisies Marion had brought still sat on her mother's side table alongside a vase filled with beautiful roses.

"Did Briony bring you the roses?" Marion asked.

Vera cast a blank gaze in their direction. "I don't know, dear, but they're lovely, aren't they?"

"Very pretty." Marion was sure the roses would be from Briony's garden.

"How are you, dear?" Vera's bright look almost made Marion think she was her old self.

"Terrible really," Marion said.

"Oh, that's no good. Are you eating properly?" Vera asked.

"I'm well, Mum, but…I'm sorry for all the grief I caused you when I was young," Marion blurted.

Vera looked puzzled. "That's a funny thing to say. You were such a lovely child. Headstrong but happy."

"Something I wrote for the Back to Badara time capsule wasn't so lovely."

"You always did have messy handwriting." Vera brushed her hand over her skirt.

"I've hurt Sarah Townsend and cousin Gloria and I feel so bad about upsetting Briony."

"It's not difficult to upset Briony, dear." Vera leaned closer. "You know her mother had to resew her wedding dress three times till Briony was happy. Goodness knows what she'll be like once she has children of her own."

Marion sighed. "I wish you could tell me how to fix this."

"Fix what, dear?"

"The upset I've caused." Marion knew she was wasting her breath.

"Pfft! Who hasn't caused an upset?"

"I guess we all do but they're not all as insensitive as mine." Marion pictured again the hurt faces as the stupid news report was read out.

"All you can do is apologise with true remorse. And a thoughtful gift can show positive contrition." Vera looked directly at Marion and held her pointer finger straight in the air and wagged it firmly. "But don't make excuses. It just sullies things."

"Okay."

Vera seemed to be firmly in the present. Marion didn't dare interrupt this rare occurrence.

"If people won't accept your apology, that's their problem, not yours."

"Right." Marion nodded.

"And don't leave it too long. Always best to clear the air as soon as possible." Vera leaned forward and adjusted one of the roses in the vase. "Briony's a funny one. Always likes the best. She had her eye on my dinner set, you know, but I think things like that should always go to the daughter." Vera turned to Marion, her face puzzled again. "I can't recall where my dinner set is?" She glanced around. "Perhaps Briony's taken it. I haven't seen it in a long time."

"You gave it to me when you left your Wirini Bay house, Mum."

"Did I?"

"You don't need it here." Marion felt guilty about the dinner set. She'd never liked the fine china with its navy edges, gold fila-gree and maroon flowers. It hadn't left the back of the cupboard where she'd put it when her mum had sold up to move to the home.

Vera's gaze returned to the roses. "They're lovely, aren't they? Did you bring them for me?"

"I think Briony did," Marion said. Her mum had slipped off into the circle of repetitive conversation they often had, but Marion felt a small comfort. Earlier, when Vera had talked about upsets and apologies there'd been a glimpse of the matter-of-fact, sensible woman she'd once been. Marion missed that woman very much.

She thought about her mother's words all the way home. She wasn't sure where it had come from but Vera's wisdom had risen to the surface when it was most needed. Marion had been so worried about the hurt she'd caused that she hadn't been able to focus on how to fix it. Her mother's brief moment of lucidity had helped. Now she had the bones of a plan. She'd get each woman a gift, something thoughtful, and then she'd visit each one person-ally at home, hopefully when they were alone.

The gift couldn't erase the words of the news report but a small something personal for each woman would make Marion feel as if she was apologising with her heart as well as her words.

Len's ute was at the back gate when she arrived home. She looked at her watch. She hadn't prepared any food and it was well after lunchtime. Hopefully he'd found himself something.

One of his boots was lying on its side on the back step and the other was at an angle against the wall. Normally they sat in a tidy pair beside the back door.

"Len?" she called as she let herself in.

"Yes." His voice was a croak she could barely hear. "In the kitchen."

She rounded the door to find him slumped in a chair. His appearance wiped all thoughts of her own problems from her mind. His face was as white as his bushy eyebrows, his thinning hair was damp and plastered to his head and one sleeve of his shirt was ripped right off.

"What's happened?" she asked as she strode towards him.

"I'm okay, duck," he said.

"You don't look it." Marion inspected her husband. There was a bit of blood and bruising on the pale skin exposed below his shoulder and fine beads of perspiration on his brow and above his lip.

"What have you done? Where does it hurt?"

He shook his head slightly. "I'm not hurt."

"No pain in your chest, or jaw or arm?"

"Got a fright, that's all."

She quickly filled a glass with water and watched him closely as he took some sips. His fingers trembled and she wrapped her hand around his and helped guide it to his lips then back to the table. It frightened Marion to see him look suddenly old and vulnerable.

"I'm going to make you a cup of sweet tea," she said. "While you tell me what's happened."

"I was trying to get the last bit of the fence done." He scraped the fingers of his left hand through his hair, dragging the few fine strands back from his face. "Had a bit of a run-in with the post-hole digger."

"Oh, Len!" The missing sleeve suddenly made sense. Once again she inspected him closely. The bruising and the beads of blood formed on his broken skin had left a pattern of matching curved lines. "What were you doing using that on your own?"

"Blake and I didn't get it finished yesterday. I came to get you but you weren't home."

"I went in to see Mum. You weren't nearby when I left. I sent you a text." She'd been in a hurry, thinking of her own problems. Now there was another line to add to her overflowing list of things to atone for.

"It didn't matter. There were only three holes left to dig. I was on the last one. I don't remember what happened except that I was almost done and next thing my sleeve was ripped from my shirt."

"Thank God it did." Marion prodded gently at his bare shoulder with her fingers. It could so easily have been his arm ripped from his body.

Tears formed in his eyes and his lip trembled. "Maybe I'm getting too old for this."

She crouched down beside him. "You're not old, Len, but perhaps it's time to retire. Find something else to fill your time that doesn't involve using dangerous machinery."

"I don't know what I'd do without this place."

"Oh, Len, you silly old bugger. You'll find something else to do. You're so handy and you love your golf and your fishing. We could go and see the kids more often."

Marion felt the eagerness that had deserted her begin to bubble again inside. She'd struggled with her own retirement and if Len retired as well she'd thought they'd both rattle around together with little to do, but maybe there was some kind of future together she hadn't thought of. And if they left the farm she wouldn't have to spend her time in Badara.

Two tears overflowed and rolled down his cheeks leaving a trail through the fine film of dust on his face that thankfully had some colour back in it.

"I don't know what I'd do without you, duck."

She frowned at him. "I'm not going anywhere."

"You've been different since you finished school."

She struggled to stand again, wriggling her toes to get the blood flowing in her legs. "I'm home more."

"Not much. It seems like you want to be anywhere but here... is it me? We've weathered so much together but I'd understand if—"

"It's not you, Len." She turned away from him and made his tea and her coffee. She couldn't explain her restlessness to him. The last thing she wanted to do was add to his distress. Besides, she'd already hurt several people around her and she couldn't bear to hurt Len as well. They'd both suffered enough.

He was still studying her as she brought their cups back to the table. She put two biscuits in front of him.

"Get some sugar into you," she said as she sat. "There's extra in your tea as well."

They were silent a moment, Len sipping his sweet tea and munching a biscuit while Marion stared into her coffee wishing it could tell her what to do.

"Perhaps I am ready to give up farming."

Her head shot up. "Really?"

"But I'm worried." Len's face wrinkled in a frown. "If we sell this place, then what?"

"I don't know. It scares me too." Marion sipped her coffee. Even though she didn't do much of the farm work it felt a bigger change than retiring from teaching had been. It wasn't only their livelihood but their home they'd be giving up. "It's not as if it'll happen suddenly. Let's think on it."

He reached a hand across the table. "And we'll decide together?"

She placed her hand on his. "Of course."

Later that afternoon when Len was off working, Marion was startled by a knock at her back door. She hadn't heard a vehicle. She stuck her head into the passage as Blake stepped inside.

"I didn't hear your car," she said.

He brushed a kiss across her cheek. "Would you have let me in if you had?"

She met his raised eyebrow with one of her own. "Come in," she said and led the way back to the kitchen. "Would you like a coffee?"

"No, thanks. I won't stay long. I drove in the top gate and caught Len up at the shed."

"Did he tell you about his near miss with the post-hole digger?" she asked as they sat.

"Yes. I told him if he needs help to let me know, for a few more weeks anyway. I'll be here a while longer."

"That's great."

"Gab wants to meet everyone but he can't come for a couple more weeks so I thought I'd stay on. That's if you don't mind me extending my stay in the shack. I can pay some rent."

"Rubbish." Marion batted a hand at him. "You're welcome to it. We don't use it much once summer's done. Just the odd weekend. It's better to have someone there so the mice don't take over."

"I think we got rid of them. I've only trapped a couple since I've been there. The woman at the coffee shop in Port Kent said she'd had trouble with them too, a month or so ago but not now.

And she's heard about me taking a fitness class and asked me if I might do one there. We're going to hold it first thing Thursday mornings at the boat club." He scratched at his chin. "I really called in to see how you were doing."

"I'm okay."

Blake shifted in his chair and cleared his throat. "I've heard a bit about the time capsule thing."

"I guess your mum's still upset with me."

"Mum seems to be upset with everyone at the moment."

"She's still not come to terms with your news?"

Blake shook his head. "You know, I think she believes this is a life choice I've made." He sighed. "That I can somehow choose not to be gay."

"I'm sorry."

He drew back his shoulders. "Anyway I'm not here to talk about me. I came to see if you'd come back to the fitness class."

"I can't, Blake. I upset people and I've got to put that right before I can face them as a group again."

"Is there anything I can do?"

"That's very kind but no. Somehow I have to fix this myself."

"I don't know what else happened, but we got the gist of what you wrote about Mum's parents."

Marion hung her head.

"It's in the past, and from what Chelsea said a lot of people knew about it anyway. We think Mum's making a mountain out of a molehill." Once more he sighed. "As usual."

Marion lifted her gaze to Blake, who was studying her with such a compassionate look she felt like crying, only she wouldn't. She was done with that. "I've hurt your mum and some of the other women. I have to make recompense."

"Exercising isn't the same without you."

Marion steeled herself against the sorrow that settled like a lump in her chest again.

"Perhaps you'd like to come to the Port Kent class," Blake said. "We're starting this Thursday."

She pondered it a moment. It'd be a totally different group of people, no doubt. Some she'd probably know but not closely. "Maybe."

twenty-two

Paige's phone was vibrating on the upturned box beside her. It was Thursday, the week nearly gone and a beautiful day outside. She'd decided to do some more weeding in the backyard. Levi was playing in a dirt heap nearby with his trucks. She glanced from her son to the phone. It wouldn't be Niesha, they'd only spoken a few nights ago. She eyed it with suspicion as she'd got into the habit of doing again, but as she bent closer she was relieved to see Dane's name on the screen.

"Just wondering if you and Levi are busy," he asked as soon as she answered.

"Not really," she said, looking from her dirty shorts and knees to Levi, who'd been adding water to his dirt tracks and was now splattered with mud.

"Dad's taken a load of sheep to market and Mum and I are shifting a mob over to the other property. We could do with an extra hand and Mum suggested you."

"Me? I don't know one end of a sheep from the other."

Dane laughed. She was beginning to like that warm-hearted sound.

"You don't have to worry. We need someone to drive ahead on the road with the flashing light. It's easy. Mum and I can do the rest. There's a small creek where we're going. No water but it's a nice spot and Mum suggested we have our lunch there."

"Oh." Paige hadn't even thought about lunch yet.

"To tell you the truth, Mum and I could probably manage with the dogs but she suggested I ask you and I pounced on it. You and Levi will brighten her day."

Paige liked Sarah's company too, and it wasn't as if she had much else to do. "We'd love to come."

"Great! Please don't bring food. Mum will have that covered."

Paige wasn't sure exactly what to expect but the day turned out to be a lot of fun. She'd driven alone in the lead car. There'd been a small hiccup when they'd wanted her to drive a farm ute but she'd never driven a manual so they'd swapped the warning light to Sarah's automatic. Levi had ridden with Dane in the ute, perched on Kodie's booster seat so he could watch the dogs and the sheep. Sarah had brought up the rear in another ute and by the time the sheep were shut into the paddock she'd set out a picnic under the trees in a dry creek bed. Levi had spent his time between mouthfuls of food playing with the dogs and begging someone to push him on the rope swing hanging from the bough of a large gum tree.

When they'd finally eaten more than enough of Sarah's food and washed it down with coffee from a thermos, Dane had said he was going to check some water troughs. Levi had been keen to go with him and Sarah had suggested she and Paige collect the breadmaker from Chad's house. Paige strapped Levi into the ute beside Dane. The little boy was so excited it took her several attempts.

Sarah leaned in and gave him a biscuit. "One for the road," she said.

They waved as Dane drove off, both dogs barking their excitement from the tray.

"He has the most beautiful deep brown eyes and lovely curls," Sarah said gently. "Is he like his father?"

"Very." The breath hitched in Paige's throat.

"You can tell me I'm being nosy but you know so much about my family. Do you mind if I ask why you aren't with Levi's dad now? Didn't it work out?"

Paige chewed her lip against the sudden prick of tears as the memories came flooding back through the small gap in the door she couldn't quite close on them. "Ari was an amazing guy. We clicked instantly when we met, about six years ago. He wasn't bothered I was already a mother of two. He loved kids and he was great with Jayden and Kodie. We'd been together three years and he badly wanted more kids. I loved him very much but…he was killed a few days after Levi was born…a motorbike accident…on his way to visit us in hosp—" Her voice caught in her throat and the tears overflowed.

"Oh, my dear girl, I'm so sorry. I didn't mean to upset you." Sarah put a consolatory arm around her shoulders as Paige dug in her pocket for a tissue.

"It's crazy." Paige stabbed at her cheeks with the tissue. "I can go weeks sometimes without crying and then suddenly…"

"It overwhelms you."

Paige nodded.

"Grief isn't something that completely disappears. We slowly replace it with new, happier memories."

Paige wasn't sure she'd done that but with Niesha's help she'd got on with her life. "Three kids gives me something else to focus on."

"What about Ari's family? Levi must be a comfort to them."

"Ari was from New Zealand so I'd never met his family until after he…His parents and siblings and their families all came for his funeral. It was overwhelming. They were nice people but they were so deep in grief they pulled me down further. I had a newborn and two grieving children to look after. I couldn't look after Ari's family as well. They tried to keep in touch but…I guess I haven't been good at it. They send Levi cards and gifts for Christmas and birthdays…" Paige had given them her new phone number but she hadn't yet passed on her new address.

"You've had a tough time," Sarah said.

"Moving here helped."

"You don't have family of your own?"

"My parents and siblings live on the Gold Coast. I'm the black sheep. We keep in touch but we're not close."

"And Jayden and Kodie's family?"

"Jayden's father and grandparents shut me out when I told them I was pregnant and…I'm ashamed to say I got caught up with the wrong crowd before Kodie came along. Her dad turned out to be a dipshit and I never met his family." She stared at Sarah through watery eyes. "I don't want my kids to know that though."

"Good heavens, of course not. Children have no control over being brought into this world."

"I've never regretted having Jayden and Kodie even though they were unplanned. I've told them both the relationships with their dads didn't work out."

"And then you met someone good who embraces you and fatherhood and he dies." Sarah squeezed her shoulder. "You're an amazing young woman, Paige."

"I don't feel amazing." Paige sniffed.

"You've done a fine job of raising those three kids and almost on your own. It can't have been easy moving to somewhere as isolated as Badara."

"We needed to get out of the suburbs. I was worried about Jayden. He was hanging around with some boys who were trouble."

"You moved a long way."

"I found the place one day on Google." It had been after one of those scary phone calls from Lucinda and she'd been desperate to move on. "The rent's cheap, we love the house and yard and the kids are settling in at school. Jayden's struggling with some of his subjects but he seems to have come to terms with the move. It's not easy for a teenager."

"Zuri says he's going well at football practice."

"It's so weird. He's never been all that sporty. He used to have a skateboard but he's never played football."

"Sport's a good way for him to make friends, for your whole family, really. The sports club's very social. And you're welcome here whenever you'd like to come. Don't wait for Dane to invite you. I'd be happy to see you…and the children, any time."

Paige blew her nose and shoved the tissue in her pocket. "Thank you, we'd like that."

"I grew up in Wirini Bay but I knew Badara well. It was a busier town back then. There was a general store, post office, garage, farm shop, even a bakery. That was where you live now. Farms have got bigger and towns have shrunk but I still like it here – the space, the fresh air, the quiet lifestyle." Sarah tipped her head to the side. "Well, almost quiet."

"I'm sorry about what happened after fitness the other week." Nerves fluttered in Paige's chest. She'd been wanting to talk to Sarah about coming back to the class but hadn't known how to begin. "Do you think you'll come again?"

"I don't know. Jean did ring me about it. I gather there was more read out than what we heard."

"It seems so."

"I found it difficult to go out into the community after...after what happened with Chad. Perhaps a downside of being here. When you live in a place all your life and suddenly your personal details are laid bare for everyone to see...and then Marion bringing up more from my past..."

"Marion's not coming any more."

"Such a shame. We've not been close friends but you can't live in a district like this and not get to know people. She acts tough but she has a heart of gold. I'm sure she'll be feeling terrible over the whole thing. She's like her parents – a hard worker for the community, and she was the one who started the fitness group. I keep myself busy enough here. And with Chad gone and two properties to run there's always something the men need help with." She looked at her watch. "You'll have to head off to collect Kodie soon. We should go over to Chad's place and get the breadmaker."

"Gosh, yes, the time's flown." Paige had been having such an enjoyable day. Even the heart to heart with Sarah had felt like a release. "Are you sure you can spare the breadmaker?"

"It's gathering dust. Everyone I know who wants one has one. Let's put away the picnic things and we'll drive over."

They packed up and drove across the creek, pulling up outside the fenced yard. Paige had seen the house in the distance when they'd arrived. Sarah led the way through the gate and along a cement path running through what once would have been lawn but was now dirt and dead weeds.

She paused inside the door, straightened her shoulders then continued through the laundry into a bigger room that was an open-plan kitchen–living area. Their footsteps made a hollow tapping sound on the floor. Even though Sarah led the way, Paige felt as if she was trespassing and that someone else would appear at any moment.

Sarah opened a door to a small walk-in pantry. "We took out all the perishables, of course, and we've been gradually removing the rest but I don't know what to do with it. Our daughter-in-law took what she wanted but there are things she didn't need or maybe she felt weren't hers. It was such a difficult time…here's the breadmaker."

Sarah carried the stainless steel box-like machine out and sat it on the bench beside an empty glass vase, a stack of recipe books and a jar holding a few kitchen utensils.

"If there's anything else you'd find useful please help yourself."

"Oh. No, but thank you." Paige didn't mind second-hand things but it felt wrong to be looking through someone else's house.

Sarah began opening and closing drawers then finally rummaged in one. "Here it is. I knew the instructions would be here somewhere." She slipped the manual inside the machine.

Paige glanced around. "It's a lovely house." Even though the blinds were closed the room felt light and airy. There were signs everywhere that a family had lived here. On the way in she'd noticed a bucket of pegs on the laundry bench, a small basket of cleaning cloths and an old towel hanging on a hook. In this room there were still photos and artwork on the walls, a basket of toys on the floor by the bench and books stacked in a bookcase. A large rag doll was propped in a corner and there was a glass cabinet with ornaments and pretty cups inside it. Even though there wasn't much furniture, she still had the feeling that the house was simply waiting for its owners to return.

"The house was built and transported in before Chad married." Sarah moved to the wall with the photos and stopped in front of a large family portrait. "I spent a lot of time with my grandchildren."

From where Paige stood she couldn't see their faces, but the photo was of a man and a woman with three children between them.

"You must miss them," she said.

"Every day." Sarah turned back abruptly. "Such a shame the place is empty but Dane says he's happy in the cottage. Maybe Zuri will move here one day...or one of Chad's children. They loved it here." She ran her fingers over the bench, leaving a trail in the dust, then brushed her hands together briskly as if she were eradicating more than the dirt from her fingers. "The place needs a proper clean-out but...I don't like to come here and the men aren't worried about it." She lifted a hand in the air. "I'm sure there'll be something Levi would like in the boys' room."

Sarah disappeared up the passage before Paige could protest and was quickly back with a box that had *Farm Play Set* printed across the top.

"I bet he'd have fun with this." Sarah held it out.

Through its clear front Paige could see a truck, a tractor, animals and all sorts of farm-related items. "We couldn't..." Paige shook her head.

"They left so much stuff behind and Chad's kids are too old for these things now anyway." Sarah lifted her gaze to Paige. "Please let him have it."

"Thank you," Paige said. "He'll love it."

From beyond the house they could hear a vehicle and dogs barking.

"That'll be Dane back," Sarah said. "Are you okay to carry the breadmaker and I'll lock up?"

Levi was so excited by Sarah's gift he hugged her around the neck and kissed her cheek so long Paige had to pry him away. There were tears in Sarah's eyes and Paige felt them brim in her own. This was as close to being spoiled by a grandparent as Levi had got.

twenty-three

"You haven't said much since we left the accountant." Marion studied Len, whose eyes were firmly fixed on the road ahead. They'd just made the hundred-and-fifty-kilometre round trip for Friday morning appointments with their accountant and bank manager.

"There's a lot to digest."

"Don't take too long. We're not getting any younger."

Marion hoped for a smile but Len remained solemn-faced.

"The bottom line is we have my super, the money from the farm if we sell, and I know it's not ours yet but one day the shack at Port Kent," Marion said. "We're not millionaires but we'd be comfortable with enough money for some travel and to visit the kids."

"I know, but...you've admitted it's been difficult for you to retire. How do you think I'll go?"

"You're seventy next birthday and I'm only eighteen months behind you. I think it's time we found out before we're too old to do it."

Len was silent as he turned into the driveway. In the garage he cut the engine but kept looking ahead.

His stillness made Marion suddenly fearful.

"What is it, Len?"

She was even more worried when he turned to face her and there were tears pooling in his eyes.

"I don't know. Selling up seems so final. This place isn't much, I know, but it was my dad's and his dad's before him."

"I understand how that must feel but neither of our kids wanted to be farmers." Marion squeezed his hand. "I'm not going to force you to make a decision, Len, but after today's meetings I've made one for myself."

"And what's that?"

"Once Blake leaves, I'm moving into the shack at Port Kent." She removed her hand from his and sat back.

"Why?"

"I need a change."

"Is it because of what happened with the time capsule thing?"

"Partly – I'm not running from that any more, but it's made me think further about what next. We've lived all our married life on this farm and I'm weary of it. Going to the fitness class at Port Kent last Thursday opened my eyes to change."

"You'll get back to the Badara group."

"Maybe, but it's not about what happened there, it's about our life here and the future. In Port Kent I can walk on the beach, take up some sport – one of the women asked me to join their croquet club. I can pop to the shop if I'm out of milk, call in for a coffee at the cafe."

"You left me once before to live at Port Kent."

"That was totally different and you know it." It surprised her that Len had brought it up. Marion didn't want to go over old ground. There was no point.

He tapped his fingers on the steering wheel. "So how will it work if I'm here and you're there?"

"I'd like us both to move to Port Kent, but if you don't want to sell the farm it's not far away. I'll still spend some time here and make sure you're fed and watered. But I need a change of scenery, Len. Port Kent would give me that, both of us if you agree to come, and we'll still be close to Vince's family...that's if he and Briony ever talk to me again. We can still go to church in Badara and keep those ties. You don't have any family here. The only thing keeping us on the farm is you, Len."

"We don't own the shack."

"It's a technicality. It will be mine one day." Marion didn't like to think about that though, as it would mean her mother was no longer with them.

"So you're giving me an ultimatum?"

"No. We've dithered over this idea of selling up for so long. Since I've retired I haven't been able to settle and now I've realised I don't want to live on the farm forever. And after the time capsule business, well, it's made me think I need a change."

"I can't believe you're letting that get to you. All you have to do is apologise and everything will go back to normal."

"I hope my apology will be accepted, for sure, but what I don't want is to go back to life as it's been." She straightened against the seat. "I need a change, Len, and I hope you'll come with me but I'll understand if you won't."

Len studied her a moment then shrugged and opened his door. "I've got some troughs to check."

Marion remained where she was as he walked away. She hoped she was making the right decision. She collected her handbag and the shopping from the boot, then turned at the sound of a car behind her. It rolled to a stop and the door opened.

"Jean?"

"Hello, Marion."

"What are you doing here?"

"I've come for a quick word. I won't keep you long."

"You're lucky you caught me – we've had some appointments and we're only just home."

"Let me help with these." Jean took one of the shopping bags from Marion's hand and walked beside her to the house. "I must admit to a little subterfuge. I rang Len and he told me you'd be home about now."

"Okay." Marion raised her eyebrows. "Sounds like I'd better put the kettle on."

"I don't want to hold you up."

"You're not."

Len stuck his head in. "Hello, Jean. Marion, I've got the troughs and a few other jobs to do. I'll be back about five."

"Bye, Len." Jean smiled sweetly at him.

He waved back but didn't make eye contact with Marion.

Jean settled herself at the kitchen table as Marion brought over the cups and a plate of biscuits.

"Now what's this about, Jean?" Marion asked as she sat opposite.

"I want you to pull yourself together, set things back to rights and come back to fitness and mahjong."

"Is that all? Shall I work on world peace while I'm at it?"

"I don't want your sarcasm, Marion." Jean sat up primly and folded her hands together. "You're too good a woman to let this go on and not fix it."

Marion sighed. "I am working on it. It's just that I feel truly dreadful and it bogs me down."

"I'm sure it does, but that's because you're such a good person."

"Am I though? Up until that blasted time capsule was revealed I thought I was. But if I could say those terrible things back then, maybe there's still some of that in me and I don't see it."

"You didn't write that report on your own."

Marion was reminded of what her mum had said. "Do you remember Gail?"

"Of course I do. She didn't have an easy life, poor thing, and then to die so young…"

"What do you mean her life wasn't easy? We had a lot of fun together. In primary school the most fun was when Gail was allowed to come home with me on the school bus. We'd go off into the scrub and play all kinds of adventure games, climb trees, make cubbies. And I used to enjoy being allowed to help out the back at their garage sometimes. Gail didn't like tidying the shelves but I loved making sure all the parts matched the numbers on the boxes and packets. And when I went away to boarding school we spent most summer holidays together. The best times were when we caught a ride to Wirini Bay and spent the day at the beach with other teenagers."

"They're the things you remember, but if Gail was here she'd have had all those times when you weren't together to tell you about."

"What do you mean?"

"Her parents were hard workers. They ran the garage and put in long hours and Gail often had to look after her younger brothers and sisters. I remember her mother trying her best to make sure Gail got a few breaks, like going to stay at your farm when she was younger and then by the time she was at high school her brother was old enough to fill in if she went off with you."

Marion frowned. "Gail never complained to me."

"When you were younger she probably didn't think on it much but as she got older I'm guessing she became aware of how different her life was. She went to school all day then worked for her family when she got home. Her father was a stern man and a hard taskmaster, and Gail being the eldest bore the brunt of it. She worked hard and he rarely allowed her any money. I think as she got older she rebelled behind his back. A few things happened around town that were attributed to her but never proven."

"Like what?"

"Mainly things went missing – Gail had a jealous streak, and had so little herself. I caught her one day wheeling a bike along the street. It was brand new. I knew it wasn't hers because I'd seen the excitement when the girl two houses down got it for her birthday. Gail told me she'd been allowed to take it for a ride, but she wasn't friends with the bike's owner. She returned it because I watched her, but a month later the bike disappeared and was never seen again.

"A few things like that happened – I said I had my suspicions but couldn't be sure until the ruckus when money went missing from the till at the garage. Poor Billy Brown had been in moments before and Gail's dad hauled him back and made him empty his pockets. He didn't have the money but he was asked not to return to the garage. I'd bet my bottom dollar Gail took the money."

"How old was she?"

"Good lord, I can't remember that. Mid-teens perhaps?"

"There was a trip to Wirini Bay when she splashed money about." Marion frowned. She remembered it because Jean was right – Gail rarely had enough money to buy one ice cream let alone a ticket to the movies. Marion often shouted her. "This particular day she'd had enough money to buy ice creams and soft drinks for everyone and she'd insisted on buying me a ticket to the movies even though I had my own money for it."

"You know, I always wondered about that fire behind their garage too," Jean said. "They never found out who started it but it had been deliberately lit."

Marion shook her head. "I was hating myself for being so unkind about everyone in that news report but now I feel even worse. My friend was hurting so badly and I didn't know it."

"Gail was good at hiding things."

"Now I think about it, Gail was the one who dictated most of that news report. I feel terrible for poor Billy Brown and the Devons, who were simply trying to make ends meet. How tough their lives must have been and Gail and I..." Marion shrugged. "The Devons are long gone from Badara. I can't apologise to them, but I suppose Billy...or William, as he prefers now—"

"Would have no idea what you were talking about. He's gone on to do very well for himself. Anyway, you've made up for your brief moment of spite over the years."

Marion snorted. "How?"

"Your many acts of kindness. The hours of tutoring you've done, and I know you didn't charge those families who were doing it tough."

"How would you know?"

"I keep my ear to the ground. How many batches of sausage rolls have you made and delivered to people needing a hand or a cheer up? How many offers of rides for people when it was out of your way to take someone home? How many sets of footy scarves and beanies have you knitted and donated? It's a long time since Grant played footy but you always help in some way. And what about the library books for dear old Cliff?"

Marion shrugged. They were all such easy things to do. She'd never thought to add them all up. Who did?

"Then there're the fundraisers you organised at church to support families sending kids to Wirini Bay for high school or to Adelaide for uni. It was you who set up that small scholarship."

"We'd been through it with our two. I knew how difficult it was to come up with the funds."

"And you used that empathy to make life easier for others."

"Don't lay it on too thick or they'll be calling me Saint Marion instead of the devil Marion."

"My point is you've done so much for this community you can't let a bad decision from your childhood ruin all that."

Marion sighed. "It's not really up to me, is it? I can apologise... and truly mean it, but my apology may not be enough."

"I have great faith in you...and the others." Jean smiled her sweet smile.

In that instant she reminded Marion of Vera. How grateful Marion was again for that small window of clarity her mum had managed when they'd spoken last.

"I've given it a lot of thought," she said. "I'd planned to visit Sarah tomorrow, first thing, and then Gloria in the afternoon. I have a gift for them."

"That's a good idea."

"It was something Mum said that made me think of it. I need to speak to Paige as well but I'm a bit stumped about something to give her."

"And Briony?"

"Of course I'll apologise to Briony, but once again I'm still thinking on the gift." Materially Briony had everything her heart desired. Marion always found her difficult to buy for on birthdays and at Christmas. "And she's already so distressed about...there're a few family issues happening there. I'm really not sure how to go about it yet."

"Unfortunately, I think some of Briony's actions or even her fears came from her mother."

"I didn't know Jill very well," Marion said. "They only lived in Badara a short time before they moved to Wirini Bay."

"I was very fond of Jill but keeping up appearances was so important to her. It was almost like that cleaning thing some people have these days."

Marion looked sideways at her. "Cleaning thing?"

Jean waved a hand in the air. "You know where they repeatedly clean and tidy."

"You think Jill had obsessive compulsive disorder?"

"I think there was definitely something, and after my brother's affair—"

Marion clapped a hand to her head. "Oh, my dear lord. How could I have forgotten that Briony's dad was your brother? I've been so worried about upsetting everyone else and I didn't even think about what effect my words had on you."

"You didn't say anything about Colin that wasn't true, unfortunately." Jean straightened her cup. "He was my oldest brother and he did his best to make up for his mistake but...I do think he may have continued to wander. He just made sure it was a lot further away."

Marion winced.

"Anyway, Jill was more obsessive than ever after the affair and their move to Wirini Bay. Colin bought her a fancy house and all sorts to go in it, along with expensive clothes. He was trying to make up for his indiscretions, I suppose, or maybe out of guilt, I don't know, but to Jill, keeping up appearances became paramount. Wherever that family went they were a well-oiled machine: well presented, smiling, impeccable manners." Jean sighed. "I think to some extent Jill's insecurities became ingrained in Briony."

Marion had what she could only describe as a light-bulb moment. "So that's why she always has to have everything just so, and why she always wants everything to be perfect, and why she wouldn't want people to know about Chelsea's marriage break-up or Blake's—" Marion coughed, pretending she had a tickle in her throat.

"It must be so hard on her, trying to be perfect all the time," Jean said.

"I'm not sure how I can get her to forgive me if her insecurities are so ingrained."

"You'll think of something." Once again Jean smiled. "Thank you for the lovely chat and the cup of tea but I must be off. Keith likes his dinner at five thirty and I haven't even planned what we're having yet." She tucked in her chair. "I don't suppose I can convince you to come to fitness on Tuesday?"

Marion shook her head. "But I am going to Blake's class at Port Kent on Thursday."

"I hope you'll come back to us soon then. And mahjong. Claire came last week. She doesn't know about the time capsule stuff and neither do the other players. We'd love you to come. Keith fills in for you but he hasn't really got a good grip on the game."

"I'll see how I go." Marion was non-committal but she felt a genuine glimmer of hope.

twenty-four

A little after ten on Monday morning Marion pulled in at Paige's house and nearly drove away again when she saw another car parked in the drive. Then she realised it was Sarah's car. Marion had intended to visit her next. Even though she'd planned to speak to each person individually, perhaps it was fortuitous that these two women were together. They'd left the hall together after Sarah's part of Marion's awful spiel had been read out and so she may as well apologise to them together.

She loaded up her cane basket and made her way to the back door. As she knocked on the screen the luscious smell of bread baking wafted out to greet her along with the murmur of voices.

Levi came running to the door then ran away again. "It's the sausage roll lady," he shouted.

"Who is it, Levi?" Paige called then opened the door. "Oh, hello, Marion."

Sarah appeared, framed in the kitchen door behind Paige.

"I was hoping to speak to you both, please," Marion said. "I won't keep you long."

Paige glanced back at Sarah.

"Of course," Sarah said.

Paige held the door wide for Marion to step through and she followed Sarah back into the kitchen.

Levi was at a kindy table with cookie cutters and a lump of playdough. He ducked his head when Marion smiled at him. She put her basket on the table.

"I'm teaching Paige how to use the breadmaker," Sarah said.

"I tried on my own the other day. My first attempt was a dismal failure." Paige wrinkled her nose. "More like rock bread. I asked Sarah if she'd give me a lesson. We've already improved on my attempt." She waved at a loaf of bread sitting on a cooling rack. "And we've started a second loaf."

Their attention was drawn to the machine whirring away on the bench as the conversation stalled.

Marion looked down as she felt a tap on her hand. Levi was staring up at her, his big brown eyes wide. "Did you bring sausage rolls?"

"Levi," Paige chided. "Mrs Addicot's only called in for a minute."

"I have actually, Levi." Marion took two Tupperware containers from her basket and sat them on the table. "There's one box for your family and the other is for yours, Sarah."

"Oh, that's nice." Paige reached out then back as if not sure whether she should accept.

"You didn't have to," Sarah added quickly.

A small hand slid towards one of the containers.

"Don't touch please, Levi," Paige said.

Marion took a deep breath. "I've come to apologise for the hurt my news report caused, and the embarrassment." The two women glanced at each other then back at Marion. She steeled herself and met each of their gazes. "I am truly sorry. I would like us to continue our friendship…but I will understand if you don't feel you can."

"Marion, really I—"

"Please, Sarah." Marion held up her hand. Her stomach was in knots but they hadn't thrown her out so she wanted to press on. "Just one more thing. I brought the sausage rolls as a peace offering but I have something else for you both which I hope you'll receive as a token of my remorse and my hope that we can continue to be friends."

This time Sarah remained silent as Marion handed her a small cardboard box and Paige an envelope.

"You don't have to open them now but they may need some explanation."

Once more the other two women glanced at each other. Paige was the first to open hers. She drew out the page Marion had designed and printed on her computer.

"An IOU for tutoring." Paige looked up. "I don't understand."

"Jean mentioned that you were worried about Jayden struggling a bit with his schoolwork. I may be able to help, but it's up to you and Jayden of course. Or perhaps with your little girl if she needs any help."

"Or bread-making lessons." Sarah nudged Paige. "Marion's repertoire is much better than mine."

"Thank you, Marion." Paige clutched the paper to her chest. "That's a lovely gesture."

"Can I have a sausage roll now?" Levi grumbled.

"That's not nice manners," Paige chided.

Sarah set her box on the table and lifted the lid. "Battleship?" She took out two small sets of the game.

"One set is for you and one for your grandchildren," Marion said. "You mentioned you struggled with what to do when you video chat with them."

"We can play battleship! What a great idea. We used to play games together a lot when they were on the farm but I couldn't think how to continue that when we're so far apart."

"You'll have to post them one set, of course, and there's a list of other suggestions that might work for video chats in the box. You've probably thought of some of them yourself but there might be something…"

Sarah took out the page. "I have tried reading stories but only the two little ones sit still for that. I Spy's a good idea. And telling jokes. Jim will be on to that. He's even more awkward than me on the video calls." Sarah chuckled and continued reading. "Play card games, help with homework, oh, and listen to music practice. Why didn't I think of that? Chad's oldest boy is learning guitar." Sarah hurried around the table and hugged Marion. "Thank you. There are some great suggestions here."

Marion remained rigid as Sarah stepped away.

"Your apology is accepted, Marion."

"And by me," Paige said. "Although I don't see why you needed to say sorry to me."

"It must have been awful for you to be caught up in it," Marion said.

"Paige and I have talked about it." Sarah glanced at Paige, who gave her an encouraging smile in response. They seemed to have developed a bond and Marion felt a brief pang of envy for their closeness.

"In a way you did me a favour," Sarah said.

That was the last thing Marion had expected to hear.

"I told Jim about my baby girl before we were married," Sarah said. "And we'd always intended to tell our boys when the time was right...but when is it ever the right time? Once they were in their teens it was just too hard but I became more anxious about it. I thought if my daughter was going to come looking, it would be when she was older. I've lived with it hanging over my head for so long and your report forced me to tell them. It was a shock for them to learn they had a big sister. Dane was disappointed I hadn't told them before and Chad...well, he's got bigger issues to deal with." Sarah sighed. "So you see, Marion, you may have forced my hand but it was a release."

"But other people know about it now."

Sarah shook her head. "After what my family's been through the last few years, I really don't care any more."

Paige gave Sarah's shoulder a brief rub. The sound of the breadmaker filled the silence.

There was a tap on Marion's hand again. She looked down into Levi's pleading eyes. "Pleeeze can I have a sausage roll?"

Marion looked to Paige.

"I guess it's almost morning tea-time."

Levi jumped up and down. "Sausage roll. Sausage roll."

"Wash your hands first, please."

The little boy dashed out of the room and was back so quickly Marion suspected he'd only waved his hands under the tap, but she lifted the lid on the container and lowered it for him to reach. He took one and then a second in his other hand. Before his mother could protest he bit into one and then the other.

"He's a doer, that one," Sarah said.

Levi looked up at Marion with the most angelic smile. His big brown eyes shone with delight.

"Thank you," he mumbled through a mouthful of sausage roll.

"You're welcome, Levi," she said.

Paige put the kettle on and Sarah peered at the bread machine. "I never know whether it's okay to lift the lid but even though our first loaf was okay it hasn't risen quite as well as I'd hoped."

"It won't hurt to open it in the mixing cycle." Marion looked at the timer. "Around twenty minutes in is a good time to check. May I?"

"Of course," Sarah said.

Marion lifted the lid and they all crowded round. She picked up the spatula beside the machine. "There's a bit of unmixed flour in the corners – you need to get rid of that." Marion poked the dough with the spatula. "It looks okay. It wouldn't hurt to check again in about twenty minutes. You want to be sure it's sticking and pulling away." She shut the lid.

"Told you Marion was the expert," Sarah said. "Did you ever use it to make hot cross buns?"

"I did."

"I was telling Paige she should give that a go."

"Easter's less than two weeks away." Paige grimaced. "I think I'll stick to trying to get the bread right for now."

"Easter will be here before we know it," Sarah said. "Do you have plans, Paige?"

"Not really. It's the start of the school holidays. I'm hoping the nice weather will hold so we can get out a bit and maybe have a few trips to the beach. The kids loved the afternoon we had at Port Kent."

Sarah suggested a few other places Paige could visit with the children and Marion marvelled that almost a whole term had passed since she'd retired. Usually she'd know the date and what week of the school calendar it was but she'd left all that behind and she realised the time had flown by. Not quite how she'd thought, but she hadn't been without something to keep her occupied.

The three women chatted over coffee and cake, and before Marion left she helped Paige with the next bread-making step. Levi had come and gone during the time they sat chatting. At one stage Marion had seen him sneak another sausage roll. The other two hadn't noticed but she caught his gaze as he turned away. They stared at each other a moment then she winked and he grinned and shot back to the lounge.

As she was saying goodbye he came running out again and flung his arms around her waist. She felt a sudden ache for grandchildren she wondered if she'd ever get.

"Thanks for the sausage rolls."

Paige reached forward. "Oh, I'm sorry, Marion. His hands are probably not clean."

"Good heavens, that doesn't matter." Marion patted Levi's back and she felt his little hands patting her in rhythm before he shot away again.

She left the two women to their baking, both relieved and buoyed by their acceptance of her apology.

It was quiet in Paige's house and she felt rudderless. Her kitchen was spotless after Sarah and Marion had finished tidying up, despite her protests that they didn't have to. She had two loaves of bread cooling on the bench, what was left of Marion's sausage rolls in her fridge for tomorrow's lunches and a full container of rock buns that Sarah had brought, well, almost full – Levi had already eaten a couple.

And Sarah had reminded her that it was almost Easter. Paige had been carefully buying some Easter treats and hiding them away but now the thought of that and the school holidays bothered her. They'd been in Badara almost four months and the time had flown by but she wasn't sure what they'd do for two weeks without the regular routine of school.

She looked into the lounge. Levi was curled up on the floor in front of the TV fast asleep. He was obviously exhausted from using his considerable charm to entertain Sarah and Marion all morning. And Paige had no idea how much he'd eaten. Every time she'd looked around Sarah or Marion were passing him something.

She put her gran's crocheted rug over him and took the opportunity to rest herself. The big old couch was so comfy she nestled back, then, acknowledging the heaviness of her eyelids, she rolled sideways, her sluggish gaze on Levi's face, angelic in sleep.

She'd been so determined to keep her little family together and safe from the hurt of broken relationships, she hadn't thought of it from the point of view of anyone else. Watching Levi with Sarah, and even Marion, dancing attendance on him and his surprising farewell hug made her sad for her parents, who hardly knew their grandchildren. It had been mostly their choice but watching Levi today she felt a pang of regret that Ari's family – Levi's family – were so far away in New Zealand. It wasn't easy but she'd believed she'd managed her little family unit well. Now she wondered what her children might be missing without extended family. Perhaps she should have tried harder to keep Levi's in his life? She updated them every Christmas and thanked them for their gifts afterwards and after each birthday, but Levi was nearly four. Like Jayden and Kodie had before him, he would soon be asking questions about his dad and extended family.

Paige hugged a cushion to her stomach and curled herself around it as a huge wave of loss surged through her. "I miss you,

Ari, so, so, much," she murmured and gave in to the tears she rarely shed for the man she'd loved.

Marion pulled up outside Gloria's house and sat a moment, gathering her thoughts. She'd been on such a high after leaving Paige's place. She'd stopped in briefly at home to collect the gift and sausage rolls for Gloria; however, it was a twenty-minute drive to Gloria's farm from Marion's and as each kilometre had slipped away so had Marion's bravado. They were cousins and even though they'd never been close, the hatred on Gloria's face when she'd flung the page from the time capsule to the table was still etched in Marion's mind.

Marion hoped Gloria would be on her own. She and her husband had three sons who were well into their twenties and all still lived on the property. It wasn't big enough to support five adults so the two older boys worked in Wirini Bay and were unlikely to be home, but the youngest worked full-time with his dad.

She picked up the container of sausage rolls and the envelope she'd stopped to collect from her place on the way. With her hands full it was a struggle to unlatch the gate with its wire contraption that replaced a broken latch. She hadn't been to Gloria's place for years but the outside had the same unloved appearance it always had. An assortment of boots, helmets, motorbike parts and tools littered the back verandah. The door beyond the screen was open and she had a grainy view of the empty kitchen. Music and the sound of someone counting drifted from somewhere further inside the house.

Marion drew in a breath and knocked. For a moment nothing happened and she was about to knock again when the music stopped and she heard footsteps.

Gloria pushed open the screen door. "Well, well, well. You've got a cheek turning up here."

Marion steeled herself against Gloria's hostile glare.

"May I come in please? I won't keep you long."

"If you must." Gloria moved back.

Marion stopped the screen door with her elbow as it swung swiftly and stepped inside. Unlike the verandah, the kitchen was neat and tidy. There was a lingering savoury scent of something baking and a couple of pies cooled on a rack.

Gloria turned to face her, and Marion realised she was wearing gym clothes and her face was red and sweaty. Gloria folded her arms across her chest and waited.

"I've come…" Marion's voice croaked. She cleared her throat and started again. "I've come to apologise—"

"Humph!"

"I'm sorry for the hurt that news report caused." Marion had decided there was no point in saying she hadn't written it. "And I know it's not much but I've brought you a small gift and some sausage rolls as a peace offering."

"Sausage rolls! The way people carry on you'd think you were the only one able to make them."

"Your savouries are delicious, Gloria. Mine are not meant to replace them. It's just something I wanted to do for…" Marion shrugged.

Gloria's arms remained firmly folded and her glare didn't falter.

Marion put the container on the bench with the envelope on top. "There's something else there for you. A small gift. It's my way of saying this apology comes from my heart. I never meant to hurt you."

"Didn't you?" Gloria flung out her arms. "You and Gail always looked down your noses at me, your poor little cousin. I know you laughed at me behind my back. That fake news report confirmed everything I've always known about you, Marion. You're so full of yourself."

Marion took a small step backwards. The force of Gloria's words was almost a physical blow. And once more she recalled it was Gail who'd done the whispering but Marion hadn't stood up for her cousin and for that she was sad.

"Nonetheless, I'm sorry for what was written."

"You think I care two cents for what you thought of me fifty years ago?" Gloria spat. "Or what you think now even? You can stick your apology."

Marion scrambled to come up with a suitable response. She'd known Gloria would be still upset but she'd hoped a heartfelt plea would assuage her a little. Then Vera's words came back to her. *If people won't accept your apology, that's their problem, not yours.*

Marion drew herself up. "Thank you for listening, Gloria. I hope I'll see you again soon."

"Not if I can help it," Gloria muttered.

Marion turned away.

"And I hope you're not planning on coming back to fitness, Marion. You'll be in a group of one if you do."

With those words echoing in her ears, Marion let herself out.

She was surprised by the tremble in her knees as she hurried along the path. The gate took an age to open as her fingers fumbled with the makeshift wire latch. Finally, she was back in her car and driving away. She was sorry her cousin had reacted so badly. It was understandable Gloria would be upset, but she was wrong about Marion looking down at her. They were simply very different people. They'd always tolerated each other but not been good friends. Just because there was a blood connection didn't mean they had to like each other but now it seemed Gloria wasn't prepared to give any leeway at all.

Marion clicked on the radio. The strident sounds of upbeat classical music poured from the speakers and she turned up the volume.

twenty-five

Briony lay on her gym mat and tried hard to relax as Blake was suggesting but she couldn't settle. They'd had a particularly hectic workout this morning and she was exhausted from both the exercises and maintaining a watchful eye on Blake. Near the end he'd changed the music to a sedate selection that included flute and pipe and the resonating sounds of a didgeridoo. He'd stepped them through some relaxation techniques but she couldn't let go of the thoughts that continually whirred in her head.

Briony was struggling to cope with everything that was happening in her children's lives and yet they all carried on as if marriage break-ups, homosexuality and dating older men with children was normal. On top of that, Vincent had been at her to make up with Marion, as if Briony had been the one to cause the upset. Briony had turned the other cheek to Marion's bossiness and sharp words on many occasions over the years but this time she'd gone too far. This morning he'd been cross with Briony. He'd said she wasn't trying hard enough to see anyone else's point of view. She'd been hurt by his words. She who bent over backwards to accommodate everyone else was being accused of not thinking of others and yet something about what he'd said lingered, undermining her confidence.

Fitness class wasn't the same since the time capsule's contents had been revealed. Even though Marion wasn't there, Briony felt as if the other women looked at her differently. Today they'd had a good group, the usual crew, and Chelsea had come again plus a few extras. Word had spread about Blake's classes.

She peeked at him now as he moved quietly about the hall, speaking softly about letting go of busy thoughts. She'd become more aware of his instructing skills today, proud of the way he'd included Jean in the trickier balance exercises by showing her how to incorporate the chair and the way he'd quietly helped Gloria adjust her squats to get them right. He'd suggested less strenuous moves for Jac who had a sore back and he'd demonstrated harder versions of the exercises for some of the more agile attendees.

"Time to wriggle those toes and fingers now, girls," he said. "Wake up those limbs, roll over and slowly get to your feet."

There were a few groans.

"Can't I just stay here?" Jac pleaded.

"Take your time," he laughed.

Once they were all on their feet he took them through some stretches and they were done. As always, at the end of his class everyone clapped. Two of the younger mums strolled over to him and Chelsea joined them for a chat. They were all a similar age and had probably been in some of the same classes at school over the years. Briony had lost track of who fitted where.

"How good to have a few new young ones along." Jean nodded in Blake's direction. "He does such a good job, doesn't he?"

"He certainly made us work today."

"I just go at the same pace regardless. At my age it's not good to get up too much of a sweat." Jean chuckled. "I might strain something."

Briony patted at her damp neck with her towel.

"It's nice to see Sarah back again," Jean said. "I wonder how many will stay for lunch? We're quite a group today."

The young ones all laughed loudly at something and Jean drew Briony to the side.

"Have you spoken with Marion?"

"No."

"Oh, that's a pity. You two are family and you've done so much together in the past. It would be a shame to let something as silly as that old time capsule come between you."

"I didn't find it silly. It was unkind and hurtful gossip. Now my children have heard some terrible lies about their grandfather that they can't unhear. I find it hard to forgive Marion for that."

"You forget that Colin was my brother as well as your father. I knew him better than most and sadly the gossip was based on fact."

Briony glanced around but everyone else was in their own little groups chatting. "How can you say that about your own brother?" she hissed.

"I don't mean to upset you, dear, but someone has to tell you the truth. Your dad was a lovely man but he wandered."

Briony clapped a hand to her mouth.

"Jill, God rest her soul, worked extremely hard to hide the truth and I worry she may have passed that trait on to you." Jean pinned her with a penetrating gaze full of concern.

Briony shrunk back and sucked in a breath between her fingers. It wasn't as if she hadn't known. In spite of her mother's hard work at keeping up appearances, the school playground had been a difficult place for Briony in her pretty dresses and shiny shoes. Other kids were quick to tell stories if they thought it brought her down a peg or two. She'd heard every rumour about her dad but she'd never mentioned it. Instead Briony had taken her mother's lead, put on a smiling face and proceeded as if they were the perfect family.

"Hello, Aunty Jean." Chelsea crossed the room to join them. "Mum, I'm catching a ride with Blake."

"Okay."

"Are you all right?" Chelsea frowned at her. "You might have worked a bit hard, you're looking pale."

"I'm fine."

"Have you had plenty of water today?"

"Yes." Briony waggled the water bottle she clutched in one hand.

"We're going to put the kettle on and have some lunch," Jean said. "I assume you young ones aren't staying?"

"We're all going to Paige's place for a catch-up. We haven't seen each other for ages."

"Lovely for her to mix with some people closer to her age, not just us old dears," Jean said.

Chelsea joined the young group heading to the door. Blake waved and Paige said she'd see them all next week.

The noise volume in the hall lowered suddenly with only half-a-dozen women left.

"You have three wonderful children, Briony," Jean said. "Concentrate on the here and now, not what's been."

That was what Jean didn't understand. The here and now was as troublesome as the past.

"Ready for lunch, girls?" Gloria called.

Briony was thankful for the interruption so she could escape Jean's scrutiny and even happier when Jean settled in next to Gloria and chatted away. By the grim set of Gloria's mouth Briony was guessing Jean was imparting more of her conciliatory wisdom.

Paige couldn't believe she had all these people in her house. Blake was the only male besides the kids but he knew almost everyone. Like Chelsea he'd grown up in Badara with Jac and Jo. Only the third woman, Beth, was new to the district like Paige, but she'd married a bloke they'd all gone to school with so she had a connection. Jac had collected her baby, toddler and four-year-old from her mum and Jo her little girl from a friend, and Beth had collected her son from pre-school at the same time Paige had got Levi. He was loving having kids his age to visit. They were all busy with the assorted toys in the sunroom off the kitchen.

The three women who were mothers all had food with them, and between them and Paige they fed the kids and created a picking plate of cheese, dips, crackers and fruit for the adults to share around the kitchen table. The conversation was all about people Paige didn't know. She thought longingly of similar catch-ups she'd had with Niesha and a few other neighbours. Times changed and she was going to do her best to form new friendships. She sat back, simply enjoying some company around her own age.

"Why did you move to Badara, of all places?" Jo's question brought her into the conversation.

Paige gave her usual spiel about needing a tree change and the appeal of the old house when she'd found it online.

"What have you been doing with yourself?" Chelsea asked. "I grew up in the district but Badara's the back of beyond."

"Maybe for you." Jac had been feeding her baby and lifted the tiny bub to her shoulder, gently patting her back. "Some of us like it here."

"I don't mind the quiet," Paige said quickly. There'd been a spark between Jac and Chelsea a couple of times during the conversation over lunch.

"How long are you back for, Chelsea?" Jo asked. "Your lovely man must be missing you."

A look passed between sister and brother.

"Chels came home to spend time with me," Blake said.

"Must be cosy at your place with you all living at home."

"I heard you were staying at Port Kent," Jac said to Blake.

"That's right. Mum's been watching too many home reno shows." Blake laughed. "She's turned my room into a library. It's a work in progress."

The kettle boiled and Paige suggested they take their coffees into the lounge.

Beth admired the rug on the couch just as the older women had on their visit. "I've been learning to crochet recently," she said.

"My gran made this." Paige raised one corner and inspected the well-washed squares. "I wish she'd had a chance to teach me. I'd like something to do at night when the little ones are in bed."

"You should join the CWA," Beth said.

"Why would she want to do that?" Chelsea scoffed.

"Don't knock the collective wisdom of the group," Jac said.

"It's a gossip club."

There was a heartbeat's silence while Paige thought back over the lunch conversation and Chelsea quizzing the others about people they'd grown up with and how quite a few personal details of other people's lives had been shared around the kitchen table. What had that been if not gossip?

"I joined when they had the guest speaker from the flying doctor," Jac said. "The CWA hold some great fundraisers and not all of the money goes out of the community. They bought that new bench at the kindy and helped fund the garden around it."

"I joined to learn how to crochet," Beth said. "There are so many skills among the group of women who go."

"I'd love to learn." Paige filled the brief pause that followed Chelsea's raised-eyebrow look. "My gran was always going to teach me but we didn't get the chance."

Her grandma had been her one beacon of kindness when Paige had fought to keep Jayden. Like the rest of the family, she'd been shocked to discover Paige was pregnant at sixteen, but unlike the rest of the family she'd recovered and been so excited to hold her great-grandson. She'd crocheted Jayden a feather-weight shawl and Paige a rug. She'd not lived long enough to meet Kodie and Levi but they'd been wrapped in the precious shawl, the next best thing to their great-grandma's arms. And the rug had been used and washed so much Paige was fearful it would fall apart one day.

"My mother-in-law used to spin and she left a cupboard full of homespun wool when she moved out of the farmhouse," Beth said. "Last year I mastered the quirky beanie but I've seen photos of some fabulous scarves and one of the ladies is going to show me how to dye the yarn so I can add some different colours. And, you know, the hot tip I learned: the best place for wool is op shops. Find some jumpers that have been knitted with good quality wool and unravel them. One of the ladies has made this amazing rug with knitted squares, all from old jumpers."

"Knitting's my thing," Blake said. "I taught myself during the UK lockdown."

His comment drew another raised-eyebrow look from his sister.

"Trust me, stuck in a tiny apartment without a few hobbies like knitting and keeping myself fit I'd have gone completely mad."

"What was that like?" Jac asked. "We had it easy here in comparison."

Paige was relieved Levi came in at that moment wanting more food. It hadn't been the same as Blake's experience, but living in Victoria she had enough lockdown stories of her own without listening to more.

When Paige returned from the kitchen the others were making moves to leave.

"How much longer are you staying, Blake?" Jo asked.

"A few more weeks."

"We'll have to find a replacement instructor before you leave us."

"When I first started we had someone called Courtney," Paige said.

Jac screwed up her nose. "She was the reason we didn't go. She's a piece of work, that one."

Paige had to admit she hadn't enjoyed Courtney's class as much as Blake's but they didn't have a lot of choice out here.

"Well, girls, you might have to suck it up and get used to her." Blake gave Jac a playful pat on the back. "I will have to go back to Sydney eventually. I've got my feelers out for a couple of jobs there."

Beth's little boy came in whining about a toy one of the others had.

"Time to go, I think," she said. "Kindy always wears him out."

The group disbanded, gathering up anything they'd brought, and Beth, Blake and Chelsea headed off while Jac and Jo went to the sunroom to round up their kids.

Beth stopped at the front door. "Would you like me to let you know about the next CWA meeting?" she asked. "Jac and I are the youngest but the women are a cross-section of ages and I've found everyone very welcoming. They even take it in turns to run a creche." She gave a tentative smile. "You seem to be settling in well but I didn't find it easy moving here from Perth. Perth's isolated but at least it's a city."

"Thanks," Paige said. "I'd like to give it a go."

"Let's swap phone numbers."

They did, and after final farewells Paige wandered back inside, smiling to herself over the fun morning she'd had. Halfway along the passage Jo and Jac came into view, their backs to her as they bent over her family photo.

"Do you think Dane would be interested?" Jo spoke in a hushed tone.

"That poor family's been through so much already without adding more kids to the mix. And if that story about Sarah is true, they could have another member of their family turn up out of the blue."

"You've got to wonder how they kept that quiet for so long."

"Sarah Townsend would be the last person you'd expect to have a secret baby."

Paige thought she'd heard Sarah's name mentioned earlier when Jac and Chelsea were in a huddle. Obviously someone had been blabbing. She trod heavier on the wooden floor.

Jac and Jo straightened abruptly. Their blonde ponytails flicked in unison as they turned to face her with quick grins.

"Lovely family snap," Jo said.

"Is Jayden enjoying footy practice?" Jac asked.

Paige pulled her own fake smile to hide her annoyance. "He hasn't started yet. Next week, I think."

"Our hubbies have been back at practice for a while." Jo patted her stomach. "The excesses of summer to work off."

"There's been nothing but complaining about aches and pains," Jac added. The baby in the capsule began to make stirring noises. "Speaking of complaining. This little one will want to be fed again soon."

"We gave the kids two more minutes," Jo said. "They're having such a good time they didn't want to leave."

Jac picked up the capsule. "Time's up, kids," she called.

Paige couldn't wait to see them off. They were nice enough but their propensity for gossip annoyed her. By the sound of it, news had spread about Sarah's teenage pregnancy. And had they been insinuating she and Dane might be an item? How dare they? The last thing Paige wanted from a man was an intimate relationship. She'd had three and they'd all ended in heartbreak. Her cheeks warmed and her annoyance returned. Of the four women who she'd let into her home, Beth had been the only one Paige had felt truly comfortable with. She hoped Beth felt the same way.

twenty-six

Marion's landline rang. She stopped polishing the glass, debating if it was worth getting down from the stepladder. Then she thought even a telemarketer might be a welcome diversion from cleaning windows. She couldn't believe she was so desperate for something to do that she'd been driven to washing windows. Once again she'd been sad to think she was missing her Tuesday morning fitness club. She'd been determined to take her mind off it with a big project. The house windows hadn't been cleaned for years. Len had raised his eyebrows when she'd said no to his question about her attending fitness and that she was washing windows instead but he'd made no comment. In fact, he'd hardly said anything of significance since they'd returned from their accountant meeting the previous week. Any attempt of hers to broach the subject of selling the property had been met with silence.

The insistent ring of the phone won. She picked up.

"Hello, Marion."

"Jean." Marion wasn't sure she should have answered. No doubt she'd be in for one of Jean's kindly lectures.

"You'll be pleased to know the CWA are happy to convene the stalls at the family games afternoon for the Back to Badara Festival."

"Great." Marion had given little thought to the festival. It had all been soured by the reading of her news report and the fallout that had ensued.

"And we had a big group at exercise class. More young ones. It's a pity you weren't there."

"My absence might be the reason for the bigger numbers."

"Nonsense. Blake's the reason. I don't know what we'll do when that boy goes back to Sydney."

Marion murmured her agreement. She was enjoying Blake's company beyond the classes. She'd miss his regular visits and their occasional catch-up at the shack. More than her she worried for Len. He and Blake had become so close during the last few weeks.

"Briony said she hasn't seen you since you left fitness group."

"You know why."

"But you've caught up with Sarah and Gloria?"

"You're well informed."

"You might get a call from Sarah. She was sorry you weren't at class."

"I don't imagine Gloria was, or Briony."

"Gloria can be a tough nut to crack but life hasn't been easy for her."

"I know as well as anyone how hard Gloria worked to send those boys away for their further education. She cleaned the school for years and worked part-time at the pub at Port Kent to help get enough money together. She still works hard cooking and cleaning for them all."

"She's a fair person. She'll come round eventually. And I hope you'll see Briony soon. That'll be everyone covered and you can come back and join us again. Time is marching on and there's so much to plan and do for the festival. Do you use Facebook?"

"A little."

"Paige has set up the site or platform or whatever it's called. She used my ID to make it so now I'm on Facebook. Can you believe it? Evidently she needed that so she could make a separate page for our festival. It's called Badara Community News. She said it meant anyone could join and keep sharing news even once the festival is done."

"Good idea."

"Well, dear, I'd best be off. We hope you'll come to mahjong tomorrow. Keith especially. He's not keen to keep filling in. He's worried I'll ask him to wear a skirt next."

Jean's cheerful chortle brought a smile to Marion's lips.

"I'll let you know tomorrow."

Marion replaced the handset and turned to look at her gleaming kitchen window. She'd only done half the house, deciding to take down the curtains and wash them at the same time. She'd lost her momentum now.

Sometime in the middle of last night she'd had a brain wave about what she could give Briony as a conciliation gift. Now that that was sorted there really was no reason to put off visiting her sister-in-law, except Marion would prefer the house wasn't full of extra family.

Len and Vince spoke regularly and Len had reported Vince was trying to keep out of Briony's upset with Marion. She retrieved her mobile phone from her bag and selected her brother's number.

Vince answered almost immediately. "What is it, Marion?"

"You sound stressed."

"I've got several jobs on the go and not one person here to help me."

"Briony's not home then?"

"Yes, she got back just after lunch but she had some jobs of her own to do and she's been so uptight lately I decided to leave her be. If one of my children were at home it'd be helpful, but Maddie's off somewhere with a damn horse and Chelsea and Blake have gone to Port Kent for a bloody coffee. Sometimes I wonder why I'm busting my arse."

"Did they know you needed help?"

"There's always work to be done."

"Perhaps you need to be more specific with your expectations."

"I don't have time for a lecture from you, Marion."

"Very well, I won't keep you. I was hoping to call on Briony to apologise and try to mend the bridge."

"Well, good luck with that."

"You don't think this is the right time?"

"To be honest, I don't know when the right time would be but she's home alone so now's as good a time as any."

"All right."

"And, Marion…good luck."

Marion stared at the blank screen. Vince rarely sounded so despondent. Between him and Len and the fallout from the time capsule her world was a cheerless place at the moment. It made her all the more determined to call on Briony. The two of them had got their men through the bad times of poor wool prices, drought years, floods and every other thing farming had thrown at them. Surely they could come together again now to sort their men out.

Only half an hour later Marion pulled up at Briony's. She took the container of sausage rolls from the esky but couldn't manage the gift she'd brought as well, so she decided to leave it in the boot for the moment.

She followed the path through the beautifully manicured garden. It had been a mix of all kinds of plants in Vera's day, more cottage garden in appearance, but Briony had removed some, added a few drought-tolerant varieties and created more structure. Marion admired her work. Gardening was something she'd never enjoyed. At her place there was a bit of lawn, some hardy Australian natives and a few tough plants like daisies and lavender.

The back door opened.

"I thought I heard a vehicle," Briony said. "I'm expecting a delivery. I was hoping it would be my new couch."

"Only me." Marion held out the container of sausage rolls. "I've come to apologise."

Briony pushed the door wider but ignored Marion's offering. "You'd better come in then."

Marion stepped into the cool interior of the old stone farmhouse. It had been her childhood home but she no longer felt any nostalgic connection. Briony had made so many changes since she'd moved in. The door to Blake's old room was open.

"The couch is going in there." Briony waved her hand half-heartedly as she passed.

Marion glanced in at the room that had once been Vera's sewing room then Blake's bedroom and was now lined with sets of bookcases.

"It looks lovely," she said but Briony didn't acknowledge her comment.

"Would you like a coffee?"

It was getting late in the day for Marion to drink coffee but she accepted the offer, hoping it meant that her sister-in-law was at least open to a chat. Briony busied herself at the machine and Marion sat at the table. She put the container of sausage rolls to one side wondering how she was going to start the conversation now that she was here.

"Did you call on Vera last week?" she asked.

"Of course I did."

Marion blinked at the force of Briony's words. "It wasn't an accusation, purely a question. She had some lovely roses. I thought they'd be from your garden but you know how she is, five minutes after you've gone she forgets you've been there."

"They were the best of what I had left in the side garden." Briony carried the mugs of coffee to the table and set one down in front of Marion. "Your mum planted those roses so I like to take her some every so often."

"It's kind of you."

"It's no trouble. Vera's always been good to me."

There was a challenge in Briony's look as if to say *unlike her daughter.* Or perhaps Marion was simply feeling guilty.

"I'm sorry for the things we wrote about your family in the time capsule news report," Marion said.

Briony looked down at the coffee mug she gripped with two hands.

"It was the stupid stories of two silly teenagers," Marion went on to fill the silence. "It was unkind and I'm ashamed to admit my part in it."

Briony continued to look at her mug.

"You're my brother's wife. You're my favourite sister-in-law." Marion paused briefly, waiting for Briony's response that she was her only sister-in-law, but Briony remained silent. "We've been good friends for so long. I hope you can forgive me."

Finally Briony looked up, her gaze falling harshly on Marion. "If we're being honest, good friends is probably an exaggeration, don't you think? We're in-laws, our family is small, we live in a small community. Families should always show a united front."

"Are you saying your sisterhood is all an act?" Marion said.

"I'm saying we're both sensible adults who know the score and do what we have to." Briony's look was calculating.

"I agree we're not close friends and in each other's pockets, but if you're trying to retaliate and hurt me by saying we haven't had friendship over the years...well, then you've succeeded."

This time it was Briony who flinched. She quickly looked back at her mug.

"What about all the days before children when we camped together?" Marion said. "The fishing trips, the holidays, and then our kids being born, the special milestones, the shared child-minding and all those shack holidays together. Helping each other when parents died, and all the times when your husband or mine was sinking under the weight of whatever was happening on the farm and we collectively supported them through it. I didn't do that to keep up appearances, Briony. I did it because I cared for you."

"All right!" Briony lifted her head. Big tears rolled down her cheeks. "You don't have to lay it on. Of course I remember all that."

"Then please don't let something I wrote fifty years ago that I don't even know was true spoil our relationship."

Briony sat perfectly still across the table. Marion's plea appeared to have fallen on deaf ears. She was ready to give up and go home when Briony's hand snaked out and peeled the lid from the container. She removed a sausage roll and took a big bite. "Mmm! Chicken. You know I love these more when they're cold than I do hot," she mumbled through her mouthful.

Marion slid one from the container and took a bite. "I do too."

They smiled at each other as they ate. It was a small tentative step towards reconciliation.

Briony chewed some more then swallowed. "Thank you, Marion."

"You're welcome. You can keep them all for yourself or share them with your family, I don't mind."

"I meant for your apology but, yes, also for the sausage rolls. I will do my best to put it behind us."

"I'm glad."

"I was trying to protect my children from the gossip of the past."

"I understand, and they would never have heard anything from me if it hadn't been for that wretched time capsule."

Briony picked up her coffee. "Ugh! It's cold. Here," she reached out a hand for Marion's mug, "I'll make us a fresh one."

"Before you do I have something else for you."

"It's really not necessary."

"I hope you'll accept my gift in the spirit it's given. I truly want to show my remorse in a tangible way. It's in the boot of my car and it'll take two of us."

"Okay." Briony eyed her warily and followed her outside.

They lifted a sealed box each from Marion's boot. "Careful, they're heavy."

"You've got me intrigued now."

As soon as they'd set the boxes on the table, Briony ripped the sticky tape from one and peered inside. "Oh, Marion," she gasped like a child opening a parcel from Father Christmas. "Your mother's dinner set." She lifted the top plate from the box and held it to the light then clutched it to her chest. "I've always loved this dinner set. How did you know?"

"Mum told me how much you liked it."

"But she gave it to you when she shifted."

"I know, but I have so much stuff I truly don't need it. It's been shut away in the cupboard, which is a shame. It's Albert Meakin so—"

"Alfred!"

Marion frowned.

Briony turned the plate over and pointed to the writing on the back. "Alfred Meakin and the design is Hamptons."

"Whatever it is, Mum and Dad were given it when they were married and Mum loved to use it for family gatherings. It should be on display and used again. I know Mum would agree if she still had all her marbles."

Briony clutched the plate to her again. "I've always loved it. This is so kind of you, Marion. I promise I'll take good care of it." She put the plate carefully back in the box and dashed around the table, throwing her arms around Marion and kissing her cheek.

Marion stood rigid as a statue then slowly raised her arms and gently patted Briony's back. She was glad Briony was talking to her again but they'd never been ones for too much hugging and kissing.

"Bugger the coffee," Briony said. "It's after four. Let's have a glass of wine."

Briony glanced towards the boxes against her kitchen wall. It had been very generous of Marion to give her the dinner set. Maybe it was that or perhaps it was the wine but Briony was finding it easier to move on after Marion's apology. She'd only let her in because Vincent had insisted. Marion's reminder about all the things they'd weathered together had swayed her. They were family after all, and family had to present a united front.

Briony was so relaxed she found herself suggesting Marion should come back to their Tuesday fitness club.

"We had more than a dozen there this morning. It was a great class."

"I've been going to Blake's class on Thursday mornings at Port Kent, but I must admit I miss the Badara group."

"You could do both."

A vehicle pulled up outside and Briony crossed to the window. "It's Blake bringing Chelsea home."

"Do you want me to go?"

"No, of course not." Briony watched to make sure Blake was getting out of the car and not just dropping his sister off. They both paused as another ute arrived. Briony returned to the table and whisked the glasses away. "I'll get rid of the evidence though. Madeline's home too. It's a bit early for everyone to settle in for a drink. I've still got dinner to prepare."

"You're lucky you have your children close."

Briony shut the dishwasher door on the glasses and turned back. "Am I?"

"I thought once I retired we'd be off to visit our kids, make a holiday of it now that I'm not governed by school terms, but I didn't factor in the farm."

"I know what you mean. These men are hard to lever away from the property. And I guess harder for Len; at least we have Madeline—"

"At least you have Madeline for what?" Chelsea asked as she strolled in, closely followed by Blake.

He stopped in the doorway, looked from Briony to Marion and smiled. "Hello. Good to see my two most favourite women are together again."

Briony felt a ripple of pleasure to be included in his genial words.

"Oh, yes," Chelsea said. "Hello, Aunty Marion."

"What's this about me?" Madeline was two steps behind her sister.

"It doesn't matter," Briony said. "Did you two have a nice catch-up with your friends?"

"We did," Blake said.

"Kind of," Chelsea added. "There was a lot of gossip."

"To be fair, we asked lots of questions about people we haven't seen for years." Blake sat beside Marion.

"Jac always was one for the inside goss on everyone. Even back at school. Now that I think of it, I'm pretty sure she was the one who told me about Grandad."

"Chelsea!" Briony did not want that topic brought up again.

"She told me Sarah Townsend had a baby when she was in her teens and it was adopted out."

"Really?" Madeline's eyes widened.

Briony met Marion's worried look.

"Well, she certainly is a gossip," Briony said. "I hope you didn't tell her you and Brandon are having a break."

"Mum!" Chelsea jabbed a finger at her own chest. "I can tell or not tell people as I choose. And word will be out that Blake's gay soon as well. Jac asked Blake that many questions today, I'm sure she's worked it out for herself."

"How would she know?" Blake said.

"If the conversation about your pre-lockdown lifestyle in London wasn't enough—"

"I mixed with plenty of straight people doing the same stuff."

"What about the hasty change of your ex-partner's name from Brian to Breeanne. It was so obvious, Blake."

"I'm not used to hiding it." He glanced around. "Except here."

Chelsea turned on Briony. "This is what happens when you keep things secret. They end up being a bigger deal than they should be."

"No, this is what happens when you don't follow the rules."

"What rules?"

"The rules of life."

"Oh, for f—"

"I have to tell you all something," Blake cut in.

Briony steeled herself against yet more bad news. She'd be sorry if he was leaving but maybe it would be best for now.

"My...Gab is coming next week, in time for Easter. He'll be staying a week or so with me at Port Kent." Blake looked to Marion, who nodded.

The back door banged and heavy footsteps pounded along the passage. Vince appeared in the doorway, his hat still on his head and his—

"Vincent!" Briony snapped. "Your boots!"

"To hell with my boots! What are you lot doing?"

Briony paused. Vincent was rarely so visibly angry. Something had really upset him. "The kids have only just arrived home from—"

"That's it! I've had it up to my armpits. This farm goes up for sale and I'm retiring."

He spun around to leave. "Oh, hello, Marion. Didn't see you there."

"Vince." Marion nodded but he'd already stormed back out the door. His boots thudded along the new hall runner then the bathroom door shut with a bang.

"What's got up his nose?" Chelsea asked.

"He probably needed help today and I wasn't here." Madeline had the grace to look guilty.

"He only has to ask," Chelsea said.

"I guess we've all been coming and going like we're on holiday," Blake said.

"We are."

"Not for much longer," Briony said. "And if you're all staying for dinner you can help prepare it in a few minutes."

"It's about time Maddie stepped up," Chelsea said.

"I do lots around here," Madeline snapped.

Marion pushed her chair back from the table. "I'd better get going."

"I'll see you out." Briony followed her, grateful for the interruption. "Sorry you had to be caught up in all that."

Marion had reached her car. She turned back. "I know our relationship has taken a battering so you probably don't want to hear advice from me."

"But you're going to give it anyway." Briony folded her arms. "Vincent will calm down."

"This isn't about Vince." Marion grimaced. "It's about Blake. I'm only adding to what Chelsea said. When you keep a secret you have to bury it so deep no-one can ever find out, and as we've recently discovered that's not easy. Blake's a young man wanting to live his life in the best way for him. It might not be the choice you'd make for him but you should accept him for who he is. Don't try to hide it or you might lose him altogether and set local tongues wagging when there's no need."

Briony forgot Marion was bossing her again. Instead she was mesmerised by the sorrow etched on her sister-in-law's face rather than by her words. She placed a hand on Marion's arm. "Is everything all right with you, Marion? Len and the kids are okay?"

The vulnerable look was replaced by Marion's usual steely determination. "They're all fine. As I said, I miss Grant and

Roxanne but that's life. You let your kids make their own choices and sometimes that takes them far away from you." She straightened. "But they're not on a wooden ship sailing off to a foreign land. How awful it must have been for mothers hundreds of years ago." Her lips turned up in that strange grimace that was Marion's smile. "Thank goodness for modern technology."

"That's true."

Marion got into her car and lowered her window. "Thanks for today."

"I'm glad you came. And say hello to Roxanne and Grant from us when you talk to them next."

Briony waved Marion off, not certain what kids making their own choices had to do with sailing ships. Sometimes Marion spoke in riddles. Briony turned back and studied her home then took a deep breath and marched back inside. She had to sort out what was going on with Vincent.

twenty-seven

Marion wasn't sure which of her feelings was the strongest: gratitude for Briony's acceptance of her apology, sorrow for not having seen her children in a long time, envy of Briony having family all close by, or worry for Len, for his fear of leaving the farm and for the secret they'd kept for so long that was suddenly bearing down on her all over again. And Vince had nearly blown a gasket. Marion worried about him too. Their dad had died after a heart attack when he was not much older than Vince.

She was so lost in her thoughts she didn't hear Len come inside but the sound of water running in the bathroom made her look at the clock. Five thirty and she hadn't thought about dinner. By the time he arrived in the kitchen she'd defrosted some beef and pork sausages and was starting on her quick and easy meatball lasagne.

"That smells good," Len said.

Marion smiled. Onion cooking always smelled good. "I've had a busy day so it's only one of my one-pot wonders tonight."

"You know I enjoy whatever you make."

Marion turned back to the sausages she'd been breaking apart to create instant meatballs.

"How did you get on with Briony, love? All good there now?"

She put the lid on the pan and turned it down to simmer.

"I think so. At least as far as Briony and I are concerned. I'm not so sure about how she's accepting what's going on with her children though. And Vince is sounding stressed. I think that whole family need to sit down and have a big conversation about their future. He stormed in and said he was selling up."

"He's mentioned it a few times."

"To you?"

Len nodded. "I think he's frustrated that Madeline won't make a commitment. She says she wants to take on the farm but they've got a huge property. She couldn't manage it on her own, and now Chelsea's marriage has failed he's worried about her. I told him it's Briony and the kids he needs to be discussing it with. You're right, duck, talking it through is the only way they'll sort it out."

Len sat at the table, a huge sigh escaping his lips.

"What is it, Len? You haven't had another accident, have you?"

He shook his head but offered nothing more.

Marion took two beers from the fridge and passed him one. "We've been pretty good communicators over the years."

He pulled the top from the can and raised it in the air. "You've taught me about communication."

She raised hers and took a sip. "I don't know. Your mum was a pretty good talker."

He spluttered and wiped beer from his chin with the back of his hand. "She sure was but I'm not sure that my dear mum did a lot of listening."

Marion smirked and silently apologised to her mother-in-law, but at least Len was smiling now.

"What would she make of me selling the farm?" he said quietly.

"You've decided to sell?" There must be something in the air today. First Vince's outburst and now this.

He nodded. "I was going to talk to the agent but then Ted's spoken to me about buying the place."

Ted was their neighbour. He owned property almost all the way around them. "Would make sense for him to buy it."

"If this year's a good year, and all the old timers are saying the signs are there, we might be better off to sell and make a clean break."

"If you're sure?"

"I thought it was what you wanted."

"Len, it's your farm."

"Ours."

"Yes, but I don't feel the same way about it that you do. I don't want to force you off but, yes, I think you should leave while we're still fit enough to do a few things. And I don't want to live in Badara. Not that I'd ever thought we'd retire there, but the goings-on of the last few weeks have made me realise I could never move into town. Not that town anyway and Wirini Bay's too big. I like Port Kent and you do too. You know all the golfers and you'd soon pick up other things to do."

"I think I could make a go of it there."

Marion spirits rose with the possibilities. "If we sold the farm we could knock down the old shack and build a nice new house."

"It's not yours yet."

"But Mum's left it to me."

"And last time I visited she was still alive."

"We've been over this, Len. Vince doesn't care about the shack. They don't holiday there now the kids are grown up and he only ever stays if you're there. In his eyes it's already mine."

Len put a hand in the air. "You know how I feel about it, Marion."

When he said her name like that she knew there was no point in pushing it. Len rarely dug his heels in, but he had when it came to ownership of the shack. She decided to change the subject.

"I think someone from our fitness group has let on about Sarah having the baby all those years ago. Chelsea and Blake came back from a get-together with some of the younger locals and it had been mentioned."

"That young woman in town, the new one – Paige, was it? Maybe she's said something."

"I don't think so. She's not the gossipy type and, besides, she and Sarah have formed a friendship. They seem quite close, actually."

"Briony has always been a stickler for no gossip and I'm guessing it wasn't Jean either."

"Which just leaves Gloria."

"Could have been someone else who's known about it."

"Bit of a coincidence it gets a mention not long after the blasted time capsule reveal." She was glad Gloria had stopped after she read out the piece about her. If she'd continued on like Jean had…A shiver wriggled down Marion's spine. The old news report was gone. She'd watched Jean burn it.

"Gloria's had a tough life, duck. Growing up with two rough-and-ready brothers – I know they're your cousins but they weren't gentlemen. Then having three sons of her own and living in that all-male household and working day in, day out to look after them all and help with the finances. Gossip gives her something to take her mind off all that, I guess."

"It doesn't make it right."

"Of course not, and here we are maligning her and she may not have said a word."

Marion pursed her lips. Len always saw the best in people.

"Speaking of not saying a word," he said. "How do you think things are going with Blake and Briony?"

"Still not good, I gather. She loves her son but she can't accept his sexuality. And she's determined it needs to be kept a secret."

"That's what Vince says."

"You two have been talking a lot by the sound of it."

Something about the way Len looked away and offered to get them another beer bothered her.

"We usually only have one beer a night during the week."

"I feel like another."

"Okay, thanks." She waited for him to sit again. "When exactly were you and Vince talking?"

"He rang me to check in about the post-hole digger incident. Blake had told him about it." Len gave a sheepish shrug. "Reminded me to ask for help when I needed it."

"He can talk," Marion snorted, thinking of the kerfuffle her brother had made with his fiery entrance. "What did he say about Briony and Blake?"

"That would be gossip if I told you."

"No, it wouldn't. You didn't overhear the conversation, you were part of it, and you're sharing with me. I'm your wife and Vince's sister. Did Vince ask you not to tell me?"

"No."

"Well then?"

"Vince is worried about Blake."

"Naturally."

Len avoided her gaze again.

"He doesn't want him to have to hide who he is."

"Of course he shouldn't."

A pained expression crossed Len's face and he looked down.

"Len?"

His finger tapped agitatedly on the side of his can, then slowly he lifted his head. Deep lines of sorrow etched his face and tears pooled.

"Oh, no, Len." Marion struggled to her feet. She knocked over her almost empty can but she ignored the beer that trailed across the table. "Tell me you didn't...you couldn't have..."

"We talked about Blake, duck. We're both worried about him and Briony's unrealistic expectations. You know that."

"But you told him more than that, didn't you?" Marion was finding it hard to breathe now.

"He's known for years." Len looked at her imploringly. "I told him a long time ago."

"How long ago?"

"When you left me."

Marion clapped a hand to her head.

"I know we were keeping it between us, duck. It was what we both wanted but you've got to remember how scared I was back then. You were living at Port Kent and I thought I'd lost you for good. Vince called in here one day. I was a mess and...it just...it just spilled out."

"My brother has known about you...me...about us all these years?" Marion was glad it was a while since she'd eaten or she was sure the contents of her stomach would have erupted like lava from a volcano. Somehow she got to her feet, ignored Len's worried look and tried not to stagger as she walked away.

twenty-eight

Levi and Kodie were having a great time on the playground with several other kids. Paige had driven Jayden the couple of k's out to the oval for his first footy practice and as soon as the little ones had seen the kids and the playground beside the clubrooms they'd begged to be allowed to play.

Paige's original idea had been to drop Jayden, take the younger ones home for a bath and early dinner and then they'd go back for Jayden but she'd been foiled by the brightly coloured playground. It was large, with lots of equipment. She wondered if they were allowed to use it any time. It was a pity the small playground in town wasn't half as well equipped. While the kids played she stayed in the car also watching Jayden and the rest of the team do a series of exercises. Her dad had been a Titans fan and Ari had barracked for the Warriors so she'd watched a bit of rugby league in her time but she knew little about Aussie Rules.

Jayden's eagerness to play the game had been the catalyst she'd used to get him to agree to have some tutoring with Marion. He remembered her as the stern woman who'd brought the sausage rolls and he hadn't been keen but Paige had shamelessly used footy as the carrot to get him to try.

A squeal from Kodie drew her attention back to the kids. She was scrambling up a small rock wall to avoid the child chasing her. They were having so much fun Paige knew she'd have trouble getting them to come home.

She got out of the car and waved to them. "Five more minutes!"

There were groans so she knew they'd heard her but they hardly paused in the game they were playing.

"It's a great place for kids," Dane said as he walked over to her.

She grinned. "I don't know how I'll get them home."

"I've come in with Zuri. A few of us are doing some jobs while the boys train."

"You don't play?"

"Nah, the leg I broke in the accident always gives me curry. I watch from the sidelines these days and help out as team manager. I'm glad I caught you though."

They were both distracted by a yell from the playground.

"Part of the game, I think," Paige said and looked back at Dane. "Was there something you wanted?"

"No, well, yes…I wondered, are you going to be around over Easter?"

"As in this coming weekend?"

"Yeah."

"We don't have any plans."

"I wondered if you'd like to have a pub meal with me. Just us."

"Oh….I…"

"Bad idea."

"It's not." Paige recalled Jac and Jo's conversation. She didn't want Dane to be under any illusion she was looking for a man in her life. "I enjoy our friendship but I'm not looking for anything more. My focus has to be on my kids now. I don't have time for—"

"Woah!" Dane held up a hand. "I'm offering dinner at the pub, not a lifetime commitment."

Paige winced and the familiar heat warmed her cheeks. Why did she have to be one of those people who glowed like a beacon when they were embarrassed? "Sorry," she muttered. "Only I overheard some women talking about...well, you being single and me..."

"Let me guess...Jac?"

"Right first time."

"She's always on the lookout to set me up. Her heart's in the right place but that's not why I'm asking you out. I remember how difficult it was to have some adult time when Zuri was little, and I was lucky enough to have family nearby. I can't imagine how much harder it must be for you on your own with three."

"Oh." Paige wished she had a shovel to dig herself a hole to hide in. "That's very kind of you but—"

"Mum's offered to come and sit with your kids. We could go Friday or Saturday night to Port Kent pub or there's a couple of options in Wirini Bay."

She hadn't been for a proper meal out in a long time.

"It wouldn't be a late night," Dane said. "Just two single parents taking a break from wrangling kids."

"It must be tough managing a seventeen-year-old."

"Almost eighteen, and you'd better believe it." He smiled. "You don't want to know what's ahead of you."

Paige was swayed. "Two friends out for a meal?"

"Sure, and my shout, please."

"Oh no. I can't have free childcare and a free meal."

Levi let out a wail. He was sprawled on the bark chips at the bottom of the slippery dip, his solid little legs kicking up and down.

"I wondered when he'd lose his biscuits," Paige said. "He was tired before we got here. Time to go."

"So you'll come?" Dane asked.

Levi's wailing was drawing the attention of other parents. Kodie was standing beside him, arms folded with a face like thunder. At least if he was making all that noise Paige was sure he wasn't truly hurt.

"Yes, thanks." She headed towards her son.

"I'll call you."

She waved and walked faster. Levi was yelling even louder and trying to kick Kodie who was screaming back at him. Dane's offer shone like a beacon of pleasure compared to the evening she had ahead of her.

Briony checked the casserole in the oven. She and Vincent would probably be the only ones to eat it. After she'd come back inside from seeing Marion off, Blake had left for Port Kent, Chelsea had shut herself in her room and Madeline had gone out to see to her horses. Briony had prepared dinner by herself. She knew the girls would come for food eventually but they could dish their own. At the moment it was her husband who needed her support. He'd feel better with some food in his stomach and perhaps a beer or two.

She went in search of him and was surprised to find he wasn't in the house. He'd showered and changed and she'd thought he'd be watching TV but he was nowhere inside. She tapped on Chelsea's door and when there was no answer she poked her head in.

Chelsea had her back to the door. Briony could see she had her phone in her hand and her earbuds in.

Vincent must have gone outside. It was so unlike him to not say where he was going. She pressed a hand to her chest against the small niggle of fear that stirred inside her. He'd been a bit uptight lately. She knew they had differing thoughts over what was best for their children and that had been a sticking point but he was obviously bothered about the farm too. Once Madeline had settled back at home and shown interest in working the property they'd discussed the future and her taking it over. That was a few years ago now. She'd been their farm worker since then but it was a huge commitment and her heart was with her horses. They hadn't done any further planning.

Briony went outside and looked around. Where would he be? She went to the horse yards. Madeline was brushing Miss M. Briony ran a hand down the horse's neck.

"Hello, lovely," she said. She'd hardly spent any time with Madeline's newest horse. "How's she settling in?"

"Fine."

"Have you seen your dad?"

"Not since he had the tanty." Madeline stopped brushing. "I didn't know he wanted my help today. I wouldn't have gone out if I had."

"I know. We'll sort it, don't worry. He must have had a bad day. You know your dad doesn't normally have a temper. I've made a casserole if you're hungry later."

"Thanks, Mum. I've got a bit to do here then I'll be in."

Briony went to the sheds. She called Vincent but her voice was blown back to her on the balmy breeze. A shed door rattled, birds sang, the branches of a large gum waggled but each time there was no answer her anxiety ratcheted up another notch.

She walked back towards the house thinking she'd get her phone and try ringing him. On a whim she ignored the back gate, walking around the house to the front yard, and that's where she found him.

"Vincent!"

He was sitting at the cast-iron table and chair setting they rarely used on their front verandah, which was also rarely used. He looked startled as she strode towards him.

"I've been looking everywhere for you." Her relief at finding him came out as anger. "What on earth are you doing out here?"

"Calm down, love. I told Chelsea I was going to sit out the front."

Briony took the three steps to the cement verandah and pulled out the heavy chair beside him. "She didn't pass on the message. I've been looking everywhere for you."

He patted his top pocket. "You could have rung me."

"I was just going back for my phone when I saw you."

"Sorry about losing my temper," he said. "I've apologised to Chels and Blake." Once more he patted his pocket. "I'll talk to Mads when she comes in."

"What's this all about?"

"Did Blake tell you about Len nearly losing an arm the other day?"

"No!" Briony immediately thought of Marion's words before she left and the worry on her face. "Surely he's not hurt or some-one would have told me."

"Luckily just a scare. He got hooked up by the post-hole dig-ger. His shirt gave way before his arm got caught."

"Thank goodness."

"Good view across the valley from this verandah. We hardly ever look at it, do we?"

"I do. It's what we see from our bedroom window." She studied his profile as he continued to gaze at the vista in front of him. "What's going on?"

He turned back to her, and even though he'd showered and washed the grime from his face, he looked weary.

"I got fed up today. Every job I tried to do I needed help with and the kids were all off stuffing around. Then I thought of Len using the post-hole digger on his own and how that could have ended in tragedy. Once upon a time I wouldn't have given it a thought but now... he and I aren't getting any younger."

"Len's several years older than you."

"I know, and I'm not ready to retire yet but we have to seriously work out when that will be and what we'll do. None of our kids are going to take on this farm." He looked back at the view. "I was born and raised here. I love this place but I have to admit some days I wonder what I'm still doing here."

"You're tired," Briony said quickly. She'd been so wrapped up in what was happening with the children she'd not been keeping an eye on her husband. "I'm here to help and you know Madeline is available, you just have to let her know what you want. And goodness knows how much longer Chelsea will be here for but she can earn her keep too."

"All this stuff with Brandon's been tough on her, love."

"I know."

"And Maddie's looking for a place closer to Wirini Bay for the horses."

"Since when?"

"A while now, I gather."

"Why didn't she tell me? Why didn't you?"

"I only heard about it yesterday and not from Maddie. I ran into one of the real estate guys when I was in the Bay. He told me to let her know about a block going on the market soon. I haven't mentioned it yet. Haven't really had a chance."

"Is that what's upset you?"

"I was hoping she might have talked to me about it or you."

"No-one's talking to me."

"I am."

"The kids all think I'm something from the ark, but I can't help it, Vincent. Family business is family business, no-one else's."

"We don't want to force our kids to lie."

"I'm not."

"If Blake can't be himself, bring his partner to visit, then you are."

"So you think it's okay for our son to have a homosexual relationship?"

"I think it's okay for him to be who he is without worrying what we think. There're plenty of people out in the world who will judge—"

Briony lunged forward. "That's why I want him to keep it to himself. I want to protect him." She remembered her primary years when one of the local football heroes was outed. She hadn't even understood what a homosexual was then but she remembered the crude remarks and the whispers. He'd moved away but his siblings were teased mercilessly.

"You can't protect him from everything, love. You'll only make things worse when it inevitably becomes known. This is the one place he should be able to feel comfortable in his own skin. Here, with us, his family."

The lump in Briony's throat forced tears to her eyes. "I just never thought that, that we'd…that our children…"

"That we'd have a daughter on the brink of divorce, a gay son and another daughter in love with a divorcee with a ready-made family."

Briony groaned and put her head in her hands. Vince's warm hand pressed on her back then rubbed gentle circles. "We have to let them live their lives, love. If we don't, they won't want to be around us."

"You think!" She lurched up and flung out her arms. "Where are they all if not around us? They keep coming home."

"Not for much longer, by the sound of it."

"So I have to be something I'm not to accommodate my children's lives."

"You don't have to be anything but the loving mum you've always been. Our kids are who they are and we have to accept that rather than try to hide it like..." He glanced away.

"Like my mother did, you were going to say."

He shrugged.

"Can you imagine how hard it was for us living in a small community and dad behaving as he did? My mother believed in her marriage vows even if he didn't. Family and home were the most important things to her."

"Nothing wrong with that. Times were different then. Just like they were different for gay people but now we're far more accepting of difference."

"Do you honestly believe that Badara has changed that much?"

"It doesn't matter. It's what *we* believe that does." He stopped rubbing her back and squeezed her hand.

She gave him a watery smile, wishing with all her heart she could see life as he did. Vincent was her rock and it had frightened her for a moment when he'd disappeared. Getting him back on track was her main priority. She might not be able to change Blake's sexuality and he was never going to come back to the farm, but she had two daughters who might and they needed to know they had to pull their weight and help out.

twenty-nine

Marion ran on autopilot, making scrambled eggs for breakfast. Last night she had done something she hadn't done for many years. She'd slept in the spare room. Not that she'd had much sleep. Her conversation with Len had played over and over in her mind and when she'd finally dozed off she'd jolted awake again, realising she hadn't dreamed his disloyalty.

"Good morning."

Marion glanced behind her. Len was standing at the end of the table as if waiting for her permission to sit.

"The eggs are nearly ready."

"I'll make some toast."

"It's in already."

"Coffee?"

"I've got one. Your tea's in the pot ready to go."

He sat and she brought his plate of scrambled eggs to the table. She looked at her own, thinking she'd prefer to let it congeal on the plate than sit with Len but that would be childish and after only picking at her dinner the previous night she actually felt hungry. She sat and took a sip of her coffee.

"Did you sleep?" he asked.

"Not much."

Len poured his tea, picked up his knife and fork then set them down again.

"This shouldn't change anything between us, duck."

"What? That you couldn't keep the promise you made me. Not even for a short time."

"When I made the promise we'd keep our secret I'd already told Vince. I know I'm gutless but I was terrified if I told you he knew, you wouldn't stay."

"There've been plenty of opportunities for you to tell me since."

"I know."

"You remember when the counsellor suggested I have someone else to confide in?"

"Yes."

"I chose not to. I couldn't think who I'd share such a huge secret with. And all this time you've had someone besides me to be your confidant."

"I haven't really. Vince and I have never discussed it since. He knows, that's all."

Marion had always imagined once the cat was out of the bag there'd be no stuffing it back in. And yet Vince knew.

They ate their breakfast in silence. When they were finished and Marion picked up her coffee, Len spoke.

"Vince and I wondered, if we told Briony—"

"Hell, it's never-ending. Why not put a notice up on the front gate?"

"It's just a suggestion, duck."

She met her husband's tender look and the anger leaked from her but she was unsettled. They'd been a team, the two of them, for so long. She couldn't imagine that changing and yet the prickly feeling still gripped her from time to time, like it was now.

Marion's phone rang. She picked it up without checking the caller.

"Marion, it's Paige. I hope this isn't a bad time."

"Not at all."

Marion paced the kitchen as Paige explained the reason for her call. By the time they'd made some arrangements the prickles had been smoothed away by anticipation. She was glad Paige had taken up the IOU. She was quite looking forward to doing some teaching again.

"I gather that was about tutoring," Len said when she put down the phone.

"Yes. Paige wants me to work with Jayden. I'll go to their place after majhong today."

"So you're going to play again?"

"I thought I would."

"I'm glad. Things will return to normal soon enough. You'll be going back to the exercise class next."

"I'm enjoying the Thursday group at Port Kent."

"Why not do both?"

"Perhaps."

Marion had mended most of the hurts she'd caused but there was still Gloria. Marion didn't want to be the reason she stopped going to fitness. The day Marion had called on her, she'd thought Gloria had been doing a home workout. Gloria's life had been filled with male pursuits, first with her brothers and then with her husband and sons. She took little time for herself, working hard for her family. She obviously enjoyed exercising. Fitness club may be something Gloria needed more than Marion.

"I'll be working up in the shed this morning." Len pushed his hat to his head. "Ted's going to call in for an informal chat about the property."

"Oh?"

"It's only a chat. Will you be home? I thought I'd bring him in for a cuppa."

"I'll make some biscuits."

Len pecked her on the cheek. "Thanks, duck."

She listened as he pulled on his boots and set off along the path. Only a few weeks ago she'd been so restless, wanting change in her life and not knowing what. Now there was so much change afoot she was even more unsettled, and the biggest change of all was Len wanting to share the secret they'd kept, well, she had at least, for so many years.

The prickly feeling returned with a vengeance. It was as if something hung in the air she breathed, spreading its unsettling tentacles and sapping her of purpose. Marion straightened, took some long slow breaths and began to clear up the breakfast things. She had dishes to do, a batch of biscuits to bake and then some prep for her first session with Jayden. Having a plan helped soften the prickles inside her but she knew they would still be there waiting.

"I'm glad you've come back to mahjong." Jean was washing up after their afternoon tea and Marion was wiping.

"I have missed it."

"Keith said to thank you. He's much happier out in his shed than playing mahjong."

"Claire's picked it up quickly."

"Yes. She's an asset. A pity her husband's only acting principal."

"Word is the previous incumbent might not come back after her leave. If that's the case, the job would be advertised and Richard can apply. And I think Claire's a possibility to take over the exercise class with the right encouragement."

"Will you be there on Tuesday?"

Marion stopped wiping the dainty china plate she held in her hand. "I'm not sure."

"We had a large group this week." Jean's eyes sparkled. "About a dozen of us and all ages. Courtney would have been impressed."

"Gloria's still upset with me and I think she needs the class. I can go Thursdays at Port Kent."

"There's that good heart of yours thinking of others again."

Marion baulked. She didn't feel as saintly as Jean portrayed her.

"I've put Gloria on notice," Jean said. "The whole group actually. We need you back on the team. It's more than the fitness class. We've got the Back to Badara Festival to plan and no-one, not Gloria or any of the others, has come forward to take on your position as convener. I assume you're still happy to hold the role?"

Marion had had plenty of time to think about that over the last week. She'd come up with several ideas for it but wasn't sure she wanted to be front and centre.

"As long as I'm not the one making speeches and leading the parade."

"I'm sure there'll be plenty of dignitaries lining up for that. Now, if you're not going to come to class we'll need to find another time to hold our meeting."

"Why don't I come for lunch after the session next week? Gloria can still have her class and if she wants to avoid me she can excuse herself from lunch."

"That might work. Although I will be cross with Gloria if she can't forgive and forget by then. We need her on the committee too."

Marion glanced at her watch. "I have to head off to Paige's place. I'll give you a ring before next Tuesday."

"Paige told me you were going to help Jayden. That's so good of you, Marion."

"Today's a trial session to see how we get on together. He's not keen to be tutored so it might not work out."

"I have every faith in your ability."

Marion smiled but she wasn't so sure of her skills in this case. She'd been a middle school teacher for a long time and she knew only too well with young teenagers that you could lead a horse to water but you couldn't make it drink. She felt Jayden was going to be a hard nut to crack.

Levi was first to the front door when she arrived.

"Did you bring sausage rolls?"

"Levi!" Paige was right behind him.

"I didn't this time, Levi, but I did bring something else for you to share with your sister."

"Let Mrs Addicot come inside first." Paige put a restraining arm on her son and opened the door wider.

Before she'd left home Marion had rummaged in the bag of rewards she still had from her days in the classroom. She'd found a couple of supermarket collectable toys she'd thought the two younger ones might enjoy. There were four still in their wrappers, which she handed to Levi.

"What do you say?" Paige growled before he'd had a chance.

"Thank you," he said then whirled around and ran down the passage. "Kodie! Kodie! See what the sausage roll lady gave us."

"I'm sorry," Paige said. "I think you're always going to be the sausage roll lady in his eyes."

Marion laughed. "The way to a man's heart is always through his stomach."

Paige waved her arm sideways. "I've set up a table for you and Jayden in here."

It was then Marion noticed Jayden leaning against the frame of the open door to the shop, his dark eyes sullen. "Hello, Jayden." She smiled.

He straightened and nodded hello. He was wearing a *Rocket League* t-shirt and a footy club beanie and looked nervous despite his casual stance. She relaxed a little. *Rocket League* and footy were two things she knew something about. She was glad she'd put a couple of packs of footy cards in her bag. He might think he was too old for them but it was worth a try.

"I thought it would be quiet in there," Paige said. "And I'll keep the other two out of the way."

"Fine by me." Marion followed them into the shop where a picnic table and two chairs were set up on a mat beside the counter. Several books, pens and paper were laid out on the table.

"I didn't know what you'd need." Paige was hovering behind them. "And I've put your Tupperware container on the counter too, so I wouldn't forget to give it back."

Marion's gaze swept from the table to the countertop where her plastic box sat. "This'll be great. Mostly I'd like to chat with Jayden today." She looked back at the boy, who was doing his best to look tough. "Find out what he needs help with and how I can assist."

By the time she was driving home again Marion was feeling more confident, at least about her ability to work with Jayden. She'd done most of the talking but gradually his more relaxed body language and whole sentence responses, instead of one or two words, had shown her his interest was at least piqued a little. It was early days but she thought some of his learning issues were more about lack of confidence and not wanting to ask than his actual ability to learn. He'd moved schools a few times and probably been one of those students who'd slipped through the cracks. It was a boost to Marion's own confidence to feel she hadn't lost her touch.

Paige stuck her head around Jayden's bedroom door. He was sitting on the floor with some cards spread out around him.

"What have you got there?" she asked.

"Marion gave me some footy cards."

"Mrs Add—"

"She told me to call her Marion, Mum."

"Okay." Paige had thought Marion would be the kind of person who was a stickler for formality.

"She gave me these footy cards. And she reckons she might have a team scarf I could have."

Paige sat on the floor beside him and picked up one of the cards. "That's nice of her. How did the lesson go?"

Marion had given Paige one of her grimacey smiles and a hidden thumbs up before she'd left. After that Paige had been busy with dinner and putting the young ones to bed. She hadn't had a chance to speak to Jayden about the tutoring session.

"Okay. We didn't do much work. Just talked about footy and *Rocket League*." His face lit up. "Marion's played *Rocket League*, Mum. She knows all about it."

"Wow! She's way cooler than your mum then."

He gave her a kind smile. "You're cool, Mum. You worry too much, that's all."

"Do I?"

"I'm old enough to help more, you know."

Paige took in the earnest look on her thirteen-year-old's face and her heart nearly broke. "You do help. You're the greatest big brother."

"But you're always doing stuff for us and buying us things and I know we don't have much money."

"We get by."

"We had to move because of Levi's grandparents trying to take him away from us." His young face creased deeper with worry. "New Zealand's a long way away. They won't find us here, will they? What would we do if they took him?"

Paige was instantly guilty for the worry she'd caused Jayden. He shouldn't need to be so burdened at his age.

"It's not so bad now. They're happy just to hear he's okay."

Jayden's look was sceptical. "You don't have to keep it from me, Mum."

"I'm not." Paige's guilt deepened. At least it was true she wasn't keeping anything about Levi's family from him. There was a book lying beside Jayden on the floor. "What's that?"

"Marion gave it to me. It's a graphic novel."

Paige picked it up and flicked through the pages. Jayden wasn't a confident reader. She quietly thought Kodie at eight was probably a better reader than he was. "Have you read any of it?"

"I read some with Marion. It's about a teenager who's a spy. It sounds good. She suggested I try reading some each night before I go to sleep."

"It's nearly that time now. Would you like me to read some with you?" She couldn't remember the last time she'd read with Jayden. Probably before Levi was born. He'd been nine then and putting himself to bed.

"Nah, that's okay. I can do it myself." He stacked up the footy cards.

She put an arm around him and kissed his cheek. "Goodnight then."

"Night, Mum."

Paige stopped at the door for one last glance as Jayden got to his feet.

"You're okay for Marion to come again?" she asked.

"Yeah." He shrugged. "She's all right."

Paige smiled as she went back to the kitchen. She'd take the high praise on Marion's behalf. For all she was a stiff and distant person, Marion seemed to have connected with Jayden and Paige was hopeful that would be good for her son.

thirty

Briony and Chelsea had a production line going in the kitchen. They were making savoury tarts and slab cakes. They'd have an extra lot of mouths to feed with crutching coming up soon and Briony wanted to restock the freezer. Vincent and Maddie had gone off to give the air seeder a going-over and Chelsea was going out later to help with stock work, but for now Briony had her to herself. There were things to be discussed. Vincent needed labour and if the girls weren't going to supply it maybe they needed to employ someone else. Before she put them all in a room together and talked future plans she needed to gather some intel. Briony was on a mission to sort her family out and she was starting with Chelsea.

"Have you heard from Brandon lately?"

"Not for a few days." Chelsea stopped pressing the pastry round into the flan. "His mum rang last night. They still want me to go back."

"How're you feeling about that?" Briony asked.

"I'd go back if things were like they were when we first married. I loved working on the property with Brandon and we'd been talking about setting up a stud. You know how much I enjoyed genetics at uni. I thought we had such an amazing future." Chelsea's shoulders sagged. "Until the ice ruined everything."

"They know about his drug-taking?"

"Yes, but they're in denial. They didn't see him every day like I did and when Brandon's on the drugs he can be a great guy. It's when he's run out that everything goes bad. It's a downward spiral affecting his health. This has all come out of the blue for them. They think I'm overreacting."

"The times when you left...why didn't you tell us?"

Chelsea pursed her lips and Briony braced herself for what she'd realised was coming.

"I couldn't, Mum. I didn't tell anyone but a close girlfriend. I couldn't admit my marriage wasn't working and then Brandon would get back on track and we'd be fine for a while. We didn't talk about the drugs. I didn't want to sound like a nag and push him into taking more. We just got on with it, I suppose...We were..."

Briony felt sick. "Keeping up appearances."

Chelsea nodded.

The realisation that her daughter had learned to keep secrets like she had hit Briony like a rock to the head. She pulled her daughter close. "I'm so sorry, Chelsea."

Chelsea eased back and screwed up her face. "What for? You didn't make Brandon take the drugs."

"And neither did you. But I fear I have taught you too much about hiding what's really going on."

Chelsea's eyebrows raised and her mouth dropped open. "I didn't want to admit my marriage wasn't working but once I came home and you all knew...well, now it really doesn't matter, does it?"

"Do you still love Brandon?"

"Of course I do. It's the drug-addicted Brandon I can't cope with."

"Do you think he still loves you?"

"He says so."

"What about rehab?"

"I've suggested it but neither he nor his parents think it necessary."

"So his parents don't understand he's got a problem?"

"I think they accept that he takes drugs but they don't realise that he's dependent on them. That's how I was to begin with, but it hurt our relationship and it will hurt his work too eventually. His parents are worried about what happens if I don't come back. If Brandon and I...you know...divorce."

"You know you have a home here if you need."

"No offence, Mum, but I think you and I would kill each other if we lived together and I'm not sure if I could work for Dad forever either."

"Hmm. So if you don't return to Brandon what will you do?"

"I don't know what but I know it's not here, not long-term anyway. Badara's too small for me these days."

Briony suspected it always had been. She paced away from Chelsea then turned back. "I'd like to give Brandon's parents a piece of my mind. Putting all this pressure on you when it's Brandon who's at fault."

"They're nice people, Mum. I shut my eyes to his drug-taking for a long time too. He's told them he's stopped and they believe him."

"But you don't?"

Chelsea shook her head. "And I think while they're protecting him and not facing up to it he'll keep using."

"You need to tell them he has to clean up his act or you're leaving him and you want half the property."

"Mum!"

"What are you going to live on? You've worked on that place as long as Brandon has. If you have to make a fresh start you'll need some money."

"But his parents put up the equity. It would hurt them badly."

"No more than if Brandon continues on this drug spiral. It might force their hand to face reality. And if he's honest about wanting you back, he might find the strength to admit he has a problem and do something about it."

Chelsea's face was a mix of hope and fear.

Briony gripped her by the shoulders. "I feel this is my fault."

"Brandon taking drugs?"

"No, you not wanting to tell people about it. I understand why you kept it to yourself but your dad and I, even Maddie and Blake, that's different. We're family, we're here to support you."

"Oh, Mum." Chelsea fell into her arms and sobbed against her chest.

"It'll be all right." Briony hugged her tight.

"What's happened now?"

Madeline stood in the doorway, a worried look on her face. Briony was pleased to see she was bootless, at least.

"Nothing's happened," Briony said. "We're just clearing the air and sorting a few things out."

"I'm okay." Chelsea gave her nose a long, loud blow.

Madeline still eyed them both suspiciously. "Dad wants to get started on the stock work soon. He sent me in to see if you've finished baking."

"We haven't," Briony said. "But that's okay. Chelsea's made a good start. I can finish on my own." At least Chelsea had been clear that, no matter what, she wouldn't be staying on to help with the farm.

Madeline turned away.

"Will you be home tonight, Madeline?" Briony asked.

"I guess so. Why?"

"I'm doing a headcount for dinner."

"Okay."

The sisters set off together and, having ticked Chelsea off her list, Briony went back to her baking and her plans to tackle Madeline.

It worked out easily in the end. After dinner Vincent had an Ag Bureau meeting and Chelsea wanted some time alone in her room. Madeline helped clean up the kitchen and was heading off to the television when Briony stopped her.

"I'd like a chat," she said and shut the kitchen door on the rest of the house.

"What about?" Madeline's wary look returned.

"This and that. Would you like a coffee?"

Madeline tipped her head to one side. "Maybe another glass of wine?"

"Okay." Briony needed no encouragement. Wine may assist the conversation she had to have with her youngest. She poured them one each and they sat at the table, both taking tentative sips.

"This is about your dad and—"

"Oh no. He's sick, isn't he? He's been—"

Briony held up a hand. "He's perfectly fine but he can't run this place on his own."

"Oh." Madeline took another sip of wine. "I know that."

"Your dad's a good operator but not so good at mapping things out and allocating tasks when it comes to family."

"I've been a bit distracted lately but we've got a plan now."

"You have?" Briony was pleased Vincent had finally made a start on sorting their future. Perhaps she'd jumped the mark with this conversation. "What did you decide?"

"We've made a list. I suggested we put a whiteboard up in the office but we haven't got that far yet so it's still on paper, but it's a who and what for the next month or so."

Briony's earlier relief was swamped by concern again. "That's a start but it's not quite what I meant. I'm talking long-term planning. You've met this man—"

"Cameron is his name."

"I know. And we hear you're looking at property near Wirini Bay."

Madeline sat back then, her big brown eyes wide in her pale face. "We're only looking. We thought we could have our own place with some land for the horses."

"He's got money, has he?"

"Not a lot."

"And you?"

"Some." Madeline's shoulders slumped further. "I was going to ask you and Dad to be guarantors."

"So your picture of the future doesn't include staying on this property?"

"I could still work for Dad. It wouldn't be a big drive each day."

"I see. And you haven't talked any of this over with your dad?"

Madeline shook her head. "Cameron and I wanted to have our own plan in place first. There's no point asking you for help if we don't have a proposal properly mapped out."

"I can't believe you've done all this with a man we don't even know."

"You do know Cameron."

"Hardly, and you certainly haven't done anything about improving on that situation." The conversation was heading in a different direction to what Briony had planned but there was no helping it. "Don't you think it's about time you brought him to meet us?"

Madeline pushed back her chair. "Listen to yourself, Mum. You can't even say his name. Cameron! His name's Cameron. Is it any wonder I don't want to bring him here? You've already made up your mind about him." She flung open the door and stormed out.

Briony put her head in her hands. She'd been determined to lay some groundwork for Vincent so that they could all discuss the future of the property and prepare a roadmap for the way forward. She'd certainly been buoyed by her talk with Chelsea earlier in the day. At least her eldest was clear she didn't want to return permanently to the farm. Somehow Briony had derailed her chat with Madeline and it had ended up going completely awry.

Briony's wine glass was empty. She tipped the remains of Madeline's into it and took a large gulp.

thirty-one

It was quarter to six on Friday night. Dane and Sarah would be here soon and Paige still wasn't ready. She'd fed the kids early and bathed the two younger ones, who were in their PJs. It was only then that she gave some thought to what she would wear. She didn't have a dress. She lived in shorts or jeans. Jayden's question from the day before had thrown her. She'd waited till she'd firmed up the day and time with Dane before she'd told the kids she was going out for a meal. Jayden had wanted to know if she and Dane were dating. She'd made it clear this was two friends going out for dinner without their kids, but now that she was getting ready she felt awkward. Paige wondered if Zuri had asked the same question and what Sarah thought about this dinner date... non-date. She mustn't even think the word.

Now as she stood in front of the mirror in her newest pair of jeans holding up various shirts, she realised she wanted to look her best and questioned what that meant. Was she simply enjoying the opportunity to put on something nice or was she also trying to impress Dane?

"You should wear the t-shirt."

Paige glanced around. Kodie had slipped into her room and was sitting on her bed holding out the short-sleeved top Paige had discarded because the night was cool.

Paige smiled. Kodie was the last of her kids she'd expect to give fashion advice. "I like that one but I need sleeves."

"Wear your jacket." Kodie slid from the bed and crossed to the clothes rack, pulling on the sleeve of a checked jacket. It was a tailored op shop find that Paige had worn a lot in Melton but hadn't needed in Badara yet.

"I'd forgotten about that." She discarded the shirt she'd been going to put on and tugged the t-shirt over her head. Kodie brought her the jacket and she slipped it on.

They stood side by side looking in the mirror. "You look nice, Mum."

"Thanks, Kodes." Paige gave her daughter a hug and kissed the top of her head. They smiled at each other in the mirror, Paige filled with a mix of guilt and love for her daughter, who was obviously growing up fast. They didn't very often have one-on-one time. She'd have to try harder to achieve that somehow before Kodie suddenly became a teenager like Jayden.

There was a knock on the front door.

"I'll get it!" Kodie shot to the bedroom door and looked back. "Lipstick," she said and then was gone.

An hour later Paige and Dane were settled at a table at a pub in Wirini Bay. Dane had introduced her to a few people they'd passed on their way in – he seemed to know half the dining room. He'd insisted on shouting her a drink. She'd opted for champagne and he'd bought a bottle, pouring them a glass each.

Paige had a couple of quick mouthfuls. She was still a bit nervous about their dinner and the bubbles helped her to relax. She hadn't thought about all the people here who would know Dane. Their table was in the centre of the room and she was aware of curious glances flicking their way.

Dane took a sip from his glass and set it back on the table. "I used to drink champagne with my sister-in-law sometimes, to be social. I learned to like it but Mum rarely has a drink and Dad's a beer man so I don't drink it much any more."

"Your mum seems to miss her. It sounds like they were good friends."

"They were very close. More like mother and daughter. The break-up hit Mum the hardest of all of us, I think. Not only did her golden-haired boy crash and burn but it caused such terrible fallout, including Mum losing close contact with her daughter-in-law and grandchildren."

"It must have been tough on you all."

"Sure was."

A couple of young men passed by and said hello to Dane.

He nodded after them as they moved away. "They're mates of Zuri's. He wanted to come in with me to catch up with them but I explained this was a kid-free night."

Paige wondered what Zuri's reaction to that had been, but she didn't ask. "I've never heard the name Zuri before," she said.

"Neither had I until his mother dropped him on my doorstep, but I'm not a Marvel fan."

Paige frowned.

"You're not either, I'm guessing. Zuri is a character in a Marvel movie. We watched it together when he was about Jayden's age."

"You're still not a fan?"

"No." He grinned. "What about your kids – did you pick their names?"

"Yes and no. Jayden's dad wasn't on the scene so I'd made a short list. My mother looked at it and scoffed at Jayden so that was what I named him. Kodie's dad picked her name. She's actually Dakoda. I didn't realise at the time but he'd been watching *Fifty Shades of Grey* and she was named after Dakota Johnson."

"I thought Dakota was spelled with a 't'?"

"In the case of Dakota Johnson, yes. I wasn't very well after Kodie was born so her dad filled out the paperwork. Turns out besides not being able to keep out of trouble he couldn't spell either. He didn't hang around for long, which was for the best. Last I heard he was in jail for robbery. I shortened Dakoda to Kodie. It has a softer tone to it. Not that there's anything soft about my little girl but I think the name suits her. Levi's dad Ari, the kids and I chose Levi's name together. We knew he was a boy. Ari wanted Jayden and Kodie to be involved. He stuck paper on the fridge and we all added names we liked when we heard them. Ari made it so much fun. There were all kinds of names there but somehow we all agreed on Levi. I think Ari may have swayed the kids with bribes 'cause he knew it was my favourite."

"Sounds like Ari was a good bloke."

Paige folded the paper serviette in front of her. "He was."

Dane picked up his glass and raised it. "To absent friends."

Paige went to take a sip from hers and was amazed to see it was empty already. Dane refilled it.

"That had better be my last. I don't drink very often. It'd be awful if you had to help me out of here."

Their meals arrived at that moment.

"Some food will help," Dane said.

They talked about all sorts over their meal. Paige told him about growing up on the Gold Coast and he told her about growing up on a farm in rural South Australia. They discussed their favourite movies – there were several they liked in common – and whether the book should come first. Like Paige, Dane was a reader. When it came to music, they had few commonalities. Dane was a hip hop fan and Paige favoured pop but they both agreed on some blues music they liked.

Their empty plates had been taken away and Paige was on her third glass of champagne when she realised she was enjoying herself very much. Adult conversation with someone around her own age was stimulating. Although for the last little while she'd been doing most of the talking. The alcohol had loosened her tongue. She'd just been blathering about Jayden and his need for tutoring.

"Marion helped Zuri when he was at primary school. She's a bit standoffish with adults but she seems to strike the right chord with kids. I reckon Zuri was around year four or five and he was struggling with reading. She helped him get back on track."

"She certainly must have what it takes. Jayden is happy to have another session."

"He's picked up footy quickly. He's got a great kick on him already. Did his dad play?"

"Not that I know of. He wasn't sporty at all."

"I find it weird that Zuri has this whole family we hardly know. I sometimes wonder, when he says or does things that are totally alien to me, if some things are inherited. It must be tricky with three lots to keep track of."

"I don't know Kodie's extended family at all and only a little about Jayden's and Levi's. I've been as up-front as I can with my kids about their parentage." Paige took a sip from her glass. She wasn't being totally honest about that but she was doing her best. "It has been difficult with Jayden's other grandparents, Lucinda and James. Their only child, Rufus, who was Jayden's dad, died after an accident last year. They thought Jayden should see his dad and wanted us to go to the hospital, but Rufus was brain dead and on life support. I couldn't put Jay through that. That phone call, to tell me Rufus was in hospital, was the first time I'd spoken to them since I was pregnant with Jayden and they told me to have him terminated."

"Hell, Paige, I can understand why hearing from them would have been a shock on several counts."

"Now they want to be part of Jayden's life. He's only met Lucinda and James once, briefly, a few days after the funeral."

"Did he go to the funeral?"

Paige shook her head. "I gave him the option but he'd never met Rufus so he didn't want to go."

"I don't blame him."

"Jayden didn't know how he was supposed to feel. I just told him his dad and I were too young. Rufus knew about him. I sent a photo each birthday until Jayden was four when Rufus asked me not to send any more."

Dane shook his head.

"Ari was more a dad to Jayden and Kodie than their own fathers ever were. In my head I call them 'co-creators'. Neither of them did anything to earn the title 'dad'."

"What made Lucinda and James suddenly change their minds?"

She shrugged. "They told me they'd always wondered about Jayden."

"You don't believe them?"

"No. I know what's really going on." Paige took a sip of her drink. She'd never told anyone this stuff but maybe she needed another point of view. A man who understood single parenting, was easy to talk to and happened to be sitting opposite.

"I decided I would go to the hospital and see Rufus. My parents gave me the money to fly back to the Gold Coast with the kids. Rufus and I had gone to the same primary school so Mum and Dad knew his parents and had heard about the accident." Paige gave a wry smile. "They looked after the kids and I went to the hospital. My parents had only met Levi once before. Quality family time, my mother called it."

Paige took a steadying breath. "Jayden knew I was going but as I said he didn't want to go with me. In the hospital there was a family room on the ward for people with someone in Rufus's situation. I heard Lucinda crying before I reached it and James murmuring responses. I hung back, not sure whether to go in or not. She was sobbing about losing Rufus and saying Jayden was their only descendant, and how they had to get me to let Jayden live with them. I even heard the word custody! Rufus wasn't even dead and she was plotting to steal my son to replace her own."

"You're kidding!"

Paige shook her head. "I don't know what role I was going to have in her little family plan but it didn't sound good. I almost knocked over a nurse in my hurry to get away."

"But you said Jayden met them?"

"Even though I didn't want him to, Jayden was curious. We met them together at a cafe before we left the Gold Coast. He was nervous. I was anxious too, given what I'd heard. James was fairly subdued but Lucinda alternated between being gushy and crying. It was all very awkward. When we left Jayden told me he was glad he'd met them but he didn't need to see them again."

"So what does he do when they make contact?"

Paige drained the last of her champagne and put the glass back on the table. The dining room suddenly seemed quiet. She glanced around and saw there were only a few diners left.

"Gosh, what's the time? We promised your mum we wouldn't be late." She pushed back her chair.

Dane's look was quizzical but he said nothing more. Just before they reached the door, a group of women burst through it, talking at high decibel and giggling.

"Dane!" one of them cried and threw an arm around him. "What are you up to?" She glanced at Paige. "Date night!"

"You sneaky devil," said another.

Paige's cheeks began to warm and then she recognised the last two women coming in the door, Jo and Jac.

Dane had managed to extricate himself from the first woman and introduced Paige to the three she hadn't met. They were all very tipsy.

"Girls' night out?" Dane asked and the women responded with hoots and whistles.

"It's Jo's birthday."

Paige had been hanging back but she noticed the birthday girl badge pinned to Jo's shirt.

"We've done a pub crawl." Jo giggled. Her eyes were bright and her face flushed. "We had a meal at Port Kent, shots down the road at the Royal and now cocktails here."

"Come on, Jo." The three at the bar were beckoning her.

Jac brought up the rear. "The downer or the blessing of breast-feeding." She shrugged. "I'm their desi. I think I'll be glad in the morning." She smiled at Paige. "Looks like you've access to a babysitter. I'll give you a call next time we have a girls' night."

"Jac!" one of the women called and was waving a glass at her.

"My lemon soda awaits." She waggled her fingers. "Night, you two. Don't do anything I wouldn't do."

Paige was glad to step outside and feel the cool air on her hot cheeks. Neither of them spoke as Dane turned his ute and headed out of town.

When his voice broke the silence it startled her. "I think you might have to be prepared for a few rumours about us. Those women have been trying to hook me up with someone for years. They'll be over the top about seeing you and I out together."

"It wasn't a date."

"You and I know that."

Paige stared at the bush along the side of the road illuminated by the headlights. She'd tried so hard to keep her private life private but it was difficult in a small community where everyone seemed to know everyone else.

Dane cleared his throat. "You didn't finish telling me about Jayden and his paternal grandparents."

"Nothing more to tell, really." Paige stared ahead but she sensed his quick glance in her direction.

"They gave up?"

She sagged, suddenly weary of the pretence.

"No. Lucinda turned up at my place at Melton the day before Christmas holidays last year. The older two were at school and Levi was playing outside. She'd brought a ridiculous pile of gifts for Jayden and wanted to see him. We argued. I sent her off, hid the parcels and didn't tell Jayden but she came back that evening. She was so determined she tried to force her way inside, started calling out for him. Thankfully the two younger ones were asleep and Jayden was next door at his mate's." Paige gripped the seat as she recalled her fear of losing her child.

"I took off first thing the next morning on the pretext of a short holiday. I found a cheap cabin and we stayed the night. I knew Lucinda wouldn't stay in Melbourne for long so I kept the kids away from home for the weekend, but then she started ringing me nearly every day."

"So you moved to Badara?"

Paige sighed. "It wasn't a good environment where we lived either. Our house was in poor condition. Lucinda was offering Jayden so much I panicked..." She stiffened. "There was a bloody PlayStation among the things she'd bought him."

"You thought she might convince Jayden to what...go with her?"

"Maybe."

"What did he say about it?"

Paige hesitated. "He doesn't know."

"Okay."

"But my bloody mother has given Lucinda my new number and she's started ringing me again. The latest offer is to send Jayden to Rufus's old school."

"On the Gold Coast?"

"Yep." Paige's lip quivered and she sucked it in. The last thing she wanted was to be crying. She stared hard at the road ahead. "I hate them, you know. I hate them so much for not wanting Jayden in the first place, for ignoring his presence for twelve years and then for wanting him to replace the son they lost, for using their money to offer him things I never could."

The white lines on the road flicked out of the darkness and beneath them for several beats.

"That's a lot to be dealing with on your own." Dane's voice was so soft she strained to hear it.

He was right, and yet weighed down as she was by the burden, Paige felt just a little bit lighter for having told someone.

"I'm sorry. I've never said all that out loud before. Your ears must be tired. I feel as if I've been talking half the night about my problems."

"I get it. I only had one kid to bring up but there's a lot of second-guessing yourself. Dad was my listening ear."

They'd reached Badara and Dane turned into her street and stopped in front of her house. Paige was amazed at how quickly the time had gone by. She'd enjoyed herself but now in the sudden quiet without the drone of the engine she felt awkward again.

"I don't know about managing your situation." He broke the silence. "But if it helps I'm always happy to listen."

"Thanks. And thanks for your company tonight. I haven't had a night out for so long."

He grinned. "I enjoyed it too."

thirty-two

Marion pulled up at the side of the hall. She was early but she wanted to be the first to arrive rather than walk in when the others were already there. In the end it had been Blake who'd convinced her to come for the class rather than just the meeting. He'd rung the day before full of excitement. Gab was on his way and Blake wanted to hold a family get-together at the shack so they could all meet him.

They'd talked about the fitness class and Blake had been adamant things would go back to normal once she returned to the sessions. It wasn't so much what he said but his attitude that had spurred her to return. When had she lost her gumption? Somewhere between finishing work and the time capsule reveal? Somewhere in there she'd become less sure of herself, restless, searching for something that was missing in her life but so hard to find when you didn't know what you were looking for.

She let herself into the hall and stopped to take in the seats neatly stacked along one wall, the slight difference in the seams where the floor had been lifted, the piano that had been moved back and now sat to the side of the small stage. She tapped a foot on the floor – the old-time dance group would be pleased the hall was usable again. She suspected Jean and Keith had probably paid their nephew some money towards the work, just like she and Len had covered most of the cost of a replacement window the previous year.

The sound of a vehicle pulling up out the front pushed her to unroll her mat. She was relieved it was Briony first in the door and then Claire. It would be good to have a few people here before Gloria arrived. She wasn't sure what her cousin's reception would be – another sign of her insecurity. A year ago she wouldn't have given it a thought.

"Good to see you, Marion." Jean had come in the back way through the kitchen.

Blake arrived and then a couple of young mums and then Paige and Sarah, who both came straight to Marion to say hello.

"And I've brought your container back." Sarah dug the Tupperware box from her bag. "We all appreciated your sausage rolls, thank you."

They were quite a crew before Gloria finally arrived. She barely acknowledged Marion and took up a space on the other side of the group near the front.

Blake started his music and had them all following his movements, breathing steadily in and out, stretching their arms in giant circles to Bryan Adam's sultry tones singing 'Heaven'. Even though Marion had been attending Blake's Thursday sessions in Port Kent and she knew some of the women there, it wasn't quite the same as being at the Badara group she'd founded. Then again, if Len agreed to sell the property and they moved to Port Kent, would she still come to Badara? Len had gone quiet on it all again. Another reason for her to be unsettled.

"You need a chair for this exercise, Marion." Briony put one beside her.

Marion glanced around. Blake was looking at her expectantly. She'd been so lost in her thoughts that she hadn't heard his next instruction.

"Thanks," she said to Briony and focused on the class.

They'd taken their last cool-down breaths when they heard the distant sound of a siren.

"Surely that's not an ambulance," Jean said.

Chelsea went to the door. "Sounds like one."

They all milled about, unsettled. The nearest ambulance station was in Wirini Bay and hearing one at Badara was a rare occurrence. Marion was aware of Gloria keeping her distance in spite of the upset.

The siren grew louder then suddenly stopped. They all looked at each other.

"That's somewhere in town." Jean's usually serene face had a worried expression, mirroring the same concern on all the other faces.

"I'm going to see who it is." Chelsea shot out the door and they heard her car pull away.

Everyone else continued to pack up, picking up mats, stacking chairs, making small talk. They were a close-knit community and Marion imagined they were all like her, wondering where they'd last left their nearest and dearest. She thought again of Len, out on the farm working alone and the day his sleeve had been ripped from his shirt. It could easily have been so much worse, and even if she'd been there to call one, the ambulance would never have reached him in time.

Outside a vehicle pulled up. They turned as one at the sound of footsteps and Chelsea burst back in.

"It's Mr Carter."

The air was a mix of sighs and murmurs.

Marion felt guilty at her small sense of relief. Mick wasn't a close friend of hers, but Len was a pal. Then she remembered he'd planned to call in on Mick this morning. "Do you know what happened?" she asked.

"Something to do with his diabetes. I saw them load him into the ambulance. He was out to it." Chelsea looked to Marion. "Uncle Len was there."

"He was planning to have a catch-up with Mick this morning."

"Keith visits him on Thursdays," Jean said. "Poor Mick misses his wife terribly. He's never been good at managing his diabetes."

"Uncle Len said to ask if you'd go and mind the shop, Mrs Townsend."

"Of course." Sarah gathered up her things. She had a quick word to Paige and then left. They were so obviously very comfortable together. Once more Marion felt that small sense of something missing in her life.

Paige stood on the edge of the group, feeling very much an outsider, especially now that Sarah had left and the other younger women too.

She was startled by Jean giving a couple of short claps.

"Mick's in safe hands but perhaps you'd all join me in a prayer for his recovery."

Paige stood awkwardly as around her the other women bowed their heads. She bent her head and stared at her shoes. She'd never been to church, never thought to pray for anyone, but there was something comforting about the circle of women all focused on Jean's words asking for God to keep Mick safe and return him to them soon.

Paige wasn't sure about God but if the collective power of these women was anything to go by, Mr Carter would be fit and well in no time at all. She hoped so. She felt bad she'd had unkind thoughts about him now. She hadn't realised he was a poorly managed diabetic.

The man who'd lived next door to them when Kodie was a baby often became unwell when his wife went to stay with her mother. Now that Paige thought about it, the similarities were obvious. He used to get irritable easily, often complained he was tired and had headaches. She'd not known Mr Carter very well so had thought his behaviour was part of his personality but now she understood he was unwell. She found herself murmuring 'Amen' with the others and hoped there was someone listening to answer their request.

"Now we'd better get on and have our lunch and meeting," Jean said. "Paige will have to go and get her little one soon."

"That's okay," Paige said. "Beth is collecting him to go to her place for a play date."

"That's lovely, dear." Jean led them to the supper room where they pooled their lunch and got started.

There was a brief moment when Jean asked Marion to continue in her role as committee chair and Gloria let out a small harumph and wriggled in her chair as if she was going to stand but then stayed put. Paige wondered how things would go but had little time to reflect as Marion got the meeting efficiently under way. They'd all made progress with their roles.

Jean had made a map of the town with places of significance, which included the old bakery and almost every second building, it seemed to Paige. She also said the CWA had agreed to convene the family games day and plans were well under way for that.

Paige passed on Sarah's request to let them know the sporting clubs were on board to help with that as well.

"The black-tie dinner will be the highlight." Briony consulted her notebook. "The dance group are keen for us to have old-time dances."

"I don't know if I'll remember how," Gloria groaned.

"What kind of dancing is it?" Paige asked.

"Military two-step, barn dance, foxtrot, modern waltz, all the old favourites we used to do."

Gloria groaned again and Jean clapped her hands in delight. Except for the waltz, Paige had never heard of any of them.

"They're happy to run a few practice sessions for those who aren't dancers or need a refresher," Briony went on. "I've asked the RFDS committee in Wirini Bay if they'd like to do the food as a fundraiser and they're keen. And the Port Kent men's shed group will run a bar. That takes the pressure off our small community. This room is small so I thought we'd have the dinner in two sittings and a light supper towards the end of the night."

"You have been busy," Marion said.

"It's exciting to think we can all dust off our jewels and high heels and finery and dress up. We so rarely get to do it."

Paige looked down at her tatty fitness clothes and shifted in her seat. She would have nothing to wear and even if she could go, everyone would be involved so there'd be no-one to look after the children.

"Oh, and I've even got a red carpet and a photographer so we'll get lots of photos on the night."

"We should make sure there's a photographer at all the events," Marion said.

"I'm sure the *Country Courier* would send someone to cover the weekend." Briony tapped the newspaper folded on the table in front of her. "Isn't there a resident journalist in Wirini Bay who supplies articles for this area?"

"When they remember we exist," Gloria huffed.

Marion ignored her and glanced at Paige. "The Facebook page you made is gaining in interest."

"Yes, well done, Paige," Briony said. "A few ex-residents have commented on it already. It's certainly helping spread the word."

"I'm guessing the *Country Courier* would have an archive," Paige said. "They run that weekly column about past events. What do you think about asking them to see if there are any old photos from the last Back to Badara and do a story on it to promote the next one?"

"That's a good idea," Marion said and the others nodded in agreement. "Well, if that's everything—"

"I did have one more question." Paige faltered as Marion's probing look fixed on her.

"I've noticed Badara doesn't have one of those big structures announcing its name at the entrance to town."

Everyone was staring at her now.

"You know, like Wirini Bay has with the fish as you drive in, and Port Kent has the sailing ship," Paige continued. "Badara is part of the same council, isn't it?"

The women looked at each other. Finally Jean spoke up. "The council did prepare a plan for one but no-one could agree on what should go on it so the sign has never gone ahead."

"That's a shame."

"To be honest, I'd totally forgotten about it," Marion said. "It caused such a ruckus. When was it…three years ago?" She looked to Jean.

"I think so, probably. Paige is right. It is a shame. The council would get it done for us if we could just agree."

"It would be nice to have it in place before the Back to Badara Festival," Briony said.

"I don't remember being part of the discussion." Gloria glanced at Jean.

"There was a Badara and district meeting held here in the hall. It would have been at least three years ago." Jean tapped a finger to her lips. "I think there were about forty people here representing the town and wider community."

"But if no-one could agree back then how will you get them to now?" Gloria said.

They all went quiet.

"What kinds of things were suggested?" Paige asked.

"The council favoured a design with wheat and sheep on it, I think," Marion said.

"We have some lovely birdlife here," Jean said, "and several people from town wanted a bird design."

"Wasn't the footy club in favour of a footballer to represent Basil Williams?" Briony frowned. "You know the fellow who played league football and won a Brownlow."

"That was a long time ago," Gloria said. "Our region has also produced a very talented netballer and a tennis player since then."

"You see." Jean held out her hands, palms up. "This was our problem before. No-one could agree."

"What would happen if you had a design that represented the town's name?"

"Badara!" Gloria scoffed.

Once more all eyes turned to Paige. Heat spread across her cheeks. She was the newcomer here and the junior.

"Go on, dear," Jean said.

"I'm sure you all know this already but I did some research and Badara is the Barngarla name for a species of gum native to this area."

There was silence as the other four women glanced at each other.

"I suppose we did," Marion said.

Briony shrugged. "If I did I've forgotten."

"There are lots of trees along the roadsides," Paige said. "I don't know if they are the exact species."

"There are still patches of natural scrub on most properties," Briony said. "And of course the reserve's not far away."

Jean clapped her hands gleefully. "They planted trees as part of the Back to Badara fifty years ago. Perhaps we could do that again."

"The area discussed for the sign has enough space to plant trees behind it," Marion said.

"Good luck." Gloria folded her arms. "If people couldn't agree on a design last time how—"

"I think Paige's idea has great merit," Marion said.

"So do I." Jean beamed at Paige.

"Would you work with me on a proposal for council, Paige?"

"I've never...I don't know how to..."

"I know how to do the proposal and you've got the backup information." Marion glanced around the group. "I think last time there wasn't enough pre-planning. The entrance sign was thrust on us and we didn't really own the ideas. I'm sure we could do it better this time and get most people on board."

"I agree," Jean said.

Briony nodded.

"I suppose." Gloria sniffed.

By the time Paige left the hall she wasn't sure whether she was happy her ideas had been accepted or worried about the extra work she'd created for herself. Beth wasn't dropping Levi back until school pick-up so she had two hours up her sleeve. It was an amazing feeling but going home to an empty house after her busy morning didn't inspire her.

She walked past her street and down the next and was pleased to see Sarah's car was still parked outside the postal agency.

"Hello," she called. The shopfront was empty but every light was on.

Sarah came from the house behind the shop. She was carrying a broom and a handful of cloths. "Oh, Paige, hello. I'm sorry I missed the meeting." She stopped to look around. "Where's Levi?"

"Play date at Beth's." Paige noticed the post office end of the front counter had been tidied and cleaned. "Any news about Mick?"

"I rang the hospital and he's doing okay but he'll be there a few days while they sort him out."

"What are you doing?"

"The place was such a mess. I've made a start but it's overwhelming. I've been wanting to give the shop a good going-over for years but the house is worse. It's a wonder Mick hasn't made himself sick sooner living like that and there's no decent food in the place. He'll probably tell me off when he gets back but I owe it to his dear wife to try to help and since he's not here…"

"What can I do?"

"Would you mind helping?"

"I'm a free agent for the next two hours."

"Divide and conquer, I think," Sarah said. "If you start on the shop I'll tackle Mick's kitchen."

The job wasn't finished by the time Sarah called it quits. "I think we've done enough for today. I'll drop you home."

Paige waited outside while Sarah did a last check that everything was secure. At least they'd made a dent in the dust and grime and they'd agreed to meet again the next morning to continue. Then in the afternoon Marion was coming a bit earlier than her scheduled time with Jayden so they could work on the Welcome to Badara sign proposal.

Paige was happy her life in Badara was suddenly busy and she felt as if she was fitting in. After the school holidays she was going to her first CWA craft meeting with Beth. She and the kids were all making friends. Kodie had been invited to a birthday party in a few weeks and Jayden joining the footy team meant they'd soon be involved in much more. Jac had told her about the social calendar the club put together for the footy and netball season. It sounded fun and would be something to look forward to on weekends. Money was tight but she was managing much better now that they were settled.

It was only the worry of Jayden's paternal grandparents that spoiled the picture. She dug her phone from her pocket. She'd had a text message from them yesterday, and another first thing this morning. Today's text had said they only wanted to talk. Paige had snorted in disgust when she'd read it. They were still trying to control her life after all this time. She'd blocked the number and deleted the message but she knew Lucinda wouldn't give up easily. The dread of them finding her spread its tentacles of fear, spoiling this new life she'd made.

"Are you okay?"

Paige startled at Sarah's voice. "Of course." She shoved the phone back in her pocket.

"Hop in."

Sarah drove the short distance to Paige's place and switched off the engine. "I'd love a quick cuppa before I go home. Do you have time?"

"Sure. Come in."

They were soon settled at the kitchen table with a cup of tea each.

"Sorry you got dragged into the cleaning," Sarah said. "I really appreciate your help."

"I didn't mind. You'd already made the counter look better by the time I got there. I didn't realise there was a coffee machine under all that stuff at the other end though."

"When Mick's wife was alive she'd bake biscuits or cakes on mail days and you could buy a coffee. It used to be a bit of a gathering place for people. That's all stopped since she died, of course. She was the one to work the machine. Mick did the postal agency stuff, and if they were away I covered that for them but working that coffee machine was beyond me." Sarah took a sip of her tea. "I rarely go into the agency these days. I feel guilty about that. I should have kept a better eye on him but he rebuffed help. He's not coped well with the loss of his wife."

"I feel bad too. I thought Mick was a grumpy old man with personal hygiene issues."

"Don't be tough on yourself. That's the way he appears. It's only because I've known him for years that I know there's another side to him." Sarah sipped her tea again then asked gently, "Is that why you looked so worried before?"

"Before?"

"When I came out of the agency you looked like you had the weight of the world on your shoulders."

"Did I?" Paige shifted on her chair, not meeting Sarah's gaze.

"I hope you think of me as a friend, Paige, and I'm the last person to pry. Dane didn't tell me what you two talked about the other night but he did say he admired how well you managed three children on your own. It reminded me of the brave face he'd put on even when he was having the toughest of days with Zuri. I was nearby, of course, but it was his dad he unburdened to. I know you've said you're not close to your family and it made me wonder…well, if you ever needed help or someone to listen…"

Paige glanced up. She considered Sarah's concerned look only briefly before she started to talk. Her worries about Jayden came pouring out. Like she had with Dane, she told Sarah everything, from having to fight to keep him in the first place, to the present demanding requests from his paternal grandparents.

"Yesterday's message was an offer to give him a phone and pay for it. Apart from the fact that I don't think it's necessary for a kid his age, I couldn't afford it if I did. There are so many things they're offering that I never could."

"They're mourning their son. Perhaps it's their way of trying to appease their guilt at rejecting you both to begin with."

"You're such a kind person, Sarah, but I know them better. They didn't want me to have Jayden and for twelve years there's been silence, no interest in him or offers of support and now they're throwing money at me to get what they want. And they want Jayden." Paige's lip trembled.

"You poor thing – this is a terrible burden to carry on your own. Perhaps it's time you told Jayden about it."

Paige shrunk away from the idea but Sarah leaned closer. "You've seen firsthand what keeping secrets can do to a family. Jayden's a smart young man. We had a good chat the night you went out. He worries about you."

"Why?"

"Sometimes as parents we're so busy protecting our kids we don't think they see what's going on. He understands how tough it is to raise three kids on your own. I think he's smart enough to see his grandparents' gifts for what they are. If he finds out about their offers later it might cause problems."

"You want me to tell him his father and his grandparents cut us out of their lives and wanted nothing to do with us?"

"Perhaps not quite like that but maybe he needs to know his grandparents want to be in touch now, that they're offering things and your reasons for thinking it not a good idea."

Paige sat back and pressed a hand to her forehead.

"I don't know how much Dane's told you about Zuri but Dane was devastated when he found out he'd missed all those early years. He would have stood by Zuri's mum and we would have helped too. He's always been honest with Zuri. He took it hard when his brother revealed his double life." Sarah took a steadying breath. "And when he found out he had a half-sister...he's not upset about that, but about the fact that we kept it from him. Secrets have a way of revealing themselves when you least expect it. I know I'm interfering but my advice is to be as honest and up-front with Jayden as you can."

"Gosh, I have to go." Paige leaped to her feet.

"I'm sorry, I've overstepped—"

"No, you haven't at all, Sarah. I really appreciate your wisdom. Only I've realised it's almost school pick-up time."

"Of course, sorry I've held you up. I should get home too. I hadn't expected to be gone most of the day when I left this morning."

Paige waved her off then hurried along the road towards the school, Sarah's words recirculating in her head. If only it was as simple as she made it sound. Paige could talk to Jayden about his grandparents' requests – but then she'd have to confess to the lie she'd told him that it was Levi's grandparents who'd been pressuring her. She'd always been strict on her children telling the truth and now she'd be showing herself up as a liar. The school bell sounded across the oval as she turned the corner. Paige put her head down and started to jog.

thirty-three

Marion waited in the old shop while Jayden went to get Paige. It was a busy time of night for a young family and she didn't want to intrude. She'd had a good session with Jayden but next week would be school holidays and while Marion was keen to keep up the momentum of what they'd started, she wasn't sure what Paige's plans were for the break.

She ran her hands along the old wooden countertop. It was smooth and dustless and shone in the light from the fluoros overhead. Paige must have cleaned it up. Marion turned her back on it and glanced around the empty room. It was such a pity old buildings like these went to rack and ruin. Paige's landlord was lucky to have such a good tenant.

Paige dashed into the room, her face flushed and her hair dishevelled. From somewhere beyond Levi was yelling at Jayden to go away. "Sorry." Paige shut the door to the passage. "It's the witching hour here. Levi's in the bath and he's so cranky tonight even that's not calming him down. Is everything okay? Jayden said you wanted to talk to me."

"It's nothing much. Just about lessons in the school holidays."

Paige flinched as someone started pounding on the door.

"Mum!" Kodie bellowed. "Tell Levi to stop yelling. I can't hear the TV."

"Sorry." Paige winced at Marion.

"Mum!" There was more banging.

"Kodie, come away," Jayden yelled. "Mum's busy."

Marion glanced towards the door. "Perhaps I could help with something."

"Oh...no...that's okay."

"A game of cards or a story? Just while you get Levi sorted. I took up your time earlier working on the proposal for the sign."

Paige dithered and there was another thump on the door.

"Would you?" she said. "Kodie loves cards. She's into Uno at the moment and Jay and I are sick of playing with her."

"I'd be happy to."

Paige opened the door and the two of them stepped together into the chaos.

By the time Paige had calmed Levi, got him out of the bath and into pyjamas, Marion, Jayden and Kodie were on their fourth game of Uno. Jayden had hovered nearby to begin with and then had joined them after the first game.

Paige carried Levi into the kitchen on her hip. He looked tired but brightened immediately he saw Marion.

"It's the sausage roll lady."

"Hello, Levi. No sausage rolls today."

"I want to play." He squirmed in Paige's arms.

"No, Levi," Kodie grumbled. "You don't know how."

"Yes I do." His little chin jutted forward.

"Will you help me then, Levi?" Marion asked and without a blink he scrambled onto her lap.

Marion was momentarily surprised. Little children rarely took to her easily and she couldn't remember the last time she'd nursed one. They finished the game and played one more, Levi sitting on her lap and playing the card she directed him to while Paige finished preparing their meal.

"Pack the cards away now, Kodie," Paige said. "Dinner's ready."

The younger two happily sat up to steaming bowls of macaroni cheese while Jayden hung back.

"Thanks so much, Marion," Paige said. "I hope I haven't made you late for your own dinner."

"It's only Len and I. We can please ourselves when we eat. Bye, kids."

Jayden and Kodie mumbled farewells drowned by Levi yelling, "Goodnight, sausage roll lady."

"I have to get him to learn your name." Paige walked with her along the passage.

"Why? There are worse things I could be called and indeed after teaching teenagers for almost thirty years I've certainly had several less appealing monikers."

They stopped at the front door.

"You wanted to talk to me and we haven't had a chance."

"That's all right. It was just about my next session with Jayden." Paige frowned.

"It's school holidays next week."

"Oh, of course. I keep forgetting."

"I didn't know if you'd planned to be away but if not, I'm happy to continue our sessions. I wanted to talk to you about it because I don't want Jayden to feel pressured. It's the holidays and he's entitled to a break but he's making such good progress already."

"I see."

"It would be good to keep the momentum going. And I don't mind making it a different time during the holidays if it suits better."

Paige's tired face lit in a huge smile. "That's so good to hear, thanks, Marion. I'll talk to him."

"No pressure. He's a teenager and not all that keen on study so I don't want to push him too hard."

"It's such a relief to have someone else who understands him."

Marion tipped her head to the side. "You know I'm only as far as a phone call away...if you ever want to chat...or if you need someone to come and help. I know I'm much older than you but I do remember how busy life was with kids, especially at dinner time. Worse when Len was seeding or harvesting. It felt like I needed four extra sets of arms and legs at this time of night."

"Thanks, Marion." Paige's smile widened. "I'll be in touch about the tutoring."

Marion turned her car for home. It wasn't far and she'd sent Len a text that she'd be late but the aroma of Paige's cooking had set her stomach rumbling and Marion felt ravenous. She hadn't done any meal prep before she'd left other than to defrost some mince, so dinner would be a while away.

To her amazement, when she opened the back door she was greeted by a delicious smell. Something was cooking. In the kitchen Len was at the stove, a wooden spoon in his hand and a tea towel tucked into the front of his trousers. He looked up from the pan he was stirring, his bushy eyebrows like mini verandahs over his sparkling eyes.

"What's going on here?" she said.

"Staff meeting."

Marion frowned and then she remembered. When she was teaching she'd always be late home on staff meeting night and Len had cooked dinner if he got in first. Then it had become their little joke. If she was late home for whatever reason and he cooked they'd called it staff meeting. He hadn't done it since…some time last year, she assumed, when she'd still been working full-time.

"What are you cooking?" She wandered over to take a look. Len didn't have a huge repertoire.

"There was mince in the fridge." He grinned. "So far it's mince, onion and a dash of Worcestershire sauce."

"A bit of extra liquid, seasoning and a few veg and it'll do." Marion washed her hands and took out some vegetables.

They stood side by side preparing the meal together.

"I don't mind cooking, you know," Len said as he put the lid on the simmering pan and Marion took them a beer each from the fridge. "Perhaps I could get some lessons in retirement. I'm not too old to learn, am I?"

"Of course not. I'd be happy for you to cook more. I get fed up with trying to think what we should have each night."

Len took a sip of his beer, a thoughtful look on his face.

"You're going to retire, are you?" Marion made light of it. Len hadn't mentioned selling or retiring again since Ted's visit and Marion didn't want to push him.

"I've been talking to Ted again."

"Have you?"

"He suggested if I'm not ready to sell that he lease our place."

Marion set down the beer she'd been about to put to her lips. "What a great idea."

"It would mean we'd have income and more time to plan our next move."

"Why on earth didn't we think of it ourselves?"

"I don't know. The old case of not seeing the wood for the trees maybe."

"He wouldn't want the house?"

"No. Just the land. This could be home base and we could come and go as we please."

"Oh, Len." Marion felt lighter than she'd felt in ages. "Wouldn't that be wonderful. When would he want to begin the lease?"

"As soon as. He wants to do the seeding."

"Oh." Marion's excitement was tempered by the droop of Len's shoulders.

"I may well have sown and reaped my last crop."

"What about the sheep?"

"He doesn't want them. We could sell some, agist some, for a while anyway until we decide what we want to do."

"I think it's such a good idea, Len. We wouldn't be burning all our bridges and wouldn't it be wonderful to be free to go and spend extra time with our kids?"

"That's what did it for me in the end." He gave a wry smile. "Besides your threat to move to Port Kent. We hardly see our kids any more and I don't know about Roxanne and Darcy but it sounds to me from our conversations with Grant and Erin that they're getting clucky. If we are lucky enough to have grandchildren I want to spend time with them."

"Me too, Len." Marion reached for his hand. "I don't dare say anything but I'd love a grandchild. Tonight when I was at Paige's place, helping her with the kids, I enjoyed myself. I had all of the fun and none of the responsibility. That's what grandparents say, don't they? Levi's such a funny little bloke. I didn't tell you he calls me 'sausage roll lady', did I?"

Len shook his head.

"Kodie's a stern little thing but as bright as a button and Jayden acts tough but he's a great kid and truly cares for his younger siblings."

"How's the tutoring going?"

"He's doing okay but I really think he'd do well with some male role models."

"Didn't you say he's been with the Townsends a bit?"

"Yes, but they live a long way out of town. Today he was so animated about the time he got to drive their ute. It set me thinking."

"Uh oh."

"You're great with kids, Len. Remember when we used to do that country home hosting through the church? The kids loved riding on machinery, seeing the animals, helping where they could. I think Jayden would enjoy it and if he came out and did some jobs we could pay him some pocket money."

"Woah. Ease up, Marion. You're making it sound like it would be a regular occurrence."

"It could be. At least while we're still here. I was thinking we could ask them out for a barbecue over Easter. The firepit on the edge of the scrub hasn't been used in years and it'll be the end of fire ban season. The little ones could have an egg hunt in the scrub. They'd love it."

Len shook his head and smiled. "I don't mind us having a barbecue, duck, but let's hang off on signing the lad up for slave labour until we've had a chance to meet each other."

The lid of the saucepan rattled hard and Marion jumped up to check it. She adjusted the heat and gave the contents a stir.

"There's something else we need to talk about," Len said as she sat back at the table. "I've also been talking to Vince today."

Marion's excitement dropped. Len looked serious. "What about?"

"Blake."

Marion nodded.

"We, Vince and I, think it might benefit Briony to know our story."

Marion leaped back to her feet. "We talked about this. I know you've told Vince and he's obviously kept it to himself but—" Her hand flew to her cheek. "All those conversations you had with Blake. Have you told him as well?"

Len shook his head. "I simply listened and offered support. I didn't want to add to his load."

Marion blew out a breath. "No good will come of telling Briony."

"But what if we could help save Briony and Blake's relationship?"

She stared at her husband. The years had worn him down, his hair was grey and thinning, his face lined and his shoulders not quite as straight as they'd once been, but he was still the same man she'd fallen in love with. They'd stuck together through trying and life-changing episodes. Could he be right about this?

"Times have changed, duck. Thank goodness. There's a chance it will be of no help to Briony and Blake's relationship at all…but what if it is?"

She sagged back to her chair.

"You're not sorry, are you, Marion?"

"For what?" Her brain scrambled to think what else she might have done lately.

"That we stayed together."

Relief whooshed from her, leaving behind an edgy shiver. "No. We both know it hasn't been easy and we've both had to make compromises. Some people would say we're crazy to stay together but…" She reached across and covered his hand with hers. "You're my best friend, Len."

"Let's try to help Briony. We've weathered so many things. I think we can cope with Briony knowing the truth about us."

Marion pursed her lips and let out a sigh. Who knew what was right in this crazy life?

thirty-four

Briony felt sick. It had nothing to do with the car or the noise of the other three occupants. Vincent, Chelsea and Madeline were chatting and laughing as if they were going on a Sunday bush picnic. That's not what they were doing. It was a Friday night barbecue at the Port Kent shack and Gab was going to be there.

She thought she'd come to terms with Blake's announcement of his homosexuality. The last couple of weeks she'd been busy and life had almost returned to some kind of, if not normalcy, steady rhythm. Except for the hiccup of her trying to talk to her girls about the future, but even that hadn't ended as badly as she'd thought.

Chelsea was communicating with Brandon and her in-laws without becoming emotional, Madeline hadn't brought Cameron home to meet them yet but there was talk of it and Blake had settled into a routine as if he was home for good. All three children had sat down with Vincent and worked out job-sharing. There'd been no more talk from him about selling up. Briony had been lulled into a false sense of security.

Then had come Blake's phone call saying Gab was arriving on Thursday in time for Easter and they were all invited to a meal

Friday night to meet him. Briony had been able to deal with Blake's homosexuality when it was just him, but now the reality of his lifestyle was about to meet hers and she was quite sure they didn't mix.

Len and Marion's vehicle was already at the shack when they pulled in. Vincent had barely stopped the car when Madeline and Chelsea leaped out, carrying on like a couple of excited school-girls. Briony stayed put as they took a salad each and hurried inside. Vincent took the esky from the boot and appeared at her door. When she didn't open it, he did.

"You okay, love?"

"Of course." She forced her legs to turn and lift her from the car, then made her way to the boot to retrieve the tray of sweets she'd spent all afternoon baking.

Vincent gave her shoulder a squeeze. They'd talked the previous day after Blake's call about the importance of making Gab feel welcome regardless of their personal beliefs. She'd agreed then but now that she was about to meet him, her resolve to act normally was eroding with every thump of her heart against her chest.

Before she could catch her breath, Vincent was ushering her inside and there they were, her son and his partner, his male part-ner, waiting arm in arm to greet them. Her heart thumped harder.

"Mum, Dad, this is Gab."

Vince reached out a hand to shake Gab's while Briony clutched the tray she was holding with both hands and forced a smile to her lips. Gab was taller than Blake, fair with ruggedly handsome features. The kind of bloke she'd hoped Madeline might bring home, not her son.

There were hellos from Marion and Len who looked comfort-able on the lounge, a drink already in their hands. The girls were helping themselves to drinks. Briony carried her tray of sweets to the kitchen.

"Welcome to our part of the world, Gab," Vince said. "Have you ever been this way before?"

"I've never been to South Australia at all. Adelaide looked a pretty city from the air but I hadn't known the connecting flight over to here was going to be such a small plane." He screwed up his face.

Blake buzzed up with a drink for Vince and gave Gab a quick hug as he passed. "Poor love. He hates flying at the best of times."

"And then when Blake picked me up from the airport it was an hour's drive to get here, but it was great to see the countryside from ground level. And from what I've glimpsed the coastline is fabulous. I can't wait to see more." Gab smiled at Briony. It was a warm, guileless smile, seeking a response. "I'm looking forward to visiting your property and seeing where Blake grew up."

Briony shied away from his gaze and glanced around. "Did anyone bring in the cob dip?"

"Don't tell me you brought more food, Mum," Blake said. "I told you not to bring anything."

"It's Good Friday. I made a seafood cob. It just needs the oven to crunch the bread. Oh, and Marion's Tupperware. I'll go and get it." Briony dashed back to the car before he could argue further. Outside she took her time getting the box she'd tucked the hot bread into, taking long slow breaths of fresh sea air. Once the churning in her stomach had slowed she took a final breath, composed her face into a smile and walked back inside.

Marion sat alone on the couch observing the goings-on in the room. Len had got up to chat with Vince and Gab. Blake was beside himself with excitement. Marion hadn't seen him sit still since they'd arrived at the shack. He and Gab had been standing arm in arm when first Marion and Len and then about five minutes later Briony, Vince and the girls had arrived.

Gab was relaxed and appeared comfortable meeting Blake's family while Blake flitted like a butterfly between each person, providing drinks and offering food. He hadn't wanted anyone else to bring anything but of course they had so the table was groaning with a fine spread and there were enough drinks for twenty people. Like Blake, Briony was finding it hard to sit still. She'd dashed out to the car not long after she arrived to collect more food and Marion's container then came in with the food only to dash back out again for the Tupperware. Marion glanced at her carry bag. The corner of the container poked out of the top. That was three back. Only one to go and it was unlikely she'd see that one again. Her gaze returned to Briony at the kitchen bench. She and Blake were fiddling with a cob loaf and bread to go in the oven.

"Hey, Briony," Gab said. "Let Blake do it and come and sit down. I'm sure he's learned all there is to know about food from you. He's a domestic goddess."

Briony hesitated and blinked at Gab, who was patting the seat beside him.

"I...I..." Briony crossed to the window. "Gosh, look at that beautiful water. I haven't walked on the beach for ages. I might go for a quick one – before it gets dark, if you don't mind. Back in a minute."

"Mum," Chelsea groaned but Briony didn't stop.

The screen door clicked shut behind her and the rest of them stood around like the cast of a play who'd forgotten their lines.

"Did I say something wrong?" Gab asked.

"No," Vince said. "Briony's been a bit...she's had a lot on her mind lately." He looked at Len. They both looked to Marion.

"Should I go with her?" Blake said.

"No," Len said. "Marion and I will. You all have a lot to catch up on. We won't be long."

Marion gaped at him. Surely he didn't think now was the right time. He took her arm and guided her outside before she had a chance to object.

"What's going on, Len?" she hissed.

"You need to talk to her about us, Marion."

"Now?" They were walking along the verandah towards the track that led to the beach.

"I think so."

They both watched the lonely figure on the sand, moving along the water's edge. Marion of all people knew what a burden it was to keep up appearances. She was suddenly weary.

"Okay. I'll do it."

Len squeezed her hand then brushed a kiss across her cheek and she set off down the path to the beach.

Briony was only dawdling so Marion caught her easily.

"Everything all right?" she asked as they drew level.

Briony stopped, startled, and brushed at tears on her cheeks. "I can't do it, Marion." Her face was ashen. "I can't sit and watch them together. Blake is prancing around so obviously, so..."

"In love," Marion said gently.

Briony shuddered. "Everyone else seems to have accepted it, even Vincent, but I can't."

"Blake's still your son."

Briony stared out to sea. "I've seen what's happened to people when there's a hint of difference, especially if it's sexual difference."

"Times have changed, Briony."

"Have they? For all we say that there are still people in this community who scoff and make jokes when homosexuality is mentioned."

"I wonder if it would help you to seek professional counselling."

"What!"

"It might help you understand your son better and keep your relationship with him healthy."

"I don't..." Briony pressed her lips together.

"Counselling helped me."

"With what?"

"Can we sit a moment?" Marion asked. "I need to tell you something."

They'd stopped not far from an upturned dinghy pulled up at the base of the sand hills. Marion looked from the boat to Briony. She thought of Len, the secret they'd kept and the impact that had had on their lives. It hadn't been without its difficulties but in the main they'd made it work successfully. She hoped Len was right about speaking out.

Briony frowned but allowed herself to be shepherded. They plodded through the soft sand and settled on the little boat.

Marion stared at her feet, seeking strength. The only time she'd spoken about this before had been when they'd told their children. It had been difficult. She swallowed, trying to create some moisture in her dry mouth.

"Len and I...our marriage is different..." Marion's chest tightened.

"I'm sure we're all a little different." Briony shifted on the boat.

"Len...Len identifies as gay." The words rushed out and with them Marion's strength.

"This is not a time for joking, Marion."

The sand at Marion's feet seeped over the toes of her sneakers as she pushed hard at the ground to stop her body moving with the spinning in her head.

"Marion?"

Briony's voice came from a long way away. A hand gripped her shoulder.

"Marion? Are you all right?"

She gasped in a breath, then took in another, slower and steadier. The dots before her eyes faded away.

Briony was peering at her. "Oh my lord, Marion. You're being serious, aren't you?"

Marion nodded.

Briony pulled away. "Why would you tell me that?"

"Len thought...and I agreed...we thought if you knew our story you might think differently about Blake."

"Why?"

"We hoped you'd want a better life for Blake—"

"No! I meant why would you marry a homosexual?"

Marion looked at the horror on Briony's face and prayed again Len was right.

"I didn't know Len was gay when we married. He denied it to himself, let alone anyone else. Life for homosexuals was very different when he was a young man in the seventies. This is a small community. He was an only child, his parents would have disowned him, the church would have turned against him. Private consensual sex between same sexes was only decriminalised here in 1975 and even later in other states." Marion shook her head. It was hard to imagine how different life had been then. "He decided to deny his homosexuality."

"It's possible then." Briony's look of horror had changed to one of hope.

Marion clenched her teeth. Briony still didn't get it. "Not without a lot of heartache."

"I don't understand. What happened? How did you find out? Why would you stay together if he was…"

Why indeed? Back when Len had first come out to her, Marion had questioned everything about her marriage. "I was thirty when I came back from overseas for your wedding. I was tired of travel, a bit homesick and Dad wasn't in good health. You and Vince were so happy I suddenly thought settling down was what I wanted to do. The teaching job at Wirini Bay came up and I met Len again. He was such a different man from the shy gangly boy he'd been when I'd left, and so different to the men I'd had brief relationships with. He'd not travelled much but he was well educated and thought broadly on lots of topics. He was funny and generous, and he spent time courting me. I fell in love with him." She glanced at Briony. "I still love him."

"How did you find out he was…you know?"

"It was about seventeen years ago – our kids had left home and both Len's parents died in quick succession. He was so sad and I couldn't seem to reach him. I was really worried about his mental health and one day he broke down and everything came tumbling out. I think he was emotionally exhausted and it was a release for him to tell me."

"What about you?"

"I was shocked, upset, angry. I think I went through every gamut of emotion. It's such a huge betrayal when the person you love turns out not to be who you thought they were. I left home."

Briony frowned. "Where did you…oh, was that when you spent a couple of months here at Port Kent? I always thought that was a bit odd."

"We had a lot to work through. It was a hugely difficult time. Len didn't want to leave our marriage. He said he'd made a commitment to me, that he loved me and didn't want to lose the life we had together. I finally decided I didn't want to leave either. He was my best friend. We'd been through so much together. I searched for some kind of help and discovered a group in Sydney. We made a couple of trips to attend counselling and we had phone hook-ups."

"Do Roxanne and Grant know?"

Marion nodded. "Once we'd sorted ourselves out we decided we should be honest with our kids. They're happy for us to do what makes us happy but once we both committed to continuing our marriage we decided no-one else needed to know."

"But now you've told me."

"I've only recently found out that Vince knows."

Briony clapped a hand to her mouth.

"Len admitted to me it was way back when he thought I was going to leave him. You know what good friends those two are. Vince called in and I wasn't there and Len was obviously down. Vince kept on at him to open up and he did."

"My husband has kept this a secret." Briony pushed to her feet. "Oh no. Is he gay too?"

"Of course not." Marion swallowed her brief flash of irritation. Sometimes Briony's thought patterns were beyond her. "It wasn't his secret to tell."

Briony glared at her a moment then stalked off down the sand to the water's edge. She stood perfectly still, her back to Marion. After a moment she moved off along the beach, stopped, turned and retraced her steps. Marion stayed where she was, watching Briony pace. Finally, she turned, slowly moved back to the boat and came to a stop in front of Marion.

"I don't understand any of this." Briony threw out her hands. "But I'm the odd one out. Vincent has obviously been able to cope with your news and now Blake's. He takes the curve balls the girls throw us in his stride and both of them seem okay with a gay brother." She sat beside Marion again. "I'm terrified, Marion. What's wrong with me? The family I thought I had is falling apart."

"Not falling apart...perhaps they're not living the life you'd thought. It's been a hard lesson but I've learned the only person I can control is me."

"But I don't understand why Blake is gay?" Briony clapped a hand to her mouth. "He wore a lot of Chelsea's hand-me-downs and played with the girls' dolls. Was it my mothering?"

Marion tried to smile. She knew sometimes people thought her smiles more like a scowl. She forced the corners of her lips higher.

"I asked the same question once," she said. "Was it something about me that had made Len gay? But now I know that's ridiculous. He was that way from childhood. I don't know what makes one person gay and another heterosexual. It's in each individual's make-up. Nothing you or I did made Blake or Len gay."

Briony pondered that a moment. "How could you stay married?"

"The counselling was a huge help. Finally I realised I wasn't angry at Len but at the family and culture that made him hide who he was. It takes two to make a marriage work and the bottom line was we both wanted it to work. We had to decide what we could live with and what we couldn't accept. I wouldn't have stayed if Len was looking for extramarital flings. He assured me he wasn't. We'd both had relationships before we married but neither of us had been with anyone since. Len didn't want to leave me for a man so..."

"So you have…you know…"

"Sex?"

Briony cringed.

Marion paused. She'd come this far, what did it matter if Briony knew the rest. "Right from the start sex was never overly important in our relationship. Neither of us were virgins…I can't say I enjoyed my early experiences and Len felt the same."

"So he's had sex with a…a man?"

"And a woman. He tried hard to deny his true sexuality. When we met there was so much more to our attraction, we became good friends, we had a lot of other things in common. When the sex happened it was because we both thought the other expected it. And when Len married me he was doing as his family and community expected and the church back then. We built a good life together, we had our children and I truly had no idea what Len was hiding until he opened up after his parents died. I don't think either of us ever had a high libido. Sex was a small part of our relationship." Marion paused. It hadn't been for some years now but she and Len still shared a bed, cuddled and remained close. "I've never been interested in anyone else and Len has never been unfaithful to me."

"You act like a normal couple."

"You're not the only one who can keep up appearances – but what's normal anyway? Who really knows what anyone's marriage is truly like? Is anyone's relationship like the images we're bombarded with in the media?"

"But you've remained together."

"It all took time and patience. For a while there was grieving for the loss of the life I thought I had. I'm certainly not saying it's been easy. That's why I've told you all this. It's too late for Len. He had to quietly deny his true self. Seventeen years ago he declared he valued the life we had together and he didn't want to give that up. It's less of a burden for him now that I know but…" Marion leaned closer. "Don't make Blake hide what he is. These days there's no need."

"There's still prejudice against gay people. I don't want him to be hurt, to have his life made harder."

"I know there are still small-minded people who snigger or are even homophobic and some who think their faith denies it, but life for Blake and Gab as a gay couple in this country…if they love each other…well, they've as much chance at happiness as any couple, heterosexual or otherwise."

"Mum?" Chelsea's voice echoed from further along the beach. Tucked up at the edge of the bush and sandhills they were out of sight.

Briony grabbed Marion's hand. "I don't know if I can do it."

"What are you really afraid of, Briony?"

"I don't want my children to be seen as different," she sobbed. "To be sniggered at and talked about, like…like I was as a child."

"Oh, Briony." Marion shook her head. "That was your experience. Life is different for this generation. You can't stop your children from living their best life in case they get hurt. All you can do is support them."

Briony looked at her through tear-filled eyes. "I don't know how!"

"You're a wonderful mother," Marion said. "You'll find a way."

"There you are." Chelsea came into view and turned up the beach towards them. "What are you two doing?"

"Having a catch-up chat." Marion stood and dusted off her jeans while behind her Briony wiped her eyes.

"Brandon's mum just called." Chelsea waved her phone in the air. "Brandon's agreed to rehab and they've asked if I'll go back and help on the property while he's away. They want me to meet them in Adelaide to talk."

"That's good news," Marion said when Briony remained silent.

"He says he's going to do his best to get cleaned up. He loves me, Mum, and he wants to do everything he can for us to stay together." Chelsea flung herself against Briony and sobbed. This time Briony's tears overflowed and she slowly lifted her arms and wrapped her daughter in a hug.

Marion smiled and gave them both a quick squeeze. "That's good news indeed."

Much later Marion and Len were in the car driving home from Port Kent. Marion was thinking about sausage rolls. She'd taken the last dozen from her freezer for the meal at the shack. She had the ingredients to make a big batch tomorrow, and after all that had happened tonight she was thinking she might get stuck into making them when she got home, even though it was late. Something about the repetitive process was soothing. She'd lost herself in baking sausage rolls many times over the years.

"How do you think tonight went?" Len broke the silence.

"I like Gab," Marion said. "He seems a good match for Blake."

"What about Briony though?"

"She did her best."

"She kept staring at me."

"You wanted me to tell her."

"I know. How did she take it?"

"It was a shock, of course. For both of us really. I didn't imagine I'd tell anyone else once we'd told Rox and Grant. Revealing our personal life to Briony was quite…difficult."

Len reached across and squeezed her arm. "We could have done it together but I thought that might be a bit much for her."

"I agree." Marion thought back over her conversation with Briony. "You know what her initial reaction was, once she'd got over the shock of you being gay? She thought if we could live a lie then Blake could too."

"Hell." Len's fingers drummed the steering wheel. "I hadn't thought of that angle."

"I told her all the reasons why it wasn't a good idea."

"You don't believe that, do you, Marion? That we're living a lie?"

"You can understand why she thinks we are."

"My feelings for you aren't a lie. We made the decision together to stay together. We've made our relationship work and that's not a lie."

"I know, Len. I'm just saying that's how Briony saw it." She studied him in the light from the dash. His face was contorted as if he was in pain. "Do you want me to drive?"

He shook his head, his gaze firmly fixed ahead. "I'm a coward hiding in a heterosexual marriage."

"You don't believe that." Marion stared at his profile. "*I* don't believe that."

His shoulders sagged.

"We've had a good life, Len, enjoyed our work and community. We've got two fabulous kids and their partners. You're not regretting that now, are you?"

"No. I wasn't brave enough to admit to my homosexuality in my youth. A lot of sad things happened for those who did. The only thing I regret is not being open with you earlier."

"There's no point to what ifs and maybes now." She glanced at him again. "But I'd stand by you if you wanted to—"

"I don't."

Marion swallowed the lump that had formed in her throat.

"You're a wonderful woman, Marion."

"Oh yes, I believe they call me Saint Marion after the time capsule reveal." She spoke with sarcasm to lighten the mood and was relieved when his lips turned up in a smile.

"You're my Marion and that's all that matters," Len said. "We might not have the usual type of marriage but we have a special bond I wouldn't trade for anything."

Marion basked in the warmth of his words. Since she'd retired, or perhaps for longer than that, she'd become focused on herself rather than them. She vowed in that moment to work harder at that.

"Do you think Briony will come round?" he said.

Marion sighed. "We did a lot of talking. Blake isn't going to hide who he is or his relationship with Gab. I told her she'd be the one to miss out if she couldn't accept that."

"I guess it will take more time."

"I don't think there's anything more we can do. It's truly up to Briony now."

They lapsed into silence, staring into the darkness beyond the headlights. Marion was still uneasy she'd told their story to Briony. Marion and Len had made the choice to maintain their relationship and keep their personal life to themselves. It had been one of her conditions that, other than their kids, she and Len told no-one else about their marriage. It was nobody else's business, except Vince had known, and now Briony. Marion felt as if she was teetering on the edge of a precipice, like she had seventeen years ago when Len had first admitted he was gay.

"You look worried, duck."

"We're too old to be the subject of gossip. I don't want people turning the good life we've made into something they discuss and pick apart and question."

"Neither do I, but I think it was a risk we had to take. Blake's a great young man. I hope we've helped."

Marion recalled Blake's bright smile as they left. "I hope so too."

"Besides, knowing Briony as we do and her propensity for keeping up appearances, she'd be the least likely to tell anyone else."

Marion relaxed back against the seat. "You're right about that."

thirty-five

Briony checked her lipstick and tucked a wayward piece of hair back into place. She'd escaped to the bedroom to take a moment for herself after the busy day and before she needed to do the final prep for dinner. The rest of the family were sitting out on the back verandah enjoying the last of the afternoon sunshine and a few drinks. Every now and then a raised voice reached her or a laugh. They all appeared to get on so well with Gab. It was just her who was still struggling.

Blake and Gab had come to the farm in time for lunch. The previous evening she'd discovered Gab was vegetarian but ate fish. Briony had been up early preparing a finger food lunch: sandwiches, zucchini slice, tuna and spinach tarts, and cheese and veg muffins. Then the three men had gone off to do a tour of the property. Gab had been keen to see it all.

They were staying on for dinner and Madeline was bringing Cameron. The pressure of feeding seven, two of them practically strangers, had made Briony anxious and she'd almost spun out when she realised her standard lamb roast wouldn't suit Gab.

He'd assured her he'd be happy with a plate of vegetables but Chelsea had helped her find a recipe for a mushroom and butternut pie. It was in the oven now along with the lamb and the vegetables and a large apple crumble. Keeping busy had stopped her thinking too much about Blake and Gab's relationship and Marion's disclosure.

Briony still couldn't get her head around Len being homosexual and Marion being his wife, but when she thought back it explained a lot of things about Marion. She had been much more carefree in her younger days, before Roxanne and Grant had left home. After that Marion went full-time instead of only teaching part-time. It all coincided with what she said about Len's admission.

"Briony?"

Gab's call from the back of the house startled her. She brushed her hands down her skirt and stepped out into the passage.

"Oh, there you are." His tall frame was silhouetted against the open door beyond him. "Sorry, I didn't mean to bother you."

"You're not."

Gab shoved his hands into the pockets of his jeans. "You and I haven't had much of a chance to talk and I wanted to…" he shrugged, "know a bit more about Blake's mum."

Briony put on her best smile. "It has been a busy twenty-four hours, hasn't it? Shall we sit in here a moment?" She gestured towards the kitchen. "I've got a couple of things to finish."

"Can I help?"

"No, no, you sit." She shooed him towards a chair. "I'm just doing a few last-minute things."

"You've got a beautiful home," Gab said.

"Thank you. Where are you living now that you're back in Sydney?"

"With Mum. She kept the house when my parents divorced. It's huge, and now that both my sisters have moved out she says she rattles around in it. There's a separate apartment below the main house where my gran used to live so I've taken that over." He gave a small smile. "I've asked Blake to move in with me."

"I see."

"I'm sorry my turning up has been difficult for you."

"Not at all." Briony smiled and turned back to the bench.

"I get how confronting this all has been for you," Gab said. "You haven't seen Blake in person for years and he arrives home, tells you he's gay then springs me on you."

"I…" She glanced over her shoulder then back to the packet of gravy mix she clutched in her hands and opened the top.

"It must have been a shock to find out Blake was living a different life to the one you'd always thought he was."

"It was a bit of a surprise."

"A bit!"

He laughed sharply and Briony jumped. The powder shot from the packet, some of it showering the bench.

"Now I know where Blake gets his diplomacy from." Gab appeared beside her and reached for the fork. "Do you mind if I mix the gravy? Blake says it's one of the jobs I can manage."

Briony passed the saucepan. "I'm sorry. It's just so far removed from my expectations," she said.

"Don't be sorry." Gab added water to the gravy powder and stirred. "My family have known I was gay nearly as long as I have. I warned Blake it wouldn't be easy for you…to suddenly discover he's gay when he's never given you any indication."

"I guess there wasn't going to be any easy way for him to tell us. And it's only me who's taken it so hard. I must seem like an out-of-touch fuddy-duddy."

"I'm not sure what a fuddy-duddy is."

"Old-fashioned."

"I'm thinking a different world view, perhaps." Gab moved to the stove. "Would you like me to put this on now?"

Briony shook her head. "Not yet, but I wouldn't mind a glass of wine. There's a bottle in the fridge. Will you join me?"

"Sure."

Briony set out the glasses as Gab opened the bottle and poured. He was easy to be with. She could understand why Blake...why Blake loved him. It was so difficult even to think the word love but she had to convince herself before she could be open about it.

They took a glass each and sipped.

"A nice chardy," Gab said.

Briony waved to a chair. "Shall we sit?"

They took a seat opposite each other. Gab swirled the wine in his glass, studying it before turning his gaze back to her.

"You need time, Briony. Blake and I haven't given you that but he's hurting. And what hurts him hurts me." Gab's easy-going persona slipped away, his look serious. "I want to tell you about a friend of mine. She's in her mid-twenties and last year she finally got up the courage to tell her parents she was gay. Their reaction was denial and they told her she had to shut out any homosexual feelings. She loves her parents, wants them in her life and to keep their love and approval she has tried to hide her true sexuality. It's been a disaster for her, she spiralled into depression, lost her job and two months ago...she overdosed—"

Briony gasped. "Is she..."

"She was found in time. It was a cry for help. She's making a slow recovery back to health, supported by good friends and extended family who were there for her once she opened up. The thing is, for her to be a healthy productive human being she can't see her parents. It would be detrimental to her well-being while her parents continue to deny her sexuality and they're missing out on life with their beautiful daughter. So sad for them all."

Briony pressed her fingers to her mouth. "Blake would never…"

Gab shook his head "Blake's confident and comfortable in his own skin. He came out a long time ago…just not to you."

Briony pushed her fingers tighter against her clamped lips.

"I didn't tell you about my friend to scare you," Gab said. "Blake has me, he has good friends and he…he has a supportive family. I don't want that to change for him." He pinned her with a searching look.

Briony sagged back in her chair as the ramifications of denying the truth hit home. Was making her son hide his true self worth what she would lose…what they'd all lose? She thought of Len and the life he'd denied himself. She was so grateful times had changed.

"I can see you might need longer but—"

"You're not going to leave, are you?" Briony realised she didn't want that.

"Not straight away. I've got another week off. We'd like to spend as much of that week with you as we can but if it's too hard…"

She drew herself up. "Of course it's not too hard. If we weren't such a full house at the moment you know you'd be welcome to stay here."

"Next time," Gab said. "And I hope you'll visit us in Sydney."

"We haven't been since Blake lived there last."

"I can take some time off to help show you around."

"I haven't ever asked what you do for a living," Briony said.

"I followed in my parents' footsteps. I'm a doctor. That's how Blake and I met. We were both volunteering at a centre for homeless youth."

"Blake's never mentioned that." Since he'd been home and told them he was gay they'd not really had an in-depth conversation about anything else.

"Blake's a great guy and he says I am too." Once more Gab's warm, open smile lit his face. "I hope I can get to know you all better and you me. My family are a huge part of my life. I think Blake built a kind of wall between family and his personal life. It was easy for him to do while he was living overseas but now that he's back in Australia...well, I know he's longing to rebuild those family connections, to be his true self with you. No matter what, he's still your son."

"He is." Briony knew it was still going to be difficult to accept what she thought of as the new Blake, but she also realised that when she forgot about what anyone else thought, her love for her son was the most important thing.

Footsteps sounded in the passage. "Gab? Mum?"

"In here, Blake." Briony stood up.

He stuck his head around the door. "I wondered where you'd got to."

"I was helping your mum make the gravy." Gab grinned.

Blake's smile changed to a look of horror. "Don't let him near it, Mum! His gravy's always lumpy." He strode towards the stove.

Gab stood and intercepted him, pulling him into a hug. "Your mum and I were having a chat."

"That's good." Blake glanced at Briony. It was a tentative look, almost questioning. "That roast meat's smelling good. Do we need to help with vegetables? Gab can do that but I'll do the gravy."

"The veggies are done. We were just having a drink."

"Don't mind if I do." Blake poured himself a glass.

They settled back at the table, Blake close to Gab. The two men smiled at each other. Briony saw the look they exchanged and something clicked inside her, like a switch flicking. Her son was in love and she was happy for him. She was so surprised she took an extra large gulp of wine and nearly choked.

"Are you all right, Mum?"

"Yes." She coughed and adjusted the small vase of roses in the centre of the table, diverting the attention from herself.

"Are these from the garden at the side of the house?" Gab asked.

"Yes, do you like roses?"

"His place is full of them," Blake said.

"It's a passion Dad and I share and I'm enjoying picking it up again now that I'm back in Australia. Dad planted lots of bushes and there are quite a few of the older varieties. Like in your side garden."

"Blake's nanna planted them."

"Dad lives in a high-rise apartment now but he still calls in regularly at home to maintain the roses. And talk to them." Gab winced. "I'm not sure I should have mentioned that this early in our friendship."

Briony laughed. "Roses do need special attention."

Chelsea and Vince came in and paused briefly before Vince said, "Looks like the party's moved inside."

"This was my first drink." Briony held up her almost empty glass. "I'd like a refill, please, and the table needs setting."

Gab topped up the glasses while Blake and Chelsea set the table.

"Where did this dinner set come from?" Chelsea was holding up one of the side plates that Briony had already stacked at the end of the table.

"It was your nan's. Aunty Marion dropped it off the other day. She doesn't use it and she knew I liked it."

"You better look after it. I quite like it too." Chelsea held the plate out, moving it from side to side so the gold edge caught the light and sparkled.

Gab picked up a plate. "Alfred Meakin – your nan has good taste."

"Why should you get it, Chelsea?" Blake said.

"I'm the oldest."

"But you wouldn't look after it like I would."

Vince joined Briony at the sink, a smile on his face. "Some things never change. Maddie's checking on the horses, then she'll be in." He brushed a kiss across her cheek. "Apart from the sibling rivalry, things look like they're going okay here?"

Briony glanced over as Chelsea teased Blake about always putting the glasses in the wrong spot and then he reminded her how she'd once blown her nose on a serviette.

"I was six." Chelsea groaned and Gab laughed.

"Yes." Briony smiled. "I think things are going fine."

"Cameron should be here soon. It's pretty serious between him and Maddie."

"You've been talking to them?"

"He called in the other day. When you were in Badara."

"You didn't mention it."

Vince shrugged. "I'm glad Maddie's bringing him tonight. It'll be good to get to know him better."

Briony took a deep breath. "Yes," she said and almost truly meant it.

By the time dinner was over Briony was exhausted. A combination of making sure the food was good – everyone had assured her it was – and the tension of trying to make the right conversation. Sitting back now, watching the others gathered around her kitchen table, she had to admit it was a happy exhaustion.

Chelsea had a smile that had hardly left her face since the call she'd received from Brandon the previous night. He was going into rehab after Easter and she wanted to see him before that. Evidently he couldn't have visitors for two weeks after he went in.

Blake was instructing Gab in the finer details of the difference between rams and wethers, with a bemused Vincent looking on, and Madeline was murmuring who knew what in Cameron's ear. He was a good-looking chap. Briony could understand why her daughter would be attracted to him. Madeline would be thirty next year. Well and truly old enough to make her own decisions, even if Cameron was twelve years her senior.

This was Briony's family. It was not the picture-perfect family she'd imagined when she'd first married and had children, or thought she'd had only a month ago, but then she was beginning to understand there was no such thing as a perfect family. They came in all shapes and sizes. Briony had been so fixated on what she thought family should be, she'd missed the reality happening in front of her.

Tonight, after Cameron had arrived looking so nervous, his hand trembling as he'd shaken hers, she'd made a vow to herself she would try her best to simply go with the flow.

The sound of tinkling on glass drew her attention to the end of the table, where Cameron was standing. He cleared his throat, glanced at Vince then down at Madeline.

"Mads and I have some news to share," he said.

Madeline flung out her left hand, fingers splayed to reveal a sparkling ring on her finger. "We're engaged."

Chelsea squealed and hugged her sister. Blake and Gab lined up to do the same. Briony glanced at Vince, who winked at her. So that's what that earlier cryptic chat had been about. Briony was pleased Cameron had spoken with Vincent first. It was old-fashioned but nice.

A champagne cork popped and glasses were handed around as they toasted the happy couple. Briony hugged Madeline and then Cameron.

"I'm thrilled for you both," she said, and this time she believed she meant it.

thirty-six

Paige's heart was fit to burst it was so full as she watched her children hunting along the edge of the Addicots' patch of scrub to find Easter eggs. Kodie and Levi scoured the bushes and tree branches, squealing with delight each time they discovered another bright foil-wrapped egg. Jayden trailed behind them carrying a basket and trying to look reluctant but was unable to wipe the smile from his face when he pointed out an egg in a tricky spot or hoisted Levi up to reach one in the fork of a tree.

"This is so kind of you, Marion," Paige said.

"Len did the hiding."

"And you, Len, thank you."

He waved from the edge of the small fire he was preparing to light later.

Levi yelped again and held up a bright red egg.

"Gosh, that's a lot of chocolate." Paige laughed. "I'm glad you explained it's a sharing basket. Levi had already eaten way too much chocolate before we'd even had breakfast."

"Hopefully Blake and Gab will put a dent in it when they come, and my brother has a sweet tooth too."

When Marion had rung to ask them out for a campfire barbecue she'd mentioned that Briony, Vince and Blake were coming too, and Blake's partner Gab, who Marion had made a point of explaining was male. Paige wasn't totally surprised that Blake was gay. He'd been rather evasive about his personal life the day he'd had lunch with the others at her place but some of the things he'd said had made her wonder. Not that it was any of her business. She was surprised that Marion had felt the need to tell her in advance though. She guessed it was more of a big deal to the older generation.

"I've got a couple more things to get out of the ute," Marion said.

"Can I help?"

"No, I'll be fine. You watch the children. It's not much."

Paige wandered in the direction of the kids, who hadn't done any triumphant egg waves for a minute or two.

Len joined her. "I'd better give young Jayden a nudge in the right direction. I don't think I went as far as they are now but there are a few scattered on this side."

"It really is kind of you both to do this."

"We used to come out here for an egg hunt when our kids were young and a few times after that for church gatherings or visitors, but we don't seem to have many young ones in our lives at the moment. They brighten you up, don't they?"

Kodie yelled at Levi, who was taking the wrapper off one of the eggs he'd found.

"That's one way of looking at it," Paige said.

"I'll go and 'egg' them on." Len chuckled at his joke as he set off.

Paige turned back to the cleared area where tables and chairs were set out. Marion was unpacking a basket of things on a long trestle table. Paige tried not to feel bad about her dip platter and potato salad but Marion had insisted she didn't need to bring anything else.

"Sausage rolls as well," Paige groaned. "Levi won't want to leave."

"I couldn't live up to my name if I didn't have sausage rolls for him."

The breeze ruffled the paper serviettes Marion had put out and Paige put some cutlery on them to stop them blowing away.

"I think we'll need that fire later," Marion said. "Amazing how suddenly the weather has turned. Oh, look, here they come."

Kodie and Levi were skipping and running back in their direction. Kodie was carrying the basket of eggs and Jayden and Len were following along behind in deep discussion.

"Look at all the eggs we found!" Levi yelled, his lips coated in chocolate.

Paige and Marion admired the colourful haul.

"Levi's eaten two already," Kodie said.

"Goodness, that's enough then." Marion took the basket and offered it around. "Everyone else can have two then we'll put them away until the others come. I've brought some morning tea for us."

Paige and Len took an egg each and Kodie and Jayden two then everyone lined up for a sausage roll and a drink.

"I'm taking Jayden for a driving lesson in a minute," Len said.

Once more Paige's heart felt full at the smile on Jayden's face.

"Can I come?" Kodie asked.

"Not this time," Len said. "It can only be the two of us when Jayden's learning but I'll take you all for a ride after lunch."

"That patch of scrub where you found the last lot of eggs is a great place to make cubbies," Marion said.

"Let's do that, Levi."

"Yes!"

They ran off as Len and Jayden headed to the ute. Len set Jayden up behind the steering wheel and Paige followed their progress as they bunny hopped away.

"He can't do any damage out here," Marion said. "Our kids learned to drive in primary school. It's a necessary skill when you live on a farm."

"He'll be a better driver than me," Paige said. "I've never learned to drive a manual."

The two women sat on camp chairs with the remains of their coffees.

Marion screwed up her nose as she sipped. "Sorry, it's only instant. I've got a pod machine back at the house."

"I didn't expect to find a coffee machine out here."

"There's not even one in Badara these days. It used to be quite a hub of activity on mail days. Poor Mick. I don't suppose you've heard anything?"

"Sarah told me on Thursday he's coming home after Easter. She plans to help out for a while till he's properly back on his feet."

"That could be never. His heart's not in it. He wants to sell and move down the coast near his daughter. Trouble is the place is such a mess."

"Not any more. Sarah and I have given it the once-over."

"That's good of you."

"She's trying to find out if she can get the coffee machine serviced too."

"And how's the bread making going?"

"Mostly successful." Paige screwed up her nose. "I had a failure the other day but I think I left out the salt."

"Not the machine's fault then." Marion grinned. "I've typed up the proposal for council about the Welcome to Badara sign. I'll send it in after Easter. It's a great suggestion, Paige, with a lot of support already. I'm sure it'll get the go-ahead."

"I hope people don't think I'm the newcomer having too much to say."

"It's a very sensible idea and I think sometimes we need some fresh eyes. The old ways don't always work."

Happy voices drifted from the scrub and from beyond it they heard the faltering sound of the ute engine.

"I know I said it earlier, but this is really kind of you and Len. The kids are in heaven."

"I'm only sorry we haven't asked you out here before. It's been a bit warm to do anything in the scrub but I know how much kids enjoy farm machinery and animals."

"I held everyone at arm's length when we first came."

"But you're settling in now?"

"We are. You were right about joining the sports club. Jayden's loving learning to play footy and Kodie's going to play netball. Everyone's been welcoming. The fitness club's expanding and I'm even going to join the CWA when school goes back."

"Good for you."

"Beth's told me all about their craft group."

"They asked me to join the craft group when I retired, but apart from knitting, which I don't do well, I don't have a crafty bone in my body. They meet once a fortnight, don't they?"

"I think so."

"Will you need childcare?"

"I'll start when school goes back – Beth said there's a creche for younger ones."

Marion sat up. "You could go to the next session if you like. Bring the children here first. Jayden can have another driving lesson and I can find plenty to keep Levi and Kodie busy."

"Oh no, I couldn't..." Paige really wasn't sure how that would go. For all her kids were having fun, she wasn't sure about leaving them totally in Marion's stern care.

"I'd enjoy it, truly."

Paige thought about the night Marion had played cards with the kids and how well they'd got on. Now Marion's look was so imploring Paige felt bad saying no.

"I'll find out when the next meeting is."

The ute trundled sedately back along the track. Jayden's head was just visible above the steering wheel.

"Look at that," Marion said. "Didn't take him long to get the hang of it. Oh, and that looks like Vince's vehicle following."

A four-wheel drive pulled in beside the ute and they both rolled to a stop.

"We're a bit early," Vince called as he and Briony got out. "But the girls aren't home so we thought we may as well come over."

"It's good timing," Len said and gave Jayden a gentle nudge. "This young fellow's just got through his driving lesson with flying colours and now he's going to help me light the fire."

Marion was pleased to see Paige's smile was as wide as Jayden's.

"Chelsea's gone to Adelaide to meet up with Brandon and her in-laws, and Madeline and Cameron are with his parents," Vince said.

"Vincent," Briony chided. "People aren't interested in all the details. The girls said to say hello to everyone."

Kodie and Levi came running back. "I found a real egg," Kodie said and lifted her hand to reveal a small cream egg with brown speckles.

"Len's the one to ask about that," Marion said.

"It's got a hole in the end," Kodie said.

Len crouched down for a closer look and the two children leaned in. "That's a willie wagtail's egg."

"How do you know?"

"I've been watching birds since I was younger than you," Len said.

Levi's hand shot out and he trailed one finger along Len's eyebrow. "Why have you got hair there?"

"Levi!" Paige chided.

Len laughed and wiggled his eyebrows up and down. "Just lucky I guess. More hair on my brows than on my head these days."

Both Levi and Kodie inspected him closely then Kodie returned her interest to the egg. "Why was this on the ground?"

"Perhaps it fell or blew out of the nest," Len said. "There are all kinds of birds here. If you walk quietly through the scrub and listen you'll hear them and if you look carefully, you might notice some different nests."

"Can you come with us, Jayden?" Kodie asked.

"We have to light the fire first," he said.

"That's right," Len said. "We have to get it roaring so it will make us some nice coals for our barbecue later. After that we can take a walk and see what we can find."

Len struck a match and for a moment all was quiet as they watched, mesmerised by the flames as they leaped up through the tinder-dry branches.

The three women were sitting, Paige on the edge of her chair as Levi kept darting close to the fire to add yet another stick. Finally, Len took a large stick and drew a ring around the fire.

"No-one can go closer than the circle," he said.

Levi nodded sagely and stayed back.

"There's a first," Paige muttered.

"Len will be a wonderful grandfather one day," Briony said.

The excitement that Marion had temporarily buried in the busyness of the morning rushed to the surface. "We have some news on that front." She looked at Len, who beamed back at her.

"Grant and Erin rang last night," he said. "They're having a baby in August."

"How exciting." Briony clapped her hands. "We've good news too. Madeline and Cameron are engaged."

Vince popped the top of a beer can and passed it to Len. "Not too early to wet the baby's head, is it?"

"No, but perhaps a bit early to be drinking," Briony said.

"Sun's over the yardarm." Vince looked at his watch. "Nearly."

Blake and Gab arrived then, and once they'd heard the news about the baby they produced a bottle of champagne. Marion ignored the time of day and took one of the offered glasses.

The men and children gravitated to the fire and the women to the seats.

Marion raised her glass. "A wedding and a new baby to look forward to."

"Cheers to that," Briony said and Paige added her voice.

Blake turned back at that moment and lifted his glass in a mock toast before Gab took his attention.

"You'll be sorry when they go back to Sydney, Briony," Marion said. "I know I'll miss them."

Briony gave her a grateful look. "Yes."

"And we won't have anyone to run our exercise classes.' Marion screwed up her face. "I'm thinking I'll have to eat humble pie and ask Courtney if she'd come back."

"What about Gloria?" Paige asked.

"Gloria?" Briony scoffed. "I don't think she even likes doing exercises. She's always complaining."

"I think that's bluff," Marion said recalling her recent visit to Gloria's house. "What made you think of her, Paige?"

"She dropped into the postal agency the other day and was talking to Sarah." Paige's cheeks went pink. "I overheard part of their conversation but I think Gloria's been doing some instructor training."

"She has."

They all looked up at Blake, who was standing in front of them with the champagne bottle.

"Anyone need a top-up?"

Paige declined but Marion and Briony held out their glasses.

"What do you know, Blake?" Marion said.

"You're not to say anything. But you'll find out next week anyway." Blake leaned in. "I've been helping her with her fitness instructor's course. She's keen and very good."

"Who'd have thought it?" Briony said.

Blake tapped a finger to his lips in a gesture of silence and returned to the fire.

Marion sat back. She was pleased for Gloria but not sure where that would leave her. Gloria's ongoing hostility might make attending the class untenable if she were to be leading it.

"I've had some responses to my requests for quotes for the dinner dance," Briony said. "I'm getting close to finalising the ticket price. It'll be at least one hundred dollars a head."

"Oh," Paige said softly.

"That seems a lot," Marion said.

Briony sat a little straighter. "There's the food and we need people to serve it and clean up, the band, the photographer, flowers, decorations."

"Sounds like you're planning a wedding," Marion said.

"It's something people will want to dress up for."

"Another expense."

Briony's face fell.

"I don't mean to be a wet sponge, Briony, but we do want the dinner to be in a price bracket that's doable for most. Half of Badara are on some sort of pension or government payment." Marion glanced at Paige. "And before you get upset, I'm simply making a statement of fact, not an accusation. There will be lots to spend money on that weekend and I know we have a limited number of people who can attend the dinner but we do want it to be as inclusive as possible."

"What do you suggest then?" Briony asked with a hint of huffiness.

"Perhaps we could look at ways to cut costs. Decorating, for instance. The hall walls will have photo displays from the past. Do we need anything else?"

"Flowers."

"It'll be spring. Everyone's gardens will be full of flowers." Marion glanced around. "Several of the natives here in the scrub are flowering then and I bet plenty of other farms would be the same. I'm sure we could come up with more than enough flowers."

"I see." Briony shrugged. "You're right, of course, we do have lots around us to draw from. And the band doesn't have to be as expensive as the one I was planning on, I suppose."

"Have you thought about the group that play for the old-time dances? They don't ask for much."

"I had them on my list. I'll follow them up."

"And surely we could find an amateur photographer who'd like the chance to take photos on the night without charging too much. If a few happy snaps don't turn out it won't be the end of the world. The *Country Courier* will also have a roaming photographer there over the weekend."

"You're right," Briony said again. "Perhaps I was channelling my inner mother of the bride."

"You'll get your chance at that again soon," Marion said. From the corner of her eye she noticed Paige tapping a finger to her lips. "Please speak up if you've got something to add."

"All suggestions welcome at this point," Briony said. "I seemed to have missed the mark."

"It's just an idea about the dress code." Paige wriggled forward on her chair. "I probably won't go to the dinner anyway, but...well, as Marion said, money might be tight for people. I love op shopping and I thought instead of a black-tie dinner you could call it an Op Shop Chic dinner or something like that. People can still be glamorous and they'd be supporting sustainable fashion." Paige chewed her lip, studying them closely.

"Why?" Briony said.

"So that people don't feel pressured to spend a lot of money on—"

"No, I mean why won't you come to the dinner if we make it a lot cheaper? You're a committee member. You shouldn't miss out."

"Childcare?" Marion raised an eyebrow at Paige.

She nodded.

"I'm working on that too," Briony said. "And it'll be free. I've already got Madeline rounding up some friends. She doesn't want to go to the dinner so I said she could help with other jobs. I'm even trying to get Blake to come back for it and lend a hand. I

should remind him now that Gab's here. They might both come."
Briony strode off to the campfire.

Paige looked a little startled.

Marion grinned. "Whether you wanted to or not, Cinderella, you will be going to the ball."

thirty-seven

"Apologies from Zuri, mate." Dane stepped through the back door Jayden held open as Paige came out of the kitchen. "One of his friends called over at the last minute, but maybe you can come out our way sometime during the holidays."

Jayden shrugged and glanced at Paige, trying to hide his disappointment. They'd been expecting both Townsends for their evening meal.

"We can work something out," she said. Zuri had some games on a Switch he'd offered to play with Jayden, who'd been looking forward to it ever since it had been mentioned.

"Tell Dane what you did at Marion's yesterday."

Jayden's smile returned. "Len's teaching me to drive. He said I can go out again during the holidays for more lessons."

"That's great, mate."

"And he says I can help feed the sheep."

"Dane!" Levi came flying from the lounge and wrapped himself around Dane's legs.

"Hey! Levi!" He high-fived the little boy, then Kodie who'd followed her brother.

"Back to the lounge," Paige said when Levi started to get silly. "I'll bring you some ice cream in a minute."

"With sprinkles?" Levi asked.

"Yes, with sprinkles."

Jayden dragged his feet but followed the two younger ones back to the lounge where ABC Kids was playing.

"Sometimes the age gap between them is more challenging than others," Paige said.

"Sorry Zuri didn't come."

"He's a young man. I expect he's got a life of his own."

"He's been looking forward to it. I think he's kind of enjoyed taking Jayden under his wing." Dane lowered a small esky to the floor.

Paige put her hands on her hips. "I said this was my treat."

"I don't expect you to buy me beer." He lifted the lid off the esky. "And I brought a bottle of champagne as well. Just in case you felt like some."

Paige sighed. She didn't have any alcohol in the place. "That's lovely of you. Have a seat. I'm nearly finished here."

She took the kids their ice cream while Dane popped the top off the bottle.

"I hope pizza's okay for dinner," Paige said as she took out some wine glasses. She didn't have champagne flutes.

"Sounds good to me."

"That breadmaker your mum gave me is great. I'm managing an edible loaf of bread most of the time these days, and I've worked out how to make pizza dough in it since Marion told me it did all sorts. I had a test run last night and the kids gave the result the thumbs up so I thought we'd do it again tonight. Levi and Kodie have had theirs."

They clinked their glasses together.

"Can I make my pizza now, Mum?" Jayden had come back to the kitchen. "Seeing Zuri's not here I might eat in the lounge."

His look was assessing but Paige had no idea what was going on in his head. They'd had such a good day yesterday at Marion's but he'd been quiet today.

"Sure."

"And watch something else on the TV?"

"Once the others are in bed." She looked past him to the lounge. "Five minutes to teeth clean, you two."

A wail from Levi was followed by a "yes, Mum," from Kodie.

"She loves to read so it's easy to get her to bed with her book. Levi's a bit more of a challenge. He's had far too much chocolate this weekend."

"Can I help? I read to Zuri every night for years. I kind of miss it."

"I'm sure Levi would love someone different to read him a story."

For the next twenty minutes or so there was the usual bedtime ruckus and then finally peace. Levi had fallen asleep quickly after Dane had read him way too many stories and Kodie was happily settled with her book. By the time they'd returned to the kitchen Jayden was taking his pizza from the oven. Paige sat at the table and took another sip from her glass of champagne. It felt decadent. Life was so much easier at bedtime with another adult to help.

"That smells good, mate," Dane said.

"Kodie and Levi prefer ham and pineapple but we're a bit more gourmet with our toppings, aren't we, Jay?" Paige said.

Jayden added some rocket to the top of his pizza. "We call this one the chook bucket." He grinned at Dane's raised eyebrows and Paige smiled. She loved to see her serious boy lighten up.

"Tell me what that entails," Dane said.

"First you spread the tomato stuff, sprinkle the cheese, then add some cooked chook, spring onion and tomatoes. Then when it's cooked you add rocket and a bit of tzatziki."

"You didn't mention our secret herbs and spices." Paige laughed.

"I'm having what he's having," Dane said.

Jayden took his to the lounge, shutting the door between them. Paige and Dane constructed a pizza each side by side, chatting about food they liked and disliked, joking, talking about their day, comfortable together. And then, when they were almost done, they playfully pretended to put extra toppings on each other's. Dane wanted to put mushrooms on hers, which she didn't like, and she tried to sneak his pet hate, olives, onto his.

They finally put the pizzas in the oven, refilled their glasses and sat back to wait.

"Mum said you've given the postal agency a going-over," Dane said.

"We did."

"And you got the coffee machine working."

"It needs a service to work properly. But your mum thinks she's found someone to do that. She's going to talk to Mick about me going in and making coffees there again."

"How do you know about coffee machines?"

"I trained as a barista when Jayden was little and worked at the local coffee shop. Someone always needs a barista and it was something that I could do part-time to earn some extra income."

"Not in Badara."

"No, and not since Levi was born so I might be a bit rusty. With three kids and no partner it was too hard."

They sipped their drinks and Paige contemplated what she'd said. He probably thought she was looking for sympathy.

"It's a shame Mick let the place go," she added quickly. "Sarah and Marion both mentioned people used to enjoy coming in for their mail and stopping for a coffee and a chat."

Dane nodded. "Mick came home today. Mum's going to go in each day for a while and she's put some meals in his freezer."

"She's such a kind person, your mum."

"Yep." Dane stared into his glass.

"Surely you can sound more convincing," Paige teased.

He looked up. The scar on his face always stood out more when he was being serious. "I've always felt through thick and thin Mum and Dad were rock solid."

Paige waited, not sure what he meant but certain she didn't want to hear another story about something bad, especially if it involved Sarah, who she liked very much.

"I'm still struggling with them keeping the half-sister a secret."

Paige blew out a breath and took a careful sip of champagne.

"It makes me wonder what else they've kept secret."

"Surely parents are entitled to some privacy. Do you tell Zuri absolutely everything? I don't want to tell my kids every detail of my personal life, that's for sure."

"I get that. But a half-sister isn't just about them. She's my family too."

"You may never meet her."

"I know, but what if she'd suddenly turned up like you hear happens sometimes? I only wish they'd told us a long time ago."

"I have three children, each with a different paternal background. It hasn't been easy working out what to tell them and when and what's best left alone. Your mum grew up in a different era. I get how difficult it must have been."

"So do I, but after Zuri appeared in our lives might have been a good time."

"Some women couldn't or wouldn't tell the men they later married. At least Sarah was up-front with your dad. She said she had every intention of telling you and your brother but the timing wasn't right and then time went on." Paige could relate to that.

Dane dragged his thick curls back from his head. "Families are complicated."

"Tell me about it. My parents have three grandchildren they rarely see because I'm out of favour with them. Then each of my kids has a half of their family tree they know little about. Kodie's I don't know at all. Levi's family want to be more involved. They're good people but they live in New Zealand. And Jayden's, well, they wanted him gone before he was born so they can harass me all they like but they have no rights."

"What do you mean, Mum?"

Paige swung in her chair. The champagne soured in her stomach. Jayden was standing in the open doorway. He'd come to the kitchen from the other way, via the sunroom.

"I told you about your dad's parents, Jay," she said quickly. "You've met them. You didn't really like them."

"You just said they wanted me gone before I was born."

His brow was creased tight and his eyes narrowed. She'd tried so hard to keep her beautiful boy free from the hurt and now her careless conversation had cut deep.

"They wanted you to have an abortion, didn't they?" His stare pierced her.

She couldn't look away, couldn't lie. She nodded. "I was young, only a few years older than you and they thought it the right thing at the time but they didn't allow me the choice I was entitled to. My choice was to have you – a decision I've never regretted."

"What about my dad?"

She swallowed.

"He didn't want me either, did he?"

"They don't matter, Jayden. I love you, you've got a sister and a brother who love you."

Jayden glared at her. "I thought it was weird you worrying about Levi's grandparents. They seemed like nice people and they live all the way over in New Zealand. They aren't the ones we moved here to get away from, are they? It's my dad's parents, isn't it?"

Once again his stare pinned her. She nodded.

"We didn't have to move! You could have just told me the truth!"

"Hey, mate." Dane spoke gently. "Don't yell at your mum."

"Come and sit down," Paige said. "I can explain—"

"No!"

Jayden glared from Paige to Dane then spun on his heel and strode away. His bedroom door shut with a bang and a few seconds later came the sound of his radio blaring.

Paige felt sick. She'd made up her mind to tell Jayden about his grandparents. She'd been trying for days to work out how to go about it but they'd been having such a great time over the Easter break she'd put it off, and now it was too late.

Dane shifted in his chair. She turned back.

"You see," she spat. "There are some things kids shouldn't ever have to know. Some secrets do need to stay buried!"

"Hey." Dane raised his hands, his palms to her. "I get it."

Paige flung herself forward, her head in her arms on the table. She was too angry for tears.

A steady hand rested on her shoulder. "This single parent gig is hard. Don't beat yourself up."

Dane's kindness was her undoing. The anger swirled out of her like water down a drain and was replaced with sorrow. The tears came next. She sobbed for her beautiful boy, the life he deserved and the bum life he'd got, and she cried at her own helplessness, and for not getting it right.

Dane softly rubbed her back until she stopped crying and sat back.

"Hell! The pizzas." Paige rose to her feet but he guided her down again.

"I'll get them out."

She sat in a daze while he took the well-cooked but not burned pizzas from the oven and slid them onto the chopping board. He cut them up, put them on plates and brought them to the table then sat across from her.

"I'm sorry to spoil your night," she said. "I'm a crap hostess as well as a crap mother."

"You're not a crap mum and it's not as if I've never heard a teenager carry on before."

Paige looked at the pizza. It was too hot to eat but she didn't feel hungry anyway.

Dane's chair squeaked as he shifted his weight. "I don't know if it would help..."

She lifted her gaze to his.

"Do you mind if I talk to Jayden?"

She shook her head. "Go ahead. I don't know what's best any more."

Dane smiled and got to his feet. She listened as he crossed the sunroom to Jayden's door, knocked and then the blast of music as he opened the door and closed it again. The music continued then the sound lowered.

Paige pushed back from the table and paced the kitchen. Each time she stopped she could hear the murmur of their voices but not what they were saying. After five minutes she went to the sunroom door and looked across to Jayden's room. The door remained shut. After five more minutes she sat back at the table, drained her glass of champagne and poured another. Another five more minutes dragged by before she heard the door open.

Dane came back to the kitchen alone. She pushed to her feet.

"He's calmed down."

"What did you two talk about?"

Dane shrugged. "Guy stuff."

She frowned.

"He wants to talk with you."

She took a step towards the door.

"He's going to come out in a while. I said you'd answer all his questions."

"Oh." Paige sagged.

Dane came closer and slid an arm under her elbow. "He's a good kid. Best to be up-front with him."

She reached out her other hand and latched onto Dane's shoulder then lowered her head to his chest. They huddled together in an awkward pose then Dane slipped both his arms around her and held her close, one hand firmly patting her back.

"You've got this, Paige." His voice was soft in her ear.

The tension fled her body, swept away by a wave of calm.

She clung to him, soaking in the warmth of another human's touch. When she finally opened her eyes she had to blink to clear her vision. The first thing she saw was the bloody pizzas. She eased away and Dane let her go.

"Your pizza will be cold," she said.

"I don't mind. Can I take it with me though?"

"You're leaving?"

"I told him I'd give you two some space. Jayden needs to hear the truth, Paige. It's best if it's just you two." He picked up the pizza. "I'll return the plate."

Paige nodded.

Dane came around the table, pressed a hand to her shoulder. "It'll be okay."

Paige looked back as he moved away. "Thank you."

"Any time." He smiled and let himself out. She heard the distant sound of his ute driving away and then there was nothing but the muffled voices of the TV playing to an empty room. The kitchen was a mess, all the ingredients still sitting out in case they'd wanted a second pizza. She set to and cleaned up, so lost in what she was doing she startled when Jayden spoke.

"Can we talk now, Mum?"

She took a deep breath. She was ready to tell him everything he wanted to know. She gave him a wobbly smile. "Of course."

Jayden waited for her to sit at the table then he sat opposite her. He studied the bare tabletop for a moment then glanced up. "So, we moved here so *my* grandparents wouldn't find us, not Levi's?"

She nodded. "And because it wasn't so good where we lived. I thought we needed a fresh start. I didn't tell you stuff because I was trying to protect you."

"It doesn't matter that my dad and his family didn't want me."

"Oh, Jay." Paige reached a hand across the table but he kept his firmly gripped together in front of him.

"I didn't like them that time we met," he said. "She kept trying to hold my hand. It was weird and they just seemed..." he shrugged, "fake."

"They're...different." Rufus's parents had been emotional when they'd met for coffee after his funeral. Lucinda had spent the whole time trying not to cry and she'd kept touching Jayden as if she wanted to check he was real.

"And they spoke funny."

"Did they?"

"You know, like Marion does, with that posh voice."

Paige pressed her fingers to her lips. Marion did sound a bit toffy.

"Why did they keep trying to contact you when they knew I didn't want to meet them again?" Jayden asked.

"I guess they're sorry now their only child is gone that they didn't know you." Paige rubbed her thumb between her fingers.

"But we met. What else do they want?"

"They want to keep in touch." She met his questioning look. "They've offered to give you a phone that they'd pay for so they could ring you."

"For real?" His face lit up then fell again. "What would we talk about?"

"They also want to pay for you to go to your dad's old school. It's an expensive private school with—"

"Isn't that on the Gold Coast?"

Paige nodded but she didn't stop. She was on a roll now and she was going to tell him everything. "And last Christmas...before we moved here...they sent you a pile of ridiculously expensive presents. I didn't know how I could explain that to your brother and sister who would get only what I could afford so—"

"Did they send me a PlayStation or a Switch?"

Paige sighed and nodded. "I sold it all to buy your laptop."

"Oh."

"I'm sorry, Jayden, but you needed the laptop for school."

He studied his hands, which were still gripped tightly in front of him. When he looked up his gaze was one of a much older person. "It's okay, Mum. You did the right thing."

Paige felt as if she were the child being given the approval of a parent – not that that was something she was overly familiar with.

"It's sad they never got to know what a great kid you are. We can keep in touch. Maybe one day you'd like to meet them again."

Jayden wrinkled his nose.

"We can leave it for now," Paige said. "And I'm sorry I wasn't honest with you about your grandparents. It's not always easy making decisions as a parent, especially on your own."

"Dane said that."

"My instinct is to always want to protect you from being hurt."

"Dane said that too."

"Did he?"

"Dane's a good bloke."

"He is."

"You smile more when he's around."

Paige twisted away to the pizza she hadn't eaten, still sitting on the bench. It would be stone cold but she was hungry now.

"You want to share some pizza?" she asked as she put the plate in the microwave.

"Sure."

This time they sat side by side, taking tiny bites of the now steaming-hot pizza.

"Home-made pizzas are better than those supermarket ones," Jayden said.

"They sure are."

"We used to make our own."

"That's 'cause Ari made the dough. He was a whiz at it." She glanced at Jayden. "You remember that?"

"Of course I do – I was nine, Mum."

Paige took another bite of her pizza.

"I miss Ari."

"Oh, Jay." Paige pulled him close and pressed her head to his. "I do too."

He hugged her back. They clung together for a moment then Jayden eased away. Paige brushed a stray strand of hair from his forehead.

"Kodie misses Ari too." Jayden spoke so softly she barely heard him. "She's been drawing birds again."

"Has she?" Kodie loved birds. She'd only been four when Ari had sat her down with one of those how to draw birds books and patiently stepped her through it. She had little notebooks filled with bird pictures, but she'd stopped drawing them after Ari died.

"She saw some parrots when we were feeding the sheep with Dane and Zuri and then yesterday when we went for that scrub walk with Len we saw all sorts. She's been trying to draw them." He looked at her, his eyes wide. "Do you think we could get her a bird book? You know, one of those that has pictures and tells you which bird it is."

"That's a lovely idea."

They finished the pizza before he spoke again.

"We, Kodie and Levi and me, we like living in Badara, Mum."

"You've talked about it?"

"We talk about lots of stuff. You like it here too, don't you?"

"Yes."

"But if I went to my dad's old school we'd have to move to the Gold Coast."

"If it was something you really wanted to do we could go. I could never afford a school like that."

"What's wrong with Wirini Bay Area School?"

"Nothing, it's just—"

"I'll work harder with Marion and I won't skip any more classes. I don't want to move from here."

"It's all right, Jay, I don't want to move either. I just want you to do your best. If it doesn't work out with Marion, well…" Paige shrugged. "We'll give it a few more goes and if you're not happy we can try something else to help you with your work."

"Marion's okay."

Paige nudged his shoulder. "She makes a mean sausage roll."

"Do you think she'd teach you how to make them?"

"Maybe 'us'." Paige ruffled Jayden's hair. "It's a good life skill, Jay."

thirty-eight

The first afternoon of the school term Paige was waiting outside Kodie's classroom instead of by the oval gate. She'd decided she should do that more often, and get to know a few more parents. Levi immediately headed off to the playground where a couple of other younger siblings were already playing.

After Paige had worried how they'd fill their time, the school holidays had ended up flying by. Between the Townsends and the Addicots they'd had several trips to both farms. Jayden was driving confidently already and Len and Kodie had bonded over birds, of all things. Kodie had also become friendly with a girl in her class who'd spent quite a bit of the school holidays playing at their place, and they'd had a day trip to the beach at Port Kent.

Levi had been sad to see his siblings head back to school that morning but Kodie and Jayden had both set off eagerly, Kodie with a special treasure carefully wrapped and tucked into an empty butter container.

Two women Paige didn't know were chatting together under the classroom verandah as she approached. They smiled but huddled closer and kept talking. Paige stepped up to the pinboard beside the classroom door. Several notices were pinned there, most she'd seen before but she glanced over them anyway and was startled when she heard the names Chelsea and Brandon. She glanced around. The other two women had their heads together and were so deep in conversation they seemed to have forgotten she was there.

"I heard he'd had an affair," one said.

"Are you sure, because I heard he was doing jail time."

"Maybe. Chelsea was staying on the farm with her folks for quite a while."

Paige turned back to the noticeboard and the siren sounded, drowning out any more of the conversation she hadn't wanted to hear. Briony would be very upset to know people were saying such awful things about her family.

"Hi, Paige."

She spun. Jo was walking towards her. Paige was pleased to see someone she knew.

Like Levi, Jo's young one shot off to the playground.

"I thought I was going to be late," Jo said. "I had to make a trip to the Bay for my husband and it took longer to pick up the gear than I'd thought."

"We should swap numbers," Paige said. "I'd be happy to collect your son if you ever need."

"That's kind of you, thanks."

They exchanged numbers. Since her talk with Jayden, Paige wasn't bothered about sharing her number or having her kids' photos taken. She'd rung Lucinda and made it clear Jayden wasn't interested in her offers but Paige had left the door open for him to make contact in the future if he ever decided to. Lucinda hadn't been happy, of course, but Paige had been firm and mentioned possible intervention orders and they hadn't heard from her since.

The classroom door opened and children began to stream out. Kodie's face lit up when she saw Paige.

"Where's Levi?" she asked as soon as she'd collected her bag.

"On the play equipment."

"I'll get him." Kodie sprinted off, her bag bouncing on her back.

"Hello, Paige, I'm glad I caught you." Kodie's teacher, Marina, smiled at her from the doorway. "Do you have a moment?"

Paige waved goodbye to Jo and followed the young woman inside, wondering what Kodie might have done to require a chat.

"I wanted to show you Kodie's work from today. She gave a very good morning talk about the willie wagtail nest she brought along." Marina's bright smile was infectious and Paige found herself smiling too.

"Len Addicot found an abandoned nest and gave it to her. He explained how the birds make them. The two of them spent a bit of time on willie wagtails during the holidays. Kodie loves birds."

"Well, it shows and she's obviously retained a lot of information. She even took questions after her talk, which is a first since she's been in my class." Marina's head was down as she rummaged on her desk. "This is what I wanted to show you."

She held out a sheet of art paper and Paige took it. There were sketches of two birds, excellent reproductions of willie wagtails, and they were surrounded by notes with lines pointing to relevant parts of the bird. One heading said *male* and the line stretched to the sketch with the white eyebrows. Paige smiled as she recalled Len's laugh when he'd told Kodie that was the easiest way to tell a male from a female, the bushy white eyebrows, and Kodie had replied, quick as a flash, they were like his.

"I had no idea Kodie was such a talent at drawing birds," Marina said.

"It's her thing," Paige said, her heart full to the brim for her little girl. "Levi's dad taught her and she hasn't really kept it up since he died. Len seems to have reignited her passion for it."

"She's a good worker but reserved. Today I saw a spark I hadn't seen before. I was so excited for her."

Paige wandered out of the classroom on a high. Of her three children, Kodie could be the most stubborn and she was sometimes hard to reach. She didn't remember her biological dad. Ari had been the only father figure she'd known and he'd done it well. Paige was so happy her daughter was drawing again. It was one more vindication that she'd done the right thing moving her family to Badara.

They'd only just turned the corner from the school when a car pulled up beside them.

"Sarah!" Levi jumped up and down.

After worrying her children didn't have grandparent contact they seemed to have been adopted by several sets.

"Hello, you three." Sarah leaned across and looked up at them through the passenger window.

"Have you been at the postal agency?" Paige asked. Sarah still called in each day to check on Mick.

"Yes, and the chap's coming tomorrow to clean the coffee machine. He's going to bring some new coffee he says we should try."

"Great."

"So, I thought I'd make some cakes for Wednesday and we could offer coffee or tea to anyone who comes in. Are you up for it?"

"Sure. I'd like to have a few trial runs before then though. What time's the guy coming?"

"He didn't think he'd get there till late afternoon."

"I might have to bring Kodie and Levi with me." Paige chewed her lip as she pictured Mick's response to that.

"I'll be there to help keep them entertained."

"Okay."

"How about I ring you when the serviceman arrives."

"Sure."

"I'd better get home." Sarah sat back in her seat. "Jim says I'm never there these days but Mick doesn't seem to mind me checking in on him each day."

"See you tomorrow."

"Oh, Paige." Sarah leaned across again. "It was a lovely day at Dane's yesterday."

"Yes." Paige smiled. "It was."

"The kids all had a great time."

"They did."

"You and Dane made fantastic pizzas."

Paige smiled. "I'm very grateful for that bread machine. It's so easy to make the dough."

"We'll have to do it again soon." She waved and the car moved off down the road.

Paige trailed along the footpath after her kids. Sarah was right. The kids had had a great time at Dane's. Jayden and Zuri had been glued to screens for some of the time but everyone had gathered around to prepare their own pizza topping. It had been relaxed and fun, with plenty of laughs. Dane's dad Jim loved his dad jokes like Len. They were corny but you couldn't help smiling.

Dane had said she'd soon get sick of hearing them. She'd almost said she'd like to try but had swallowed her words.

Dane had looked at her strangely then, as if he'd wanted to say more and then one of the kids had interrupted and the moment was gone. They'd packed up and gone home not long after. Her kids were settling and happy. She didn't want to do anything that might jeopardise that.

Marion and Briony were inspecting Vera's roses in the side garden as Len and Vince came back from looking at a problem with a spray unit.

"Gab took some cuttings from a couple of your mum's older roses," Briony said. "Evidently his dad has great success growing roses from cuttings. I've never had much luck."

"Have you heard from them since they left?"

"Nearly every day. Blake's had a couple of job interviews and Gab wanted the recipe for the mushroom and veg pie I made."

"Time to go, Marion," Len said. They'd made a personal visit to explain their future plans to Vince and Briony.

Vince shook Len's hand. "If my opinion's worth anything, I think you two are doing the right thing, leasing for a start."

"We appreciate your offer to agist some of our sheep." Len adjusted his hat. "Not quite ready to let everything go."

"We understand, Len." Briony hugged him then stayed clasped to him for a minute longer, giving his back a gentle pat.

Over her shoulder Len met Marion's gaze with a startled look.

"We're making a few plans of our own," Vince said.

"Oh, that's early days yet." Briony leaped back and batted a hand at him.

"It's okay for Marion and Len to know Maddie and Cameron might end up on the farm."

"One day," Briony said.

"Well, I didn't mean tomorrow. They still want to have some time with the horse property, see how that goes but they'll work with me as well. Cameron's agronomy background will stand him in good stead."

"So the property might remain in the family." Marion gave Vince and then Briony a farewell hug.

"We'll see," Briony said.

"I think it's good Vince and Briony are trying to work with Maddie," Marion said as they drove away. "Keep her and Cameron in the family business, but Briony still likes to hold things close to her chest."

"Like me with that hug. I'm not sure what that was about."

Marion chuckled as Len squirmed in his seat.

"She's being more open about Blake and Gab though," he said.

"With us at least – I'm not sure about out in the community."

"Slowly, slowly."

"I don't think Briony's got a proper handle on it all yet. She's planning to buy Gab and Blake some nice underwear for their birthdays and she asked me which department I shopped in for yours."

Len frowned.

"Ladies or mens?"

"Really!" Len said. "So it might be a bit too soon to sign her up for the Gay and Lesbian Mardi Gras?"

"Way too soon," Marion said and they both laughed.

thirty-nine

There was a knock at Marion's back door. She glanced at the clock. It was quarter past nine in the morning and she wasn't expecting anyone. She opened her door to find Gloria outside and did her best to smile.

"Hello, Marion. I was hoping you'd still be here. I wanted to catch you before fitness class."

"Come in."

Gloria looked her up and down as she passed. "You're not in gym clothes yet. You are coming, aren't you?"

"This is your first time leading...I wasn't sure—"

"If I'd be up to it."

Marion lifted her chin. "If you'd want me there."

"Oh."

Marion led the way into her kitchen. "Would you like a drink?"

"No, thanks, I'm all good. I wanted to return your container." She put the Tupperware box on the table. "And to say thank you for the voucher." Gloria wriggled her fingers at Marion. Her nails were a pretty pink. "I had a manicure yesterday. I've never had one before. It was lovely."

Marion had forgotten all about the voucher she'd given Gloria from a salon in Wirini Bay. She took in her cousin's neatly brushed hair, the healthy glow of her cheeks reflecting back from the pale pink t-shirt she wore over black leggings, and she was also sporting a pair of new gym shoes. "You're looking well, Gloria. The training and the classes must be doing you good."

"Thanks to you."

Marion's eyebrows raised.

"It was you who organised the fitness class in the first place. I found it hard work in the beginning but then I realised I was enjoying doing something just for me. I started doing extra classes online at home. Then Blake came and the routines were so much more fun. It made me think about all the women who were enjoying the classes and how sad it would be if we didn't continue."

"It's so important to keep the group going. It's good of you to take on the challenge."

"You worked hard to get it started. It won't be right if you're not there."

They sized each other up over the kitchen table.

"I accept your apology, Marion," Gloria said. "I've wished several times I hadn't read out that damned scandal sheet. I should have stopped when you said so and...well, I'm sorry."

"You don't know how many times I wished I'd never written it."

"The person responsible for most of it isn't here."

Marion frowned.

"It was Gail, wasn't it?"

Marion remained silent.

"You and I were in the same class for several years at primary school, I know your messy writing," Gloria said. "The last part of that stupid report was written in neat print. Gail wrote that stuff about me with or without your knowledge, it really doesn't matter. She was besotted with Rodney Tripp but he was a nasty piece of work. He was a typical spoiled little rich boy."

"I have to admit to wondering why Gail had liked him."

"You know I actually tried to protect her. I'd overheard him saying all kinds of disgusting things about her and I told him off. He dropped her and then spread stories about me as well. She believed that I'd shagged him and taken him away from her. I'd kissed a boy or two behind the railway shed and had a few ciggies but that was as far as it went. None of what Rodney said about me and him was true. He gave me the creeps. I tried to explain but Gail all but spat on me. She made my final year at school miserable."

"I'm sorry, Gloria."

"You weren't there. You didn't say it. And I'm pretty sure you knew nothing about it being added to that awful news report. You don't need to apologise to me any more, Marion."

Marion sighed. It was all so very sad.

"I'm not sure how many will be at class this morning," Gloria said. "But now that the school holidays are over I'm assuming some of the young mums will come back and I have to admit to feeling a bit intimidated by them."

There was a surprise. Marion couldn't imagine anyone intimidating Gloria.

"I would like some support. Claire's definitely coming. She's been my study partner. I was hoping all of the original crew would be there too: Jean, Briony, Paige as well...and you."

Neither of them were into hugging so Marion simply smiled. "I'll get changed and I'll be right behind you."

"Good." Gloria nodded and let herself out.

Marion stood alone in her kitchen for a moment, pondering all the things Gloria had said about Gail, and the previous conversations involving Gail with Vera and Jean. Marion had not seen the other side of Gail that they had. Together she and Gail had laughed and had adventures and imagined great futures for themselves. Perhaps Marion had been the friend Gail needed, someone who had accepted the funny, happy-go-lucky person that maybe deep down Gail wanted to be but circumstance had prevented.

She wondered what Gail would have made of the life Marion had lived. And what had Gail seen or heard that had made her write the things she had about Len. Maybe she'd written it out of spite or maybe she'd known something. If Marion had been aware Len was gay she was pretty sure she'd never have married him, and yet knowing him as she did now she couldn't imagine them not being together. In their own funny way they'd lived a good life, making the most of what they'd been dealt. They'd talked through the next steps and, Marion had realised only that morning, the vague prickly feeling that had plagued her since her retirement bothered her less often.

They'd found a house to rent in Port Kent, a more substantial building than the shack but still with a good view of the sea. If they liked living there they might one day knock down the shack and rebuild. Marion had tried a game of croquet, which she'd enjoyed, and they'd asked her to join the social golf group although she wasn't sure that something named 'Coffee and Cackles' was for her.

Her phone pinged with a message. Marion picked it up, read and smiled. It was from Blake. *Knees up, girls, have fun today. Good luck, Gloria. You'll be a star.*

She tucked her phone away and her gaze rested on the plastic container Gloria had left on the table. Her smile widened. Usually, she gave out her sausage rolls in small boxes, ice-cream containers or anything recycled that she didn't need back. When she'd packaged her apology sausage rolls she'd purposefully chosen to put them in her good Tupperware containers. They were something people would feel should be returned and here was the last one, home to roost.

Briony pulled up in front of the hall and dug her phone from her bag. She read her son's message and instead of a smile it brought a tear to her eyes. He'd returned to Sydney almost a week ago and she still missed him terribly. Gab had been driving the hire car when they'd left and Blake had waved from the passenger window until the car turned out of sight. To Briony it had felt like she was sending him off from home all over again. His high school and university years in Adelaide, his first job in Sydney and then off to London; it was as if most of his life she'd been waving him goodbye.

A child crying made her look up. Jo and Jac were heading into the hall with their little ones in tow. Paige had suggested they start a creche now that they had regular women attending with young ones to care for and Briony had heard they'd found someone to begin today.

She collected her things and joined them in the hall. Gloria was already set up with her sound system and headset. A few of the group had offered to put in the money to purchase it. It would be useful for other events, the Back to Badara Festival being one.

"Hello, Briony," Jean said. "Chelsea's not with you today?"

"No, she went home straight after Easter. She's got to be there while Brandon's...away." Briony pulled her best smile. "She was only here for a holiday."

"Of course, dear." Jean nodded sweetly. "And remember to ask Madeline to bring her young man around to meet Keith and I one day soon."

"I will." Briony didn't call forty-two young but in Jean's eyes she supposed it would be.

"I had a text message from Blake, earlier. Did you get it?"

"Yes."

"We'll miss him but I'm sure Gloria's going to do a fine job. And Claire's been a marvellous support for her behind the scenes."

Music blared from the speaker. They all jumped. Claire fiddled with a dial and the volume went down.

"Sorry, everyone," Gloria's voice squeaked from her headset. "Had it up a bit loud."

She smiled towards the door. Marion entered, followed by Paige and Sarah.

"It's just marvellous, isn't it," Jean said. "We'll be a good group again today."

The three women said hello and moved on but for Paige. "Is it tomorrow you're heading to Adelaide?" she asked.

"Yes," Briony said. "And I've got your list packed, don't worry."

Paige smiled. It was genuine and lit up her face. So different to the almost haunted look she'd had when Briony had first met her.

"Briony, I feel a bit awkward asking you this but I heard some rumours about Chelsea's husband at school pick-up. I hope Chelsea's okay."

Briony glanced around – no-one else was close. "What kind of rumours?"

"One was that he was in jail."

Briony frowned.

"And the other was that he was having an affair."

"Neither of which is true."

"I didn't think it was. I would have spoken up but I didn't know what to say."

Briony sighed. Chelsea had been the one who'd said they should be up-front about Brandon being in rehab to nip any rumours in the bud. They'll only make stuff up, Chelsea had said, and had suggested hearing about his addiction might help someone else. Perhaps she'd been right.

"Brandon has a drug addiction," Briony said. "He's in rehab. Chelsea is supporting him and we're hopeful he'll be back on his feet soon." She looked Paige in the eye. "If you hear people making up stuff again you can set them straight."

"Okay." Paige nodded. "I will."

"All right, everyone." Gloria's tone was more modulated now that she and Claire had fiddled with the sound system. "Let's get started." She switched on the music and INXS singing 'Never Tear Us Apart' pounded from the speaker. The Port supporters cheered in equal volume to loud groans from the Crows fans.

Briony winced. Gloria could have a mutiny on her hands before the warm-ups were started.

"Come on, you lot, no nonsense," Gloria commanded but with a cheeky smile on her face. "It's a jolly good beat to warm up to. Let's get walking on the spot. Don't lift those knees too high yet. Zip that core. Put a smile on your dial." And she started singing along.

Briony eyed Gloria closely. She hoped she didn't think their expensive speaker and headset were a karaoke machine.

Gloria picked up the pace and after several minutes of warm-ups she upped the sound and the beat of the music. Suddenly 'Let's Get Physical' was playing and they were doing knee repeaters and heel kicks like they were spring chickens.

Briony had thought she could take or leave the fitness classes when they first began but now she wouldn't miss it. Gloria was thinking she might run a second class during the week, perhaps early evening to cater for some of the working women who were keen to join, and Briony thought she'd go to that too if it happened.

She looked around at the wonderful mix of women moving to the beat like a poorly choreographed ballet group. Her gaze stopped at Marion, who was looking her way. Marion's lips turned up in that odd grimacey smile of hers and Briony smiled back. Over the years she'd often found her sister-in-law distant and a little bossy but Marion was right – they were family and they'd shared so much together. Briony felt humbled that Marion had entrusted her with her secret in an attempt to help Briony's relationship with Blake and for that Briony would always be grateful.

The session flew by and the energy was electric when Laura Branigan's voice burst from the speaker singing 'Gloria'. Everyone belted out the chorus, kicking their legs and raising their arms in time to the music. The flesh and blood Gloria beamed back at them. When it ended everyone clapped, then there were a few moments of quiet as they lowered to their mats ready for ab work. There were one or two giggles when the music changed to 'You Sexy Thing' and Gloria had them doing star-jump movements while lying on their backs. The giggles turned to cackles as legs and arms flung out of kilter and finally Gloria had to call them to a stop. In the brief silence as the music ended a series of staccato pops erupted from Jean's direction.

"Oh, pardon me." Jean's look was surprised.

"Thanks for the applause," Gloria said and everyone, including Jean, burst into laughter.

forty

Paige helped herself to one more of her sandwiches made with the bread she'd baked. It wasn't bad, even if she was praising herself. Around her in the hall supper room, the other members of the Back to Badara Festival committee were finishing their lunch. They were ready for their meeting to finalise the finer details before the events went public. It was already May and they needed to get the information out so bookings could begin. These five amazing women who she'd kept her distance from and even felt a little terrified of when she'd first come to Badara she now recognised as friends.

Jean reminded Paige of her grandmother, listening to all points of view and running her smoothing words over any ruffled feathers. Marion and Briony both still scared Paige just a little but she knew behind Marion's brusque exterior there was a thoughtful, caring person, and Briony's penchant for wanting everything to be just right was a valuable trait when you worked with her on a committee. Gloria had taken on the fitness class and made it better with her changing music and routines. And as well as a Port Kent session and their regular group, she now ran two other classes in

437

the hall. There was an early evening class and she'd managed to get a few of the guys along to a men's only group which always ended with a beer, cheese and crackers. Marion said Len loved it. And then there was Sarah, who Paige felt closest to. Perhaps it was that they'd both become mothers as teenagers, albeit with different experiences, but they had a strong connection and enjoyed each other's company. Dane had pushed his mum to look for her daughter but sadly the file had been firmly closed. Sarah was philosophical about it. She hoped it meant her daughter was totally happy in the life she was leading.

Paige's own mother had surprised her by getting in touch more often and suggesting a visit soon. She was sceptical but Sarah had encouraged Paige to keep the communication going, reminding her of the importance of grandparents even if they were distant. Paige couldn't help wishing her mother was more like Sarah, who was smiling brightly at her now from across the table.

"Shall we make a start on today's meeting?" Marion said and the chatter dropped away.

"I'd like to report that Paige and I submitted the proposal re the Welcome to Badara sign and it's been approved by council, providing it has the support of at least fifty per cent of rate payers."

Gloria groaned.

Marion held up a hand. "Thanks to some astute canvassing by Paige and I over the last two weeks we've got the numbers."

There was applause from around the table and Jean, who was sitting next to Paige, gave her a pat on the shoulder.

"Council is hopeful the sign should be ready to unveil at the festival," Marion said. "Any other reports?"

Gloria flipped up her hand. "I have. The welcome barbecue for Friday night is under control. The butcher in Wirini Bay will cut me a deal on the meat and ditto for the bakery with bread. The

Lions Club have offered to cook and the sport's club have offered extra people power and to have their bar open."

"Thanks, Gloria."

"The dinner dance is to be called Op Shop Glamour Ball," Briony said. "I've booked a fabulous old-time dance band and tickets are fifty dollars each."

Everyone agreed it was an acceptable amount.

"There are ten buildings on our walking trail now," Jean said. "And, of those, five of the occupants, including Paige, have agreed people can look through if they ask." Jean passed around copies of a rough map she'd made.

"The sporting club have the Saturday afternoon fair under control," Sarah said. "They want to keep it family orientated and have old-school events, like the egg-and-spoon race, three-legged race and sack racing, but they also want to have a few things like goal shooting and kicking and they're working out prizes."

"The CWA have got the food stalls organised." Jean glanced down at her notepad. "And they're planning some stalls for local arts and crafts. Several artisans from our district are interested in taking part."

"Oh, I forgot about the bar," Sarah said. "They wanted to know if we would like the bar open in the clubrooms during the afternoon."

"Let's think on that," Marion said. "We don't want to lose people from the fair to go and prop up the bar all afternoon." She checked her watch. "If no-one has anything else to report, I propose we end there and reconvene in a month. I don't think we need to meet as often until the festival gets closer."

There were murmurs of agreement and people began to pack up.

Briony turned to Paige. "I forgot to say I've organised some dance classes but I can't seem to get the young ones interested.

I was hoping you, being a committee member, might come along with Dane and then a few other younger ones might give it a go."

Paige opened her mouth, closed it again. She wasn't sure about attending dance classes, let alone with Dane, but Briony had moved off before she could object.

"Dane's a great bloke and I think he's come out of his shell since he's been seeing you."

Paige startled at Marion's softly spoken words.

"Seeing me?"

"Dating, going out, whatever you call it these days."

"I've had three men in my life who've left me with three children. I love my kids but I don't want any more heartache."

"I understand that. But life's a risk. Everyone, even Sarah, can see you and Dane work well together."

"Sarah?" Paige glanced at the others. Sarah was deep in conversation with Jean and Gloria.

"Don't worry," Marion said. "She hasn't said anything she shouldn't. She was just telling me the other day how happy Dane was when he was doing something with you. You've had a lot of sorrow in your young life, he has too, but you shouldn't let that stop you trying again. Four years is a long time to be on your own." Marion smiled a soft, kindly smile very different to her usual contortion.

"Paige, come and look at this." Briony was standing by a large box she'd carried in earlier. "When I was in Adelaide last week catching up with Chelsea—"

"Oh, I meant to ask you," Jean said. "I heard something awful about Brandon the other day," Jean lowered her voice, "that he was in jail. I squashed it as gossip but I did wonder, is everything all right there?"

Her gentle question startled Briony for a moment then she found her voice again.

"Brandon has a drug addiction. He's committed to Chelsea and their life together so he's gone to rehab. It's early days, of course, but he's going well so far."

"Oh, the poor thing," Jean said and Sarah and Gloria mumbled similar sentiments.

Marion moved across and stood beside Briony. "He'll get through it. His family and ours are giving him every support."

Briony caught Paige's eye and smiled.

"Now, what's in this box?" Marion said.

Briony opened the box wide. "Those op shops you suggested I visit, Paige, were absolutely full of fabulous treasures. I got several jumpers for you to use for your crochet as you asked." She took out a bag and waved it at Paige then hoisted a huge glass vase from the box. "This will be perfect for the main floral arrangement beside the red carpet." Once she'd set it carefully aside she took out a bundle of soft shell-pink fabric. "Chelsea and I saw this and we couldn't leave it behind. I hope it won't be crumpled but I needed something to wrap around the vase."

She lifted a coat hanger in the air and a dress billowed out and fell in a pale pink cloud.

"Isn't it pretty?" Jean said as Briony twirled the coathanger back and forth. The gown swished, the movement creating soft swirls of fabric.

"I do hope it fits you," Briony said. "Chelsea thought it was your size."

"Me?" Paige said. "I don't wear dresses."

Briony frowned. "What on earth were you planning to wear to the Op Shop Glamour Ball and the dinner?"

"Try it on," Sarah said, her eyes bright and sparkling.

"Now?"

"Oh, yes, please do." Briony pushed the dress towards her. "It would be perfect for the dinner if it fits."

Paige looked to Marion who gave her a smug smile. "You can use the kitchen to change."

Paige found herself being firmly guided in that direction by several sets of hands. She shut the door on the supper room and examined the dress. She'd never worn anything like it. When her friends had been going to school formals, she'd been pregnant and the next year looking after a baby. She'd not had a reason to dress up in something as beautiful as this.

"We're waiting," Marion sang from beyond the door.

Paige moved away into the open space between the bench and the back door leading to outside. She took off her sneakers, then her t-shirt and leggings and stepped into the dress. It was lined with some kind of cool silky fabric that slipped over her skin. The straps were made of the same sheer outer layer and held the bodice snugly in place. Paige was relieved to see the straight neckline covered her cleavage – she already felt exposed just wearing the dress. She reached around for the zip but could only get it part way up. If only Niesha was here. She wondered what her friend would make of her in a dress.

The door from outside opened. She whirled around, the full skirt floating out as she did.

"Paige?" Dane stood in the doorway. He twisted away. "Sorry."

She put her hands to her neckline as heat flooded her cheeks. She was covered but she felt naked. "What are you doing here?"

"Mum had a flat tyre and she drove the ute in," he mumbled over his shoulder. "I need it to pick up some things in the Bay so I was dropping off her keys. I'm sorry." He gave a quick glance over his shoulder. "I tried the front door but it was locked. I didn't realise you'd be..."

"Briony got this dress from the op shop and they wanted me to try it on. It's all right. I'm clothed. You surprised me, that's all."

Dane turned around and the heat surged in her cheeks again as his gaze swept her from top to toe.

"I've never seen you in a dress. You look...well, you always look good but the dress...it's amazing." He took two steps towards her.

"Actually, you could help me," she said and turned. "I can't get the zip up the last little bit. Not sure if it's stuck or..."

The touch of his fingers through the dress as he tugged at the zip were like an electric shock. She gasped.

"Sorry. This isn't something I've ever been asked to do before."

"It's fine," she gulped as a tingling sensation spread over her shoulders and warmed her all over.

He fiddled a bit more then Paige felt the pressure of the zip sliding into place.

"There." His fingers lingered on her back.

She turned and he was so close they almost touched. His eyes searched hers and he leaned a little closer.

He kissed her so gently at first she barely felt it. She kissed him back, realising Marion was right – this was something she'd wanted for a while now. The kiss became more urgent and deepened; their hands began exploring each other.

"What are you doing in there?" Gloria called from the other room and they jumped apart.

Dane grinned and backed outside. "I'll call you later."

The door shut and before she could breathe it flew open again. He held out a set of keys. "Can you give these to Mum?" His smile widened. He kissed her again and then he was gone.

There was a tap on the other door. "Are you okay, Paige?" Briony called. "Do you need help?"

"No." Her voice squeaked and she cleared her throat. "I'm coming out now."

Gloria gave a piercing whistle and the women turned as one.

Heat burned her cheeks as they all told Paige how wonderful she looked.

Sarah tipped her head to one side. "Pink is definitely your colour."

"I hope Dane can find something worthy of being your escort," Marion said.

"I'll make sure of it." Sarah winked.

Paige twisted away from their gaze and the dress floated out around her. She almost giggled out loud. If they'd stuck their heads in the kitchen a few minutes earlier they'd have got a surprise.

"You look like a princess," Jean cooed.

"A princess who needs some shoes," Gloria said. "The grotty gym socks don't quite complete the outfit."

Paige poked first one socked foot and then the other from beneath the dress, and joined in with the others as they laughed.

Once Paige would have taken Marion's words about a possible relationship with Dane and Briony's gift of the dress as interference or pity but now she recognised them for what they were – kindness and friendship. Paige had run away to Badara to hide from family but instead she'd found a family and a home. She touched her fingers to her lips, smiled and allowed herself to believe she'd found something more.

THE COUNTRY COURIER

22 November 2022

Blast From the Past With Back to Badara

Badara residents past and present reconnected at the Back to Badara Festival on the weekend, 52 years after the festival was last held.

More than 300 people flocked to a variety of events over the three-day celebration, as festivities kicked off with a welcome barbecue at the Badara Community Sports Complex.

"After spending my formative years in Badara, it's my great honour to open this festival on behalf of the town," District Mayor William Brown told the crowd in a stirring opening address.

"Badara was a welcoming and supportive community to me in my youth, and it still is to this day.

"Welcome back to Badara, and congratulations to the committee for your hard work putting this weekend together," Mayor Brown said.

By Saturday morning the streets of Badara were a hive of activity as festival-goers took walking tours of the town and visited significant buildings.

Some buildings' current occupants opened their doors, giving visitors a glimpse inside for a gold coin donation. This was a nostalgic journey for several older visitors who had grown up in the town and had not been back in many years.

One such visitor was Max Wilson, Badara's last baker. Mr Wilson's former bakery now houses the local postal agency and a cafe open three days a week, run by current owner Paige Radcliffe.

"Seeing the old bakery again was a blast from the past," Mr Wilson said.

"It's great to see the house is still lived in, and the old shop is back in use again."

Saturday afternoon saw the crowds move out to the Badara Community Sports Complex for a festive community fair.

The Op Shop Glamour Ball lived up to its name. Convener Briony Hensley said more than 100 people attended the ball, donning a fabulous array of op shop–sourced suits and dresses.

"We really want to reduce our impact on the environment, so the op shop theme seemed a natural fit," Ms Hensley said.

"Once Chaz's Old-Time Dance Band started up people really got into the dancing too – everything from waltzes to foxtrots to polkas."

The dinner was held in two sittings, in the supper room added to the hall along with the kitchen in the late sixties. Both rooms have recently been updated.

And the pews were full for a service at the Uniting Church on Sunday morning, with morning tea afterwards hosted by the Badara CWA. Attendees were able to enjoy the sunshine sitting outside in the newly planted Badara Memorial Garden behind the hall. Named in recognition of the district's first people then settlers, the garden is filled with specially selected local native species suited to the Badara region's climate.

Community service announcement: Some readers may remember that a time capsule was buried at the previous Back to Badara. Committee member Jean Chesterfield reports that unfortunately the capsule's contents were destroyed by water and pest damage, and nothing was recoverable. The committee has decided against organising a new time capsule.

Photo above: Paige Radcliffe with her children, Jayden, Kodie and Levi, stand beside the newly erected Welcome to Badara sign. Paige is credited for coming up with the idea of the gum tree design that was inspired by the town's name. Badara refers to a species of gum in Barngarla language.

Photo top right: The Back to Badara Festival Committee, (L–R) Gloria Chapman, Sarah Townsend, Jean Chesterfield, Briony Hensley, Paige Radcliffe and Marion Addicot, chair.

Photo bottom right: Jean and Keith Chesterfield sit on the bench seat they donated for the Badara Memorial Garden.

Photo left: District Mayor William Brown is treated to a plate of sausage rolls by committee chair Marion Addicot at the community fair.

Photo below: (L–R) Prince and Princess of the Op Shop Glamour Ball Dane Townsend in a black tuxedo and Paige Radcliffe in an A-line pink chiffon gown. Queen and King of the ball Marion Addicot in floor length midnight blue satin and Len Addicot in a seventies-style powder blue suit.

Personal Notices

Birth	Engagement	Wedding Thanks
Len and Marion Addicot, formerly of Badara and now of Port Kent, are overjoyed to announce the arrival of their first grandchild, a daughter for Grant and Erin Addicot, in Perth. Welcome, Verity Rose.	**Hensley – Vassos** Briony and Vincent Hensley of Badara and Ann and Janus Vassos of Sydney are delighted to announce the engagement of Blake to Gabriel. We wish you both a future of love and happiness.	**Radcliffe – Townsend** We would like to thank family and friends for joining us at our surprise wedding party. Thanks for sharing our special day and showering us with your love. Paige and Dane.

acknowledgements

Keeping Up Appearances was the perfect title for this book in so many ways. We all do it to some extent, be it in the community, at work or even at home. If you are lucky enough to be a parent, it's a lifetime journey, and sometimes the words *I love you as you are*, are the hardest to say. Thank you to those people who shared personal anecdotes with me to help inform this work of fiction.

The town of Badara doesn't exist in reality but, if you've ever lived in the country, I'm sure you'll recognise it. Badara is any rural area where people work hard to keep their identity alive and their community together, supporting each other through the highs and lows. For the hall in the centre of this story I imagined the halls from my childhood at Butler Tanks and Ungarra on Eyre Peninsula where I attended many school concerts, dances, strawberry fetes and community events. My parents were married in the Ungarra hall, which is still in use today thanks to the efforts of the local community (that for many years included my sister Vivonne) who understand the importance of providing a space where people can come together. Here's to the ongoing success of local halls.

I used words from Barngarla language for some of the place names in this book. The places are fictional but the language was spoken in parts of Eyre Peninsula, South Australia and I acknowledge Barngarla people as the traditional owners of that land.

I also want to acknowledge fitness classes, the instructors and attendees, who nurture our physical and social needs. Keeping active in a group is such good fun. All you need is a space, an instructor and willing, and even not-so-willing participants to make it happen. Of course all of the instructors and the attendees in this story are works of fiction but I'm very grateful to the many real-life instructors and fellow fitness enthusiasts I've spent time with over the years. There's something about doing our best to keep our bodies strong and active that unites. Thanks for your encouragement and camaraderie and, for better or for worse, none of you are in this book – but I would like to say a big thank you to reader and supporter Kerryn Eacott, who is also a fitness instructor. Kerryn read an early draft to give feedback re the various fitness activities I've described. As always any deviations from reality are of my own making.

I've made a Spotify playlist which includes the songs mentioned in the story and a few more to give you an hour of fitness and relaxation. My profile is Tricia Stringer and you can search for the playlist as 'Keeping Up Appearances'.

This year marks the tenth anniversary of my first publishing contract with Harlequin Australia, now part of HarperCollins Australia. I'm forever grateful to the talented publishers I've worked with over that time, Haylee Nash, Sue Brockhoff and now Jo Mackay. For this book in particular I would like to acknowledge and thank Jo and my fabulous editor Annabel Blay who helped me tease out the finer details and as always make the story better – this book is for you.

Of course Jo and Annabel are part of a fantastic wider team. Thanks also to the keen eyes of proof-reader Annabel Adair; to the clever design team headed up by Mark Campbell and specially to Christine Armstrong and Darren Holt for another stunning cover; to publicist Natika Palka; Jo Munroe, Eloise Plant and the marketing team; Karen-Maree Griffiths and the sales team; publishing executive Johanna Baker; and head of publishing Sue Brockhoff – what a fantastic crew. I am so grateful for you all and the fabulous work you continue to do.

The end result is another great book for you, dear readers, to enjoy. Thank you for reading, and for sharing your enjoyment with others, and with me. I love to hear from you.

My very grateful thanks to the book reps, booksellers and librarians who continue to champion my books. Pandemics and extreme weather events don't make it easy but somehow you keep the light shining for the reading community.

To my wonderful band of fellow writers, thank you for your friendship, timely wise words, humour, cheer and support which all helps keep me afloat.

To dear friends and family who keep on showing up at events, purchasing my books, recommending them and sometimes even adjusting their position in bookstores, I value your encouragement so very much.

And last but never least are my beautiful home team, Daryl, Kelly, Steven, Harry, Archie, Dylan, Sian, Jared and Alexandra. Thank you for always stepping up when I need you – Sian, your help with the newspaper articles for this book was much appreciated, and thanks Kelly for the playlist suggestion. There are so many ways you all support and inspire me. Love you to the beach and back.

book club questions

- There's a saying that the nice part about living in a small town is that when you don't know what you're doing someone else does. Is this a positive or a negative and why?
- Some of the characters in *Keeping Up Appearances*, such as Marion and Briony, had to work very hard to hide their secrets. How did this affect their relationships with family and friends?
- Paige moved her children part way across the country to hide from a difficult situation, something she didn't feel empowered to face. How did moving to Badara make that better or worse?
- There's often an invisible wall in some communities between those who were born there and those who move in. Do you think this impacted Paige? Discuss.
- Briony made decisions that others didn't like, to protect her family. Why do you think she did this and what impact did that have on her relationships with them?

- First Len, then Marion and Len, kept a huge secret. Why did they choose to do this? What impact has it had on their life together?
- Marion did something as a teenager that she regrets as an adult. Has this happened to you?

Turn over for a sneak peek.

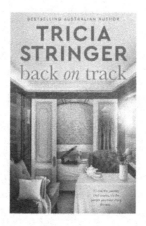

back *on* track

by

TRICIA STRINGER

Available October 2023

one

One night in February – Paddington, Sydney

The deep blue of evening slowly descended over Sydney, creating a momentary lull as the day departed and the night took over. In Paddington a small group were gathered for drinks under the pergola at the back of Ketty Clift Couture. Jazz played and, as the light faded, fairy lights winked and blinked to life. They momentarily distracted Ketty from the speech she'd been about to make. She loved fairy lights. There was a certain kind of magic in them that even at seventy-one still filled her with the frisson of anticipation.

She gazed up at the twinkling strands looped beneath the vines covering her courtyard and followed the trail of one string that wound down the verandah post and stopped beside a pot containing a lush green tomato plant. It was covered in small fruit, round and bright red like the baubles on a Christmas tree, and the colour of the silk dress she wore.

The gentle clearing of a throat brought her attention back to the women gathered before her. Tien, one of her seamstresses, was looking at her closely. "Are you all right, Miss Clift?"

Tien had been seventeen when she'd first started working at Ketty Clift Couture. Now at forty-eight, no matter how many times Ketty insisted she call her by her first name, her employee stuck with the formality.

"Of course."

Ketty ignored the disbelief in her smile and swept her gaze over the group before her, each with a glass of their preferred drink.

Her second-in-command, Judith, stood to one side stiffly holding a glass of wine, and at the other side of the small group stood Lacey, Ketty Clift Couture's young designer and deft jack-of-all-trades. Funny how their drinks reflected their personalities. Judith could be as crisp as the pinot grigio she gripped while underneath dwelled a kind heart. Lacey was as sparkly as the champagne she held but could never be described as frothy.

Between them stood the three women Ketty called her engine room – these were the women who cut and sewed with careful precision. Ketty's three long-serving seamstresses smiled back at her. Ning, who'd been with her from the early days of Ketty Clift Couture, held a glass of icy lemon squash. Tien, who was approaching twenty-eight years of service, held a glass of apple juice, and Birgit, who'd been there nearly half as long, had champagne like Lacey.

Ketty cleared her throat. From the moment she'd made her decision she'd been planning this Friday night get-together; from the drinks and nibbles to the carefully packed brown-paper carrier bags, one for each woman. She wanted her staff to hear it from her while they were all together and then to give them the weekend to digest her news. She knew it would be a surprise, perhaps even a shock, and now that the time had come to make her announcement she felt a little nervous.

"Thank you, my friends, for your dedication and talent and your service to our business. Last year was one of the most successful in the history of Ketty Clift Couture and it's because of all of you." She lifted her glass, putting off the moment a little longer. "Join me in a toast to you all. To us." She raised her glass higher. "To Ketty Clift Couture."

A chorus of voices joined her. Patch, Ketty's old black-and-white cat, startled from his position on a chair by the door and ran inside. They sipped their drinks and all that could be heard in the brief pause was Norah Jones serenading them with 'Come Away With Me'.

Ketty savoured the easy intimacy of the gathering. They'd worked together a long time and she was concerned that the old saying 'familiarity breeds contempt' had somehow been infiltrating the previously harmonious working environment she'd fostered. She'd noticed some of the cracks prior to Christmas. She'd been sure it was simply that they were all in need of the break over the festive season, but they hadn't been back at work long before it was more than scissors that snipped and needles that stabbed.

Not only had Ketty Clift Couture survived and evolved over the last few tough years, but each of these women had been integral. They'd been right beside her doing their part, but now something was wrong.

"We've worked together a long time." She met Ning's gaze. She'd been with Ketty since the early days, when the buildin that now housed the business and upstairs apartment had be little more than an empty relic of Paddington's bygone era.

"I have something to tell you that may come as a surprise I—"

"You're retiring, aren't you." Tien's words cut through Ke

"Oh, no," Birgit wailed. "You're not selling?"

"She is over seventy, you know." Tien sniffed.

Judith frowned, Lacey paled, Ning cried out and then they all started talking at once.

"I'm not retiring or selling." Ketty's words were lost in the kerfuffle. She put down her glass and clapped her hands. "Ladies!"

They fell silent and turned back to her. In the background Norah crooned on.

"This is something else—"

"Are you taking time off?" Birgit's eyes shone with excitement. "I know! You've booked a cruise."

"That's fabulous, Ketty," Judith said. "You didn't ever do anything special for your seventieth."

"You haven't been away in a long time," Tien said. "It's good you're doing another trip before it becomes too hard for you."

Ketty struggled to keep the smile on her face. Once more her speech had been hijacked. And what did Tien mean, 'too hard'! The last four years had been about keeping her business afloat in a constantly changing and difficult world, though she hadn't lied about the past year being their most successful. It didn't mean she hadn't longed to go on another cruise but the fact that it hadn't been possible had been beyond her control.

"That's so wonderful, Miss Ketty." Lacey beamed at her.

It was enough to snap Ketty from the sudden regret that had enveloped her. After all, not taking a cruise for years was hardly something to wallow in self-pity over. Cruising had begun again and while Ketty had kept her eyes firmly averted from the tempting offers, it didn't mean she wouldn't go again one day.

She lifted her shoulders, ready to address the group again. This wasn't going how she'd planned at all.

"That's not what I want to tell you. It's been a difficult few years but we've survived it. You've all helped to ensure Ketty Clift

Couture has survived as well. And I do wish we could all go on a cruise."

Ning shook her head and Tien looked horrified.

"Careful what you wish for." Birgit grinned

"I have a surprise for you," Ketty said. "Lacey, would you please hand out those bags." Ketty indicated the brown-paper carrier bags she'd prepared earlier.

"What are you up to, Ketty?" Judith's look was wary as she took the bag Lacey handed her.

Once more there were murmurs from the others.

"I've booked us on a train trip," Ketty blurted before they could cut her off again. "On the Ghan from Darwin to Adelaide."

The women lifted their gazes from their bags. Five sets of surprised eyes locked on hers.

"Which I'm paying for, of course," Ketty added quickly. "We depart mid-April."

"Doesn't that take a few days?" Birgit gasped.

"Four days and three nights plus two nights in Darwin before we get on the train."

Judith glanced at the others then back at Ketty. "By 'we' you mean..."

"The whole staff of Ketty Clift Couture."

talk about it

Let's talk about books.

Join the conversation:

 facebook.com/harlequinaustralia

 @harlequinaus

 @harlequinaus

harpercollins.com.au/hq

If you love reading and want to know about our
authors and titles, then let's talk about it.